# FRESH WATER

## A NOVEL

## MICHELLE S. MORRIS

MICHELLE S. MORRIS

**1**

___

Alexandra "Alex" Newberry couldn't help but be frustrated. Maybe even a smidge angry. *She* was the head of the family. Shouldn't they abide by her wishes? At least pretend? No one should tell someone else how she should grieve—or even if she should grieve at all. But that's what this had come to. Now she waited on the shore of the family island she loved for those nearest and dearest to descend like a swarm of locusts.

Alex stood in the same spot for several minutes, watchful, unmoving. Then, head back, eyes closed, she breathed in deeply and then out slowly. That glorious smell of summer. Sun, water, green growth, and, yes, dead fish. Her nose wrinkled slightly but then smoothed again.

The water in the lake arced and fell in slow ripples, its underpinnings vibrating gently, causing the wake. Light from the sun caught on the tip of each crest for a mere second, flashing brightly then gone, the effect mesmerizing—and blinding.

The light breeze, barely noticeable in its lazy transit over the lake, carried the smell of childhood. The magnificent essence of summer.

The tall trees rocked slowly with the rhythm of the breeze. She could smell the pine, see the birch leaves moving, creating their own fluttering light show when the sun caught them. The other trees—what were they? She could never remember but thought maybe cedar; another aromatic giant, protecting her island. That is how she fancied the trees, growing practically untouched for hundreds of years, guards for the land, her respite from the busy, noisy world beyond.

The woman glanced toward the closest shore. She still didn't see any cars pull onto the land connected to their shoreside dock. She breathed another lungful of fresh air, glad for the time alone before the onslaught. Her family.

Well, *some* of them were descending upon her in what she surmised was a misguided intervention of sorts. Maybe not an intervention, but a misguided assumption that she should not be alone in her time of grief.

The young had this perception of the finality of death, of its heart-wrenching emotional crippling of all in its wake. Death, though sad, held a different position in this second half of her life. It was an inevitable part of the circle, one where if a person lived life to its fullest, the joy of the time spent, and the memories kept, overshadowed the sadness.

No one should ever be crippled by the inevitable. But this next generation were not in the second halves of their lives and had not yet reached this level of wisdom. She knew what they saw was a woman who tragically lost two husbands. A woman who was truly alone for the first time in her life. They were worried. That's what it came down to—their worry. Selfless? Selfish? She wasn't sure.

A tiny flutter of guilt took flight in her belly. They didn't know the whole story. They didn't know the circumstances of her husband's death. Yet, she had no plan to tell them. Part of her was worried she might blurt it out in her frustration.

She knew their attention and insistence in coming to the island should warm her heart. She had friends who wished their children desired to spend so much time with them. Her childless friends were more envious as time marched on.

Yet she knew the truth, the truth spun into the very fabric of the universe. Every person had an infinite capacity to love and be loved. Everyone was broken in some way. Every path was chosen.

Maybe that was the source of her consternation. She knew each of their secrets. Her friends'. Her children's. Even her grandchildren confided in her. They trusted her with every joy, fear, and sorrow. She never broke their trust.

Why couldn't they trust her enough to know her own capacity for grief? "Damn it!" she shouted into the wind. "I don't need an intervention or whatever they think this will be." That flutter of guilt took another flight around her gut.

A sudden thought sprang into Alex's mind. She hadn't been looking for an idea. But that was how it always was for her—ideas entered her mind without her even trying. She had learned long ago her thought process was far more productive when she left her mind open to any possibility. The kernel pushed forward now through her minor annoyance.

*Maybe this is less about me, no matter what my children think, and more about them.*

As the keeper of their secrets, the knower of their truths, an influencer in shaping their individual character, she knew each of their trials, demons, fears.

She looked again to the lake, the trees, felt again the breeze on her face, her skin yet to show its age. That was it. She would help them heal, recognize their own truths, face their own demons, find their own peace, as they *thought* they were helping her.

That settled, Alex whispered, "Thank you..." letting the words be carried to God and the universe.

# 2

—————

"Mommy! Why is it so cold in here?" the little voice whined from the backseat.

Even the air conditioning was not keeping the strands of her straight, dirty-blonde, shoulder-length hair from sticking to her face. She puffed out an exaggerated sideways breath, trying to dislodge the hair from her cheek. It didn't work. So, she took her hand off the steering wheel and swiped at the strands angrily.

"We'll be there soon, and then you're going to wish for air conditioning," she argued. "Pull your jacket over you." She looked at her young son in the rearview mirror and craned her neck to see if the jacket was still there next to his car seat. It was.

She realized her skin was chilled, which meant the sheen on her forehead and cheeks was more from sheer nervousness. The judgment she wanted to avoid was coming too soon—judgment from her family and their perfect lives. Sure, Aunt Alex always welcomed her with open arms, but she would not be able to stand it if that calm, successful woman judged her—or worse, pitied her.

More nervous perspiration beaded under her arms. *Ugh! When did I become this woman?* She used to exude confidence. The confidence that naturally came from being loved and cherished her entire childhood. Now she thought maybe that hadn't been confidence but ignorant bliss.

Ignorant that your entire life could change with one conversation.

With any luck, her cousins would be too busy consoling their mother, the grieving matriarch, to pay attention to her pitiful situation. Maybe her husband—was she even allowed to call him that anymore?—was right.

He said she was not the woman he married. He said she did not have her own interests anymore; she was boring. He said her body was no longer the tight and contoured cheerleader he fell for in high school.

She choked on an unbidden sob as she tried to hide her sorrow and embarrassment from her young son. Besides, she had already cried enough tears in the last week. She contained her tears to the hours her son was in kindergarten and after he went to bed.

Earlier in the week she almost gave in and left for the island early, almost pulled Donovan before the final week of school ended. What would it have mattered? It was only kindergarten. But she heard her husband—was he still?—in her head berating her for not even getting kindergarten right. So, she had stayed. But as soon as the final bell rang, she had the little boy bundled into his car seat and was driving away toward the island, the vehicle packed haphazardly in her zeal to escape.

Escape meant Mark Wright would show up to a house devoid of his family. Escape meant he could not force her to sign the papers still sealed in their manila envelope, her name, Victoria Newberry-Wright, clearly typed in the center, with the legal address of his attorney screaming officially from the corner.

At least she'd been saved the embarrassment of the mail carrier—someone with whom they had gone through school—witnessing her latest failure. No, instead, Mark had dropped them on the counter and instructed her to sign them before he came back to pick them up Friday—today.

One side of her mouth lifted in a tiny smile at her slight rebellion.

She noticed a bird that seemed to be racing the car and glancing at her at the same time. As she absently stared at the soaring bird, the road's dirt edge pulled her tires toward the ditch. Startled, she jerked back onto the road, earning a shout of protest from her son.

"Mommy! Be careful! I almost lost Max!" He hugged the action figure he named himself to his chest, the jean jacket dropping to the floor.

Gritting her teeth, she glared at the bird, still next to her moving vehicle. She could swear the bird winked at her. Her younger self would have insisted it was the incarnation of her wicked-smart yet playful uncle, guiding her the last part of the way to their island refuge. That younger version of herself would also have sported a bikini top on the drive to the lake, rather than the long-sleeved, high-necked shirt she wore now. She was no longer that girl and wondered in a detached way who that ignorantly blissful girl had been.

Through the trees she caught glimpses of sunlight reflecting on the water in glistening sheets. She rolled down the windows and breathed deeply. The smells of childhood rattled something deep inside her. It was painfully comforting. The pain, she recognized with some surprise, was longing. Oh, how she ached for a "do over."

"Smell that, Van? That's the smell of summer," she said and smiled in the rearview mirror for his benefit.

"Mommy! I smell the water! It smells warm!" Every sentence seemed to be punctuated by an exclamation point. She said a small thankful prayer her innocent little boy had not begun to doubt himself and end his statements on the high note of a question. He still exuded confidence.

Suddenly, his eyes crinkled, and his nose wrinkled. "Mommy! Close the windows! It stinks like fish!"

She giggled, then caught herself. How long had it been since she giggled?

Pulling onto the family lot, she parked off the two-track and on the grass. The only other car was her aunt's. They were first to arrive.

She turned the vehicle off and stared toward the island. The tall trees swayed in the breeze, and she felt an immediate sense of connection and protection. In the back, Donovan struggled to be free of his car seat and scrambled through the break between the front seats, fingertips gripping the dash, eyes big.

Their aunt was standing near the dock on the island side, staring at the sky. Slowly Alex turned her head and looked directly at their car, a smile brightening her face, even at this distance the joy radiant.

Tory's breath jerked unevenly. Alexandra Newberry, her Aunt Alex, always seemed to have a sixth sense; she hadn't even honked the horn yet to get the older woman's attention; yet there she was.

It seemed an antiquated practice to honk the horn to signal their arrival, soundwaves racing across the water, amplifying as they got closer to the island. They all had mobile phones now, but some traditions were sacred, and this was one.

Exiting the vehicle, Donovan close behind her, she waved to her aunt and hoped the smile she plastered on her face would be enough to get through the first night with the family.

She stood straighter and locked her spine. She would not be pitied. And, with a little less conviction, she determined she would not be hurt by the judgment she expected to come.

Her aunt started the ancient ski boat, the freshly painted red hull with the lower white bottom bobbing from below the waterline, causing a flutter of excitement in her stomach.

"Come on, Van, help me get everything to the dock so we're ready when Aunt Alex gets here."

They carried their few belongings in two wheeled cases and one duffle bag. Contributions to the kitchen pantry were in a box and four plastic bags. She had a moment of doubt and hoped in her haste to escape that she remembered their new bathing suits—both necessarily larger from the previous season.

Alex pulled the ancient ski boat up to the dock just as Tory set the last box from the vehicle down on its worn wood.

Her eyebrows pulled down in thought and, eyes on the dock's graying wood, Alex mused out loud, "I wonder if I should have a new one built?" Her niece decided that wasn't a question for her and didn't respond. Alex reached up and pulled the boat close. Her fingers slipped on the rough wood, and she bit back the curse that almost made it out before she saw the little boy watching her with rapt attention. She quickly tied the boat off and lifted her finger to her mouth.

On close inspection, Tory saw the gray splinters that took reckless residence in her aunt's skin. *Yep, new dock is added to her mental checklist.* Tory's heart beat louder in her chest as she watched Alex smile widely at the little boy, who looked like he was going to dance right off the dock in his excitement.

Alex held out her arms. "Donovan, I'm so glad you came to stay! Would you like to sit next to me?"

Donovan nodded excitedly. "Yes! Please!" He jumped into her waiting arms and threw his small ones around her neck in an enthusiastic hug.

Over his shoulder, Tory mouthed, "Thank you." Then she loaded their bags and box into the boat before hopping down and finding herself enveloped in Alex's strong arms.

"I'm really glad you came to stay. It's been so long since we caught up," Alex said. "I want to hear everything."

Tory inwardly winced and put her hand to the messenger bag strapped across her body, hoping the envelope was not peeking out for the world to see her failure. Realizing the flap concealed the bag's contents, she felt silly for worrying. Of course, her aunt was just being polite. She quickly pulled a life vest over her protesting son and clipped the plastic buckles.

"Van, how would you like to help me drive the boat?" Alex asked, distracting him from the vest.

"Yes! Yes!" He pushed quickly to stand in front of the seat where his great-aunt sat. He grabbed the steering wheel.

Alex kept a loose hold on the wheel with one hand and slowly lowered the throttle lever to increase the speed to a nice slow pace. Tory knew it was much slower than her aunt preferred—she liked to go fast in all things and always had.

Alex wrapped an arm around the youngster's waist. She did not miss the pensive look on her niece's face but decided there would be plenty of time to puzzle it out, or, conversely, to just ask what was so wrong she would have the weight of the world weighing her down on such a beautiful early summer's day.

"Let's circle the island, shall we?" Alex asked loudly in Van's ear, over the sound of the wind and the motor.

"Yes!"

The island was not large, but it was not tiny either. It housed an ample cottage up the crooked dirt pathway on the hill. A nice area stretched off the cottage on the flat of the hilltop, with old school-bus bench seating under the shade of the towering trees. A boathouse, with a separate dock and all manner of water toys inside, sat on the water's edge near the main dock and small sandy beach. Several acres down an easy slope behind the cottage were home to a couple acres of forest, a dilapidated treehouse in the stand closest to the clearing. Beyond, toward the far edges of the island, was swampland that led to the lily pads crowding the edge of the lake on the natural sandbar. It was common to see small fishing boats anchored there, trying to lure the fish to their hooks. The far side of the island, the north side, was a steep hill that dropped quickly to the water.

"Look! The outside bathroom!" Donovan yelled, pointing up among the thick trees at the top of the steep hill. The boat jerked to the left, the hand still on the steering wheel moving in the direction of his eyes. "Oops!" he yelled, righting the vessel. Luckily Tory had been sitting.

"The boat tends to go where you look, Van, so it's best to keep your eyes ahead when you're in charge of steering," Alex suggested gently. She noted in her mind that it was a good life lesson as well, wondering fleetingly if her niece could use that reminder but not voicing her thoughts. Sometimes—most times—it was better for people to come to their own realizations.

"Sorry!" the little boy shouted, sounding more excited than sorry.

"That's called an outhouse, Van," Tory reminded her son. To her aunt she said, "I can't believe that's still standing."

The grayed planks were hidden, blending in with the trees surrounding it. It sat precariously on the edge at the top of the steep hill, cliff-like with the angle of descent. The back of the ancient structure stuck out into the air. It had been in use for many years, until Alex's grandparents brought indoor plumbing to their summer getaway.

"I think that will stand as long as we do," Alex mused. "It's still structurally strong. And who knows? We might need it at some point." Her mind wandered to a few summers before when one of her grandsons stuffed the toilet with so much paper that it took an emergency trip from a plumber before one of her daughters threatened to leave before their vacation ended. No indoor plumbing was a line that daughter would not cross. *Who knew I raised such a delicate flower?*

As they completed the 360-degree circuit of the island, she noticed another car pulling up shoreside. With a quiet sigh, she turned to her niece. "I'm going to drop you and Van on the dock with your stuff and go pick up the next load. I'll help you carry it up the hill when I get back."

"Oh, that's all right. I've got it," Tory insisted, sighing her own secret sigh that she'd made it so far with no inquiring questions into her life. Maybe, with so many others visiting, the questions could be avoided all together. She lifted her son to the dock, leaving the life vest behind, and heaved the rest of their belongings there too.

Alex turned and gunned the engine, racing toward shore. Donovan looked on in awe. "I'm going to drive that fast next time!"

"Sure, you will. Come on, bud, help me put as much as we can in the wagon and pull it up the hill." Her son's eyes stayed glued to the receding boat sending choppy waves out into the lake.

## 3

———

The large SUV pulled up shoreside, and the driver could not wait to exit and have a second, or three, to close her eyes and have a private—albeit micro—moment to herself. She dearly loved her entire family, but sometimes, it was all a bit much.

In addition to her children, she had driven her youngest sister and her sister's best friend after picking them up from college at the finish of their freshman year. Her half-sister, Lauren Robertson, was at an age when long monologues of great philosophical thoughts could not be contained and must be shared with all who were near. An enclosed SUV was definitely near—too near.

"Come on, move it, little people. I see Grandma coming," her son, Gavin Mitchell, called out from the third-row seating, impatiently shaking the seat back with the twins and his aunt in it.

Lauren turned and glared at him. "That's disparaging to truly little people." With exaggerated slowness, she descended while the twins raced out of the vehicle's other door, happy to be free.

Colin Mitchell, the oldest son, rolled his eyes toward his mother, Charlotte "Charlie" MacGowan—she'd kept her maiden name, just as her mother had through two marriages—and then shot her an amused grin over the vehicle's hood at his aunt's overly correct political correctness. *When did he get so mature?*

Somehow in the last year, he had taken his unfortunate "man of the house" role seriously, showing maturity in words and actions beyond his fifteen years. He turned the few steps to the back passenger door and reached up to give the chestnut-haired Harper Davenport, his aunt's childhood friend, a hand down from the third-row seating—her protruding belly first out of the large SUV.

Harper smiled her thanks to Colin, without whom she would have had a hard time with the large step. Somehow with pregnancy, her center of gravity had shifted, and she had yet to figure out where it went.

Gavin leaped out the opposite door and started after his twin sisters, who were running full tilt toward the dock where their grandmother had just pulled alongside and tied off. Colin called sharply, "Hey, Gav, bags. Now." The boy, younger by three years, stopped in his tracks and shot his older brother an angry look. Colin merely raised his eyebrow, as if to say, "Really? You're going to challenge me? Bring it on, little brother." Gavin looked down and moved to the back of the vehicle.

Charlie's breath caught in her throat and her eyes burned as she watched the brief interchange between brothers. How like his father Colin was. He even had the man's nonverbal communication down pat. She swallowed hard, remembering she did not cry. Instead, she pasted a smile on her face and joined the boys, Lauren, and Harper to begin unloading.

"I've got yours," Colin said to Harper. "You go on down to the boat."

"Really, Colin, I'm pregnant, not an invalid," she said, hands on her hips.

He smiled. "Never thought you were." He hefted her roller bag in one hand, two duffels over his shoulder, and another roller in his free hand, before quickly moving toward the boat, not bothering to argue.

Lauren's jaw dropped as she watched her nephew, who must have grown six inches in the last year, walk away. "When did he grow up so much?"

"You mean get so bossy?" Gavin grumbled, gathering three more bags and striding after the older boy. "He seems to think he's Dad."

Recognition dawned on the college student's face as she swung around to her sister, her thick, shoulder-length, slightly wavy, brown hair, swinging violently with the quick movement. "I didn't mean to bring it up. I'm so sorry, Charlie! I didn't think."

"It's okay. I was thinking the same thing about him a few minutes ago," Charlie replied. "Let's get the rest of this so we can get to the island and get settled."

"I guess I just miss Dad so much, I wasn't thinking all of you must still be grieving for James," Lauren said, a tear trailing a path down her cheek.

Charlie pulled her youngest sister, who was at least three inches taller than Charlie's five feet four inches, into a hug. "We're fine, really."

Lauren got her height and darker hair and eyes from her father, Charlie's stepfather, Hank Robertson. Hank had recently died, though Charlie knew her mother was fully capable of being on her own, no matter what her sisters thought. Their mother was vibrant, energetic, hardly in need of anyone's pity. If anything, Lauren was the one who needed support and validation. She had been Daddy's girl from the start. And unlike Charlie, this was Lauren's first time losing a father. But then, Charlie also knew what it was like to lose a husband. Like her mother, she knew life was incredibly short, so you could wallow, or you could enjoy what you had while you had it. She chose to live. It was a choice.

Shored up by remembering her recommitment to enjoy life, her back a little straighter, shoulders a little broader, chin a little higher, she purposefully marched toward the dock with her load. *Ha! Maybe Colin didn't get absolutely everything from James. Maybe there is a little— or a lot—of me in my oldest son, too.* That thought made her smile genuine. Perfect to greet her mother and deal with her sisters.

~

Two more vehicles pulled up on the grassy, shoreside property in quick succession. Through bug-spattered windshields, they could see small figures pulling and carrying luggage and supplies up the long, well-worn path toward the cottage at the top of the island. Since Alex was one of the people trekking upward, it would give them a chance to get their belongings organized down at the dock.

Aimee Dumont needed that moment to organize, to inventory, to plan her next step before the chaos of her loving, annoying, opinionated, intelligent, independent, frustrating, educated, successful... *Oh, damn. Even thinking about them causes lists in my head.*

Why did visits with her family cause every childhood insecurity to rise, as if carried by her very blood to every extremity in her body? It was ridiculous. She knew it. All the same, she shook her hands, trying to dispel the very real feeling. It still rose. Her teenaged daughter and almost-teenaged son were glued to their phones; she was sure they had not even realized they were parked.

The passengers in the minivan that had pulled behind them were already unloading, a seemingly never-ending stream of tow-headed children emptying onto the long grass.

"Aunt Aimee!" She heard the high-pitched happy cry at the exact same time a small body slammed into her legs and wrapped little arms tightly around her thighs. The towhead with long curly hair clung to her, chubby little legs now wrapped around her legs, climbing upward as if her aunt were a human jungle gym. Staving off the inevitable bruises, Aimee reached under the little girl's arms and lifted her up to sit on her hip.

"Well, hello there, Miss Harmony. Are you ready to see your cousins?" Aimee asked excitedly, matching the energy in the little girl's voice.

"I am!" Harmony shouted, already kicking her legs in an effort to get down.

Aimee heard the swish and click as the minivan door shut, the last of her nieces and nephews hurrying to the back of the vehicle to help their mother unload and get to their vacation faster. Her own offspring had yet to even unbuckle their seatbelts. She stuck her head back into the vehicle. "In case you haven't noticed, we're here."

"Mmmhhmm," her daughter muttered.

"Just a minute; I need to finish this level," her son said.

Those words took Aimee back to her older sister Charlie, who always insisted on finishing her chapter before she would move... anywhere...her entire childhood. Right now, she wished it were a book in her son's hand. She was already braced for the storm when he remembered the island doesn't have Wi-Fi.

Aimee sighed and began unloading the back of the vehicle, setting her children's bags on the ground as she found the collapsible wagon on the bottom. Once the wagon was assembled, she began placing shopping bags with fresh produce, meat, and snacks into it.

AT THE BACK of the minivan, Aimee's sister-in-law systematically pulled out the smaller bags her kids could handle. She implored them to stick close and not run off to the dock without her. Somehow, they listened. Sage MacGowan smiled a quiet smile, one meant for herself alone. She had a lot of those moments. Grateful for the little things. Just as she was grateful to be part of this large, boisterous family she had married into.

Growing up an only child, even participating by watching from the sidelines was a delight for her—one she treasured more than her new family could possibly understand. How could they? They had this ever-present joy and unconditional love for one another. Oh, she knew her hippie-want-to-be parents loved her, but they loved one another and what they called their "life journey" even more. She moved from place to place, even country to country, as a child, always an appendage to her parents' never-ending quest for peace and enlightenment.

Once, they'd left her in a ladies' lavatory in Bath, England, and did not realize until they were at the ferry in Holyhead, ready to embark for Ireland. They did turn around and go back for her, but not before she sat with a tear-streaked face in the local nick, a stoic bobby seated next to her. The woman did hold her trembling hand when Sage tentatively reached out. Her parents laughed, embarrassed, and said they thought she had crawled into the back of their tricked-out hippie van and was sleeping, and did not realize they had left her. Her parents lived the "van life" before it was a thing, and Sage, for one, did not see the allure. Even the minivan made her cringe, but with five young children, it was a practical solution—for now.

"Let me take that." Aimee appeared at Sage's side and grabbed the larger duffle bag from the taller woman, five feet eight inches to Aimee's own five feet five inches. Aimee already had their luggage at the dock and seemed happy to help her sister-in-law.

"Thanks," Sage said, already breathless from swinging several bags from the back.

"Mom, can we head down to the dock now?" eight-year-old Hudson, her oldest son, implored as he watched his two older cousins meandering their way to the water, eyes still cast to their phones.

"Sure, but watch your sisters please," Sage replied.

A haughty, exaggerated sigh reached the adults' ears as her six-year-old daughter, Indy, stuck a hand on her hip and glared at her mother with narrowed eyes, the blue barely visible. "Mom, I *can* swim you know. Sheesh! I don't need boys to keep me safe." The girl stomped toward the shore.

"Six going on twenty?" Aimee asked, and Sage noted her sister-in-law's sympathy.

"Yeah," Sage said with an eyeroll only another parent would understand.

"I don't know how you do it," Aimee said. "My brother deployed, you at home with five kids, *and* working as a nurse part-time. I would lose my mind."

Sage shrugged, throwing her naturally wavy, naturally bleached-blonde hair over a shoulder and away from her face. "I don't know, it's not so bad. Hudson is eight going on forty. Jaspar may be seven, but he's pretty serious and responsible. Even the girls seem to help one another out—when Indy isn't trying to prove she's old enough to do whatever the boys do. Savannah is so excited to be going into kindergarten and making her daddy proud. Harmony, well, she's fine being the baby and milking it for all it's worth. I think William talked to all of them about behaving and helping while he's deployed. For some reason, it stuck." Sage sighed, thinking about William and wondering where he was in the world at that moment.

Aimee nudged her. "Hey, sorry, didn't mean to make you all sad and everything."

"You didn't," Sage smiled again.

"We better get this stuff to the dock. Looks like Mom spied our arrival and is on her way over."

The beautiful wooden boat sliced through the water, cutting a path directly to them. The kids were jumping, dancing, and waving from the dock, unable to stand still in their excitement. Alex slowed before she reached them, quickly tying off and climbing onto the solid wood to hug all the grandchildren. While they greeted their grandmother, loud and excited to get in the boat, another ski boat pulled up behind them, just out of reach of the dock.

"Hey, Alex, good to see you out here. So sorry to hear about Hank," the white-haired man said. "Looks like you got the whole family visiting. How about I take a load of them over for you, rather than you making two trips?"

Alex nodded at the older man, a friend of her late parents, and still a sitting district court judge—a position his father held before him. His family had the shoreside property and cottage next to their land where they parked their cars for probably as many generations as her family had owned the island. "Thanks, judge, that would be wonderful, as long as you don't mind."

"Gives me more time out on the water," he laughed. He stage-whispered to the kids, now quiet, watching the exchange, "I was supposed to mow the lawn an hour ago. You're a good excuse to put it off. Helping a neighbor and all that."

By this time, Aimee and Sage joined the others on the dock and began loading both boats, ensuring each child had on a properly fastened life jacket. When belongings and people were parceled into the two boats, the judge shouted a challenge. "Bet I can race you around the island and still beat you to the dock!"

"You're on," Alex shouted back, feeling the adrenaline race from her chest and spread through her body as her competitive streak pushed to the surface. She quickly backed away from the dock and threw the lever down to lurch the boat forward. "Hang on, kids! We're going to win this!"

The sounds of screaming, laughter, and engines whining rolled over the water and drew the attention of those already on the island. They ran toward the water, shouting encouragement to Alex.

After circling the island, the boats pulled up close, waves from the wake crashing into the pilings of the dock and onto the shore. The kids were still happily laughing from the exhilaration. Even Aimee and Sage, each holding their long hair to stave off the worst of the wind damage, were giggling.

"One of these days I'm going to win," the judge said, frowning dramatically, then with a brilliant smile—*he must have either veneers or dentures,* Alex thought—he efficiently unloaded the supplies and precious cargo onto the dock and wished them a good stay. "Are they here for the whole summer?"

"Just the girls and the kids this trip. I'm not sure how long they'll be here, but they're welcome the whole summer," Alex said graciously, glancing toward her adult children. No one bothered to correct or amend her assumptions.

Inwardly Alex sighed, hoping the stay would be more like the boat race, wild and exhilarating, and less like the funeral they'd all attended a couple weeks prior. "We've got a lot of life to live and where better than the lake."

"Hear, hear," the judge said as he pulled away from the dock. "Too bad most people don't realize that until they're old." The last sentence echoed on the water until his engine drowned out the words.

$$4$$

Alex took a short break. In her own room, she leaned against the closed door, relieved to be temporarily away from the chaos of the others getting settled. When she took a deep breath, remembering her resolve to be there for her family, she opened her eyes and took in the bedroom in front of her.

Expansions to the cottage over the years ensured enough sleeping space in bunk rooms for all the grandchildren, with space left for guests and adults in the family.

The one room that was not changed, no matter how her recently deceased husband had suggested updates, was the master bedroom. It was the same now as when her grandparents owned the island— probably the same as when her great-grandparents and even those before spent summers and weekends at the island. The only change allowed was a new mattress to top the old wrought iron bed and the added ensuite bathroom. The same nightstands with ancient lamps that threw shadows against the darkness placed where they'd always been. Her grandmother's vanity sat pushed against the wall at the foot of the bed, the same tri-mirror stood on its surface. Even some of the same pretty metal pill boxes rested in the drawers, long ago empty, but a reminder of a different time.

No matter what anyone else thought, she found comfort in the things touched by those who came before her. Sometimes she could even smell the light scent of her grandmother's citrusy perfume or the faint scent of her grandfather's sweet pipe tobacco. Whether embedded in the knotty pine walls or simply a sensory memory, it was real for her and comforting. The ages linked forever. Death did not take the memory. Absence did not lessen the emotion. If anything, it was sweeter.

The island was her grandmother's haven, as it was hers.

She heard the scuffle of bags on the wood floors of the bunk rooms and bedrooms, zippers opened, muffled voices arguing over who got a top bunk, laughter coming from the living area. The sounds of the living. The next generations of her family. Even in her fifties now, she still found it strange that she was no longer the youngest in any room, but the oldest—by far.

The youngest and only girl in a family of three older brothers was only her first experience with being the youngest, followed by many years of first being the youngest staffer in the congressional office where she worked and later the youngest reporter on the political team of a major national newspaper. So many had mentored her, shaped her views, honed her skills, sharpened her character built on the solid foundation of her family.

She still had a hard time believing she was the mentor now and had been for years. It had been easy to fall into that role when Hank was alive. He was larger than life and liked nothing better than sharing his wealth of experience with the next generations. She preferred to lead by example, and hoped people followed.

"Grandma!" She was pulled from her musings by the sound of her grandson Cameron yelling loudly for her. Quietly she stepped out and pulled her bedroom door shut behind her.

"What is it?" she asked.

"Wi-Fi? What's the password?" Aimee's son asked. His face was contorted into aggravation verging on panic.

"It doesn't always work," she said, taking his phone from him and inputting the password.

"It's not working," he said, large blue eyes like his mother's opened wide.

"Ah, well, guess you'll need to spend some time outside with your cousins," Alex suggested with a shrug of her shoulders.

She had not really lied to the boy. She said it didn't always work, which was the truth. Why it didn't always work was another thing. She had unplugged the modem located under her bed, far from prying technology-dependent eyes. Sure, she would plug it in again, for short bursts during the day, but refused to be held captive when the island offered enough natural delights for the imagination.

"What?! Seriously?" Cameron looked truly horrified. She tried not to feel sorry for her grandson and held fast to the white lie. The twelve-year-old immediately screamed for his mother. "Mom! I need to use your phone's hotspot."

Before Aimee could answer, Colin stepped in. "Cam, why don't you get your bathing suit on? We'll go test out the lake. Come on." He winked at his grandmother as he turned to walk out the door. She suspected her oldest grandchild had caught her but leaned into the fib for her sake. Cameron stomped into the bunk room to change.

Alex had a surge of—what was it? Anger? Really, she felt anger? The emotion took her by surprise. The anger was aimed at Hank, her recently deceased husband. He's the one who insisted on installing the technology in her safe place. It was her compromise with him to spend as much time as possible at the island. He needed it to connect to his—well, their—company, a successful political analytics and marketing business, and work from the island.

Not that her grandchildren needed to know it existed, but then she remembered Hank showing Colin how to reset it last summer. *Damn you, Hank.* "No," she chastised herself under her breath, "that's not fair. Sorry, Hank. I know it's not your fault you died on me." Oh well, at least her grandson seemed willing to keep up the pretense.

As the kids changed and raced down the hill, Aimee yelled from the top, "Slow down! You might trip on one of the roots." Of course, none of them listened and continued their headlong race to the bottom.

Over the years, the tree roots had grown up in the crooked path that led from the lake to the cottage. Aunt Aimee, always worried about everyone around her. Alex often worried her second daughter would give herself a stroke by worrying about things she couldn't change or things that didn't matter. But, as Hank had reminded her, this was the way Aimee was, and no amount of worrying, chastising, or persuading was going to change who she was at her core. A nurturer. Was it any wonder she had opened a restaurant with her husband? Nurturers liked to feed people, Hank had always said. She could hear his voice in her mind.

"Why don't you finish putting away the supplies in the kitchen," Alex suggested to Aimee. "I'll watch the kids." She didn't wait for a reply and followed more slowly behind her grandchildren.

"You can't keep an eye on all of them by yourself," Aimee protested.

Without slowing her descent, Alex replied, "Lauren, Harper, and Tory are already there. Organize the kitchen, please." She waved her hand over her head behind her, hoping to end the discussion. She heard the cottage screen door slam as Aimee entered through the screened-in porch and made her way to the kitchen.

Alex smiled to herself. Small victories. That brought to mind her first husband. Ian always reminded her to relish the small victories. She could hear his strong voice now in the recesses of her mind. He died while on a mission shortly before he would have had his twenty years for military retirement—not that he would have chosen retirement. His selfless sacrifice was hard to forget, for his country, for his team. His death came as he saved several injured members of his team, carrying them one by one to the waiting helicopter for extraction, only to make himself a target.

When their son, William, insisted on the Naval Academy for college and then a military career, she had a moment of pure terror, but pushed it aside. She had her first three children with Ian, and they instilled a strong sense of duty and public service in their offspring. Charlie was fifteen when Ian died, Aimee ten, and William only nine. But they all had solid memories of their father, even though he was deployed much of their lives. That was one good thing about technology—he did call and then video conference with them, when that became available, when he could. It made him feel closer and more involved than could have been said for previous generations in the same situation.

She married Hank three years after Ian's death, something she never expected to do. The man was surely a force of nature, and their connection was strong, different than with Ian, but strong, nonetheless. He owned his own company, after convincing Alex to start it with him, wrapped up in the business of politics, something near and dear to her own interests. Even Ian had planned to eventually run for office. Now her own son, William, encouraged by Hank, had his sights set on an eventual political run. The tendrils of strategy had been forged years ago. Too bad Hank would not be around to see it through.

Alex shook her head, almost to the bottom of the path, her grandchildren's and grand-nephew's laughter pulling her from the maze that was her brain. Some of them were already splashing in the shallow water by the beach.

Noting her arrival, Colin yelled to his brother, "Race ya to the raft!" He dove off the end of the dock and began a quick stroke toward the floating raft anchored several feet out from the dock. The water was still cold after the long winter melt—never truly warming until mid-July—but that didn't dissuade the family. They'd been jumping in the lake in May and June for generations.

"No fair! You got a head start!" Gavin yelled, diving in behind him.

Andi grabbed her brother and pushed him off the end of the dock. "Come on, Cam! Let's go!"

Both began swimming, Cameron's cheeks puffed out and eyes narrowed, straining his neck to keep his head out of the water—classic signs of a sour look, one Cam had perfected. By the time they reached the raft, the scowl was replaced with laughter. Alex noted how exercise could clear the darkest soul. Not that her grandson had a dark soul, but he could be challenging at times.

"Mom, do you think the sun's UV rays are bad for the baby?"

Lauren asked, clearly hoping her mother would back up her theory. Lauren liked to be right as often as her father, Hank, did and had no qualms about voicing her opinion—any opinion.

"I don't know about that. Sunshine provides vitamin D, and I'm pretty sure that's good for mother and baby." Alex smiled. "Just don't overdo it. And use sunscreen."

Harper shot a triumphant look at her best friend and rubbed a hand over her protruding midsection. "Thanks for letting me join you, Alex." She shyly ducked her head before continuing. "I know it's not a good time for all of you. I didn't really have anywhere else to go."

"Oh, Harper, you're always welcome. And why wouldn't it be a good time? We lost Hank, but he would want us to continue on and celebrate life by living it," Alex said.

"Mom, it's okay to grieve, you know," Lauren said.

"I've grieved, sweet girl, and I'm sure I'll have more moments, but I'm good. With everything," Alex insisted in a quiet voice.

"The funeral was only a couple weeks ago." Lauren looked slightly horrified, and large tears streaked down her face.

Alex moved to her daughter's side and hugged her tightly. "Lauren, I know you miss your father. But it's okay to grieve and live at the same time. Your dad would certainly want it that way. We're still here. We still have a lot to live and give. You're just beginning your journey. You still have to finish college and decide what you want to do with your life."

Lauren, ever the youngest child, stuck out her lower lip in a pout. "I've been thinking about that. What if I take a breather from school, get a job, and help Harper with the baby?"

Harper was clearly stunned, if her dropped jaw was any indication. "When did you come up with that lamebrained idea? You are *not* quitting school on my behalf. Even I'm going to keep going to school. How else am I going to give this child the life it deserves?"

"I was thinking maybe we could get married, and then you'll both be mine for real," Lauren said.

Her friend was almost speechless. She found her voice after a moment. "Oh, no. We are not doing that, Lauren. You're my best friend and I love you. But I'm not *in* love with you, and you're not in love with me. We are not getting married for convenience. Besides, even though this didn't work out right, I still like guys." Harper huffed that last part. Her situation was not ideal in any way.

As freshmen in college, she and Lauren had very different experiences. Lauren always knew she was into girls and flaunted that fact, joining every campus organization that catered to her sensibilities, dating any young woman she desired. On top of that, her family supported her, never expecting her to be anyone other than who she was.

Harper, on the other hand, had made one bad choice, drunk at a fraternity party when her major crush paid attention to her. That attention led to embarrassing drunken fumbling in his room at the frat house and missed periods for the next three months that she didn't even notice she missed. She did miss her jeans not easily buttoning. That was when she realized something was wrong, terribly wrong.

The frat boy had wanted nothing to do with the child, even suggesting it could have been any number of his fraternity brothers' spawn. At that point Harper realized she didn't want someone so vile to have anything to do with her precious baby. Her parents were not much better. All her mother could think about, as she raised her wrist to her forehead and acted as if she might faint at the news, was what her country club friends would think.

Her parents told her if she refused to agree to adoption or abortion, she would be on her own and no longer welcome in their home. Only eighteen at the time, Harper had argued with them—how could she abort the child she could now feel moving? She was very clear that people should have that right to self-determination of their own bodies, but she, with her means and feeling the flutters, had made her choice and accepted the responsibility gladly, knowing there would be one person whom she would love unconditionally, someone she would never let down, like her parents did to her.

Harper had walked out of the large brick home where she grew up, drove her BMW back to campus, and never looked back. She was surprised her mother did not have her father repossess her vehicle, but then remembered they had put it in her name when they gave it to her as a graduation gift. One lucky move for her.

Back on campus, she had waited until Lauren sought her out and collapsed in tears in her friend's arms. Lauren, fierce as ever, wanted to puncture Harper's parents' tires, punch the frat boy in the mouth, and protect her best friend from what the world was throwing at her.

Harper had told Alex in a teary phone call how vehemently Lauren had said at the time, "Well, my family is yours now. They already love you. We'll always be there for you."

Indeed they had, even welcoming her into their home for the Christmas holiday. Hank had worked with her on a plan to live independently and not have to break into the trust fund her grandparents had left her, and thankfully, that her parents could not touch.

"I just want to help, Harp," Lauren said.

"You already have; you are," Harper assured her. "All of you are."

"You're one of us, whether you want us or not, Harper," Alex assured her and kissed the girl's cheek. "We don't disappear when the going gets tough. Not in this family."

Tory had watched the exchange silently, while also keeping an eye on Donovan with his arm floaties, splashing in the lake with the other younger kids. Her heart skipped a little; was that the feeling of hope? Perhaps? Maybe her family would stand by her too. She breathed deeply, the smell of sunscreen and lake water taking over her senses and filling her with a silent anticipation. Maybe Aunt Alex was right all those years ago when they were children. Maybe the island was magic.

**5**

_______________

Aimee stood in front of the huge stainless-steel refrigerator and looked inside. "What has she been eating? There's only cheese in here. Really, Charlie, are you going to tell me you aren't worried?"

Charlie sighed as she continued to put cans, jars, and packages of pasta into the pantry. "No, I'm not worried. If you haven't noticed, our mother is the strongest person I know. She's got soup. Crackers. Cheese. Tea. Popcorn. Tuna packets. There are bananas on the counter." She had enough drama in her life, no need to manufacture it. She had a lot of decisions to make; not that her sister knew anything about that. Not that _anyone_ knew anything about that.

"You're as bad as she is," Aimee continued. "I'm glad Hank insisted on replacing the appliances. These are great!"

"There wasn't anything wrong with the old ones, but yeah, these are nice." Charlie shrugged begrudgingly. She kind of missed the old aqua, rounded-edge Frigidaire that was there since before her grandmother was born. The SubZero seemed unnecessary. She admitted the six-burner Viking stove was a nice addition, and probably safer than the old gas stove, equally as ancient as the old refrigerator.

Alex had put her foot down at replacing the old cabinets and, particularly, the pirate-head bottle opener attached to the space between drawers next to the sink. It was at eye level for most little kids, and every one of them had grown up frightened and then comforted by the familiar pirate face. It was part of the family. Hank argued hardly anyone had a need to open bottles anymore. But Alex —and Charlie—prevailed.

Charlie remembered how their father, Ian, had made up stories about how the pirate got stuck in the cabinet, forever serving his time in their summer kitchen. He had been home on leave and able to accompany them to Michigan and the island.

The kitchen smelled of pine and oak, a little musty—and a little gamey. What was that smell? Sage threw open all the windows. Charlie hoped that would air it out. The outside seemed to seep in through the walls, claiming what had been void of humans since the last season.

The dining area, a step down off the kitchen, had been expanded since Charlie and her siblings were children to accommodate the growing family with all the grandkids. Just as the sleeping area had been expanded with bunk rooms and additional bathrooms.

The rest? It was the same as the original. Same living room with the pot-bellied Franklin stove in the middle, stove pipe reaching up through the roof, warming the cottage on those rainy, cold summer and fall days. Same books in the corner bookcases of the living room, some dating back to the late 1800s, newer books added with each generation. Same worn board games of Clue, Monopoly, Scrabble, Yahtzee, Operation, and Candyland stacked on the bottom shelves, along with decks of playing cards.

Same screened-in front porch with fish nets mounted on the white-washed paneled walls, various seashells and starfish caught in the cloth. Same wooden benches along the wall housing treasures, old boots, flippers, goggles, and snorkels, when the seats were lifted. Same blue and red wicker rocking chairs positioned to catch the lake breeze that whipped up the hill and through the trees.

Charlie took comfort in the familiar. While change thrilled her— a good thing, since she had faced so much of it—having this one place, mostly unchanged, surviving generation after generation, gave her peace and hope.

"All right, I think that does it," Sage said to her two sisters-in-law as her beautiful hazel eyes quickly scanned all surfaces and the now empty boxes and bags. "Ready to join the others?"

"Think they'd notice if we stayed up here and drank a bottle of wine?" Aimee asked wistfully.

"No one will mind," Charlie assured her. "I kind of wanted to ski though." A teasing smile curved Charlie's mouth. It was one passion the sisters shared.

"How about wine now and ski tomorrow?" Aimee negotiated.

Sage watched the play between the two, preferring to remain silent, but voluntarily sidelined. She spent a lot of her life that way. She blamed her parents for moving her during the entirety of her formative years. To herself, she admitted she preferred watching. Being part of the large family but standing just far enough to the side or behind that they still saw her as a participant, but she didn't really have to join. They could be a bit much. What if they really got to know her and didn't like what they discovered?

"Fine. Ski tomorrow," Charlie agreed. She pulled a bottle of wine from the rack and handed it to her sister, then pulled down three glasses. "Come on, Sage. We have a reprieve before we face the angry masses."

"Red?" Aimee scoffed, looking at the label.

"It's a pinot noir and none of the white is chilled yet," Charlie said practically.

"And you don't like white," Aimee said under her breath, loud enough for the others to hear.

Charlie had the decency to look guilty. "Yeah, well, there is that. I really only detest chardonnay. I can handle a Riesling or pinot grigio, but it will never be my first choice."

Aimee poured three generous wine glasses, then led them outside to the old school bus seats that leaned against the large trees on the flat at the top of their hill. The seats were brown, or maybe a red, weathered after decades of use, but still hanging in there. They had to be leather. She remembered the story her great-grandfather told about buying them from the owner of a decommissioned school bus in the 1950s.

"Are you sure squirrels haven't made these seats their homes?" Sage asked, as she sat gingerly on the edge of one, crossing her legs to make sure as little of her as possible touched the seat.

Charlie laughed. "Only ones with holes, but we repair those every summer. Most have never had holes, so you don't need to worry." Sage seemed to relax, just as she had done every year for the last decade since she was with William.

They could hear the birds singing in the trees overhead, obviously not bothered by the human intruders. The breeze was gentle and smelled of the lake and trees combined, giving it an elemental scent. The total joy of the kids' laughter and excited voices floated up the hill.

"Does Tory seem quiet to you?" Aimee asked.

"I didn't notice. It's not like we've spent any time with her yet," Charlie said. "Did you notice anything, Sage?"

"Maybe a little quiet. She's usually in the middle of things, isn't she?" Sage thought Tory was acting more like her than herself—staying on the sidelines—but did not want to overstep.

"Exactly," Aimee said.

The three were quiet after that, each caught up in their own thoughts, seemingly relaxing while they could, with no little ones under foot or needing their attention. Aimee tried hard to focus on something other than her teen and almost teen down by the water, wondering if they were having fun, hoping they were behaving. If only her mind would be quiet, allow her to truly relax. She envied Charlie and Sage, who both seemed totally relaxed and comfortable with their own thoughts. Charlie might even be asleep behind those expensive sunglasses.

Glasses drained, Aimee sighed and stood. "Guess I'll go get dinner prepped."

Charlie looked over the top of her sunglasses. "You don't have to do that, you know. You don't have to do all the cooking."

"I know. I just want to. You can help, if you want," Aimee shrugged and started back to toward the cottage. Anything to not have to go down to the lake and listen to her son complain about the lack of Wi-Fi.

Sage handed Charlie her glass and headed down the path to the lake. Charlie followed her sister, prepared to peel potatoes, or make hamburger patties. Whatever the chef commanded. She shouldn't have been surprised when her younger sister opened a cooler positioned by the sink and pulled out a large container of already cooked chicken breasts, ready as always. Aimee then pulled out red peppers, black beans, lemons, sweet corn, and the olive oil and balsamic vinegar.

"Thought I'd make a chicken and black bean salad for tonight with French bread. Can you cut up the chicken into bite-sized pieces? Oh, and I have chicken nuggets in the freezer for the little guys," Aimee informed her sister, seamlessly continuing her prep.

"You got it," Charlie said, as she reached for a sharp knife from the block on the counter.

Soon the kitchen that earlier smelled like a mixture of must and outside was overtaken by smells of chicken, spice, and vinegar.

The party at the lake trudged back up the hill to change from wet swimsuits to shorts and sweatshirts, ready for the cooler night air. All claimed to be starving. There was nothing like fresh air and fresh water to calm the beast in every child. Charlie wasn't sure her younger nieces, nephews, and cousin would even make it through dinner, possibly not even her nine-year-old twins. Sure enough, Harmony, Donovan, and Savannah all had heads on the table before the adults had finished their meal. The others weren't far behind. All in all, a good first day.

Once the kids were tucked away in bunks, the adults gathered in the living room, caught up in their own thoughts and exhaustion.

"So, Tory. What's new? I haven't seen much of you lately." Aimee intently watched her cousin.

Tory knew it was only a matter of time, but she so wanted to keep the spotlight from herself for at least another day, if not the whole trip. So, she hedged. "Not much, just finishing out Van's first year in school."

Unlike the others, Tory, Aimee, and their families lived full time in Michigan in the smallish town founded by their ancestors. However small it was, it was large enough to not see one another every day, even every week. That may have been more a design of lifestyle than town size. Aimee was caught up with her restaurant, and Tory was caught up with her son and trying to hide from the world.

Before the conversation could go further, Charlie stood and announced, "It was a long drive from Virginia. We left in the middle of the night to get here midday, so I'm off to bed. See you all in the morning. You're sharing a room with me, right, Tory? Don't worry about the light or making noise. When I'm out, I'm out. Night, all."

Even with renovations and additions, they would still need to share sleeping accommodations with so many of them at the island at the same time. That was part of the fun of summer living.

Tory took that moment to escape too, claiming the need to shower tonight rather than in the morning. Perfect. Peace for another day. She would have to thank Charlie later. Her oldest cousin was always her favorite. Though more different than night and day, the two clicked in a way Tory did not feel with the rest of the extended family. Charlie was successful. Strong. Independent. All the things Tory thought she would be herself. Until she didn't matter. Until she wasn't enough.

# 6

The sun barely rose on the horizon, cutting a path through the tall trees, creating a small glow through Alex's bedroom window. She loved this time of day. Most of her family were night owls and the early morning was always her alone time. She could organize her thoughts, plan her day, breathe deeply before anyone else's drama invaded her space. She loved her family dearly. She also cherished the brief moments of alone time over the years.

One good addition Hank had made to the cottage was creating a master bathroom, ensuite. That was the only concession she would give him in the cottage renovations. She secretly enjoyed having her own private bathroom. She could quickly shower and be ready before anyone even knew she was out of bed.

This morning would be a good one to do some painting on the landscape she hadn't had a chance to finish before the onslaught of her family. Her easel was still set in the corner of the screened-in porch, the canvas still sitting as it was the day before when she cleaned her brushes and stowed the oil paint, turpentine, and pallet in the built-in storage box. No little hands had added fingerprints.

Once in the kitchen, she found her eldest grandson seated on a stool at the counter with a bowl of cereal, already in his swim trunks and a T-shirt. His dirty blonde hair was short on the sides, slightly longer on top, reminiscent of the military hairstyles of his uncle, and late father and grandfather. Even his posture was straight and alert, though he was alone. His blue eyes were all hers and his mother's.

Without turning around, Colin said, "Here's your tea. I wasn't sure how much milk you wanted." He held out the mug with the tea bag already steeped and water steaming. Milk was sitting on the counter. She ruffled the little bit of hair her grandson had and kissed him on the cheek.

"Your Grandfather Ian used to have my tea waiting. He had a sixth sense where I was all the time and when I would join him," Alex said. The sweet memory brought a faint smile to her lips.

"Wish I'd known him. Mom brings up stuff like that all the time. Dad was like that with her, when he was home," Colin replied. He suddenly smirked. "Grandpa Hank got you the one-cup wonder so you can have your tea on demand. Or his coffee." Alex glanced at the counter and found it interesting her grandson did not use the modern technology, opting for the kettle on the stove.

"I use it sometimes," she admitted. "You okay? You're up awfully early."

"Fine. Just couldn't sleep. Gracie got scared and decided to climb in bed with me last night. Then she kicked me out of the bunk in her sleep this morning."

Alex thought it was sweet that the teenager would be so caring with his little sister.

"At least Cassie didn't join her," Alex laughed. "If you're okay, I'm going to get some painting time in before the hordes wake up."

"Sure, Grandma. Mind if I get the sailboat out of the boathouse? Maybe I'll teach the twins to sail this summer. Hudson might want to learn too." Colin rose and took his bowl to the sink, swiped the dishcloth with dish soap around it, rinsed it, and left it to dry on the ancient drying rack.

"Want me to come with you? I don't think you'll be able to lift it and rig it yourself," Alex said.

"Nah. You paint. I'm pretty sure I can do it myself. If I need help,

I'll wait until Andi or Gavin wake up. Do I need the key for the padlock?"

"It's been open since I put the ski boat in the water after the funeral," Alex answered.

The boathouse was an outbuilding down at the lake to the side of their little beach. It was green and blended nicely into the background of the trees and grasses, even the marsh grass, lily pads, and untamed stands of lake weeds. It had a regular door on landside and barn doors that opened lakeside. Lake water ran up the middle of the building with wide dock structures on either side, and any of the boats, whether speed, kayak, row, canoe, or sail, could be set in the water from where they were wintered on the wall hooks or on the wooden structures inside the building.

"Okay, I'll see you later, Grandma. If I get it in and no one is up yet, want to go out with me?"

Alex felt her heart speed up in her chest. Not only did she love when the wind was blowing and the small boat raced across the water, she was touched her fifteen-year-old grandson still wanted to spend time alone with her.

"Let's do that," she replied, kissing him again on the cheek as she went to her painting. Colin looked delighted, holding the screen door until it softly closed so it wouldn't wake anyone else, and took off at a fast pace, long legs loping down the path to the lake.

Colin was surprised to find the sailboat sitting next to the open water inside the boathouse, ready to be carefully set into the water. He lifted, dragged, and coaxed each end into the channel, using the overhead pulley to take most of the weight. Even though it was a small boat, and the building was tall, he had to raise the mast and attach the sails once it was out of the boathouse and tied off on the boathouse dock. Luckily, the pulley could be moved back and forth, and he used its leverage to position the mast fairly easily. He spent the most time rigging the sails, again glad it was a small and uncomplicated boat. It was perfect for learning, something he would teach his little sisters and cousins this summer. Just as his dad had first taught him on this same lake, this same boat.

Once ready, he raced up the hill, not even winded by the steep slope as he whispered through the screen to his grandmother, "Come on. It's ready. The others must be getting up by now. Hurry!"

She was delighted by the little secret they shared and quickly shut the tackle box she used to hold her paints and brushes, dropping the brush she was using in a Mason jar of turpentine, and closed it all in the storage box against the wall that doubled as seating on the porch. She tiptoed out of the cottage and the two jogged down the hill, giggling.

"Is it okay if I have the helm?" Colin asked, knowing it was his grandmother's preferred position.

"Absolutely, captain. It's your ship," she said, laughing. Then she tossed him a life jacket. "Guess we better set a good example in case any of the youngsters see us—or your Aunt Aimee."

Colin gave her one short nod and dutifully donned the life jacket as she did the same. Alex untied the line and pushed off from the dock while Colin used a paddle to move them farther into the lake. Then they unfurled the mainsail. It whipped in the early morning wind until it caught and, with the rudder down, Colin's hand on the tiller, they began to race at a quick clip across the lake. No one was on it yet except a couple people fishing in the recesses of the coves. No speedboats or skiers. No one on the beaches. No one on the docks.

They had the wind in their faces, Alex glad her curly hair was short enough it didn't get in her eyes too much. Both smiled and laughed until their faces ached and their sides hurt. The sound of the wind cut out any distractions that might have existed. This was where she could feel peaceful, completely in the moment, no nagging thoughts of the past and what should have been, and no worrisome thoughts of what the future might bring. Just this one glorious moment with her grandson.

In this moment, she felt closer to him than she had felt toward anyone in ages. It was clear from the pure joy on his face that he shared her passion for the water, for speed, for the clean wind, and living in the moment. She hoped he felt the same peace and was almost positive he did.

When they had circled the island, explored a couple of the coves, and made sure to sail to the far side of the lake, they saw small figures on their dock beckoning them to come back. It was Gavin with nine-year-old twins Grace and Cassie, Aimee's fourteen-year-old daughter Andi, and William and Sage's oldest son, eight-year-old Hudson. They all stood with life jackets already fastened, waiting for their turn.

"Looks like you have a crew waiting for you," Alex said. "Drop me at the dock and you can pick them up."

"No, stay, Gram. We'll just pick them up," Colin said, carefully turning to use the wind to slow their pace, moving the tiller expertly to reach the end of the dock. They had barely pulled aside when the kids began jumping aboard, excitedly talking and pointing the directions they wanted to head.

Once back out in the middle of the lake, Gavin asked, "Can I take the helm now, Col?"

"Sure. Remember what you're doing?" His older brother moved over to the bench to allow his younger brother to take his spot.

"Yep," Gavin sat up straighter and looked toward the horizon, plotting their course with his eyes. Colin secretly winked at his grandmother, giving Alex the thrill of once again being in on a secret.

Andi leaned back, face in the wind, from where she perched on the bow. She looked completely relaxed and at home. "You've got the life, Grammy!"

"It's your life too," Alex yelled back. She couldn't help but feel the weight of the last few weeks lifted and believe she was exactly where she was meant to be at this time.

**7**

_______

The wooden speedboat rocked with the gentle waves caused by the morning wind, every once in a while rubbing against the foam barriers protecting it from the dock. Charlie and Aimee worked together silently, moving the skis to the dock, unfurling and checking the rope, making sure there were no knots and that the squirrels had not chewed through the nylon over the winter.

"Double?" Charlie asked.

"Let's go single first, ease into it," Aimee replied.

Charlie nodded, jumped into the boat, and leaned over to attach one ski rope to the back, above the waterline. She had no doubt her sister could easily begin the season next to another skier but was going easy for Charlie's sake. "Hey, Cam, you want to spot for me?" she asked, trying to draw her nephew out, get him to quit looking at his phone screen, waiting for enough bars to appear for the data to stream.

The almost-teen raised his dark curly head and looked from his aunt in the boat to his mother on the dock, ready to decline until he saw the tilt of his mother's head, the firm line of her lips, and sighed,

"Yeah, okay." He dragged his feet as he moved from the grass to the dock, clearly not happy.

Aimee jumped in the water, lifting two skis in with her, adjusting as she fit them to her feet and leaned back with the rope between her skis.

"What? You're not going to take off from the dock?" Lauren called from shore. She ran up behind her nephew and bumped him lightly as she passed, causing his shoulder to jut forward before he turned it into a full-on stumble onto the dock. He went to his knees and shot his young aunt a look accompanied by a curse. Lauren rolled her eyes. "Oh, come on. I barely touched you; certainly didn't push you hard enough to fall."

Aimee looked concerned. "You okay, Cam? Maybe you should go first, Charlie; come back for me later."

Charlie shook her head. "No way. You're the queen of the skis."

"He's fine," Lauren assured Aimee. Then in a quiet voice to Cam she said, "Quit milking it. I'm the queen of the spotlight and I know you're just trying to get your mom to feel sorry for you."

Cam looked shocked but quickly stood and jumped into the boat. Charlie gave her youngest sister a knowing look. Both of his aunts had no doubt no one ever called him on it when he acted out for attention. Running a restaurant, as his parents did, took a lot of hours, and playing on their guilt, at least his mother's, was easy. It was hard to stand out in this family.

Charlie eased away from the dock, stretching the rope until it was taut, waiting for Aimee to signal she was ready.

"Hit it!" Aimee yelled. Charlie moved the ski boat forward with speed, a rush of wake pushing to both sides of the motor, her sister easily rising from the water, smiling, finally no worries.

After once around the island, Charlie took off for the widest part of the lake, picking up speed and giving her sister more of a ride. Cameron sat facing forward, looking at his phone, knowing he could get a signal somewhere. Lauren was in the front passenger seat, enjoying the wind in her face. After a bit, she looked behind, shocked to see the rope skipping along the water, no Aimee.

Lauren yelled, "We lost her." Charlie immediately brought the speed down and turned the boat. They saw a head and two skis bobbing out of the water a good distance back.

"You can't do that, Cam; you have to pay attention!" Charlie admonished. "Accidents can happen in a blink."

Lauren moved to the back and swiped the phone. "Give me that!" She shoved it into the pocket of her shorts.

"Hey," Cam protested. Then his eyes widened at how far away his mother was. He had one job, and they all knew he had blown it.

When they got to her, Aimee was laughing, "Sorry! A bee hit my face and I let go! Your turn, Charlie."

Charlie positioned the ladder on the side so Aimee could easily climb aboard and take her spot. She fastened her life vest and jumped overboard, put on the skis, and positioned the rope. "Hit it!"

And they were off again, Cam's eyes peeled on his aunt flying through the water. He could hear her laughter even over the sound of the engine. Lauren also watched carefully, now positioned backward in the back of the boat. No sister would be lost on her watch, no way, no how.

After more than enough sport to turn her arms to spaghetti, Charlie signaled to go back to the dock. Another motorboat was speeding from the far north shore, where the dockside gas station and general store stood. Coming around the island, Colin was bringing the small sailboat in, making it look easy to navigate the wind and dock at the boathouse the first try.

Charlie let go and glided to a stop, sinking down in the water, feet from the dock. Aimee brought the speedboat around, careful not to tangle the ski rope in the propeller, and tied off as Charlie lifted the skis and then herself onto the dock. The other motorboat approached at much too high a speed, waves from the wake crashing into the boats, the docks, and the children in the water—knocking Harmony over, water going up her nose—before the driver killed the engine mere inches from the dock where Charlie had just pulled herself from the water.

Sage gathered her youngest, using her hand to wipe the water from her eyes and reassure the sputtering child she was fine. Tory helped with the other children just moments before, not sure if the driver was out of control or simply reckless.

"Damn it, Tory! Where are they? You made me come all the way out here," the angry man in the boat yelled. His face was red from the blood pressure in his head, not sunburn. His knuckles were white as he gripped the line to tie off the boat and jump up onto the dock.

"Daddy!" Donovan quickly recovered from being knocked down by the waves when he heard his father's voice. He waved his water-winged arms up and down, trying to scramble out of the water and toward the dock. He came to a dead stop as his foot hit the first plank, seeing the look on his dad's face. His little eyes were huge, eyebrows jutting toward his hairline. In a panic, he looked for his mother.

Tory quickly moved from the water, carefully pushing her son back toward Sage and his cousins. "Not now, Mark."

"Oh no, you don't get to tell me no. It's your fault for coming here and not leaving the papers first," Mark yelled, jabbing the air with his finger to punctuate his words.

The adults, not sure what was happening, gathered closer to Tory. Alex carefully disembarked the sailboat and moved with purpose toward the other dock.

"It's good to see you, Mark," Alex said, ever the proper hostess. When all else failed, etiquette worked.

Mark seemed taken off guard by Alex's even tone. "Oh, hi, Alex." Then finding his steam, he continued, "Tory left without telling me and didn't sign the papers I need." Anger again mottled his face as he looked at his wife. His eyes traced her body up and down and back up again, a sneer forming. "God, can't you even cover yourself?" Disgust laced his voice.

Tory automatically shrunk before him, already covered with a long-sleeved, high-necked surf shirt and fully covering swim bottoms, so much demurer than her cousins' bikinis and French-cut one-piece swimsuits. Before she could recover, Mark grabbed her by the arms and shook her, sure to leave bruises.

A collective intake of breath sounded from adults and children alike.

"Mark, I suggest you let go of my niece. Sage and Harper, take the kids to the cottage and give them lunch, please," Alex said evenly, stepping forward. Colin matched his grandmother's steps, ready to step in. Gavin, taking his signals from his brother, followed suit, not sure what was going on. Charlie and Lauren both pushed forward, ready to take the man down, anger seeping from both.

"I'll treat my wife however I want." Mark spit out the words, clearly reading the mood of the island beachfront wrong.

"And I'll knock you on your ass if you don't let go. Now," Charlie said, matching her mother's even tone, though tension radiated from her shoulders and clenched fists.

"What she said." Lauren backed up her big sister, chin jutting forward.

Mark laughed, but not with humor. "Of course, you'd all stick together." He still hadn't loosened his grip. The closer to the man she got, the more Charlie could smell the booze oozing from his pores. *Wow, he must have tied one on last night. Or maybe he was still drinking this morning.*

"Doesn't sound like she's your wife for much longer, so you have no right to touch or speak to her unless she wants you to," Alex said, guessing what the papers were, and hoping to defuse the situation. "And you *never* have the right to put hands on a woman or child, Mark. You should know better."

"All I know is that this cow is not what I thought I was getting when I married her. Her dad hasn't even sent me his golfing buddies as clients like he should have." Mark was somewhat successful as a stock trader, sometimes. "She couldn't even keep her hot bod." Mark shook his head, as if they'd understand.

"She certainly *is* hot, you heinous twit," Lauren declared vehemently. "She had a child and still looks gorgeous! You on the other hand –" Alex stopped her before her daughter could take it further. She also took note of the way Tory's right hand moved to cover her lower abdomen.

"Yes, Lauren, your cousin certainly is a beautiful woman. But that's not why you're here, is it, Mark? Why don't we sit at the picnic table and talk like civilized adults?" She held out her arm, indicating the picnic table positioned just off the beach. No way was she inviting him to the cottage or anywhere near his son.

Tory took that opportunity to pull her arms from Mark's grasp and back away. That seemed to make him angrier. "I just need the papers."

"I haven't had a chance to read them, Mark," Tory said quietly, looking anywhere but into his eyes.

"You've had days, Victoria. Beth and I need to move on with our lives. Our baby deserves that," Mark said, the name of his successfully earning co-worker sending a white-hot poker to her core. He did that on purpose, one more way to embarrass her in front of her family. He let them know he had a girlfriend, pregnant with his child, with whom he was ready to build a life, tossing her aside.

"Days?" Alex jumped in before Tory could answer. "Mark, surely you know our attorney will need to carefully review any papers before my niece signs?" No one made any move toward the picnic table. It was a standoff by the dock.

Ignoring Alex, Mark looked through narrowed eyes at his wife and uttered the words of which she was most frightened. "If you don't sign, I will file for and get full custody of that brat you've been turning against me. Turning him against his own father; how could you do that, Victoria?" That was a lie, and everyone knew it. Tory had hoped he hadn't but knew Van probably heard far more than either of them thought he did. But Mark did this to himself with his cruelty and abuse toward his wife.

Without warning, Mark raised his hand and began to swing toward Tory's face. Charlie reached up, snatched his wrist mid-swing and turned it behind his back in a move that surprised even her. *Huh, who knew? Guess the moves James taught me really do work,* she thought, pleased with herself as she shoved his wrist toward his neck, hoping she caused him great pain. She pushed him back toward the boat he had arrived on. "Time for you to go, Mark. Tory's attorney will be in touch."

Tory had belatedly flinched before Charlie turned the bully back the way he came. She blanched and said quietly, not sure anyone could hear, "What if he follows through on his threat? What if you made this worse by protecting me? What if the court sees how ill-equipped I am to be a mother or a wife?"

Tory flinched again when Charlie pushed Mark into the boat and flung the line in behind him, watching him stumble, catch himself on the seat, and shoot one last look of pure hatred directly at her before he backed the boat from the dock and took off in an angry spit of water waves.

Tory's vision tunneled and she was sure she might faint. Sarcastically she thought, "Why not add one more embarrassing moment to the last minutes filled with embarrassing moments?" Then her vision really did fade and her knees buckled.

"Whoa, no, no, Tory, careful!" Lauren and Gavin both reached for her at the same time, keeping her from hitting the ground. They lowered her to the ground, and Lauren pushed her head between her knees. Alex gathered her niece's hair away from her face and held it behind her neck.

"What a complete dick!" Lauren muttered. "How long has he been hurting you?"

"Lauren, leave her alone. Why don't you go get a bottle of water?" Alex requested.

"I'm fine now, Alex," Tory said with a small voice, eyes tightly closed, head still hanging down.

"Everyone, go on up to the cottage and have lunch. Tory and I will be along after she catches her breath," Alex directed. Her daughters, along with the older grandchildren, silently walked up the hill, preferring to stay and support Tory. But Alex was right, she probably didn't want them so close right now.

The only sounds left after the screen door slammed shut were grasshoppers, birds, and the breeze blowing through the leaves, pine needles, and lake grass. Alex didn't seem to mind the silence, but it was killing Tory. She was so ashamed.

Before she could break the silence, Alex spoke first. "You're so strong, Tory. You always have been. But this is one fight you don't need to carry alone. We've got you."

"Strong?" Tory's tone was incredulous. "I'm anything but. You heard him."

Alex shook her head. She knelt in front of Tory, her knees creaking with age, and lifted the young woman's chin with her finger. "Oh yes, strong. You are strong. Who else could have endured what you have and still survive? Still raise a happy, healthy little boy? Protect that baby you have growing inside? Many others would have caved long ago, or let it affect their child."

"Wait. You know I'm pregnant?" Tory asked, confused how her aunt could know. She had not told anyone yet, hadn't even really processed it herself.

"Well, I saw you protect your belly and then almost faint. Kind of obvious to me," Alex said.

Tory let the fat tears streak silently down her cheeks.

"None of this is on you," Alex continued. "It's all him. Get his voice out of your head."

"Lauren said I'm gorgeous."

"She did. You are. That girl couldn't lie if her life depended on it. You're also smart. Too smart to let that blowhard bully win."

"I am?"

"You are. You are a Newberry through and through. You'll not only survive, but you will thrive. For you and your children. And we'll be here cheering you on." Alex stood and helped Tory to her feet. "So, finish crying your tears. Then go hug that little boy of yours who is probably worried about his mama. Today you can wallow. Tomorrow, we read those papers and call an attorney," Alex asserted.

Tory nodded her agreement; the plan felt right to her. It was the first thing that felt right in a very long time. Yes, she was a Newberry, and her family had her back.

**8**

———————

Another calm morning dawned. The lake air seemed to tire everyone out by the end of the day and they slept in—well, at least longer than she did. She was glad for the time to paint. The landscape was almost done. It was a rendering of the far end of the island, a glimpse of the cottage showing through the thick forest only if the trees swayed just right in the breeze.

Her sketchpad lay close by on the bench seat, pencil on top. No one knew she secretly drew her family members when they weren't looking, capturing the essence that made each who they were. The emotion is what drew her, interested her. The total of the collection, if what she saw so far came to be, would be a powerful statement—on family, on perseverance, on individuality creating collective strength. Alex began to think this may be the way she spent the next Act of her life—quite possibly the final Act—capturing stories through her art.

"Off again so early, Colin?" she asked, not turning around, but knowing it was her eldest grandchild.

"Morning, Grandma. Yeah, I'm going to get the tools and ladder out of the basement and rebuild the treehouse. Thought I'd get organized before Gav and Andi get up. Who knows, maybe Cam will help." He shrugged, knowing Cameron's involvement was a long shot.

"My father and uncles originally built that for my brothers and me," she remembered. "You sure you can handle it?"

"Not completely, but I think we can figure it out." He could measure, hammer, saw; so, yeah, he should be able to do it. It wasn't like starting from scratch. The first thing would be to replace the boards nailed to the tree that acted as the ladder. He could do that before the others were awake.

"Let me know if I can help or, better yet, call someone who knows how to build a treehouse."

"Will do." And he was off.

It was another half an hour before anyone else stirred. Sage disappeared into the kitchen and brought her coffee to sit with her mother-in-law while she painted. Like the older woman, she appreciated what peace and quiet she could get. Five children under eight, while invigorating and fun, could be a lot sometimes. Luckily, they helped take care of one another and worked pretty well as a unit. This was her time to breathe and center herself, try to remember she was but one part of a much larger universe. Once centered, she could make it through the day. *Huh, maybe something from my parents rubbed off,* she thought, surprised by the notion.

"Are you still painting?" Alex broke the silence, eyes still on her canvas.

Sage shook her head. "Haven't had time."

"Don't let it go. You're talented," Alex said. She turned her head slightly to meet her daughter-in-law's eyes.

Sage looked skeptical and stared at the calm scene outside the porch, branches of the giant trees barely swaying in the early morning breeze. She realized Alex was not painting what was in front of her. Quizzically her eyebrows drew inward. "I thought you were painting this." Her hand swept outward.

"No, the other end of the island. From my memory. We'll see how close I come. I like the light on the porch in the morning and this corner seems to be safe from inquiring young minds." Days before, Alex had anchored the boat in the lake at the far end of the island, capturing its beauty in her memory, trying to ensure each tree stayed in her mind's eye, before beginning the landscape.

The island had felt void of energy—humanity—when Alex first arrived, after the funeral. Only old memories and maybe a few ghosts haunted her imagination. She craved that emptiness, that aloneness. She needed time to gather her thoughts. Time to feel, yet she only felt the void. She was numb. She was sure a psychologist would say it was normal. She wasn't so sure. It wasn't the numbness of shock, an emotion she was way too familiar with, having experienced it with her first husband Ian's violent death. This was a void.

She had turned to her painting, bringing forth hidden emotion through the oils, only after opening the cottage for the summer. Cleaning—how could it get so dirty when no one had been there for seven months?—and putting fresh linens on the beds, sanitizing the kitchen. She would not let Aimee know the squirrels, and possibly raccoons, had made it their playground over the winter.

She kind of liked the idea of her ancestors' spirits roaming freely during the winter months, or at night. To feel so connected to the island, she had to believe more than she and her grandmother felt the same way and even from another plane they found respite surrounded by water and the familiarity of the cottage.

Brush to canvas, she shook loose the whimsy of her thoughts and concentrated on the scene she recreated: the far end of the island as seen from the lake. She could control her brushstrokes.

Sage's voice brought her out of her thoughts. "You're so strong." After a slight hesitation, her daughter-in-law added, "William looks up to you so much. I wish I had half your strength."

Alex stopped mid-brushstroke and tried to measure her words before she replied. What your children thought they saw and what was reality were not always aligned. Then she just as quickly chastised herself. Of course she was strong; she simply didn't always want to be.

"You know, you *are* strong. I know exactly what William saw in you. Think about it. He's halfway around the world, and you're raising five, well-behaved, intelligent, beautiful children, and managing everything it takes to run a household, managing finances, and ensuring those kids are well-rounded. You still find time to fill in at the hospital when they need you." Alex paused, thought for a moment. "We all feel less than sometimes. We aren't. That's self-doubt talking, and it's counterproductive. When I feel that way—and believe me when I say I do—I tell my mind to banish those thoughts. If that doesn't work, I fake it." She giggled at the end of her mono-logue. Giggled? That was unlike her.

"You? Fake it? I doubt that," Sage scoffed.

"Oh yes. Often, actually," Alex confessed. "I'll let you in on a secret. When you reach your fifties, you'll realize everyone has their own insecurities and worries, so, rarely, if ever, does anyone notice the shortcomings you see in yourself. You also realize you are enough and all that really matters is whether you're kind and do what you can to help others when you can. You've already got that part down." Alex smiled at her daughter-in-law. "William did well when he married you. I'm so grateful you're part of this family and raising my grandchildren."

Wiping a lone tear, Sage said, "I don't know what to say, Alex. I think you see more in me than I see in myself. Thank you."

"That's another thing about your fifties; you feel free to speak your mind and be brutally honest. I only speak the truth," she said and turned back to finish her painting. It was so close to finished. She was tired of it and ready to start something new.

Sage went back to the kitchen to refill her mug and begin break-fast. She could hear movement across the cottage.

IN ONE OF the bunk rooms, Andi threw a pillow at her brother. "Get up. Colin's already gone." At the same time, Gavin emerged from the bathroom in board shorts, T-shirt, and sneakers.

"Stop!" Cameron grumbled, "I'll meet you out there."

"You better. If you don't help us build it, you can't use it," Andi said.

Cameron's head raised. "Why not? It's common property."

"Nuh uh. Our treehouse, our rules," Gavin said, backing Andi. "If I can help, so can you."

"It'll be fun," Andi coaxed.

"Manual labor? Fun? I don't think so," Cameron said but got up and quickly grabbed shorts and a shirt. It would be just like his sister and cousins to enforce their stupid rule.

"I'm helping too," Cassie said, standing in the doorway in jeans and a sweatshirt, baseball cap pulled low on her forehead, hammer in hand. The nine-year-old twin was determined and ready for building.

Gavin pushed past her on his way to the cottage door. "Cass, I don't think you're tall enough to even reach the first rung on the ladder."

"Then I'll tell Colin to add a lower rung," Cassie replied logically. "Or I'll hammer one on myself." She ran to keep up with her brother's longer legs.

Several minutes behind the others, Cameron walked by his grandmother, who was putting her paint tubes in the tackle box and dropping brushes into the turpentine jar.

"Hey, Cam, have you given more thought to what you want to be?" she asked, picking up a thread of conversation they had started before Hank died.

Cameron shrugged. "Some. Still thinking about writing graphic novels or maybe video games."

"What about making movies or writing for them? Still interested in that?" his grandmother prodded.

Cam's head dropped and he stared at his shoe, kicking the cement slab below the screen door. "Yeah, but Grandpa Hank's gone now. He was going to give me a camera from his office and someday introduce me to his friends in California."

Alex reached under the bench seat to the storage below and pulled out a camera she had charged the night before. "He didn't forget, Cam. Here's the camera. He said you could also capture some good video on your phone. There's never a single path to anything you really want; sometimes you find a new route." She held out the treasure. "How about you come up with a movie or documentary while you're on the island?"

Cam looked skeptical, "Really? You think I could do that?"

"I do," Alex opened the door and handed him the camera. It was capable of capturing both video and stills.

Looking at the camera, he slowly turned it in his hands. "Thanks, Grandma." When he lifted his head, it was the first time in a long time she saw a hopeful look on the boy's face, the typical sullenness gone. He picked up his pace as he wound down the hill at the side of the cottage and around the exposed side of the basement mechanical room and storage, heading toward the forest on the backside of the cottage.

Colin held a board steady way up in the branches, kneeling on the floor of the treehouse, so his little sister could hammer it down. Not as many boards needed to be replaced as he thought there would be. He did need to add a new railing to the side that had collapsed, but the two sides with the solid walls seemed to be holding strong. He saw his grandfather Ian's initials carved on a beam in the ceiling along with his Uncle William's and his mother's and was sure it had been repaired long since his great-grandfather and great-great-uncles had built the original structure. The current repairs were a nice project for the older cousins to work on together, leaving something of themselves when the summer ended.

Cass's tongue poked out at the side of her lips, deep in concentration, determined to show her brothers she could do the work. Andi and Gavin were nailing more replacement boards on the other side of the room. Colin had the boards cut to size by the time they arrived and had installed a new crude ladder to the trunk.

It was a little daunting to Cameron, having to pull himself up the boards affixed to the tree. He backed up a bit, capturing some video and then stills of the work in progress, before shouting upward, "What do you need me to do?"

Colin looked over the open side. "Do you have your phone with you?"

Cameron hesitated. He wondered if this would be another lecture. Before he could answer, Colin said, "If you could take notes on what we need to finish the job, that would be a big help."

Shoulders immediately relaxing, Cameron pulled his phone from his back pocket, ready to take notes. Colin called out the sizes of wood, length of railing, tarp to cover and rainproof the roof, and some special features for which he would need specific tools in order to add to the structure.

"Could you look around under us and around the tree to make sure we didn't lose any rusty nails—or new ones? I don't want anyone to have to make a trip to the hospital for a tetanus shot," Colin said. "There's a coffee can for the old nails by the trunk of the tree."

Relieved he would not be climbing today, Cam eagerly nodded his agreement.

"Yeah, no one wants a tetanus shot. Those suckers hurt!" Gavin grimaced. He had to get one a few weeks before when he had run with friends through an abandoned field near their home. The nail had punctured his sneaker and sent him sprawling with the rusty iron protruding from his foot, blood quickly filling his shoe.

An hour later, out of materials and progress made, Colin called it a day and suggested they all take a swim. Hand-over-hand he lowered a rope with the tool kit tied to it to the ground below, leaving the bucket of nails in the treehouse. He moved down a couple rungs of the tree trunk ladder and waited for Cass to carefully start her climb down, positioning himself in case he had to catch her. Gavin braced himself topside, quietly telling her where to place her foot. The little girl was flexible and sure-footed, showing her brothers she could do what they could do, shorter or not. Her face broke out in a smile when she pushed her feet off the trunk after the ladder ended and landed softly on the forest floor.

"See, I did it," she said triumphantly.

"Yeah, you did good, squirt." Colin annoyed her by ruffling her hair. While her twin's dirty-blonde hair was long, hers was cut above her shoulders in a wavy bob, better to stay out of her way when she played sports or dogged her brothers' steps, insisting on doing whatever they did.

Once the tools were stored in the basement filled with cobwebs and smelling of years of mildew, they raced to the lake, swimsuits underneath their clothes, ready to join their younger cousins, aunts, and mothers in the cool water, refreshing their sweaty and sore bodies. Soon laughter and splashing echoed the joy of summer as the sounds bounced across the waves on the lake.

**9**

———

Weather and moods seemed to be inextricably intertwined.

Rain came down in a steady drumbeat on the metal roof. The chill in the air required the old Franklin stove to be stoked to warm the living area. The sky was a solid sheet of gray, as only Michigan could display—no clouds, only one unending sheet of gray, no gradations, no texture, simply light gray spread across the entire sky.

Alex preferred when low storm clouds threatened, various shapes, sizes, and shades of gray from light to dark. Still, the sound of the rain was comforting. They were cozy in their cottage, three generations cohabitating without stress or strain, for the time being.

Van, Savannah, and Indy were on the floor in a corner of the room playing a children's board game, with Grace joining in and facilitating the rules.

Cameron randomly recorded video, everyone ignoring him; it was becoming normal.

Charlie sat in a red rocking chair with her feet on the seat, book propped against her legs. Alex could not help but see the young girl

54

who used to sit in the exact same position on rainy days decades earlier, always a book in her hands.

On the couch, Cassie, Hudson, and Jaspar flipped through old family picture albums, pointing and laughing, calling out people they knew and deciding who now looked most like previous generations.

Colin sat in an old winged-back chair reading a spy novel, completely oblivious to the family around him.

Andi and Gavin played cards in their own world in the kitchen. Their laughter made its way to the living room while Sage and Tory helped Aimee make sandwiches for lunch and prepped for dinner.

Lauren sat in the living room and flipped through a magazine, bored, sighing loudly every minute or so. Finally, she held up the magazine, shaking it. "Why is this drivel still being published? It sets impossible standards for women and subliminally sends the message women are here for the enjoyment of men and can never be enough. It's a disgrace."

Alex looked up, waiting to see if the monologue would continue. She wasn't disappointed.

"These body sizes are ridiculous. No one should have to starve themselves and watch every morsel they put in their mouths. Did you know that the so-called optimal weight chart the medical profession has used for years was actually created by insurance actuaries, not by medical professionals, and not for health reasons? And why are all these articles focused on how women can improve themselves and achieve their best look?"

"No argument here, Lauren. I figure women who want that are not the people I want to hang with. Don't read it. I don't," Charlie said, going back to her book.

"Something should be done about it," Lauren grumbled.

"So, what are you going to do about it?" Alex asked.

"Me?"

"Yes, you. If something should be done, and you feel that strongly, then be part of the solution," Alex said.

Lauren chewed on her lip for a while. "Well, first of all, we should stop buying these magazines and quit supporting a flawed industry.

We need to promote more positive images of women with a variety of shapes, sizes, and skin tones, who have well-rounded interests that go beyond fashion, makeup, weight loss, and attracting a man. Serious women, powerful women, need to be depicted in Hollywood in all kinds of roles," Lauren continued, on a roll. "That's the fastest way to change the culture. We need to support women running for office—as long as they have the best platform, one that supports equality, of course—so no laws are made or repealed that are anti-equality or anti-woman. That's a start."

"Sounds like you have a direction," Alex smiled. She fervently hoped her youngest daughter would not be beaten down by the inertia that was the enemy of positive change and that she would always be a firebrand.

Before Lauren could continue, Harper appeared from the bedroom where she'd been resting, one hand holding her back and the other supporting her protruding belly. "Ummm. I don't feel so well."

Lauren jumped up and raced to her friend's side. "What's wrong. Morning sickness again?" Morning sickness was a misnomer. It came at all times of the day.

"No, I'm having lots of cramps and pain. I think I'm having the baby," Harper said, looking pale and worried.

"But your due date isn't until the end of the month!" Lauren exclaimed.

"Babies can come early, Laur," Charlie said, standing at the same time as her mother, book now forgotten.

"Did your water break?" Alex calmly asked.

"I don't think so, but I'm not really sure. I was a little wet, but no big gush or anything. But the cramps are closer together," Harper said, her pale face reddening with embarrassment. How could she not know if her water broke or not? And how come she didn't know if she was actually in labor? *These put-together women must think I'm pathetic.*

"Okay, let's get you in some rain gear. We're going to have to take the boat across the lake in the rain. Lauren, grab a duffle bag with a change of clothes for Harper. You may want to grab one for yourself in case you get soaked," Alex ordered.

"I have the outfit I want to bring the baby home in on the top of my bag," Harper said.

"Good thinking." Alex nodded as she grabbed raincoats from the hooks on the screened-in porch.

"We'll take my vehicle. The baby car seat is in the box in the back," Charlie said, pulling on her jacket. "Hey, Sage, might need you; can you come with us? Everyone else, Mom, Lauren, Sage, and I are taking Harper to the hospital. Don't know how long we'll be gone. Everyone behave and help out your aunts," she yelled so those in the kitchen and living area could hear.

Those in the kitchen raced to the porch, eyes wide.

"Want me to go instead, Mom?" Aimee asked, eager to help.

"We'll be fine. You stay here and make sure everyone eats and gets along. Colin, you come along and bring the boat back to the island, please," Alex said.

Soon they had Harper bundled and carefully helped her down the hill, so no one slid on the wet leaves and pine needles or fell in the mud. They raced across the lake to the shoreside dock. Alex got a rush of adrenaline from the speed and the need to get to the nearest hospital, which was forty-five minutes away in West Branch.

Colin idled the boat engine, watching through the downpour as they pulled out of the drive, tires spinning in the soft wet grass until they gained purchase, and raced away.

"Everything all right?" the judge yelled from his side door.

"Yes, judge. Harper thinks she's having the baby."

"Let us know if you need anything."

"Thanks! We will." Colin waved and pulled away.

In the vehicle, Lauren sat on one side of Harper holding her hand, Sage on the other calmly timing contractions and smiling reassuringly at her patient. Charlie raced down the road as carefully as she could, glad for the all-wheel drive on the wet pavement, rain coming down in torrents.

"Maybe it's those fake contractions," Lauren said.

"Not helpful." From the driver's seat, Charlie glared in the rearview mirror at her sister. Harper gave her friend her own glaring "are you for real?" look, though secretly wondering whether it was real labor or Braxton Hicks contractions. One thing she knew: the pain was real. The timing shortened between contractions.

"Just think! Soon we'll have a baby at the island," Alex said, dragging everyone from the current state of panic, pain, anxiety, to the end-state happy result.

Thirty minutes later they arrived at the Emergency Room. Two hours later, the baby sprawled across Harper's chest, skin to skin, declared healthy, cleaned from the remnants of the birth, seemingly content to be out in the world.

"That one was ready to be here," one of the nurses said, surprised at the quickness of the labor and delivery, especially for a first child. "Good thing you got here when you did."

Lauren still looked shocked and uncomfortable, the birth and the messiness associated with entering the world a little much for her, though her only job had been to hold her best friend's hand.

"You were ready, weren't you?" Harper whispered to her daughter. Daughter. That word no longer seemed so daunting. A fierce protectiveness replaced any lingering fear or doubt. She silently promised her daughter would always know she was enough; nothing could make her lose her mother's love.

"Can I hold her?" Sage asked quietly, not wanting to intrude on the new mother's time with her baby. She held a blanket in which to wrap the newborn.

"Of course," Harper smiled. "You helped get her here."

"Do you have a name yet?" Charlie asked.

"Allie," Harper said. Her eyes darted to Alex and then down at her hands, suddenly shy. "Short for Alexandra. For the strongest person and best mother I've ever met."

Alex looked stunned, then smiled brightly. "Thank you, Harper. What a wonderful compliment. I'd say you're pretty darned strong yourself." She held her hands out to Sage and reached for the baby. "My turn."

Allie looked up at her namesake, blue eyes wide for a newborn. Though Alex knew intellectually that experts state newborns can't see clearly, she also knew intuitively the two of them bonded in that moment. She would always look out for this little girl and her mother.

Agreeing to collect Harper and the baby in the morning when they were discharged, the others made their way back to the island, first stopping at the only baby store within sixty miles to buy newborn clothes, burp cloths, towels, and baby blankets, then the pharmacy for diapers and wipes. The torrential rain had slowed to a steady drizzle now. Charlie, driving more slowly on the return, was able to see the road clearly.

Lauren, who had been abnormally quiet in the hospital room, blurted, "I am *never* doing that."

"Never say never," Charlie advised, smirking.

"No, seriously, *never*. That was horrifying. And messy," Lauren said, shaking her head vehemently.

"Oh, poor Lauren, scarred for life," Charlie teased. "Dramatic much?"

Lauren scowled at her sister's back. She was not being dramatic. It really was a traumatic experience.

"It's natural. Circle of life and all that," Charlie said.

Birth. Death. They could take both, as far as Lauren was concerned. Birth was way too messy and distressing. Death was too painful and awful. She missed her father horribly. She could feel the hole in her chest when she remembered she would never see him again. Never feel his accepting arms comforting her. Never hear how proud he is of her. Never...she sighed, rubbing her chest.

"The circle of life can bite me," Lauren gritted out. Then she remembered and muttered to herself, "Oh yeah, it already has."

Alex surreptitiously reached across the front seat console and smacked Charlie's thigh with the back of her hand, hoping her eldest would get the message and not further antagonize her sister, though Alex agreed with Charlie's view of life.

**10**

———————

Alex again stood on the screened porch in front of her canvas. Contemplating. Even the excitement of the day before and the arrival of a new baby didn't deter her. Sleeping in wasn't in her blood.

Morning had dawned with the sun rising over the trees on the east side of the calm lake. The air crisp and fresh after the cleansing downpour the previous day and night. The smell of the recent rain lingered. Fish darted to the surface in their perpetual attempt to grab the insects that flew barely above the water. The loon's song carried in the early morning hour, its mate answering, probably sitting on the nest warming or feeding the babies. One lone fishing boat with two fishers hugged close to the lily pads at the remote end of the island, attempting to lure the fish away from their pursuit of insects with more appetizing treats waiting on their hooks.

Alex tilted her head, her practiced eye critiquing her painting, determined it was as good as it was going to get. The blues, greens, browns, and grays of the island landscape punctuated by spots of brighter color from the lily pad flowers floating on the water. It looked...peaceful; yes, that was the word.

She silently wondered how that had happened. Inside she raged, craved clarity, demanded answers that would never come. She would have thought the painting she allowed to come forth through her brush strokes without planning or much forethought would better reflect her inner turmoil.

*Maybe I should throw some red and orange on a canvas, drag it around with my finger. Would that better represent me? Ha.* She realized maybe —just maybe—this did represent her. Smoothing the rough edges of life, bringing order to chaos. When did she become that woman? Yes, she craved control. Yes, she protected those she loved. But the world was sometimes messy and rarely what people saw on the surface.

She sighed and listened for signs of others rising. She would rather not be left with her own thoughts this morning. The trip to the hospital yesterday, leaving her island refuge, allowed the external world to seep back into her consciousness. How long would it take to get her equilibrium? She would. She knew she would. She always did.

Later, Charlie would take Lauren to collect Harper and Allie from the hospital. Alex would stay on the island. There was a lot to prepare. She had called one of her older brothers the day before, giving him the list of what they needed him to deliver to the island.

The added benefit was Victoria would be face-to-face with her father, and perhaps the conversation that needed to happen would.

There was no doubt in her mind that the entire family would rally around her niece, should she give them the chance, just as the women from the family on the island had. Call it manipulation; she preferred to see it as a happy coincidence, facilitated by a friendly shove in the right direction.

Then there were the treehouse builders. They would be thrilled with the materials their great-uncle delivered. With any luck, the repairs and additions would last another generation or two.

Cleaning her space and brushes, leaving the canvas to dry, Alex lifted her mug and went to the kitchen for a tea refill. She stared at the individual-serving machine and narrowed her eyes. Stubbornly, she turned to the stove and twisted the control for the burner under the kettle. She knew it was a silly reaction. She liked the machine she had bought for herself at home. Here, it was another modern convenience Hank added. Another reminder of his place and influence in their lives.

Unbidden, his face appeared in front of her, her mind a powerful conjurer. Not ready to examine her reactions, she scowled at the image and waved her hand in front of her face, dispelling the face of her dead second husband and focusing on the kettle, willing it to boil.

"What's wrong? Flies?" She heard Lauren's voice before she saw her.

Unwilling to tell her daughter she was vanishing the girl's father, she ignored the question. "Good morning. Ready to pick up the baby?"

"Not really. I don't think we thought this out very well." Lauren sat on a stool at the counter, propped her elbow on the surface, and rested her chin in her hand. She waited for her mother to prepare her a mug of tea when the kettle boiled. "Harper didn't want a shower. We set up her apartment with the baby stuff she bought in one room, but where will a baby sleep here? And clothes? And diapers? I mean—"

"It's fine. I have a crib here I'm pulling out of the storage closet. We picked up the other necessities yesterday. It's all set. Relax," Alex said, knowing how overwhelmed Lauren could get with the basics of living, while her mind was brilliant with the complexities of the world.

"Wow. You did all that? Thanks, Mom," Lauren slumped in her chair, visibly relaxing.

The kettle gathered steam and started the high whistle. Alex pulled it off before it could full-on wake the rest of the cottage. A moment later she pushed a mug across the speckled counter in front of her youngest, a generous pour of milk already added. Lauren added her own sugar.

After a fortifying sip, Alex leaned on the other side of the counter and stared into her daughter's sleepy eyes, the brown color and shape very much like Hank's. As frustrated as she was with her late second husband, she would never regret the daughter they created together. "It won't be easy, Lauren. You've got to know that. But Harper has all of us, which is more than many have. She'll still be able to achieve everything she hoped before the baby; she may just have to work harder for it."

Unsaid was that it was like that for women forever—be what you want, do what you want, achieve what you want, simply work harder than the men and everyone else around you. Alex sighed inwardly at the thought. Maybe not right, but an unfortunate reality. Then, what is ever fair? Everyone has their own trials, regardless of gender or skin tone, whether anyone else sees them or not.

"Her parents are awful people," Lauren huffed.

Alex did not disagree; they seemed to live in another century with impossible standards. However, she would rather her daughter focused on the positive than the negative. Being positive and living a grateful life created a sense of power—and peace—no one could take away.

"But she's wonderful. Her baby is loved and wanted. Focus on that," Alex said. Silently, the irony smacked her in the face; she bid herself to apply the sentiment to her own life.

Charlie hurried into the kitchen and around the counter, giving her mother a half hug on her way to the kettle. "Got enough hot water left for me?" She did not give the single-serve machine a glance, homed in directly on the stove. "Ahh, great," she sighed as she poured water over a tea bag, milk on top of that.

Charlie slid back around the counter to sit next to Lauren, a side glance at the bottle opener pirate staring at her from below the rim of the back counter, ever holding his vigil over the kitchen. A twinge hit her gut. Nostalgia? Happiness? Longing? Shaking it free, Charlie didn't have time to examine her reactions.

"Want to head out after the tea?" Charlie asked. "We can have breakfast in town, if you want." Lauren nodded and at the same time a horn honked, two short blasts.

Alex winced. "The neighbors will love that." She hurried out the door, her daughters following, and headed down the hill to the lake.

She inwardly loved that her brother did not hesitate to use the age-old method of attracting the islanders' attention instead of reverting to his mobile phone. Closing in on the dock, she could see her brother back his big, black truck as close to the dock as he could get, wave to her when he got out, and begin unloading onto the dock.

"What's all that?" Lauren asked.

"Our reinforcements," Alex replied cryptically. "I told you; family takes care of family—blood or chosen."

Jumping into the boat, the three made their way to the shore, cutting a straight path through the water. Tying off on the shoreside dock, they all climbed out and hurried to help Maitland Newberry unload his truck.

"Wow!" Lauren exclaimed, eying the new crib mattress wrapped in plastic, along with a box for a baby swing and several brightly colored baby toys, sitting amongst the wooden rail sections, beams, and random lumber and hardware store purchases.

Maitland slammed the tailgate closed and faced his sister and her daughters. "When the queen calls, the liege jumps."

"Queen, hrrmmpph," Alex responded. Her brother was a successful attorney, staying in the hometown their ancestors had helped found.

"Youngest or not, you're the matriarch now, sis, the glue who holds us all together," Maitland insisted, hugging her to him.

"Thanks for this, Mait," she said, hugging him back. "Guess I'll get it back to the island."

He shook his head. "I'm coming with you. Took the day off." Truthfully, Alex didn't even know what day it was. One ran into the other in her island existence. Weekdays were no different than weekends—except, she reasoned, there were more boats on the water on the weekends.

"Excellent! Let's all get a move on." Alex looked at the load weighing down the boat and jumped in. "You two honk when you're back," she called after the backs of her daughters.

Charlie waved over her head without turning around. "We wouldn't think of summoning you any other way, Mother." Why use modern technology when the old ways were so effective, albeit intrusive to everyone within hearing distance?

Island side, the inhabitants were moving, beginning their day. Colin and Gavin were waiting when the sister and brother docked. Colin's blue eyes lit up when he saw the lumber, particularly the readymade railing sections.

"Need some additional labor?" Maitland asked. Alex could tell he secretly hoped the kids wouldn't mind his participation. He turned to her and said so only she could hear, "Even thinking about the old treehouse makes me feel years younger."

"Really?" Colin asked, eyes even wider. "You want to help?"

"Absolutely."

The boys got busy hauling the wood to the treehouse, enlisting the help of their cousins. Hudson and Jaspar helped Cassie with the lighter, smaller purchases. Colin was quietly relieved when his measurements were exact and the pre-made railing sections fit perfectly. Hauling the heavy lumber up with their makeshift ropes was heavy, sweaty work.

They could see the outline of the cottage through the trees, but it was far enough away that they could feel the treehouse was their own domain. Their great-uncle was a surprising help and even went so far as to suggest they expand the space, reinforce the beams above and below, and create lookout windows on the solid sides of the structure.

They were no longer self-conscious with Cameron pointing the camera in their direction and documenting every moment of summer.

"The tarp will keep the water out for now when it rains. But I might have some friends come out and really roof it, or maybe we should change to a metal roof. What do you think?" Maitland asked the kids.

"You don't need to do that," Colin protested.

"But I want to. This has been here for a long time. I want it to be here for many more generations. Why not do it up right?"

Colin and the others couldn't argue with the logic but didn't really want professionals coming and finishing what they started. "Will they let me help?" he asked.

"And us," Andi and Gavin said together.

"I'm sure they would," Maitland said, making a mental note to ensure it was a metal roof; that would mean no need for the kids to be suspended on a sloped roof high above the uneven ground, nailing shingles.

Colin gave one short nod, acquiescing to his great-uncle's suggestion. After cleaning up the space and checking for rogue nails on the ground, the kids stored the tools and raced to the lake, where everyone else was already gathered.

Harper and Allie were the only ones resting in the cottage, with Lauren hovering close in the living area. Lauren thought it was crazy insurance companies could make hospitals discharge new mothers and their infants the very next day—all for their almighty profits, not what was best for the mother and child. Other countries were far better equipped for and in tune with maternal-fetal health. One more thing to add to her "fix it" list.

Maitland walked more slowly toward the shore, his knees not cooperating. Gritting his teeth, it was easy to read his irritation that his age was showing.

"Grandpa! When did you get here?!" Donovan yelled and raced full tilt toward Maitland, jumping up at top speed, expecting his grandfather to catch him. Maitland dipped low and complied, raising the little boy into his arms, swinging him around, taking some of the momentum out of the strength of his leap. Pretty soon Donovan was going to have to slow it down or bowl over the adults.

Down the beach, Victoria visibly blanched. She pulled at the mock turtleneck of her surf shirt and pulled the hem of her boy-short swim bottoms, hoping the action would shield her from view. After greeting everyone else and swinging the other kids who waited their turns, Maitland plopped down on the beach blanket, looking out toward the water where the older kids were now sailing and kayaking. His eyes didn't stray to his daughter. She began to wonder if her hope for invisibility worked. She would certainly not break the silence.

Finally, Maitland spoke. "No reason to hide from me, Tory."

"What are you doing here, Dad?" she sighed.

"What? I can't check on my family?" he asked, still not looking at her. She didn't respond, so he added, "Alex asked me to bring a crib mattress and treehouse supplies, among other things."

Now she glared toward her aunt. Had she called Tory's father to force her to talk to him? "Is this an intervention?"

Alex moved closer and shook her head. "Nothing so nefarious, I'm afraid." She shot her niece a kindly smile, one where Tory looked for but detected no pity. "But never miss an opportunity. Right, Tory?"

"Did you tell him Mark showed up here and why?" Tory's irritation, bordering on panic, coming to the surface.

"She did not," Maitland assured his daughter. "Mark's attorney saw me at the courthouse and asked if I knew when you would return the paperwork. He wants to go on vacation. But I'm only here to deliver supplies." After a moment's hesitation he asked, "Why didn't you tell me you were having problems, Tory? We rarely see you anymore and don't spend nearly enough time with our grandson, unless we kidnap him for the day."

"One more failure, Dad." Tory sighed quietly, yanking the hem of the shorts even farther down her legs.

Maitland realized what Tory had said and asked, concern marking his voice, "What's this about Mark showing up? By the way, I have no idea why you'd think you're a failure, but we'll examine that later."

Alex related the incident; Tory remained silent.

"I never liked that son of a bitch," Maitland growled. "I should beat the shit out of him."

"Language, Mait," Alex said gently. The kids were all occupied, and no one could hear their conversation, but the response was automatic. Alex could admit to herself she wanted to do the same thing—maybe even take a shovel along.

"Tory, maybe you should go over the paperwork with your dad.

I'll watch Van. Mait, we already marked what we saw as problematic clauses and put in what Tory should demand. Maybe you can convince your daughter she's worth more than she thinks and now is not the time to play nice."

Tory stood, walking gracefully toward the cottage. "I guess I've been listening too much to Mark. He doesn't see much good in me at all."

"Bastard." Mait's voice was low and full of grit. "You're intelligent, beautiful, and a great mother. You're the whole package."

"Dad."

"He's the loser, Victoria. Always has been. He only says you're not those things because he wants to control you. You will not be controlled; got that? Not anymore."

Maitland hit straight to the heart of the issue. Tory was only now realizing Mark had made her feel so undesirable she no longer wanted to be seen. He had told her so often she was stupid that she was afraid to say anything of substance to anyone.

Instead, she holed away in their house—the house that was way too big, the house he demanded when she wanted a small, attractive cottage—losing what friendships she had left and cutting most contact with family.

Then the bruises he left behind during his rages cinched her desire to rarely leave the house. Charlie's insistence she join them when she talked to her after the funeral, coupled with the legal envelope on her counter, made the decision to escape to the island a purely emotional one. She needed her family. She needed to be seen for who she was. She needed to find who she was again.

"Dad." One word that carried the weight of the world. One word to express disbelief, gratefulness, and the myriad of other conflicting feelings that coursed through her in that moment.

"I'm on your side. Always," Maitland said. No room for doubt. No opening for equivocation. No space for disagreement.

The two sat at the kitchen counter, side-by-side, papers spread in front of them.

"Coffee?" Mait asked, rising to make himself a cup from the

single-serving machine, after they had made one pass through the documents. Tory could tell his blood was boiling, but he was controlling his anger for her sake.

Tory hesitated. Her father noticed. His daughter was addicted to coffee, just as he was. With those dark circles under her eyes, he had no doubt she craved caffeine at that moment. The glance to her midsection made Tory blush.

"Does he know?" he asked.

How did her father always know? She could keep nothing from him. Maybe that's why she stayed away. Not only did she not go to law school and join him in his practice—with Mark's insistence she support him through his MBA and financial certifications, and then stay home to raise their child, she never did go to law school—she felt she was a failure in her father's eyes. But staring into those eyes now, she didn't see the expected reproach, only support, and maybe some pain from being left in the dark. Oh, there it was, the anger toward her soon-to-be ex-husband.

"No." Tory sighed yet again.

Maitland made his coffee and looked for a decaffeinated tea pod for his daughter. Setting both mugs on the counter, sliding the milk jug toward her, he leaned his tall, still trim body forward. His hair was short, as it had always been, now more steely gray than dark brown at age sixty-three, his brown eyes bright and clear. No one had ever doubted Maitland Newberry's intelligence or his resolve. The man won more cases than he lost and was sage counsel for the better part of the surrounding area's population.

"First, he doesn't get the house. I made that down payment, so he can live in an alley, for all I care," Maitland said.

"We paid you back," Tory said, her voice quiet, small.

"*You* paid me back, Tory, not that I asked you to. He wasn't even working at the time."

*Huh. I did,* Tory thought. Somehow, she'd forgotten amidst Mark railing how he paid for everything, how he did everything. Come to think of it, even in high school she was not just a pretty face cheering on the football team. She was in the top five in her class and would have been valedictorian had she not spent so much time doing Mark's homework for him. *Huh.*

College was much the same. She didn't go to her father's alma mater because Mark hadn't been accepted. She went where he could play football, and she could do most of his coursework. Then came the battle when she was accepted to law school. He insisted she defer until he was set up in his financial practice. He wasn't even that good an investment broker, relying more on his colleagues' and company's acumen than any talent himself.

"What am I going to do?" Tory whispered.

"I've got some ideas, if you want to hear them…" Her father was careful with his offer. To him, she seemed fragile. Yet he saw some of the strength she used to display with so little effort return to her eyes, the set of her jaw, the shoulders that straightened from her slump.

"Okaaaay." She drew the word out slowly, as if she wasn't sure whether she wanted to hear.

Maitland laid out the semblance of a plan, including engaging an attorney for his daughter. They would make their own demands in the divorce petition. The house would go to Tory. Minimal monthly supervised visitation with Van and the baby once born. Child support, unless Mark wanted to relinquish all parental rights. Alimony until Tory completed law school—only fair since she unfailingly supported him through school.

They expected the final decree to be somewhere in the middle.

They would get pictures and Emergency Room records from the far-flung hospitals Mark insisted she travel to so no one in town would know about his abuse. They would file a restraining order.

Tory would reapply to law school for the following fall. She would work at her father's law office—something she did throughout high school and summers during college—until she got her law degree and joined the practice as an attorney. Maitland would fund school, since he never touched the funds he originally set aside for her law school costs, always hoping she would complete her education.

If she was awarded the house, she would sell it. She and the kids were welcome to move to her parents' home for as long as she wanted, but that was not what she wanted. Eventually she and her children would move to a smaller home—more to her style and what she had wanted from the beginning.

By the end of the discussion, legal document markups, and thoughts of her future before she had even come to terms with her past, Tory was completely spent, sure her tears were finally gone as she stoically faced the long road ahead.

**11**

———————

Dinner was a rowdy affair. Adults and kids gathered around the oversized dining table with bench seating. Maitland stayed for dinner, grandson Van eating primarily from his grandfather's plate, beaming up at him. That was something his father, Mark, would never have allowed.

The kids—no matter how small—had a voice, as had always been the case around the Newberry table. They could all state their opinions, joys, questions, with adults eagerly listening, contributing, and clarifying. The political landscape was a usual contender for time and this night was no different.

"Any idea when my brother is going to get out and where you'll live when he does?" Aimee asked, as she carefully surveyed the table, making sure everyone had what they needed, and no dishes needed refills. If it were up to her, the entire family would move to Michigan, to the town of their ancestors.

Sage shook her head, but before she could answer, Charlie jumped in. "He's going to have to decide where he wants to run first. Michigan, Connecticut, and Virginia are all contenders. With his service record, the party would welcome him with open arms."

"Is that still the plan?" Maitland asked. The unspoken part of his question "now that Hank is gone," but Alex heard it anyway.

"So far," Sage said. "But he isn't planning to get out of the service yet."

"It's the plan, eventually," Charlie said. "We still have the basic strategy. I'll have the team run a study to see where the most likely place would be for him to win." There were advantages to majority family ownership of the political analytics and image firm.

Aimee rolled her eyes. "Of course, you will. Maybe Sage would like a say in where they put down roots?"

Eight-year-old Hudson, Sage and William's oldest, piped in, perfectly comfortable adding to the adult conversation. "If we stay in Virginia, you'll be close to the Naval Academy when I'm there." The boy already had his heart set on following in his father and grandfather's footsteps; whether that would remain the case was yet to be seen.

"I want to move to Michigan and work with Aunt Aimee and Uncle Andrew in the restaurant. I'm going to be a chef," six-year-old Indy declared with the absolute confidence of a child. "Let's move to Michigan, Mom."

"I want to be in Michigan too. There's more family here," seven-year-old Jaspar said.

"We'll take that all under advisement," Sage promised.

"Look at you! Breaking out those diplomatic chops already. William is lucky you're his wife," Lauren joked.

Alex and her children had lived in Michigan, Washington, DC, and Connecticut at various points in their lives. All felt like home, for different reasons. She and Hank—no—*she* still owned homes in all three. She needed to remember to use the singular now; there was no "we." It would make sense for her son to contemplate an eventual run for office from one of the three "home" bases.

Picking up on a thread of the conversation, the one relating to "home," Van, eyes wide and steady, looked directly into his grandfather's eyes and asked in a quiet voice, "Can Mommy and me move in with you and Grandma? Can that be our home?" Tory caught the question and her forehead immediately wrinkled and her lips pursed, trying to keep tears at bay, her entire visage pained.

Gently, Maitland spoke quietly, hoping this would not become the next vein of the conversation, for his daughter's sake. "You're always welcome at our house, Van. But you and your mommy have a home."

The little boy got on his knees on the bench so he could whisper in his grandfather's ear. "But Daddy wouldn't come to yours. He's not nice to Mommy and me."

That did it. Maitland was going to officially beat his soon-to-be ex-son-in-law to a pulp. He cleared his throat and said, "How about you think about all the fun things you have left to do on the island and leave all the worrying to me?"

Satisfied with that answer, Van dropped to rest his behind on his heels and turned back to his grandfather's plate, ignoring his own, a smile on his chubby, tanned face.

On the dock that evening, the sun was beyond the western horizon. The moon rose bright, shimmering light tattooing the water with a magical beam. The boats gently rocked against the two docks in the gentle, rhythmic beat of the waves.

Brother and sister stood side-by-side, surveying their surroundings, drinking in the peace, smelling the cooler air that rose after the sun set. The fragrance of the water was still fresh, blending with the aroma of the summer trees standing guard.

In contrast to the serenity around them, Maitland said with venom, "I'm going to kill him."

Charlie came up behind the two, joining as opposed to interrupting their contemplation. "I'll bring the shovel."

"Stop it, you two. Don't put that into the universe. It's beneath both of you," Alex chastised. Not that she hadn't had moments filled with the same sentiment, but she pushed them away and tried to focus on what was best for her niece and great-nephew.

"Can I at least beat the shit out of him?" Maitland grumbled.

"He's more than thirty years younger, don't try. Unless he throws the first punch. Then by all means." Alex smirked.

"I think I can take him," Maitland argued, obviously remembering his younger years.

Though, her brother *was* in good shape, and Mark seemed to be drinking himself into an early grave, so, maybe...

Her brother interrupted her musing. "Okay, take me to the other side. I guess I have to leave the magic. Reality calls."

"I'll take you, Mait," Charlie said.

"Oh no! I'm not leaving you two alone to plot. We'll all go," Alex said, dropping into the ski boat.

"Sorry, she's on to us," Maitland joked, arm around his niece.

As he waved on his way to his truck, still backed up to the dock, he said, "I'll get the ball rolling on what Tory needs, including the attorney and what he'll counter to the asshole's attorney. And the restraining order." They were glad the man was on their side.

Alex steered the boat away from the shoreside dock and cut to the left, steadily increasing speed with a hand on the throttle lever, not heading the straight path to the island. Her almost shoulder-length curls caught the wind and beat time against her face. No one had said anything yet about the white beginning to show prominently at her roots.

A conscious decision, she would no longer let oppressive societal norms for women dictate her style, her actions, or, frankly, her hair. No coiffed, age-appropriate cut, straightened into submission. She was going to let the wild curls, albeit white, no longer dirty blonde, fly. Next to go would be the skirts and heels. She never liked them anyway.

The moon was bright enough they could see most other boats, if there were any, even if those boats didn't have the regulation lights for nighttime boating. Their lights shone on the dark water. Charlie stood beside her in the left-side passenger seat, her own wild curls, still dirty blonde, flying in the wind. Her daughter never cared what anyone thought yet commanded any room she entered, even if she didn't see the power of her presence herself. That gave her the humbleness that endeared her to most.

"I take it we're not heading back," Charlie said.

"Do you have something you have to do?"

Charlie smirked at her mother, her face clearly visible in the moonlight.

"Didn't think so." Alex answered her own question and smirked back.

"Faster!" Charlie urged.

"Just look out for fishing boats with no lights," Alex said and increased the speed, the bow rising before them, waves large in their wake, sure to annoy any fishers out after dark. They raced across the lake, quick turns, raced back again, over and over. Suddenly Alex pulled the throttle back and the boat came to an abrupt halt, their own wake rocking them in the swells. The momentum pitched Charlie forward but she caught herself before she smashed into the windshield.

"Maybe we should send Mark out on a boat with you," Charlie suggested sarcastically.

"Hush, you," Alex giggled. She leaned back in her seat and stared directly up at the stars. Maybe she'd paint a night scene next. Yes, the dark colors would soothe her soul, particularly with the path the moon illuminated across the water, promising something yet to be discovered. She continued to stare, moving her gaze to the island sitting vigil the length of several football fields away, memorizing the scene, searing it into her gray cells.

When her friend Maddie visited, Alex made a mental note to bring her out for a nighttime ride. The light, shadows, water, and distant shore, with its gloomy silhouettes promising some manner of humanity within, would stir Maddie's imagination; she was sure of it. The woman oozed creativity and inspiration.

That's probably why she was a successful screenwriter and producer in her own right. Who would have thought her friend from the national newspaper in Washington, DC, so many years ago would now move in West Coast circles? She was as much a part of their family as any blood relative. Age between Alex and Charlie, Maddie had her own unique relationship with Alex and each of her children, especially Charlie.

Alex took a deep breath and banished the shadow thinking to the recesses of her mind. They threatened to appear when she opened herself to the pleasant memories. Her friend could not arrive soon enough, as far as she was concerned. Adults or not, she refused to burden her daughters, niece, or chosen daughter with the weight of her thoughts.

First, she needed to make sense of the tangled web created by Hank's death. Who was she kidding? The web was woven long before his death; she was simply not privy to it until that night. "Thoughtless, stupid man," she muttered under her breath. Then another cleansing breath allowed that unwanted thought to disperse in the wind, bringing full circle her peaceful night on the boat with her daughter, staring at the sky and dark lake.

"I miss James," Charlie said quietly, stargazing, same as her mother.

"He was a good man. I miss him too," Alex said.

"Staring up at the night sky like this, everything so big, makes me think my problems are pretty small and insignificant in the grand scheme," Charlie said.

Alex weighed that sentiment in her head, testing how it felt. Slowly she nodded. "I can see that." Then she added, "But isn't that what life is? Made up of small moments, some significant, some not? All that matters is that they matter to us. Maybe that's the collective human condition—one moment, one memory at a time. Doesn't matter the size of the universe, only what you make of it, huh?"

"Yeah, I guess," Charlie conceded. Musing more, she said, "I hope he's out there keeping watch over us. I know he's in my heart and my memories—and he certainly appears often enough in my dreams. I like the thought that he's the kids' guardian angel."

"I believe he is." Her son-in-law was rare, much like her first husband, Ian, both good to the core.

"Do you miss Hank? Or Dad?" Charlie asked, the last spoken more hesitantly.

"I think of your dad every day, Charlie. That'll never change. I feel like he's a part of me."

"Was it different with Hank?"

Alex contemplated the question, not sure if she knew the bigger answer herself; the simple answer was a resounding "yes." "They were different, yes. Both good men. Your father was selfless to a fault, duty always came before any of his own wants and needs. Hank cared about others, certainly our family, but he demanded what he wanted out of life. A different approach, I guess. With Hank, I miss the man who made me feel like I was a priority." Alex hoped that was enough of an answer. Whether she was truly a priority or not, she may never know. What she wouldn't give to have never lost Ian, but wishing something she couldn't change was fruitless.

"I know death is natural, even when it comes unnaturally early," Charlie said. "I tell the kids to channel their emotions to make them stronger, not wallow. I tell them their dad will never be gone because he's a part of each of them. And I tell them I believe he's watching out for them."

"You're good at this motherhood stuff, Charlie."

"Thanks. I learned from the best," Charlie said. Then she admitted, "Feel like I'm failing most of the time though. But I keep trying. I keep getting up every morning."

"That's a huge part of life. Simply getting up, showing up, never giving up."

Both left to their own thoughts, they recognized it would sometimes be so much easier to give up—but that was not an option. That was not what they did. They were women of stronger stock, a long line of strong women before them. They embraced that and prayed they passed it on to their children.

At that moment two shooting stars, one following the other, streaked across the sky above their heads.

"If ever there was a positive sign, we just got one." Alex sighed, knowing those were dying or dead stars, light only now reaching earth, but they portended all the possibility in life.

"Maybe Dad and James are hitching a ride, waving at us," Charlie said, her lips turned up at the corners. "That would be just like them."

"Yeah, it would."

**12**

___________

Wind. Not a gentle breeze, but a gale blowing, whistling against windows probably in need of a better seal. Then came the large rain drops, splatting like a paint ball game against the glass and the sturdy metal roof.

Alex steeled herself for another day indoors. This was day three of the wind and intermittent downpour. While one day was a nice change, and two days were workable, three days became stifling. Multi-generational living made the time more interesting, always something to discuss, debate, explore. It also meant more people to keep an eye on the youngest family members.

Her phone pinged beside her on the bedside table, signaling an incoming text.

**William: Mom, plug in the internet lol**

**Alex: William! I miss you...Plugging in**

She lowered to her hands and knees on the wooden floor and reached under the bed, finding the modem plug, and blindly aimed for where the electrical outlet rested in the wall. She found it on the third try, thankful she did not have to crawl all the way under. Her knees were not what they used to be, not that she would ever admit it. She pulled herself back up with her arms.

**Alex: Done**

**William: Open your laptop and I'll video in**

Alex hurriedly opened her laptop, resting safely on her grandmother's vanity at the foot of the bed. The call came in and she could see little of the background, her son in fatigues, the edges a makeshift structure, and beyond what might be a desertscape, but she wasn't sure.

"Don't have a lot of time, but wanted to check in. How are you?" her son asked, that same dirty blonde hair as his two older siblings looking even blonder and dirtier, longer and wavier than the last time she saw him.

"All is well here," Alex said. "Sage is doing a great job. The kids are happy and healthy. Oh, and Harmony is a fish—" Alex said of his youngest daughter. "She can swim as well as the older kids now. No fear in that one."

"That's great, Mom. I miss them. A lot." William swallowed. Then he stared into the camera, unwavering, looking so much like his biological father in that moment. "But I want to know about you. How are you?"

Oh. Was her son worried about her? Seeing no pity for the twice-widow in his blue eyes, only genuine concern, she considered how to answer. She was fine. She really was. She had a lot to work out in her own mind, but very little had to do with devastating grief. Maybe later she would grieve. Or not. Death really did not strike her the way it used to. She saw it as natural, sometimes preferable, depending on the person's suffering. She also didn't think it was final. But her son was not asking that from halfway around the world. He was concerned about her grief and moving forward.

"I'm doing well. It's not my first rodeo." She tried for levity, laugh with the widow.

William pursed his lips, then gave her a crooked half smile, one side of his mouth rising. "Okay, Mom. I believe you. Better let me talk to the brood before I get kicked off."

Alex opened the bedroom door and shouted, "Sage, kids, William is on video."

They charged in from the living area, the kids bouncing up on their grandmother's bed, atop the worn red, navy, and khaki quilt created by her great-grandmother. Sage sat on the matching bench seat in front of the vanity, with Harmony in her lap.

Alex pulled the door shut behind her as she called, "I love you, William! Stay safe. I'll give you some privacy."

A few minutes later her youngest grandchildren walked through the door, quieter than when they went in, but all smiling. It was a lot. They were happy, but she understood it was bittersweet, their dad not enjoying their summer with them.

In the room, alone with her husband, if only on screen, Sage said, "There's been a lot of discussion about your future. Our future."

"Let me guess: Aimee wants us to move to Michigan, Charlie is ready to launch my political career."

"Yes. And yes. But what do you think? Maybe we should move to Michigan, be closer to family," Sage said.

William's look turned serious. "I'm not ready to get out yet, babe. Do you want to move to Michigan? Charlie and her kids are still in DC. Aimee will never leave Michigan. Mom could end up in either of those or in Connecticut. Has she decided?" Questions hung in the air.

"I don't know. I like it here. It feels like home." Sage, who had never had a real place to call home, liked the coziness of the small town. "I'm not sure about your mother. She hasn't said much, come to think of it."

William sighed. "Sounds about right. She'll keep it tight, until she's ready to make a proclamation." In a lower voice, probably hoping his buddies didn't hear, he said, "I miss you so much. I hope we get stateside before the holidays. I love you, babe."

"I love you too, William. Stay safe—" Before she could add anything else, the video picture pixilated. Then he was gone. Sage sat in the chair, a single tear escaped and rolled slowly down her cheek. Ugh. She was turning into a sentimentalist. Dashing the tear from her cheek, she took a fortifying breath, stood, and plastered a smile on her face, once again opening the door to the world.

The living room was buzzing with conversation. Her kids were excited to tell their cousins about their short chat with their father. The other kids sat, eagerly listening, all attention on the youngsters. She marveled, yet again, how this family rallied around one another. It didn't matter if they lived halfway across the country, or on the other side of the world, they were there for one another. What a wonderful gift to pass on to the next generations.

THE KITCHEN WAS QUIET, Aimee working by herself, humming along with the song she heard softly playing on the old FM radio that sat in the corner of the counter since before she was born. Created for longevity, not the obsolescence of modern technology.

Alex slipped in and filled the kettle for her tea. Once it was ready, she sat at the counter, allowing the brew to steep, and watched her daughter work. Aimee had her dirty-blonde hair pulled up in a pony-tail, moving easily, hips swaying to the music as she hummed. She was so at home in the kitchen. Happy.

"What are you going to do now?" Aimee asked, back turned to her mother. Alex knew the words sounded innocent, but her daughter was dying to delve into her life, psyche, and future.

"I thought I'd drink my tea and watch you in your element."

Aimee's shoulders heaved in a huge sigh, reminiscent of her teenage years, when Alex and her stepfather could not possibly understand anything she was going through. "You know I meant: what's next? How are you feeling? Do you need to cry? Have you thought where you'll live? Have you even processed that Hank's gone? Do I have to ask all the questions everyone else here is tiptoeing around?"

Alex inwardly cringed. Yes. Here it was. The intervention she had been expecting, though the others weren't in the room to gang up on her. This was the first time in weeks she'd been alone with her daughter, so, of course, Aimee had waited for the opportune moment.

Alex ran her finger absently over the old, speckled countertop, the one she stubbornly refused to let Hank replace with granite or stone. He never understood why she wanted those things in her home but would not allow him to upgrade the cottage; just as he would not, had he lived, understand her aversion to using the single-serve coffee/tea machine here that she used regularly at home. She thought this last was more a reaction to Hank's death and his having bought the thing, than to the contraption itself.

Through this musing, Aimee stood, hand on hip, staring at her mother, waiting. After a few moments, she wondered if her mother even remembered what she had asked.

"Mom?"

"I heard you. I'm not sure what you want to hear from me," Alex said, trying to be as honest as possible, without being offensive. Her daughter was sensitive; she and her youngest sister had that in common.

The lighting in the kitchen was a bright contrast to the outside gray and the even darker shadows cast by the trees in the storm, though the kitchen light was yellow and warm, not the harsh brightness of fluorescents.

"Let's start with how you're feeling."

"I feel fine. Good even."

"Your husband died," Aimee prompted.

"I don't have dementia. I know that," Alex said more sharply than intended, then soothed it with, "It's not the first time this has happened to me."

Aimee stayed quiet, waiting for more. Alex left her hanging a few more moments, then said, "Of course, I feel some sadness when I see something Hank would appreciate, like Lauren wanting to marry Harper because she's worried about her friend and the baby. I turn to nudge him in the ribs and he's not there. Of course, I miss some of that intimacy. But I'm not immobilized by grief. Death happens to all of us, someday. We go on. That's what we do—at least in this family. So, yes, I'm fine."

When Ian died, she was only thirty-six years old and had wanted so badly to allow the grief to immobilize her, to rail at the injustice, lament everything she would never experience with him at her side.

But she'd had a fifteen-, ten-, and nine-year-old to worry about; she had not had time to allow it to consume her. So, she buried her grief and continued to live, moving forward. It worked for her. In time, she realized she had not buried anything, but allowed the memories to bathe her in their sweetness and pain in moments alone. Even in death, she allowed the intimacy of what they had shared together give her strength to move forward.

"I knew Hank longer than I knew Dad." Sadness streaked across Aimee's face.

"You did. You were lucky; two fathers who loved you unconditionally."

"Not so lucky; they're both dead."

"No, that's not lucky," Alex said. "That's simply the way life and death go. But you were and are lucky. You know what it is to have a father—two good fathers," she persisted, determined her daughter would see the positive side of her life. And no matter what else about Hank, he had been a good father and grandfather to all the children.

"Yeah, we're lucky with that," Aimee said. "Will you miss anything else now that Hank's gone?"

Not thinking before she spoke, and hoping for a way to stop this line of questioning, Alex said, "Sex. I'll miss sex. I like sex. A lot."

"Ooh, Mother, enough. TMI—too much information. Aren't you beyond that stage?" Aimee cringed.

"Beyond it? I don't think you get beyond it if you really like it." Alex shrugged, secretly enjoying her daughter's discomfort. "Anyway, I'm not old. I'm in my fifties. You'll see someday."

Not to be thrown off course, Aimee stayed on track with her questions. "Where are you going to live?"

Ugh, the intervention continued. Alex tried her best to look as if her daughter had asked a ridiculous question and said, "I assume I'll live where and how I've been living. Why do you think that would change?"

"You don't need three houses anymore, do you? Plus the island? I thought you had those to be close to us and your grandkids, and

Hank's company," Aimee reasoned. "Why not stay here, and everyone can come to you from now on?"

Temper quickly flared and then fled. The company was Hank's *and* hers. Her money had helped build it from the beginning, and she remained an active participant, though she much preferred her writing. Admittedly, over the years, the company had come in direct conflict with her political commentary at the newspaper; she had to let go of the job she loved to keep her reputation intact. That still stung, but it was a choice. Everything was always about choice.

Houses. Back to the houses.

There was the one in Michigan, in her family for many generations. None of her three older brothers wanted to take on the old house, their wives preferring newer homes, but she loved it. As with the island, she could feel the ever-present spirits of her parents, grandparents, and ancestors. It sat on a beautiful, tree-lined street, up a small incline from the sidewalk below. The judge and his wife still owned the house across the street. Next door were their friends and Michigan political insiders; they had known Ian and been business associates of Hank's, as well as friends.

Then there was the house in Stonington, Connecticut, Hank's parents' summer home on the water he had inherited upon their deaths. A quick train or car ride to either New York or Boston. Very convenient. She guessed that was now hers. He had added her to the deed years before.

The townhouse in DC belonged to her and Ian when she first lived in the nation's capital and worked on Capitol Hill and then at the national newspaper. It was there she had Charlie. The woman next door, whose husband was a diplomat at the Guatemalan embassy, insisted on providing daycare while she worked, and Ian was eventually deployed. Charlie still spoke Spanish like a native. Alex couldn't see selling her first home.

It was not lost on her that Aimee expected her to choose Michigan, where she and her family would live nearby and not have to travel to see her. That made her smile. Her selfless daughter had a little chink in that flawless armor.

"I think it's fine just the way it is. Who knows, maybe someday William and his family will want to be in Connecticut or maybe Lauren will want the house that has been in her father's family. Maybe one of the grandchildren will work in DC and need the townhouse—it's so expensive there now, why would we get rid of something so close to everything and worth so much more than when I bought it? Maybe William will need it once he's elected...if he still pursues that path."

"Mom! Don't encourage William to go anywhere other than here!" Aimee huffed, clearly frustrated with her mother. "You're not getting any younger, you know," she said, trying another tact. "You shouldn't be climbing up ladders to change light bulbs. You should have family close by in case something happens, and you need us."

That merely made Alex's temper flare again. "Don't have me dying off already. For God's sake, I'm fifty-nine—I'm not dead. I still feel young and have a lot of living to do." People in her family lived to be well into their nineties, unless they died tragically. She was going to break one hundred, just to spite her middle daughter.

"That's not what I meant," Aimee said, quickly backtracking.

"Sure, it was. But you shouldn't. Don't worry, darling daughter of mine; if I become frail or infirm, I will knock on your door and beg for your support. Deal?"

"Well, you don't have to be so sarcastic about it. I'm only trying to be practical."

"Try for more whimsy in your life, kid," Alex responded drily.

Aimee spent a few more minutes taking ingredients from the pantry. She weighed her words, something she rarely did, thinking how to approach her own vulnerability with the woman in her life who was never vulnerable—at least never appeared to be.

Steeling herself, she pretended to organize the ingredients, not meeting her mother's eyes, as she said, "I'm worried about the kids. Andrew and I have to spend so much time at the restaurant, I don't think we're spending enough time with them."

Unlike her daughter's self-view, Alex thought they spent as much or more time with their two children than other parents did with their own.

Aimee said, "I think Andi might have a boyfriend, or maybe a girlfriend, but she's not talking to me. She used to tell me everything. Andrew is going to blow a gasket if he thinks she's seeing someone behind our back. Cam seems so sullen all the time. I don't know what to do about it."

"Let Andi know you're there if she's needs you; she'll talk when she's ready. She's been here for weeks; I haven't seen her pining over anyone, have you?" Alex suggested.

Looking toward the ceiling, exploring her recent memories, Aimee shook her head, having to agree with her mother.

"Cam. Yes, the boy's sullen. But I think he wants to be. He's got all those hormones starting to rage in his body. He's got all these cousins he sees as competition for attention rather than the support they are," Alex said. "And I'm pretty sure he's struggling with wanting to be an artist and how that fits in. He gets plenty of attention from you, maybe too much."

"Too much? We work all the time!"

"Maybe, but you still cater to him when he's there. You need to worry less. You're a great mother, Aimee. Andrew is a great father. You're both involved and balance running a demanding business with being there for each and every thing your children participate in. You listen to them," Alex argued. "You love them. They know it. That counts more than you believe."

"I love them more than anything!"

"I think it's great they have the example you two are setting. They know about hard work. Doing their homework there, helping at the restaurant, it's good family time, supporting one another. No one is ever perfect. Yep, you're doing great, my darling." Alex pounded her point home.

Aimee seemed lighter, her mother's approval ringing in her ears. She was still going to worry. It was her nature. But for now, the encouragement and praise were enough.

Changing the subject slightly, Aimee said, "By the way, I'm going to need to head into town soon to work. I've been here for a few weeks, and Andrew is starting to drown, even with the new help. And since you seem so ... I don't know ... so grounded, I guess I can go. Is it okay if the kids stay though? I'll be back as soon as I can."

"Of course! Take your time. We'll take good care of them."

"I'll leave in the morning."

A classic song came on the old radio, reminding Aimee of her childhood, when they all sang at the top of their lungs and danced around with their parents like loons. She turned up the volume, loudly blasting the familiar tune. Alex chair danced without even realizing it. Aimee faced her mother and held out her hand, "Dance with me, Mom."

Alex jumped up and took the proffered hand, both moving to the music, and began to sing, quite loudly. Others migrated to the kitchen, wondering what the ruckus was all about. They saw the two women dancing, singing, and laughing, and each joined in. Little kids bounced around, wanting to be part of the party. Teenagers and almost teenagers each took up the dance, abandoning their usual concern about appearing stupid. When the kitchen and dining area were full of moving bodies, the rest continued the dance on the screened-in porch, the kitchen door that opened to it left wide. Even Harper stood with baby Allie in her arms, joining the dance, marveling yet again how different this family was from the one in which she grew up. One classic song led to another and soon all were trying to do the Twist, the Mashed Potato, the Swim. By the time a slow song played, all were out of breath and laughing out of control.

"Let's get this show on the road," Aimee declared with a wide smile adorning her beautiful face. "Indy, you're helping me make dinner, the rest of you decide who is setting the table and then clear out of our kitchen."

Indy squealed, unable to squelch the delight that belied her six years—Aunt Aimee remembered her promise to teach her more recipes. Since she could form cogent sentences, Indy decreed she wanted to move to Michigan and take over the restaurant from Andrew and Aimee Dumont when she was older. She secretly hoped her two cousins, their children, wouldn't want to run the restaurant, and if they did, she hoped they would want a partner—her.

While some might assume Indy will change her mind several times over the years, Aimee believed the little girl and planned to do everything in her power to make one more avenue for her family to return to the town she called home.

The storm raged outside. Inside was one more day of island magic.

**13**

---

Bright sunshine shown through the tree branches. The island, green in summer splendor, woke along with the occupants of the old cottage. Furry creatures scrambled, looking for acorns and food scraps that may have been dropped by tiny hands, the unobservant little humans focused on other delights.

Andi and Colin took Aimee to the shoreside dock. Andi hugged her mother goodbye, happy to stay with her cousins. Cameron, much to Aimee's consternation, did not beg to go back to town with her, where his video games waited and Wi-Fi was unimpeded. Instead, the boy on the cusp of becoming a teenager recorded her departure on his camera, face serious, completely involved in his art. If anything, Aimee was the teary one, torn between duty to her business and desire to while away the summer with the women and children of the Newberry clan. She reminded herself she would return in a few days.

"Want to take a spin before we head back?" Colin asked, eyebrows raised daringly.

"Let's go for it." Andi hung onto the side and tucked her shoulder-length hair under her baseball hat as the speed picked up and her cousin cut around the island, leaving the younger ones shaking their fists on the shore, demanding their return. Today, Colin promised to continue their sailing lessons.

The two eldest of the next generation raced around the lake before pulling up alongside the general store's dock on the far side of the lake. Colin tied off and asked the attendant to fill the tank as he and Andi jumped up onto the dock and he ran inside the store to get the staples his grandmother sent them to retrieve. Once inside, he added the candy his mother called "penny candy"—which was a lot more than a penny now—to the counter with the milk and bread. He knew his young cousins would love the pixie sticks filled with flavored sugar, wax bottles filled with colored liquid, strings of red licorice, SweeTARTS, caramel-flavored Sugar Babies that looked like beans, Red Hots soft cinnamon pellets, jaw breakers, and tiny candy-covered chocolates that came three to a wrapper. While the lake brought back the smells of summer, these would always be the tastes of summer for children of the clan. Actually, the adults felt the same and were secretly glad the general store continued to carry these childhood favorites—minus the out-of-favor candied cigarettes—even if the sweet treats were not good for any of them. As one of their great-great-grandmothers always concluded: "Everything is fine, in moderation."

"That's a lot of candy." The white-haired man behind the counter laughed, the same proprietor since Alex was a child, though back then his hair was much darker, his face less wrinkled.

"We've got a lot of people to satisfy," Colin countered good naturedly. Through the window, he saw Andi talking with the guy filling their tank, presumably the proprietor's grandson, or maybe great-grandson. Whichever, he was flirting with Andi. She appeared to be flirting back.

"Who's running the gas pump?" Colin asked in what he hoped was a nonchalant voice.

Glancing outside, the old man smiled. "That's my great-grandson Jared. His mother dumped him with us this summer."

"Does he go to school here?" Colin asked, pumping for information without trying to seem too interested. Should Jared be flirting with a fourteen-year-old? That's all he needed to know. He thought his aunt would want him to look out for his cousin.

"Not yet. He was down state. But if my granddaughter doesn't come back, we'll enroll him here. He'll be a sophomore, before you ask." The proprietor in the VFW sweatshirt smiled, seeing through Colin's questions. He nodded toward the window. "How old is she?"

"She'll be a freshman in the fall."

The old man nodded. "Good of you to look out for your cousin. Your dad would be proud of you."

Surprised, Colin's words choked in his throat before he swallowed hard and got them out. "You knew my dad?"

"Sure did. You're Charlie's and James' boy, right? Colin? James was a good man, the best," the man said, head bowing reverently.

"I am. Yeah, he was," Colin said, gathering the paper sacks from the counter. The proprietor would have no plastic bags in his store; they always ended up polluting the lake, and he would not contribute to that insanity. "Thanks, Mr. Gillette." Colin remembered the man's name, even though he was surprised the old man remembered him, given the traffic the store must see in the summer months.

Back on the dock, he jumped in the boat and carefully set the brown paper bags on one of the passenger seats. He held out a hand for Andi. Rather than take his hand, Andi accepted Jared's tanned, grease-stained hand to help steady her as she took the long step into the boat.

"See you around, Andi," Jared said, white teeth shining a little too brilliantly in the sunlight against his tanned face as he smiled.

"Bye, Jared," Andi waved quickly, all too aware of her cousin's observant gaze.

As they pulled away from the dock, Andi turned to Colin. "What?"

"Nothing," Colin said, setting a path for the island, wanting to get the milk in the refrigerator and the sailing lessons started. He thought it was fine if Andi was a little uncomfortable with his silence —let her stew.

Some of the younger kids had planted themselves on the

boathouse dock, searching the water for the ski boat while the really little ones played in the water, awaiting Colin's return. When he pulled up and tied off the boat, he did not disappoint. Hudson, Jaspar, Cassie, and Grace jumped up and down where the sailboat waited, unable to contain their excitement. They already had their life jackets done up, ready to be given the "come aboard" signal.

Colin handed the bags to Andi to take to the kitchen and strode to the other dock. "What about you, Cam? Do you want to learn to sail this year?"

"No thanks," Cameron said, focusing on his camera and capturing a shot of his cousins boarding the boat. "Not my thing."

Colin shook his head and quickly moved the small sailboat away from the dock and toward the center of the lake.

"Remember how to hoist the sail?" he asked his charges.

"Aye aye, captain," they all responded excitedly.

He laughed. "Okay, Jaspar, how about you come back with me at the tiller. Hudson and Grace, you hoist the sail when I say. Everyone, remember to watch your heads and not get beaned. We don't need any more hospital trips."

Once the sail was raised, the lesson continued, with each child given the chance at the tiller and learning to trim the sail. The sun bounced off the water, blinding them when they sailed into it and warming their backs when they came about. From shore, the adults could hear the laughter and the intermittent orders bounding across the green-colored water.

Alex marveled at what a good teacher Colin was. His patience alone was a wonder, something she herself found hard to master.

Harper had Allie lathered with sunscreen and lying under a makeshift umbrella. "Someday that'll be you out there, little girl. Want Colin to teach you to sail?" Harper spoke with the baby as she would an adult, no baby talk in this family. Maybe that's why all the children seemed like little adults to her. Allie already reached out with grabby hands whenever she heard Colin's voice.

"How are we going to handle going back to school?" Lauren asked, ever the worrier, like her sister Aimee. "I mean, should we make sure we have classes at opposite times so one of us is always with the baby?"

"It'll work out; nothing for you to worry about. One of my professors said she and a few of the other younger profs created their own daycare and offered to add Allie for when I'm in class," Harper said.

Lauren was beginning to wonder if she wished Harper was into girls; did she have a crush on her best friend? Watching Harper so effortlessly flow into the role of mother and the obvious love she bestowed on her infant daughter made Lauren yearn to be part of it. Her own ovaries were not exploding; she had no desire to be pregnant. But she could see them creating their own small family.

She sighed, instinctively knowing she had to keep that thought to herself. Her mother and sisters were right; she needed to finish school, find her place in the adult world. If it was meant to be, it would be. In the meantime, she would be the steadfast friend. Patience had never been her strong suit, and she believed her forebearers when they claimed no change ever came about by people who were patient. She would save her impatience for her activism, once she figured what to focus on first. She was going to practice patience when it came to her personal life. At least she would try.

"That's great news, Harper," Sage said, sitting close and listening to the conversation. "Having a safe place for childcare must take a load off."

"It does," Harper agreed. "When I signed up for classes for this semester, I tried to bunch them as close together as I could and still meet my requirements. I wanted to chunk up my time and make it efficient."

Lauren was shocked to hear how much forethought her best friend had put into this. She hadn't known Harper had spent so much time and energy making the appropriate plans. Then she felt foolish. She was the one who hadn't thought it through; of course Harper had. Harper was always organized and poised. She was the planner. Lauren was the passionate, fly-by-the-seat-of-her-pants, decisions-in-the-moment girl. She was constantly reminded that she was the baby of her family, closer in age to her oldest nephews and niece than her siblings, and now even her best friend made her feel like the immature one.

She missed her dad. He would automatically sense how Lauren felt and remind her of all her good qualities—what were those again? He would reassure her that her passion was a strength this world needed. Where was he when she needed him? *Oh yeah. Dead.* That's where her father was. Dropped dead with no warning. No time for her to get used to the idea. Dead. Damn him.

Lauren jumped from her seat on the ground, ran down the length of the dock, and dove into the cool lake, swimming in long, smooth strokes to the raft, where she could be alone with her own morose thoughts. No one else here seemed to miss her dad. No one else was on the verge of tears. So, she let her hot salty tears mix with the lake water. She prayed her mother was right and that the fresh water would rejuvenate her, making everything seem less bad than she felt it was.

# 14

Another languorous day by the water slipped by, lulling the island inhabitants into a sense this calm, simple existence could last forever. The glorious days of youth, not so different for any of the generations of this family. All experienced the island's embrace, shielded from the world beyond its shores, if only for a moment in time.

In the hours before her son woke, Tory spent mornings preparing her law school applications. Lucky for her, the LSAT standardized test for law school admission she had taken and did so well on years before was still valid. If she had waited one more year to apply, she would have had to retake the test. She still had to remind herself daily—who was she kidding? several times an hour—that she was good enough. That she deserved a full and happy life. Whoever said "happy wife, happy life" had obviously never met Mark Wright. The man was a monster. She was the normal one. She simply had to remember that ... over and over again.

Alex handed Tory the mug of decaffeinated tea across the counter as she got her own caffeinated breakfast version, making sure not to spill on the laptop or papers Tory had scattered on the surface. In the early morning, Alex continued her painting of nighttime, of the brilliant sky, moon, and lake she had envisioned that night with Charlie, when all around them was quiet and dark. Now she took a break for more tea—more caffeine.

"How's it going?"

"It's going," Tory sighed.

"Proud of you, Victoria," Alex said, using the woman's full name to underscore the seriousness of her statement.

Surprised, Tory looked across the counter where her aunt leaned, elbows on the counter. "Maybe you should withhold judgment until I actually get in and things in my life move forward."

"Nope. You took the first step. The rest is just putting one foot in front of the other."

"You make it sound so easy," Tory said.

"Nothing easy about it. Which makes me even more proud of you. This? All you're going through? This stuff is hard. Really hard. But you're doing it. And someday Van and that baby you're carrying are going to know and be proud of you, too. No better example you can set for them," Alex said, brooking no argument.

Tory had a sudden thought and a flush rose on her cheeks. "We're supposed to be here for you, and here you're having to worry about me. I'm sorry I brought my problems with me."

"Don't be ridiculous! I'm perfectly fine. I have my memories. Lots of good times to look back on. No reason for me to mourn. Hank lived a full life, even if it wasn't as long as we would have liked. None of us know how much time we have left. That's another reason I'm so glad you're taking control and moving forward on your own," Alex said, pushing concern for herself to the side, as if it deserved no further thought.

Again, Tory hoped she would eventually be even half as strong as this woman, all five feet three inches of her, her indomitable attitude and constitution outweighing all physical attributes. She touched her abdomen, her pregnancy finally showing, and resolved that she would be strong.

Tory did not know her aunt was secretly capturing her in her sketchbook, in many poses: bent over the laptop with papers scattered around, lower lip caught in her teeth as she concentrated; rocking a restless Donovan when the boy woke from a nightmare; watching, carefree with the others while the children swam. Alex hoped her niece would see what she saw, once she viewed the sketches. She hoped they all saw something in themselves when her project was complete.

All the kids gathered at the lake after lunch, the morning spent playing knights and pirates in the forest—both called for the swords cut from cardboard their grandmother had fashioned for them. The youngsters were worn out and happy to splash in the lake or lie on the beach. Cassie and Hudson each took a kayak to explore the other end of the island, where marshy ground excluded exploration on foot. The island folklore held that quicksand was hidden beneath the mossy, marshy ground and would swallow unsuspecting children. While they all thought it was a made-up story, none were brave enough to test the boundaries and stayed within the forest with solid ground underfoot or skimmed the shore from the water.

Most of the older kids swam to the raft, giving them a sense of freedom from the little kids and the adults. They lounged on the raft, held up by barrels of air lashed together with sturdy rope, soaking up the sun, and talking about nothing in particular. Cameron left his camera on shore, hidden beneath his shirt, and joined Andi, Colin, Gavin, and Grace on the raft. They took turns challenging one another to see who could make the biggest cannonball splash. Then they moved on and rated one another on who had the smoothest dive.

Cameron kept glancing back toward shore before his turn, making sure eyes were on him, wanting an audience for his feats of daring. At first the women on shore would cheer or good naturedly boo for the competitors, but the younger children then wanted in on the action and demanded the attention of the adults.

"Oh no, I'm drowning, help me!" Cameron called from the water a few feet out from the raft, ducking his head under, and then coming to the surface spitting water, and then ducking below the surface again, arms waving above his head.

"Stop that right now," Andi yelled at him.

Cameron came to the surface and not so furtively looked to the shore, making sure all eyes were on him. Lauren was posed to run into the water and swim to him. He smiled and waved. "I'm okay now." Then he made his way to the raft.

"Not cool," Gavin grumbled, pushing his cousin back into the water from which he'd just climbed.

"Better be careful, Cam. Next time no one will believe you," Colin said, echoing his brother's sentiments. Cameron glared at the brothers, not appreciating their reproach. Who were they to tell him what to do? They always thought they were the bosses.

At that moment, Jaspar brought the rowboat up to the raft. Colin helped him climb up, after lifting the seven-year-old's fishing pole and the tackle to the raft. "You'll have to stand on this side, buddy, so you don't hook any of us when you cast," Colin said, placing the boy facing out toward the lake on the far side of the raft where his right-handed casting would not accidently hook anyone.

"Got it," Jaspar agreed, happy to be allowed to stay with the older kids and not be the oldest of the little kids for once. Nothing much was biting, so luckily, the line stayed out in the lake, red and white bobber many generations had used wobbling on the surface, not needing too many casts that could possibly hook a cousin by accident. For the sunfish and bluegill he did catch, Colin helped him carefully take out the hook and release the fish into the water.

Soon Jaspar tired of fishing and challenged the older kids to more water antics. They all, including those on shore, made sure to cheer and talk up his moves as they judged his water trick prowess, particularly his in-air somersault before hitting the water.

Cameron laid on the raft, declining to participate, staring at the sky. Finally, he stepped into the rowboat Jaspar had come out on and began rowing parallel to the island. Then he moved it out into the lake. He may not be interested in sailing and may have been too self-conscious to try skiing, but rowing he could do. And he could do it by himself, which suited him fine.

"Hey, you took my boat," Jaspar called, not really yelling, and not attracting attention from shore. Consternation showed on the Jaspar's face. How was he supposed to get the fishing gear back to shore? His daddy told him to always put his things away when he was done so they'd last a long time. He considered that much of the fishing tackle was older than his grandmother, so it was already positively ancient, and he didn't want to be the one that messed that up.

Not looking back and not bothering to answer, Cameron shot his middle finger back toward the raft, making sure it was hidden from those on shore.

Jaspar's mouth dropped open, unable to decide any fitting reply to that. Andi did it for him. "Nice, Cam. Really mature." Then she put an arm around Jaspar's shoulders and assured him, "Don't worry, he'll be back when he's done moping."

Those on the raft made a conscious effort not to pay attention to Cameron, instead continuing to dive and swim, splashing one another, and reclining on the raft when they tired.

"I'm going to get a ball and we can play catch in the water," Andi said before diving in and swimming to shore.

Once there, she spied Cameron's camera sticking out from under his shirt. "It serves him right," she thought, picking up the camera. After a quick test she saw how to turn it on and use the video record function. She pointed the lens toward the raft, zoomed in, and captured the others diving and pushing one another off the raft. She swung the camera across and farther out to record her brother in his lonely pursuit in the rowboat. Then she moved back to the action on the dock, only able to stand so much self-imposed angst.

From his position on the raft, Colin heard a splash. It didn't come from the shore where the younger kids were swimming, and it wasn't close to the raft. A creeping feeling climbed his spine and up his neck; he recognized what his dad had called intuition. He heard his father's voice, *"Never ignore that feeling, Col. It'll save you or someone else more often than not."*

He let his eyes carefully move systematically across the lake, taking in everything in front of him. That's when he saw the rowboat, rocking and empty. A moment later, he saw his cousin's head appear, nose just above the water a few feet from the boat and heard the low cry. "Help." The head moved as if struggling and went down again.

From shore, Andi called, disgusted, "Not funny this time either, Cam!" She was still recording.

Cameron's head appeared again, his eyes wild, arms trying to flail above his head, "Help! Stuck!" Then he disappeared below the water again.

Colin admonished the others to stay with the raft, not follow him. He dove in a crisp, shallow slice into the lake, meant to propel him forward with as much momentum as he could muster, then came up with strong, fast strokes, glad for his lifeguard lessons. Later he would make sure a life preserver was affixed to the raft, but it was too late for that now. If his cousin was faking again, he'd kick his ass later. In the meantime, that intuition and his father's voice in his head told him he had to hurry. *"You can do it, son; you'll get to him in time."*

Only once more did Cameron's head appear above the water. When he reached what he thought was the spot and saw air bubbles bursting upward, he dove below the surface and opened his eyes, hoping the lake would be clear enough to see. The sunshine helped and illuminated far enough down Colin could see his struggling cousin. Somehow the boy had gotten his leg caught in the seaweed that grew up from the bottom in parts of the lake. The more he struggled, the more the green algae wrapped around his leg, like a serpent squeezing the life out of its hapless victim.

The weeds were watery shades of green, yellow, and brown. Long and waving slowly, rhythmically, moving with the water. Except around Cameron, where the weeds' movements were fast, jerky, responding to his flailing limbs. The effect was eerie, as if the rest of the weed bed were more serpents waiting for their next victim. Colin had to ensure that victim was not him.

Lauren and Sage both ran into the water, sensing something was wrong, and began to swim, leaving the others with Harper and Tory.

Colin tried to signal Cameron to stop struggling. Colin held up one finger as in "wait" and hoped the boy understood and didn't think he was abandoning him. Colin swam behind Cameron, trying to help without Cameron grabbing him in a panic and getting them both caught in the weeds.

He tried to pull the slimy green weed from the boy's leg. That didn't work. It held even tighter. Without a knife, he did the only other thing he could think of, before panicking himself. He sunk his teeth into the strands wrapped around Cameron's calf, gnawing and biting through the bitter tasting green, pulling it apart, and finally, his lungs ready to burst, the last strand let loose. Cameron shot to the top. The younger boy was out of breath, coughing the water he'd begun to breathe from his lungs, but at least he hadn't drowned. Colin wrapped an elbow gently around his cousin's neck and swam with him to the rowboat.

"Cam, you gotta hang on to the side. Please. Don't kick your legs," Colin practically begged the younger boy. "There's too much seaweed here. I don't want you to get caught again. I'll try to pull you in." Colin's own muscles burned from the momentary lack of oxygen and exertion.

Cameron seemed to understand and passively held on to the rowboat, elbow hooked over the side, head bent, fatigued. Colin moved to a position opposite his cousin and hauled himself over the side, careful not to swamp it. It took a few tries to get Cam into the boat.

The younger boy sat on the bottom, not even on a bench seat, not saying anything, eyes closed. Colin wondered if he'd passed out from fear or exhaustion. He took the oars and began rowing to shore, his arms and legs shaking, spent after the adrenaline rush, only now taking the time to be scared.

*"You did it. I knew you could."* His father's voice was like a balm that took away the fear and replaced it with resolve to reach the shore.

Sage and Lauren were beyond the raft, but turned around once they saw Colin had Cam. The entire clan was deadly quiet, watchful. Tears streamed down the younger kids' faces as they picked up on the tension and anxiety surrounding them.

When Colin rowed up to the main dock, the adults raced to the boat and pulled Cameron out, wrapping him in a towel and walking him up to the cottage. Alex had been on her way down the path when she saw the drama on the lake play out. Now she hugged Cameron to her and then allowed his aunts to take him inside. She stayed behind, watching Colin, who sat in the boat staring out at the lake. The others swam to shore, and he remembered he needed to get the fishing gear from the raft.

Only then did Colin notice Cassie and Hudson, kayaks pulled together, each holding on to the other's craft, tears silently flowing down their faces. With resolve, he waved to them to bring it in. He pushed away from the dock and retrieved the fishing gear before tying the rowboat to the dock at the boathouse and carefully stowing the fishing rod and tackle box where they belonged.

Staring at the tackle box, he belatedly realized there was a fish knife in the box he could have taken with him and used to cut the weeds, though he hadn't known at the time the weeds were the culprit. He berated himself internally for not being prepared; his dad said to be prepared for any eventuality.

*"Hindsight is 20/20, son, no use now. You saved him. Take the win."* James' voice was clear as day to him and he wondered why it didn't bother him that he might be going crazy. He also mused if, perhaps, his grandmother heard it too; looking over to the main dock where she stood staring at him with a knowing smile, he was sure she must have. Too bad his mother was in the cottage and missed all the drama; how she would like to hear his dad's voice!

Andi still stood, recording, not even realizing that's what she was doing, taking in every one of her relatives, down to her grandma on the dock and Colin now helping Hudson and Cassie put the kayaks up in the boathouse. Everything in the proper place in the proper order.

Suddenly Andi realized what she was doing, grabbed her brother's T-shirt and took off for the cottage, camera off and in hand. That must be guilt that clawed at her insides; guilt that she had not believed her little brother was in peril and had not been the one to swim to his rescue. What kind of sister was she? She told herself she would be better.

"Let's go up, Colin," his grandmother said, holding out her hand. He suddenly noticed in the afternoon sun that her hair was going white, not gray, but pure white. "That's enough excitement for the day," she said.

He could not agree more. "Enough for my entire summer."

Once he took her hand, she pulled him in for a long hug. "You did good, my boy. So well. Your dad would be so proud of you. You kept calm and did what needed to be done. You saved a life."

"I think that means he's supposed to be mine to be responsible for —for life. Think I can throw him back?" he joked. They'd read a story about that in his English class last year.

"What I think is that your cousin is very lucky to have you." She kissed him lightly on the cheek. They both looked around the beach and dock to make sure nothing important was left out, not expecting anyone to come back today. Arms around one another, they slowly made their way up to the cottage.

Once inside, Charlie hugged her son, closing her eyes, breathing in the scent of the water and sunscreen on his skin, thankful he and Cameron did not both die during the rescue attempt. Maybe James was truly looking over them.

Pulling away, Colin said, "I gotta brush my teeth. I think seaweed's stuck. It tastes terrible."

In the bathroom, Colin stared at his face in the mirror, not sure why he thought he would look different. But the face reflected looked the same as always, even though he felt different inside. He had come to some understanding this part of the world may not be as safe as he thought. He already knew, having lost his father, that the world could be brutal, but the island was supposed to be untouched. Even nature had a dark side. Who knew? Now he did.

Once in the kitchen, Sage handed Colin a cup of hot tea, the family's go-to comfort and emergency drink—that and brandy. She had given Cameron a little brandy, no more than a thimble full, to help keep him calm and warm his insides.

Andi found her brother sitting on the couch and dropped beside him, pulling his head to her shoulder. She whispered, "Glad you're okay. You're a pain, but you're my pain, and I love you." Until that point, Cameron had been too numb to cry. Now he let the tears flow. He turned and sobbed into his sister's shoulder, soaking the T-shirt she'd thrown on over her bathing suit.

"Please, don't tell Mom." He choked out the words between sobs.

"Sorry, buddy, no can do. She always knows," Lauren said, staring at him with concern from her seat in one of the old rocking chairs.

"Let's focus on our celebration. How about that?" Alex suggested, as she stoked the Franklin stove.

"What celebration? He almost drowned," Lauren snorted.

"We're celebrating that neither of our boys drowned. That is definitely something to be grateful for, in my book."

That was it. The evening turned from the horror of a near-death experience to the celebration of the lives saved. Dancing included.

# 15

Days passed with no drama. No interventions. No near drownings. No violent soon-to-be-ex-husband sightings. Simple days with sunshine, swimming, sailing, skiing, and fishing in the evenings off the end of the docks or from the rowboat—life vests securely fastened, no exceptions.

Aimee returned for a couple days. Other than hugging her son extra tight and promising Colin his favorite dinner, she bit her tongue, followed her mother's example, and breathed in and out with a grateful heart—though she really wanted to give in to the panic practically choking her when her thoughts turned dark and imagined what could have happened.

Andi secretly showed her mother the video she had recorded on Cam's camera, the almost drowning and heroic rescue, but more importantly, Cam's sullen behavior and attempt to attract attention, any attention, even negative, that led to the mishap.

Aimee realized Alex was right. Cam was begging for attention. *Of course, she was right,* Aimee thought and inwardly rolled her eyes. Now she had to get her son to realize he should seek only good attention, or better yet not seek attention at all.

This was the summer they promised to teach Indy, Savannah, and Van to ski. Jaspar and Hudson were both accomplished young water skiers, as were Grace and Cassie. Time after time the new skiers, with their child-size water skis, face planted into the cold Northern Michigan water—until that first time they stayed up for longer than a few seconds, that first time that meant the world to them and gave them the confidence to continue the ride.

Her turn, the other kids shouting encouragement from the ski boat, Grace rose from the water lithe and smooth. While Cassie, short curly hair plastered against her forehead and cheeks, was bold, a daredevil driven by decisive action, her twin lived up to all her name promised: poised, thoughtful, and quieter than Cass. They were two halves of a whole. Where one excelled, the other depended on her for those skills, and vice versa. It worked for them. Charlie, their mother, was a little worried what would happen down the road when they no longer were together every day and had to depend on themselves for all the skills they currently shared. For now, skiing was something they both enjoyed with proficiency—Cassie laughing, shouting, jumping the wakes, while Grace smiled silently and slid smoothly back and forth over the wake, gliding, taking no notice of the rough water.

This was the first day since Cameron's brush with death that Grace was out skiing. She'd been content to swim at the island's little beach, kayak in the reeds near shore, and mostly sit in her grand-mother's favorite old rocking chair and read her books. Today she'd been ambushed by Hudson, Jaspar, and her twin, begging her to join them, towed behind the boat speeding around the lake with her mother driving. First, they'd ski and then, if there was time, they wanted to take the tubes out and be pulled on their bellies, the fresh-water spray in their faces blinding them. Fun. They wanted her to join in the fun and she had acquiesced.

Charlie was watching both forward and backward as she steered the boat, delighting in her daughter's easy grace. Aimee was the spotter this round.

"Down! She's down!" Aimee suddenly yelled over the roar of the engine and the kids' shouts and laughter.

Eyebrows knit closely together, Charlie immediately pulled up on the throttle lever and turned the boat around quickly. What went wrong in that split second? She had watched as Grace rose from the water and easily skimmed the lake water. She was fine. How was she down? All those thoughts raced through her head. Then her heart seemed to skip a beat as she saw the nine-year-old, long dirty-blonde hair in a ponytail spread behind her on the water, her body floating face up on the surface, life jacket rising more at her center, skis at her side. Charlie breathed a little easier when she saw Grace's eyes open. The boat pulled next to her; she still didn't move.

"Are you hurt, Gracie?" Aimee called out, the other kids sensed something was off and immediately quieted.

"No," Grace replied through gritted teeth.

"Then put your skis on and we'll get you up again," Aimee encouraged her, knowing the girl could easily get up on skis from the deep water.

"No thank you," Grace said.

"What's wrong? Charlie horse?" Charlie asked, rushing toward the back of the boat and peering over the side.

"Nothing," Grace gritted out.

"Swim over and climb up," her mother requested.

"Can you pull me, please?"

"Help us out here, Grace, swim a bit so we can reach you and we'll pull you up," Aimee said.

Grace grimaced but made small fluttering motions with her hands and tiny kicks with her feet, barely breaking the surface of the water, and slowly made her way closer to the boat on her back. Once at the side of the boat, Charlie and Aimee reached over and hauled her light body into the boat.

Once on the boat's floor, Grace easily sat up, gulped a deep breath, and looked out toward the horizon, not meeting anyone's eyes. "Thank you."

Potential crisis averted, the boat moved farther down the lake. Jaspar shouted, "My turn!" They waited while he jumped into the water and pulled the skis onto his feet, not an easy task with the buoyant life jacket and nothing to keep him immobile. He placed the ski rope between his skis, which now pointed skyward. Charlie moved forward slowly, taking the slack from the tow rope.

Wrapped in a towel, Grace sat quietly in the front passenger seat next to her mother. Aimee and the others were gathered in the back, shouting to Jaspar.

"Want to tell me what happened back there," Charlie asked quietly as she maneuvered the boat.

"Weeds," Grace uttered the one word and her body shivered involuntarily.

"What do you mean?"

"Weeds. I was fine, but then I looked down and saw weeds. I was over the place Cameron almost drowned," the girl said quietly.

"The weeds do grow tall in that part of the water," Charlie said, still not following her daughter. It was one of the only places in the lake where weeds reached so close to the surface. "Did you fall? Get the wind knocked out of you?"

"No. I let go."

"Why?"

Grace looked her mother in the eye for the first time, blue eyes wide, and solemnly said, "I guess I panicked. I saw the weeds and had to let go before we got even farther away from the island. Then I had to float as high as I could, so they didn't touch me."

"But if you'd kept skiing, we would have been away from the weed patch," Charlie reasoned, glancing at her daughter, trying to puzzle out the rationale.

"I didn't want them to get me," Grace replied, seeming to realize it was irrational, but it happened that way all the same.

The weight of the moment crashed on Charlie all at once. Her young daughter was afraid she would be a victim of the same fate as Cameron days before.

"Oh, Gracie, the weeds won't get you. What happened with Cam was a fluke. He was going underwater, then treading water and kicking his feet, getting himself wrapped up."

Her daughter did not look convinced. She tried again. "How about this? We won't pull skiers over that part of the lake. Will that work?"

"And you're sure there aren't more near the surface in the rest of the lake?" Grace pushed.

"I'm sure, but tell you what, I'll do some reconnaissance after you all go ashore. I mean, I'll take the boat and check out the rest of the lake, scout to see if there are any other rogue weed beds. Then we'll know. Okay?"

Grace smiled for the first time since getting up on the skis. "Okay. But I'll wait until you do the recon thingie before I get up again."

"Deal," Charlie smiled, wanting to hug her daughter, but at that moment she heard Jaspar yell, "Hit it!" She pushed the throttle forward, creating the tension needed to get him out of the water and glide around the lake.

Much like his cousin Cassie, he was a daredevil and was soon jumping the wake and trying new tricks. On one trick, where he jumped and tried to turn 360 degrees, passing the tow rope behind his back, he landed slightly off the 360 mark, caught the edge of his skis on the water and went flying through the air.

"He's down!" Aimee yelled, making a circular motion above her head to signal "turn around."

They saw Jaspar's body shoot straight up out of the water, simultaneously laughing uproariously and swiping at the water running down his face from his white-blonde hair like a waterfall. His skis were scattered in two different directions, nowhere near his body. Those in the boat, seeing he was not hurt, took the time to gather the skis before going to collect the seven-year-old showoff.

"Did you see that? I almost had it!" Jaspar spouted as he pulled himself out of the water at the ladder.

"Yes, you did! Pretty soon you'll be skiing circles around me." Aimee praised the boy. As the best water skier in the family, Aimee could see her status being challenged down the road, and, surprisingly, she was all right with that, proud even.

"I want to go!" Cassie piped up, not to be outdone by anyone.

"Not your turn," Charlie reminded her, the girl frowning at her mother but knowing she was right.

Aimee dropped into the water, motioning for Donovan to follow. He excitedly jumped in beside his aunt, his life vest popping his little body to the surface instantly. Once she got him situated with skis up, leaning forward, and tow rope between the skis, she hauled herself back into the boat.

"What do you say when you're ready?" Aimee shouted to Van.

"Hit it!"

"That's right. Say that when you're ready."

"No, I meant now—hit it!"

Charlie chuckled to herself and pulled the boy to the surface. He balanced admirably on his skis. She made sure she went fast enough to maintain the tension, but not too fast that she'd lose the boy. What Donovan didn't know was that the others were preparing for his birthday party on the island. He turned six today and thought learning to ski was his celebration.

After a couple turns in the lake, Van's little arms grew tired. He lifted one hand from the tow rope handle to his face and brought it down to let them know he was done.

Charlie followed Aimee's instruction and brought the throttle back, slowly slowing the boat, and allowed Van to hold the rope and sink down in the lake. Once at a standstill, Aimee hauled the rope, towing the boy to the boat, where he pulled the skis off and scrambled up the ladder into the boat. Aimee lifted the little skis out of the water.

"Think we better get back," she said to a chorus of groans and shouts of "no fair."

Soon the grumbling would be forgotten as they dove into the grilled hamburgers and hotdogs, and the special birthday cake Aimee had baked for the little boy.

Aimee wasn't looking forward to going back to work again the next day but was glad to be here one more night for the birthday party. Van had wrapped presents of books and toys waiting for him to open. She hoped the adrenaline would kick back in when he realized what was going on, because right now he looked ready to fall asleep in the seat, his chin almost resting on the life jacket.

Back on shore, Victoria raced down the hill to the dock. She had stood at the top in the clearing, looking down the steep back slope to the lake, through the trees, watching her son get up and stay up on skis. The sight of his mother energized him as they docked. He struggled against Charlie trying to get him out of the life jacket and onto the dock.

"Mommy! Did you see me? Did you?" he shouted, full volume, and ran off the dock toward shore, coming to a full stop in front of her.

"I saw you! You did great!" Tory said, ready to reach out and hug her child, surprised he hadn't launched himself at her as he usually did.

Van reached out and placed his hand gently on her rounded belly, still not big, but visibly showing. "I'll teach you to ski, baby. I'm going to take care of you." Then Van danced up the hill yelling for his great-aunt, asking if she saw his success on the lake.

Tory's eyes were big; she was speechless. Her son knew she was pregnant and didn't seem to have a problem with it. In fact, he was already acting like the loving, protective older brother she hoped he would be. *When did that happen?* He must have overheard her discussing it with her aunt or cousins. Maybe being around all the older kids and seeing how they looked out for one another provided just the example he needed at just the right moment. She was certainly grateful he didn't seem to have his father's tendencies—and never would, if she had anything to say about it.

Enough giving Mark any real estate in her brain. Tonight was about celebrating the birthday of the newly turned six-year-old boy who held her heart and her hope.

Later, after dinner, after cake was eaten and presents opened, Alex had logs burning in the fire pit. The smallest of the children sat in the women's arms, Aimee holding Indy, while Sage held her younger sister Harmony, Alex held Savannah, and the birthday boy tried to stay awake in Charlie's arms.

Aimee relished the smell of the water in her niece's hair and the way her body curled into her aunt. She had loved when her own two were this age—when no one was as good as Mom. The flames danced, mesmerizing them all. One-by-one, the little children nodded off, followed shortly by the older kids where they sat and woke only long enough to walk into the bunk rooms. Soon even Colin and Andi said they were calling it a night. A long day in the water, and then the sugar crash after the birthday cake Aimee baked, had taken their toll.

Colin stopped halfway to the cottage and turned around, telling Andi he would catch up. The teenager hugged his grandmother, a long, tight hug, and whispered in her ear, "Night, Grandma." Then he turned to his mother and kissed the top of her head as she sat on a log and whispered to her, "Love you, Mom." Just as suddenly, he walked through the screen door; it slammed against the frame as it shut.

"I keep forgetting to have that fixed," Alex said absently. That door had been slamming shut since she was a child. It would take a handyman or handywoman very little time to fix it, but it was never a priority, and she forgot until the next time it slammed loudly in the dark.

Soon it was Alex and Charlie in front of the fire, everyone else calling it a night.

"Do you remember much about this place from your childhood?" Alex asked.

"I remember everything," Charlie said emphatically, her lips tugging upward at the memories. "This is one of my favorite places in the entire world."

"Your grandmother would have stayed here year-round, if she could."

"I remember. She said this was our magical place, and it didn't matter if no one else could see the magic, we could," Charlie said, a far-off look in her eyes, staring into the darkness, but really seeing the previous years in her mind.

"I had forgotten she said that. I thought the magic started with me," Alex said. *Huh, amazing how the mind can bend thoughts and origins to what we desire.*

She'd spent a lot of years angry with her mother. Angry for being strong and unapproachable. Angry for the woman not recognizing her only daughter's strength. Angry for not supporting her at one of the most trying times of Alex's life. So many of her early memories were around her grandmothers and not her own mother—baking with her father's mother, stories at the feet of her mother's mother. Her mother was always working. Always trying to claw ahead in a world not yet ready to recognize women as equal to men in intelligence and competence in the workplace—even though bra burning and marches for women's rights were active movements. A world that wore her down too young.

Yet, Alex's mother did not make it easier on her only daughter. No, Alex now thought, she probably believed she was doing the right thing and making sure Alex was tough enough to handle a world that would not see the intrinsic value in women as equal for many lifetimes to come, if ever.

When Alex was at university in Washington, DC, she met the dashing sailor who was getting his own education at the U.S. Naval Academy in Annapolis. She had spent a Saturday sailing on the Chesapeake Bay with friends, one of whom had a father who owned a sailboat at the marina near the Naval Academy. They had gone for dinner at a local seafood restaurant and bar, before heading back to DC. The band had started at 8pm. Alex's memory of that day was so clear in her brain.

*A group of midshipmen from the Academy were there and flirted with the girls in Alex's group after they finished dinner and waited for the band to begin their set. One stood back from the others, leaning against the bar, watching her—at least Alex thought he was. She stayed back from her friends and watched the scene, much like the tall young man leaning on the bar. When he realized she watched him as closely and carefully as he watched her, he pushed off the bar and sauntered—yes, she thought he sauntered—to where she stood by the wall.*

*"You look a bit young to be here," the midshipman said as his opening to her, a smile playing on his lips.*

*"Maybe I just have good genes," Alex said. A sliver of anger streaked through her chest, replacing the excitement that was there moments before when she thought he might be interested in her.*

*"I'm sure you do. But are you old enough to be in here?" he asked, trying not to smile.*

*"It's a restaurant. Anyone can be here."*

*"How old are you?"*

*"I'm nineteen, not that it's any of your business."*

*The midshipman visibly relaxed. "Thank God."*

*"Excuse me?" Alex started.*

*"You're an adult."*

*"Of course, I am!" Alex exclaimed, getting more annoyed by the second.*

*"Let's start over," the man suggested. He held out his hand, "I'm Ian MacGowan. I'm at the end of my third year at the Naval Academy."*

*Reluctantly, Alex took his hand and responded formally, "It's nice to meet you, Ian MacGowan. I'm Alexandra Newberry, but my friends call me Alex. I'm finishing my second year at The American University. And before you ask, I finished high school early."*

*Ian chuckled. "I'm a lucky guy. Smart and beautiful."*

*"How does that make you lucky?"*

*"Because, Alexandra Newberry, I'm going to marry you someday."*

*Alex was shocked at his proclamation and sure he was teasing her, thinking her too young to know the difference. But as became clear, he was serious. She was immediately captivated by the man, as much as he was by her. She soon learned he was not only self-confident and handsome, but intelligent, strong, and loving, a leader among his peers. They were engaged by Christmas and married two days after he graduated from the Naval Academy.*

Thinking back, Alex laughed. Her mother had been appalled. Alex was married at twenty and pregnant a month later, much to Ian's delight and her mother's mortification. But she did it all. Her mother thought she was throwing her life away on a man, but Alex lived up to every expectation, finishing her degree, getting a good job, and keeping the home front organized and under control while Ian was deployed.

Yes, she said with satisfaction, she had done it all, despite her mother's lack of confidence in her ability to handle it. One thing she would say was that her mother adored Charlie from the day she was born, and that didn't change as Charlie grew. The two had a special relationship. Alex was not sure if her mother finally realized she had raised Alex to be this strong or if she transferred her hopes and dreams for her female legacy to her granddaughter. In her later years, the woman did tell Alex many times that she loved her and how well she had done with her life, so far. She still wasn't sure. Not that it mattered.

"She told me you're the one who holds this family together. Said I should follow your example." Charlie's voice broke through the silence in the darkness, the fire dying, only a few embers still glowing.

"She did? That amazes me," Alex said.

"Why? You're the strongest person I know," Charlie said quietly. "I'm sure she saw that in you. She did raise you."

Alex almost told her she was raised more by her father and her grandmothers but stopped herself. It didn't matter. Looking back, maybe she was like her mother. She went for what she wanted. Maybe her mother's contribution to her had been her example. Just because a lot of what her mother desired did not come to fruition— probably more because of the times than because of her mother— Alex's own life had more ups than downs. Another startling revelation: she was one more link in the legacy that was marked by strong women, generation after generation.

"Thank you for saying that. You're the strongest person I know," Alex answered her daughter.

The last glow flickered out. Charlie used the water bucket to douse the embers, to be on the safe side. The two women headed back to the cottage, each lost in their own thoughts. Alex remembering her first husband and marveling over the complexity that was her mother—what better place to contemplate the woman than here in the place that was so special to them both. And Charlie, glad her mother saw strength where she herself saw only survival, also thought of her husband, James, and wondered if he would be proud of how she was surviving.

# 16

The day was here. The window left open all night, Alex smelled the cool morning air, the hint of pine, cedar, and the lake water wafting through the screen. She stretched before she rose. Shower, tea, a little drawing, then she would have someone take her to the shoreside dock where she would get in her truck and drive the two hours to the small airport to pick up her closest friend.

Today, Maddie was arriving. She was pretty sure her daughters were as excited as she was. But she already decided she would be selfish and call dibs on the early hours of the other woman's time. They had a lot of catching up to do—alone, without children or grandchildren hijacking the conversation. Only then, would she share her friend. Alex laughed and shook her head, as if she could hold back the inevitable tide that was her family.

She had the kitchen to herself, cold even in her sweatshirt, hoping the Irish Breakfast tea would warm her soon. Unbidden, two distinctly different waves of déjà vu rolled through her chest.

One was of a cold morning on the island. Charlie, Aimee, and William still asleep, she was relishing the moment of quiet, shivering as the kettle heated on the ancient stove. Seeing her shiver, warm, strong arms wrapped around her, her back pressed to his front, sharing his warmth. She had looked over her shoulder and smiled thankfully up at Ian. "I'll warm you up," he had promised and kissed her long and hard.

The second sense of déjà vu was a similar morning at the island, many years later, the kettle yet to boil on the stove, she shivered inside her oversized sweatshirt. This time large hands dropped a sailing jacket over her shoulders and rubbed her arms, hoping to help warm her. "You know, you'd be warm faster if you used the single serving maker rather than waiting for the kettle to boil," he had said. Then Hank moved around the counter to make his own single serving of coffee, the first of many before he would leave the kitchen. He smiled at her, friendly and loving.

Alex felt like she had been punched in the gut, gasping for air, glad there were no witnesses. Damn. She rarely, if ever, compared the two men in her life. Why did those two moments haunt her this morning? She did not have time for this.

The kettle boiled and Alex quickly poured it over her tea bag. She set her sketchbook in front of her on the old counter and added shading to the drawing she had begun the day before. She held it up closer to the window and the early light beginning to filter through the trees into the eastern facing windows, tilted her head side to side, finally deciding it was ready and turned to the next blank page, starting her next drawing.

Two mugs of tea drunk and life stirring in the main part of the cottage, she closed the sketchbook, put her pencils in the hardcase designed for them, and added both to the large leather bag she would carry to the mainland. Déjà vu gone, her excitement grew—her friend would be here today.

A vehicle horn honked, two short blasts breaking the peace of the early morning. The only person Alex knew who would arrive this early was her brother Maitland. But unless he had news for his daughter that could not wait, she saw no reason he would visit during the week.

Grabbing the boat keys, she walked at a quick pace down the path to the lake. She didn't recognize the vehicle parked on their property. She shaded her hand over her eyes, as if that would help her see better. When the visitor got out of the car and waved wildly, Alex's face broke out in a huge grin and she jumped into the boat, firing up the engine, and racing across the lake, no longer caring if she woke any of their lakefront neighbors.

Waiting on the dock with a rolling bag next to her and a large leather bag over her shoulder, Maddie patiently waited for her friend.

"I was coming to get you," Alex exclaimed, taking the bag Maddie handed down to her. Maddie then stepped gingerly onto a seat and into the rocking boat, the easiest way to come aboard without jumping.

"Got an earlier flight and rented a car. Couldn't wait to leave the city. One more meeting and my head was going to explode." She shut her eyes, took a deep breath, held it, exhaled, opened her eyes and wrapped her close friend in a tight hug.

Glancing around, Maddie chuckled. "I wasn't sure if I should honk the horn this early. Was a little afraid some redneck-y neighbor might shoot me."

Alex shook her head and joked, "Wrong lake for that."

Maddie situated herself in the passenger seat, and Alex backed away from the dock.

"Want to take a ride first?" Alex said, a mischievous glint in her eye.

"You know I do." Maddie grinned in return. She liked the speed and the wind as much as Alex.

Alex immediately pushed the throttle down, the old wooden boat responding quickly to the prompt for speed, jumping forward, bow raised high, pounding against the water. Not the same effect as a cigarette boat, but close enough. Her friend's long black braids, high-lighted with subtle red streaks, flew behind her. When Alex made a hard turn, the boat dipped, water only an inch below the side.

"Woo hoo!" Maddie hollered, arms raised in the air in victory, as the boat righted and shot forward.

Alex laughed, no longer thinking of anything except the water, wind, and friend beside her. It always amazed her that the only place her mind completely stilled was when she was on the water. It didn't matter if it was sailing or flying on a speedboat. Water was her peace. Though she liked the Atlantic Ocean and found peace in saltwater sailing, there was nothing like the rejuvenation and smell of freshwater lakes. It soothed her soul, which was in sore need of soothing since Hank's death. Mind blank, endorphins in full effect, they skidded around the lake at high speed, skimming the surface of the water, bow pounding.

Too soon, they agreed they should probably head to the island. On the third circle around, they saw a few members of the family standing on the dock waving at them, cheering as loudly as if another boat had joined their race rather than their singular search for the freedom of speed, wind, and water.

"Maddie! Maddie!" Charlie's twins jumped up and down, unable to contain their excitement. Charlie and Lauren looked almost as excited. Everyone else must still be in the cottage, either sleeping or eating breakfast.

"I'm here, munchkins," Maddie said as she climbed out onto the dock and gathered a twin in each arm and hugged them to her, clearly happy to see her friend's grandchildren.

She then stood and hugged Lauren. "It's so good to see you, smart girl. You'll have to tell me all that's happening in your world."

Turning to Charlie, she hugged her and whispered, "How are you *really* holding up? It's been too long since I've seen you." She intended to ask the woman's mother the same thing once they were alone and settled into discussion mode.

"I'm hanging in there. Missed you too," Charlie whispered back before releasing the hug. Her mother's friend—her friend too, she realized—smelled like citrus and everything that brought calm to her life, and she took a long intake through her nose before letting her go. That was another childhood smell.

Bouncing the roller bag on the trail behind her as they paraded up the path marred by tree roots and rocks pushing through the earth, Alex said in a low voice to her friend, "Hope you're ready for the onslaught. They've all been waiting for you to arrive."

"I'm more than ready. All that family love; bring it on." Maddie smiled easily.

The Newberry clan did not disappoint. Kids jumping, shouting, throwing arms around her in child-size hugs, adults laughing and awaiting their turns. Breakfast all but forgotten on the table—Aimee and Indy's special chocolate chip pancakes.

"Okay, let's let Maddie get settled, and then she'll come back for breakfast with you," Alex said, trying to regain control and some semblance of order.

"You bet I will," Maddie said enthusiastically. "I wouldn't miss Aimee and Indy's chocolate chip pancakes for anything ... and is that bacon I smell?" She made a big production of closing her light brown eyes and breathing in deeply, inhaling the tantalizing aroma.

"Sure is," Indy answered proudly. "We'll make sure Jaspar doesn't eat it all."

"Hey," Jaspar protested, not at all happy being singled out as the food hog in the group. Then he sheepishly said, "I'm a growing boy, and Aunt Aimee's pancakes are amazing."

Alex led her friend to the room she'd have for her stay. The walls were knotty pine paneling, floors tiled in the 1950s, and the dresser matched the pine interior, the mirror on top marked with slight dark lines at the edges of the glass, appropriately aged. The white painted iron bed was naturally shabby chic from years of use. The pale-yellow sheets were clean and crisp. The checkered quilt on top was one created by Alex's paternal great-grandmother, yellows, blues, reds, and greens complimenting one another nicely, stitches thick and exact. Homey. That was the word that came to mind immediately when Maddie reacquainted herself with the room in which she stayed when she had time to visit in the summer—it felt like coming home. Even the smell of the water wafting through the window was familiar all the way to her bones. The haze from the two flights and long drive it took to get to the island was quickly fading.

"Do you want to freshen up or take a nap?" Alex asked her friend.

"Are you kidding? Jaspar is not getting my pancakes or bacon." Maddie laughed, her braids swinging as she vehemently shook her head.

"Come on then," Alex said, pulling her by the hand.

Suddenly Maddie stopped in the doorway and pulled Alex back. "Are you okay? I'm sorry I had to get back and couldn't stay for a few days after the funeral. Production started on the latest project and things were in disarray."

Maddie hated to even mention the excuse, true though it was. It was her reality these days. In order to make sure her projects made it to the big screen or the streaming properties, she had to stay on top of them, from screenplay to casting to production and post-production. It was so different than her days at the national newspaper where she first met Alex more than twenty-five years before. There Alex was on the political team, and Maddie covered health care, the country's cluster of all clusters.

*Maddie was fresh out of graduate school, steeped in liberal arts, raring to take on the establishment and use her creative gene. She first spotted Alex in an editorial meeting where the new news editor, thankfully not long for his job, droned on and on about what she could only describe as trite gibberish intermingled with big words, trying to make himself look smart. Alex had caught her eye across the conference table, and she knew right then she had a like-minded partner.*

Maddie remembered that day as if it were yesterday.

*As the two left the meeting, the pale woman with the blue eyes and dirty-blonde hair, curls wild to her shoulders, hurried to walk next to her. "I'm Alex Newberry, political team," she introduced herself. "I hope you aren't planning to leave after that sham of an editorial meeting."*

*Maddie admitted to herself the thought had crossed her mind, but to the woman she said, "I'm Maddie Owens, health care team. Nice to meet you." In a lower voice she said, "Glad I'm not the only one baffled by that meeting."*

*"I'm hoping he's not here for long. At least the senior correspondents and editors on our two teams are excellent. They'll be a buffer until he's canned," Alex said.*

*Wow. Maddie was a little shocked by Alex's openness. That was more honesty than she expected, but before she could say anything, Alex said, "Let's have drinks after work. Okay?"*

*For whatever reason, maybe the burgeoning sense of a kindred spirit, Maddie felt compelled to get to know this woman and agreed.*

That was the first day of the start of a friendship that had weathered marriages, divorce, deaths, job moves, opposite coasts, and career changes that spanned more than a quarter of a century.

"I'm fine, really," Alex answered her question. "I understand you have a job to do. There was no reason for you to stay. There was nothing for anyone to do." Alex had spent as little time as possible in Connecticut after the funeral, flying to Michigan and getting to the island as soon as she could.

"Fine is a word we use when we're not," Maddie argued.

"We'll have time to talk later. Breakfast now, remember?"

"Okay, I'll let it slide for now," Maddie said, threat to not let it go implied.

Both hurried out the living room door, across the screened-in porch, and through the kitchen door at the end of the porch. As promised, two seats were waiting for them. The pancakes and bacon were still warm.

"Thought you probably needed this," Aimee said as she set coffee in a large mug in front of the woman who had been a part of their lives for almost as long as she could remember.

"You know me. I mainline the stuff," Maddie quipped and took a drink of the hot liquid already doctored with soy milk and a dash of sugar. She closed her eyes in appreciation and sighed loudly. "Perfect. As always. Thank you!"

Alex's tea was already steeping at her place at the head of the table. She quietly watched her family, loud and happy, each sharing what they found important. Three generations sharing space, the food, their time, and best of all, their thoughts and ideas.

Now, with Maddie here, she felt the tribe was close to complete. The only thing better would be if her son William and Aimee's husband Andrew were here. But something about just the women

and the children felt more right than she expected when her daughters planned her self-proclaimed "intervention"—something she was
happy to say she had avoided thus far, other than the one conversation with Aimee.

## 17

As much as Alex hoped to spirit Maddie to some quiet place all to themselves, the island women conspired against her. They all sat by the water, soaking in the sun. Maddie, skin slathered in sunscreen, a surf shirt over her upper half, and large floppy hat covering her head, kept to the shade of the trees.

"I'm not going to age any faster than I have to," she declared. "This skin has to last me a lot of years. 'Black don't crack' and all that jazz, but I'm not tempting fate."

Charlie looked from Maddie to her mother, one a warm brown naturally, one a pale golden tan from the summer, and smirked at the vanity of the women. Neither had any facial lines nor looked their ages, Alex now fifty-nine and Maddie fifty-one years young. She saw some small lines at the edge of her eyes when her mother smiled or laughed—but didn't that happen to everyone? She hoped her mother's good genes passed on to her. Her mother's hair appeared to turn white overnight, and it was becoming obvious she'd decided to quit coloring it.

*So what?* Charlie thought. Why shouldn't women be revered in their natural state? Beauty had been so bastardized during the twentieth century, Charlie hoped the trend of the generations after her that demanded body-positive image and respect became the norm. Women, even so many decades after the Equal Rights movement began, still had enough to contend with, including persisting lower wages than their male counterparts for the same jobs.

Charlie mentally shook her head to clear it, the enormity of the issues she could do nothing about today weighing her down. "Hell, it's enough for me to take care of the kids, make money, and get through the day ... in that order," she muttered to herself.

Animated conversation continued. Sitting slightly out of listening distance, but hearing the voices and watching the people speak, hands and arms waving in emphasis, Sage noticed the cadence of the conversation matched the swaying of the trees. The more animated, the more wind she noticed, causing a rustle in the leaves and through the needles that was unique—as unique as the constant sound of car engines and sirens in the city. This was pleasanter, surprisingly in tune with the nature surrounding them. She absently mused if the wind and trees picked up on the rhythm of the women or the women became more animated with the uptick in wind?

*Look at that. Mother would be so proud of that thought,* Sage thought and kept her musings to herself. Sometimes she felt more comfortable if her free-spirit upbringing was not out in the open for all to notice.

Alex was happy when Maddie declared she'd had enough sun, and the two escaped to the cottage.

"I'm not even going to ask why you're heating a kettle," Maddie said as she pressed down on her pod and picked the largest size for the single serving mug of coffee. Alex's narrowed eyes and withering look let her know she was not going to get an answer to her non-question.

Tea and coffee in hand, the two escaped to Alex's room and settled comfortably on top of the old quilt with patches of red still bright, legs crossed, ready for an overdue talk.

"Spill. What's happening? Your text said the entire tribe decided to descend on you and you didn't seem happy. You're always happy when your family's around." Maddie got right to the point. Careful and diplomatic with most people, she could be direct with her old friend.

Alex took a fortifying sip of her milky tea and rolled her shoulders to release the tension. It didn't work.

"I think it was supposed to be an intervention. They seem to think I'm not grieving appropriately."

"What?!"

"Yep. I mean, they didn't say that, but I could read between the lines. Then Aimee spilled a little one day we were alone. Why the hell do they think I'm old and need to slow down?"

"Because they're young," Maddie said. "They have no idea their minds will tell them they're the same people at fifty or sixty as they are at twenty or thirty."

"Youth. Wasted on the young." Alex rolled her eyes. "I'm also perfectly capable of handling my life without a man."

Maddie leaned forward, eyes narrowing. "Yeah, tell me more about that. There's something up."

How could she explain? Where should she begin? She still hadn't figured it out in her own mind. Maybe telling the story to her friend, the one person in the world she knew would not judge, would help her bring together the fragments that wandered aimlessly in her head, looking for a place to land, wanting to make sense.

Listening to make sure the cottage was still quiet—she didn't want little ears to hear something they shouldn't—she began.

"Okay, I'm not sure I have my thoughts together enough yet, but I'll try." Deep breath in and out, she continued, "Let's start with the night Hank died."

"Okay," Maddie said, wondering where this was going.

"He didn't die at home in DC. He told me he would be out of town working on new business, some potential candidate in rural Virginia." Once again Alex chastised herself for being so gullible. The company was well enough established that new clients almost always came to them, at least until they were on board, and then field work was necessary. "He was at a hotel in DC. Less than two miles from home."

Maddie's eyes grew wide, but she kept silent, afraid if she stopped the other woman's momentum, she might not pick it up again.

"Yeah." Alex noticed her friend's reaction. A faraway stare replaced the look of determination on her face as she recalled the events of that night for Maddie. Suddenly she was transported backward, as if she were there.

*The townhouse in DC, with its rich colors, overstuffed couches, heirloom wingchairs, leather chairs and ottomans, heavy curtains in deep, warm colors, and lots of wood, was a great place to be alone with her own thoughts. That's what she thought when Hank said he would be out of town for the night.*

*This had been her house with Ian, her first husband, and Hank's overwhelming personality always seemed a little big for it. He seemed to recognize that and was always quieter here, less boisterous, more reflective. But he was gone for the night, and she was going to take the downtime to work on an idea that had wormed its way into her brain. The idea for a book. Somehow, she knew Hank would not be impressed.*

*Sure, he loved her mind, but preferred to use it to the advantage of their clients, making the clients seem more articulate than they really were, developing individual voices for future and current leaders that pulled them out of the crowd. Writing fiction was a waste of her beautiful brain, according to Hank; unless she collaborated with her friend Maddie and wrote a screenplay that would get lots of viewers and make lots of money.*

*Ian, on the other hand, had always encouraged her more creative pursuits. Why would she make the comparison between the two? Why now? That was not something she ever consciously did. It disturbed her that she couldn't put her finger on why.*

*Lost in her creative thoughts, hurriedly jotting down ideas before they disintegrated, afraid she might miss something that could be critical to the plot or the disposition of her characters, Alex was not aware of time.*

*The phone rang at two in the morning. She was annoyed it took her away from her productive night alone, even for a moment. She was sure it was Hank just getting in after a late night catering to another potential candidate.*

*"Hello," she said, distracted, seeing Hank's name on the caller ID.*

"Mrs. Robertson?" *a small voice, male, practically whispered into the phone.*

*The name was her first clue this was not a normal night and not a normal phone call.* "It's actually Ms. Newberry. I didn't take my husband's name—the first or the second time." *She was annoyed having to explain this yet again to someone.*

"Alex..." *the man's voice wavered.*

"Who is this?" *Alex asked, sensing something was off.*

"Um, this is Jeff Mullins. There's a problem."

*Alex now recognized the voice, though faint, of her husband's administrative assistant. Hank had gone through several that lasted a week or less after his long-time assistant left the year before. Apparently, her gregarious husband was not so easy to work for. She suspected his mind worked too fast for most other humans to keep up. He finally settled on Jeff, and the young man had been in his job for six months, surviving fine, as far as she knew.*

"What kind of problem?" *Alex asked, curiosity winning over her need to continue her creative process.*

"Um," *He stopped talking and she was pretty sure she heard a sob. He cleared his throat, but still spoke in a whisper,* "I don't know what to do."

"Maybe you should ask Hank," *Alex said, trying to be helpful. Hank must have overwhelmed the young man.*

"That's the problem. I can't." *A choked sob again came through the phone speaker.*

"Well, why not? I'm not in Virginia. I don't know what I can do from here," *Alex said, not for the first time wondering why people couldn't just get to the point. It would save so much time and alleviate misunderstandings.*

"We're not in Virginia either." *The voice came back, hollow.*

"What? Where are you?"

"We're at a hotel in Dupont Circle."

*Now, really confused, Alex wanted to reach through the phone and shake the young man.* "No, Hank's in rural Virginia meeting with a potential candidate."

*"We had dinner with the candidate here," Jeff said, seeming to be glad to have one answer.*

*It felt like a knife seared through her belly. Lies. She did not lie and expected the same from others. To lie, it was best to keep as close to the actual story as possible; it was easier to remember that way. Why that thought passed through her head at that moment could only be attributed to intuition; Hank did meet with a candidate, just not where he said.*

*"What, exactly, is the problem, Jeff?" She could certainly think of a few problems on her own but doubted that's why Jeff called with Hank's phone.*

*"Hank's dead."*

*Okay, she definitely did not hear that right.*

*"Did you call 911? Didn't the bartender notice a problem?"*

*"We're not in the bar. We're in a room."*

*"Why is he in a hotel room when he has a perfectly good bed here?" Alex asked, still not comprehending what happened.*

*"Please, Ms. Newberry ... Alex ... please, just come. I don't know what to do."*

*"You need to call 911. He might not be dead. They might be able to revive him," Alex insisted.*

*"He's cold," Jeff said. Alex could feel him shudder through the phone.*

*"Text the address and room number. I'll be there shortly," Alex said, realization hitting her, glad she had not bothered to get undressed earlier; that would waste more minutes.*

*She walked up the avenue in the blackness of night, sky dark, only the streetlamps, long-since converted from their original gas, providing pockets of light and deeper shadows. Any other night she might be frightened of the shadows, but tonight she was too preoccupied with confusion and anger to notice. She had enough presence of mind to hope she'd find a taxi roaming the deserted streets, trolling for a late-night fare.*

*Not knowing what she faced, she did not want to worry about parking around Dupont Circle, and she didn't want the potential trail of a rideshare. Why? She didn't know. She just knew it might be important. She laughed without humor as she realized maybe the fiction she had been creating sparked her cloak-and-dagger approach.*

*Luck had been on her side, as far as cabs, anyway. She walked quickly through the lobby, ignoring the skeleton crew on the hotel night staff, punching the elevator call button, and making her way to the room number Jeff had relayed.*

*The door was ajar when she got there, the flip-over lock keeping it open. She slowly pushed it open, closing it completely behind her, hoping Jeff got the room right and she wasn't walking into an amorous scene with oblivious lovers. That thought almost sent her reeling backward, knees buckling, but she caught herself. Lovers. Why did that word stick in her brain?*

*Alex turned the corner, realizing it was a suite. She saw Jeff sitting still as death in a chair in the farthest corner of the room. His clothes looked haphazard, not at all like the sartorially astute young man who worked for her husband. Stepping a few more steps into the suite, she could see through the open bedroom door. The large lump in the king-size bed must be Hank.*

*Slowly, one booted foot in front of the other, she made her way to the side of the bed. Hank was on his back. Mouth slightly open. Eyes shut. She quickly realized he was naked. She reached down and touched his neck, skin cold to the touch, carotid artery still. Yep, dead. Damn. Jeff was right.*

*"I...I found him like that," Jeff said, his voice close behind her. So intent on her task to prove her husband was still alive, she hadn't heard him enter the bedroom.*

*"Why was he here at all?" Alex asked. All she could think was he had too much to drink over dinner and decided to get a room instead of potentially bothering her. But no, that couldn't be right. Hank never drank to excess.*

*"We had the client dinner. He drank a little too much, between the wine and whiskey..." Jeff started and then tapered off, shrugging.*

*"Why are you here? How did you get in the room this late to check on him?"*

*She noticed condom wrappers partially hidden between the lamp and the alarm clock on the nightstand, and reality suddenly dawned on her.*

*"You didn't have to be let in. You were already in here. You 'found him' because you were already in bed."*

*Jeff hung his head further. "Yeah."*

*He continued, voice a little stronger. "We fell asleep. When I woke up, he was cold."*

*Alex stopped. A shudder began to crawl up her spine; her husband had been holding someone else in his sleep.*

*"He didn't expire while you were fucking?" Alex asked, almost wincing as the word left her tongue. She hated that word. Now she may decide to use it more often if she could get a reaction like the one she got from Jeff. He looked like she'd slapped him.*

*"No!" he said emphatically, the loudest she'd heard him since he called.*

*"Were there any drugs involved?" she asked dispassionately, almost like she was back in the newsroom interviewing a corrupt politician.*

*"No!" Another loud response. "Only wine and whisky, for him. I had a few Cosmopolitans before we came up here."*

*"We have to call 911," she said. Turning to look him straight in the eye, she asked pointedly, "Are you prepared to tell them exactly what happened? We can try to leave it at you 'found him,' but depending on the autopsy, they may know someone else was in the room."*

*"God, no, I don't want anyone to know! Do you know how hard it was to call you? But Hank always said if anything ever went sideways, to call you and you'd know what to do." Jeff had no idea he said too much.*

*Alex narrowed her eyes, fists clenching at her sides. "You mean this wasn't a one-off? You've been sleeping with someone else's husband for how long?"*

*"He meant if something happened with a client!" But then a guilty look streaked across his face, one moment pale and the next he flushed, red moving quickly up his neck to cover his face. "It wasn't the first time. I guess for the last few months."*

*Quickly Alex's mind reviewed all the times Hank was "out of town" with clients in other locales and wondered if all were a lie.*

*"I'm sorry. God, I wish I'd never said yes," Jeff said.*

*"You're telling me my husband came on to you?" Alex stated, teeth clenched.*

*"Yes. Well, I mean, I was attracted, but he's the one who suggested a liaison," Jeff said, using the French word, as if that would lessen the impact of what he delivered.*

*Alex straightened, tipping her head from side to side, trying to loosen the tension in her neck and keep the headache looming behind her eyes at bay. She had dealt with enough crises in her position with the political firm to be able to handle this, even if it meant simply laying it all out there. "Listen, I don't have the energy for this. What's done is done. Now we have to deal with the fallout."*

*Jeff nodded and visibly relaxed, glad to see she moved from affronted spouse to professional crisis manager.*

*"I'll call 911. I suggest you put those condom wrappers in your pocket or get rid of them in the lobby trash. The last thing I need is to have some overly ambitious detective decide the injured wife came to the hotel room, found her husband with his lover, and decided to off her husband. By the way, you better figure out how you're going to get rid of the used condoms too." She was aware she spoke in the plural and pushed the feelings down.*

*"He flushed them before," Jeff said. Then he had the good grace to be embarrassed. He grabbed the foil wrappers and shoved them deep into his trouser pocket.*

*Alex nodded. "We aren't going to lie. That's where this all went wrong to begin with. We're just going to say the minimum necessary. Got it?"*

*"Yes, ma'am."*

*"Don't call me ma'am."*

*"Sorry," he whispered again.*

*When the police arrived, one of the officers called in the detectives. Just to be on the safe side, she reasoned—high-profile dead guy, leave no "t" uncrossed. Alex was relieved to recognize one of the detectives, Charles "Charlie" LeBrandt, someone who had been at the Naval Academy with Ian.*

*Charles and his partner got the story, short as it was, from Jeff and Alex.*

*"Alex, did he have a bad heart or was he at risk for a stroke? Anything that made you suspicious he could die?"*

*"No, nothing at all," Alex said truthfully.*

*"Mr. Mullins, why did you call Ms. Newberry and not 911?"*

*"I panicked; I'm sorry. My boss was cold. Dead. And Mr. Robertson always said to call Alex for anything I wasn't sure about," Jeff answered, sticking to the truth.*

*"The officers will wait here until the medical examiner arrives. Without*

*a known illness or pre-existing condition, I'm sure they're going to want an autopsy. They'll want to rule out poisoning or suffocation, blunt-force trauma—anything like that," Charles explained. "We may need to speak with you both again."*

*"Got it." Alex nodded. She briefly wondered if anyone found it was strange she hadn't cried yet. She would be wondering about that. Great. She may have made herself a suspect if foul play were involved. Wait. She hadn't considered that. What if Jeff had suffocated or poisoned him? No, that couldn't be right! The young man was way too unnerved ... unless that was an act. Ugh! She watched too much crime drama and read too many spy thrillers. This was the real world. Admins did not off their bosses with nothing to gain; and there was certainly nothing to gain here, but a lot to lose.*

*Charles then switched out of cop-mode and wrapped an arm around Alex's shoulders. "You're going to be okay, Alex. You're great in a crisis. But do you want us to take you home? Our shift is ending now. I know you, and once the shock wears off..."*

*"You know what? I would really appreciate that," Alex said and leaned into Charles' tall, lean body. Somewhere her brain registered he was amazingly muscular for a man over 60. Must be a hangover from his naval career; or maybe detectives had to meet physical standards. Or maybe it was simply Charles. Hank, though tall and not fat by any means, had been getting a bit soft; the product of a lot of rich, client dinners, she supposed. And not much exercise lately. Well, unless you counted fucking your administrative assistant.*

*Charles asked the officers to get Jeff a lift home, the young man obviously not holding up as well as the dead man's wife.*

*"How's that goddaughter of mine?" Charles smiled, speaking of Charlie. Her oldest daughter was named after him, her first late husband Ian's best friend. First late husband. What a morbid moniker.*

*Oh no. The mention of her eldest daughter reminded her she had to break the news of Hank's death to her children. Someone would need to be with Lauren when she learned the news; the others would be fine. How was that going to work? The girl was in the final semester of her college freshman year in Michigan, while Alex was in DC.*

"*Charlie is hanging in there. You should give her a call,*" *Alex said. She then said, stress making her voice tense,* "*Charles, Lauren can't hear this on the news.*"

"*There wasn't an ambulance and not a large police presence at the hotel, so no news media were alerted. You may be okay for now,*" *said Charles' partner, someone with whom Alex had been acquainted over the years through Charles.*

"*Okay, that's good. One less thing to worry about,*" *Alex said and huffed out a long breath.*

*Charles had lost his wife to cancer a few years before, so losing a spouse was something with which he was all too familiar. When they got to Alex's home, he sent his partner home and went inside with her. Without asking, he fixed her a cup of tea with milk, coffee for himself, and then sat next to her at the counter. Alex was numb.*

"*Alex, have you thought about what Hank was doing in that hotel room?*" *Charles asked carefully.*

"*Is this Detective LeBrandt asking or my friend Charlie?*" *Alex asked astutely.*

*Charles pinned his lips together before he said,* "*A little of both, I guess.*"

"*Thanks for being truthful, at least.*"

"*How about you give me the same courtesy?*"

*Alex sighed.* "*What do you want me to say, Charlie? We both know Hank was bisexual. But when he asked me to marry him, he promised me I was the one with whom he'd been in love, even when Ian was alive. He said Ian got to me first. Now he's dead, I find out that might all be a lie?*" *The words came spewing out.*

"*Do you think he had something going with his assistant? Otherwise, why was he at a hotel?*" *Charles persisted.*

*Alex laughed without humor.* "*That would be the best bet, wouldn't it? I feel like I don't know anything anymore, Charlie. I didn't see my husband in bed with another man, but that would be the odds-on favorite, right? You know, he promised me it was only me. I told him before we married that I'd understand if he didn't want to limit his options and call off the wedding. He told me I was being ridiculous. Then I made him promise that if he ever wanted to be with a man—or even another woman—that he would give me the courtesy of divorcing me."*

*Charles pulled the woman against his broad chest and held her head. Alex felt hot tears in her eyes, her throat burning, but no tears came. "Why can't I cry, Charlie? What's wrong with me?"*

*"Not a thing, Alex. You've had a big shock. I'll just sit with you until you're ready to go to bed; then I'll go. You okay with that?" He kissed the top of her head, comforting the woman too numb to feel anything except confusion and anger.*

## 18

"How did I miss that, Maddie?" Alex asked, eyes coming back into focus and staring her friend in the eye.

"Holy shit. That's some crazy stuff," Maddie said, eyes huge, in shock at the story.

"Maybe he only married me for the money to start the company," Alex said, saying one of her greatest fears aloud for the first time.

"That can't be right." Maddie frowned. "We all saw it. Hank was in love with you. He adored you. Besides, his family had a boatload of money."

Alex shook her head. "Before his parents died, he was left a small trust and the summer house in southeastern Connecticut. His dad left all his money to his favorite charities. He believed his son needed to make his own way."

The magnitude of that statement hit Maddie. No wonder her friend was feeling off center. Anyone, under the circumstances, would question their entire relationship. Maddie moved so her back leaned against the wrought-iron headboard. Alex followed suit, once again staring straight ahead.

"No, I don't believe that. He loved you." Maddie decided, picturing all the times over the years she'd seen the couple together, including when she stood up for Alex when they wed. She also knew Ian for a few years before he was killed, when he was home from deployments, and knew the two marriages were different, but that didn't mean the second one was bad.

"I don't know anymore. I think he did. But he talked me into founding the company with him awfully early in our relationship. Hell, if I hadn't, I'd still be writing for the newspaper."

"Maybe, or maybe you would have been out at the same time the news business downsized and the most experienced reporters were the first to go," Maddie argued, though she doubted Alex would have been on the cut list. "Besides, he could have asked you to go into business with him; he didn't have to marry you."

Alex weighed that thought, tossing it over in her mind, seeing how it felt. "I suppose that's true. And I know he adored Lauren and even loved my other kids."

"True, he did. He never would have started planning William's political future if he didn't love him and didn't believe in him." Maddie carefully formed her next thought before voicing it. "Do you think maybe this Jeff guy was a one-off? You know, Hank starting to feel his age, proving his virility and ability to attract someone younger."

"*Much* younger," Alex followed immediately. Her eyes darkened again. Softly she replied, "No. It wasn't a one-off. He was with that little twerp for months."

Alex continued, eyes getting that faraway look again, wincing as she brought forth a painful memory. "Jeff wasn't the only one. Remember the funeral?"

"Of course. I wondered what it was that Hank's old assistant said to you that got you so upset, but there were too many people around for me to ask." Maddie remembered.

"You saw I was upset? Did anyone else notice?" Alex asked, hoping she'd kept a better poker face than that.

"I know you, Alex, of course I knew you were upset. But I'd guess everyone else thought it was the weight of the funeral, if they saw anything at all," Maddie assured her. She urged, "Tell me."

*Alex chose to have the funeral in Connecticut, far enough away that there would be little speculation in DC and close enough that anyone who really wanted to come could be there.*

*Charles told her the medical examiner had released the body—no blunt force trauma, no signs of strangulation, no poison, and no drugs in his system on which he could have overdosed. He did have more than his usual consumption of alcohol in his system and still in his stomach; Alex thought it was probably to dull the guilt of lying to his wife. He also had an aneurysm, a weakness that had probably been in his brain since birth and decided to rupture that night. Really bad timing, but no nefarious causes at fault, Charles assured her.*

*Then she had him cremated. An urn was easier to carry to Connecticut than a casket. The one reason she thought of putting him in a casket and burying him instead of cremation was that he wanted to be cremated. The idea of worms eventually eating his corpse made him physically ill. She thought it sounded delightful, a perfect follow-up to his lies. But, in the end, she couldn't do it. Unfortunately, she didn't have a truly mean or vengeful bone in her body. She was a naturally forgiving person.*

*She, again unfortunately, always saw the reasons why something may have happened or why someone did what they did. Right about now she considered the gift a curse. She did the right thing and respected the man's wishes for his remains. The urn would be buried next to his parents' graves in the picturesque Mystic cemetery on the Mystic River. The ancient trees provided shade and protected those bodies of souls long departed. The breeze would blow off the wide, curving river, rustling branches and leaves, as the water flowed out to sea not too far down. Constant movement. Continual renewal. Cocooning the ashes and those buried there in comfort and peace behind the wrought iron gate and stonemason's walls.*

*Charles accompanied the family on the train from DC with Alex— Charlie and her kids, Lauren and Harper, Sage, William, and their kids. William, in between missions, got permission to come home in time to take the train with his family for the ceremony and burial but had to fly out to who knows where the next day. Aimee, Andrew, and their kids closed the restaurant—small towns understood family emergencies—and flew out to meet the others.*

*The service was held at the Old Mystic United Methodist Church. It was a beautiful, cool spring day. White clouds drifted sporadically up high against the backdrop of a bright blue sky. She could smell spring in the air, new growth after being dormant in winter, the first cutting of grass, and the fragrant spring flowers. Everything shouted renewed life and prospects. She felt empty and confused. Then that damn hawk flew overhead, dipping its wings down toward the earth, catching her eye, drifting for a bit, before flying toward the sea.*

*She was surprised when everyone at the church made the trek to the graveside ceremony down the road. There were a lot of people. More than she had expected. But then again, Hank had a lot of friends and even more business associates. A large percentage of politicians across the country owed their success to their company. They didn't know what she knew, or maybe they did, and she was the only fool.*

*Jeff was there. He avoided her. That was fine with her. He cried. Then he disappeared with another young man directly after the graveside ceremony. Good riddance. She hoped he would not show for the wake at Hank's favorite local restaurant.*

*Her youngest daughter, Lauren, needed the wake part. She needed to see people celebrating her father and sharing stories of his life. Alex just wanted to leave for Michigan and go to the island. It would still be cold on the lake, but she would manage.*

*Her family walked away to the line of cars. She lagged behind, staring at the scene around her for one more moment.*

*A man walked up to her, hands shoved in his trouser pockets. He was tall and lean with a shock of dark wavy hair, clipped much shorter on the sides, the temples showing the slightest hint of gray, eyes covered with impenetrable dark sunglasses. "Hello, Alex."*

*Hank's former assistant had been scarce since he left the company a year ago. His departure still made no sense to her. The man had been there and been loyal since they started the company twenty years before. He was now in his mid-forties. Yet one day Hank told her he had decided to leave; he was ready for a new challenge. Clay Bryant had rarely been away from Hank's side, traveling with him for client field work, keeping the perpetually moving Hank organized, always one step ahead, devoted to Hank the entire tenure of his relationship with the company. He was always polite with Alex, but she could feel his standoffishness and had from the beginning. But as long as Hank was happy and well cared for, she never questioned his choice in assistants.*

*"Clay. It was nice of you to make the trip. I didn't know if you got my text."*

*"Yes. Sorry for not responding. I'm back in Connecticut now," Clay said, voice flat. He stood in his dark designer wool slacks, sport coat, and dress shirt, looking more like an aging runway model than an assistant. She too wore designer wear, courtesy of Hank's shopping sprees on her behalf: black trousers, black lightweight turtleneck sweater and trendy black jacket, matched with pearls and black patent leather loafers. Maybe she was not dressed exactly like a grieving widow, but she would never wear a dress again, so this was how she moved these days.*

*She had forgotten he and Hank both grew up in Connecticut. "Well, I'm glad you could make it. I'm sorry we hadn't seen you in so long. I hope you can come to the restaurant. I know Lauren will want to see you."*

*Clay studied her, pursing his lips, searching for something, though she didn't know what. Finally, he spoke, "You really don't know."*

*"Know what?" Alex asked. She really needed this to stop, she could not take more confounding statements. She was used to being in control and she had none since this entire nightmare started.*

*Something akin to a strangled chuckle left his throat. He pulled off his designer sunglasses and looked toward the sky before staring straight at the woman. "I didn't leave for more of a challenge, Alex. You were more than enough of a challenge for me. But you won, didn't you?"*

*Her head was beginning to spin; she could feel a migraine coming on. Why couldn't people use straight talk? Was that really so hard? "I have no idea what you're talking about, Clay."*

*Out of the corner of her eye she noticed they were the only ones left graveside. Maddie was standing at the cars with the rest of her family and Charles.*

*"Huh. You don't. He never did have the guts to tell you."*

*"You're going to have to stop talking in circles, Clay. Either that or I've got to get going," she said, trying to keep the frustration from her voice.*

*After all, this was someone who had been a big part of their lives for twenty years.*

*"That's right, you like candor. Well, let me enlighten you." He leaned close and she could see his eyes were bloodshot and puffy, tears still welled. He had obviously spent a lot of time crying over his friend and former boss. "I left because he refused to leave you. He loved me, but he wouldn't leave Alex." Her name sounded like a curse from his mouth. "Oh, he said he loved you too. But it wasn't the same, was it? You couldn't give him what I did— pure passion and freedom to be who he was. Unconditional love."*

*Alex was speechless and simply stared at him. He probably thought she was holding back angry words, but she wasn't. She couldn't get a word out if she tried.*

*He continued, sounding more forlorn, beaten. "But then, I couldn't give him what you did—a family and respectability. He never could get over the respectability part. He was so afraid of his father being disappointed in him, even from the grave, that he was willing to live his sham of a life with you."*

*Kicked in the gut. That's how she felt. She needed to breathe. Oh, how she wanted to yell at Hank right now, rail against the lies that brought them to this point.*

*Deep breath in, she finally found her voice. As always, when faced with confrontation or contempt, she became overly quiet and even toned. Only when pushed past her limit did she lose her composure and eviscerate her opponent with her words. She was past her limit today emotionally, but not with anger toward Clay, so she could still appear composed and poised while talking to the man with whom her late husband had apparently been in love. She almost felt sorry for the younger man.*

*"I'm sorry for your loss, Clay. You're right. If I'd known, I would've let him go. I knew he was bisexual, but he told me he was in love with me, and I was enough. I told him even before we married that if he ever wanted to be with anyone else, I would give him a divorce. I even would have remained friends. Because we were friends. We were always friends."*

*Clay hung his head and then looked in her eye. "Damn you, Alex. I really want to hate you. I've always wanted to hate you, but I never could. I still can't. You've always been so selfless, with everyone. It wasn't fair he didn't tell you. Not to me, not to you, and especially not to himself. But he said he loved you and made a choice. He thought we could keep going, keep our secret; I'd still be the family friend, Uncle Clay to Lauren. But I didn't want to be a secret anymore, so I quit my job and I quit him. I thought he'd come to his senses and follow me."*

*"How long were you having an affair—or I guess I should say, how long were you in a relationship with him?" Alex dreaded the answer even as she asked the question.*

*"The entire time, Alex. We started seeing one another when we worked together before you formed the company. Then he hired me. It was so much easier to be together when we could travel together, and no one wondered why. It worked so well you didn't have a clue. Alex, smart, brilliant, Alex, you didn't have a clue. I so wanted you to figure it out," Clay lamented.*

*There it was. The next punch to the gut she knew had to be coming. This wasn't something new, later in life; he had lied to her and cheated their entire marriage. He lived a dual life, and she was a fool.*

*"He didn't go after you?" Alex couldn't help but ask.*

*"No. Oh, he called. Asked when I was coming back. I told him when he confessed to you. He thought I'd give in. I thought he would do the right thing. I waited too long. Now he's dead." Clay's voice was even but a few tears rolled down over his high cheekbones.*

*"Is everything all right over here?" a deep voice asked from behind them. Alex was so involved in her own misery she hadn't heard Charles approach.*

*"Everything's fine. I was just paying my respects to the widow, Charles," Clay said and turned his head to stare at the gravesite, no longer looking at either of them. He quickly walked away, mumbling his parting words over his shoulder, "I'm sorry, too, Alex. Tell Lauren I'll see her at the restaurant." Then he was gone.*

*"What was that about?" Charles asked, carefully watching Clay's departing figure weave in and out of headstones.*

*"Grief and regret, I think," Alex said cryptically.*

*"Tell me all about it later. Right now, your kids are waiting, and we need to get to the restaurant." Charles placed a hand on her lower back and steered her toward the cars lining the cemetery's drive.*

*She took one more look back at the Robertson family plot and glanced up, unsurprised to see the hawk, sitting high on the tree branch, staring at her. Damn bird. Why did Hank have to want to "fly like a hawk" when he died? Couldn't he have picked some less disconcerting symbol? Then she allowed the pressure on her back to lead her away.*

Maddie was enthralled and appalled at the same time. This could not be happening. Her friend was living a movie script. She remained quiet for quite a while. So did Alex. Alex finally turned to her and shrugged.

"See? What am I supposed to think? Was my marriage a complete lie? Were there others? Was he cheating on both me and Clay at the same time? Who was Hank? Really, who was he?" Alex demanded.

"Before we dissect that, I have to ask, did you and Hank have a sex life?" Maddie came out with it, bracing herself for the retort.

"Yes! I thought we had a decent sex life, often. Like, really often. It wasn't as passionate as with Ian, but frankly, no one will ever top that." She looked at her friend incredulously. "I wouldn't live in a sexless marriage, Maddie. You know me better than that."

Maddie burst out laughing, "Thank God! I mean, I assumed you were, but with that load of heavy crap in the background, I wasn't so sure."

"Oh yeah. And the first thing I did after the funeral? I got tested to make sure that lying husband of mine hadn't given me some sort of disease. I saw the condoms, but you can't be too careful, you know?"

"I'm glad to see you were still thinking straight." Maddie's tone was sardonic as she tried not to smile.

"That's it. I don't think I am. None of this makes any sense. How could I have been such a blind fool? I still have the same unanswered questions: Did he marry me for money? Did he ever love me? Why did he marry me? Was he gay and not bisexual? Did he only say he was bisexual because it would be more acceptable to our generation? Why didn't he divorce me? Why? I hate that he's not here to face the inquisition." Alex pounded the mattress with her fists. She relayed most of this to Charles after the funeral, before he made his way back to DC, and she left for Michigan, but that had been a simple reporting of what she learned, no analysis included. He told her she could call anytime if she needed someone to talk to or even vent to.

Instead, she kept all of this in, waiting for an epiphany or Maddie's arrival, whichever came first.

Maddie sighed and turned, moving her body in front of Alex. "First of all, you weren't a fool. You were upfront and honest with your expectations. You trusted what he told you to be true, as should be expected. He was the fool and the only one to blame in this mess. Second, I do believe he loved you, in his way. Who knows? Maybe he loved both you and Clay. You can love more than one person at a time, even be *in* love with more than one person at a time; whether society accepts that or not is another issue. Or maybe he was a greedy bastard who wanted it both ways and was spoiled enough to expect to get it. We'll never know. Third, does it matter?"

Alex started to nod her head yes and then slowly changed to shaking her head no as Maddie shook her head no, braids swaying and the little beads clacking together as they moved. It was a strangely comforting sound.

"Can you change anything that happened?" Maddie asked.

"No," Alex reluctantly conceded.

"No. Then let it go. You can't change the past. You may never know the whys. What we do know is that you have an amazing family, part of which you created out of love with that man. And you have an amazing best friend—me. You can live in the moment and let go of all the shadows in your mind, enjoying the time you are blessed to have with the tribe here with you under one roof, and every moment yet to come. Don't let the unanswerable questions of the past cast doubt over your present and future."

Alex narrowed her eyes, light eyebrows reaching inward. "When did you get so smart?"

"I've listened to you talk to your kids all these years," Maddie joked. "Seriously, something I've heard you say for years is a big lesson you need to remember right now: don't wallow. Let any challenge make you stronger, or at least more resilient and empathetic."

Alex ran her hands through her wild curls, wrapping her fingers around the hair and pulling. She had to feel more than numb. Her scalp tingled, the pulling becoming uncomfortable. At least she felt *something*.

Suddenly, knowing didn't seem as critical. Suddenly, she was feeling some of the peace she usually only got from being on the water. And, suddenly, she wasn't so angry at Hank. She felt kind of sorry for him not having the courage to own up to his own truth, if that's what he avoided, but she wasn't ready to feel totally sorry for him—yet. That would come, probably quickly, since it was already kicking into her psyche.

"Okay." Alex nodded once at Maddie and moved to get off the bed. "Good talk."

Maddie laughed and rolled her eyes. Luckily, she had years of practice understanding "Alex-speak" and reading her friend.

"If that didn't work, I was going to suggest we burn him in effigy in the firepit before I leave," Maddie deadpanned, to which Alex burst out laughing.

**19**

---

Lauren slid down the wall, ear close to her mother's door, straining to hear any other earth-shattering revelations. The red painted, two-panel bedroom door was solid, but with the quiet in the cottage, she could hear the voices behind it.

She wasn't far behind Alex and Maddie when they made their way back to the cabin. Originally, she was on a mission from Aimee to ask if they wanted to go skiing later; then she made the mistake of listening to see if she would be interrupting anything before she opened the door. She never got that far. Hearing the discussion stopped her where she stood, completely frozen and unable to leave or announce her presence. Sitting on the floor, knees close to her chin, she tried hard to keep the sobs locked in her chest, though she could not stop the salty tears that fell like twin waterfalls down her suntanned face.

Since the autopsy results, Lauren had kept a secret fear deep down that her body harbored a similar anomaly that killed her father and would someday—sooner rather than later—kill her. She was afraid to bring it up, worried her family would think she was a hypochondriac or being ridiculous. Didn't the doctor say it could have been there his whole life? Didn't it then merit the possibility that he could have genetically passed that weakness to his only child?

That morning when she awoke, the possibility of an aneurysm was the worst thing in her life, other than her father being dead. But now? Now she discovered the events surrounding her father's death were not what she thought. She was told he was at a business meeting and died in the hotel—not a lie, but not the whole truth.

Her father lied to her mother their entire marriage. He might have been a gold digger. Her parents' marriage could be—probably was—a complete sham. That's how she interpreted what she heard. Did that somehow negate her worth or lessen their love for her if their love for one another was not what she thought?

How could her father do this to her? He knew she was gay. How could he let her feel like she was the only one in the family who struggled with that realization?

All these thoughts spun in her head, making her dizzy. The tears fell faster.

BY THE TIME Harper found her, Lauren sat frozen on the floor, eyes red and swollen, snot running down her nose, waterfalls still falling silently from her eyes, unable to tear herself from the door. Harper's first instinct was to knock on the door and get help, but as she got closer and heard the muffled voices, she instinctively knew it was a serious conversation that shouldn't be interrupted. They thought they had privacy.

If something was really wrong with Lauren, such that she needed medical attention, she would walk in and get help. First, she had to find out what was wrong.

Harper pulled Lauren to her feet, wrapping an arm around her, and walked her down the hall to the bedroom they shared with her baby.

"Are you hurt?" No answer. "Can you walk?" No answer.

Well, she was walking, so that was one mystery solved. Harper didn't see any blood, so she didn't think her friend was hurt. That left one conclusion in Harper's mind. Coming from a house where her mother had made eavesdropping on her and her father into an art form, Harper was well-acquainted with the reproachable practice. Rarely did anyone hear the whole story or understand the context when they eavesdropped. Almost always, they came away with ill-gotten secrets, hearing something they shouldn't have.

Pushing the door shut with a gentle click, the ancient door mechanism engaging, Harper sat her friend on her bed, handed her a box of tissues to clean up her face, then sat down beside her, the old mattress dipping with their weight. She demanded, "Why are you a mess? What did you hear?"

Lauren's eyebrows rose. Through breathy sobs, she asked, "How do you know I heard anything?"

"I know you. And you know my mother. So, tell me right now or I'm going to get *your* mother, because you're scaring me," Harper threatened. She knew how to apply pressure that would make Lauren talk.

Lauren broke down again, sobbing out loud this time, and related the entire overheard conversation in halting sentences that almost drove Harper mad. Given the seriousness of the topic and her friend's reaction, she could hardly complain about her delivery. Instead, she did what she observed Alex do time and again over the years; she listened, every once in a while nodding her head or making an acknowledging noise, just to let Lauren know she was still there and taking it all in.

Well, this was not what Harper expected Lauren to reveal. She was not sure what she had expected, but it was not this. She always envied Lauren's relationship with her parents and their relationship with one another. Her own parents had made it quite obvious their marriage was arranged as a business transaction, not undying love—though she had to admit a kind of distant affection had grown between them, or maybe a product of familiarity born out of years of responsibility. Even so, unlike her parents, Hank and Alex seemed to enjoy one another's company, love one another, be great friends. That couldn't have been faked. Not twenty years' worth.

Lauren looked younger than her nineteen years. Forlorn. Child-like. She continued talking, and Harper had to focus. It was hard to focus on an entire monologue spoken while crying.

"I'm so sorry, Lauren," Harper said, one arm around her friend's shoulder, hugging her.

"How could he do this to me?" Lauren wailed. "Why did my mom keep this from me? It was my dad who died. Did he even want me? Maybe I was a mistake. He let me think Uncle Clay was this great friend." More loud crying.

The more Lauren's abject sorrow turned to a rant, the less patience Harper had. She still felt sorry for her friend's sorrow and grief, but not the direction this was taking.

"I like girls, Harp. I've always liked girls. How could my dad not tell me? How could he let me think I'm the only oddball in the family?"

Harper was taken back that her self-assured, take-no-prisoners, bulldoze-through-life friend felt anything other than accepted and adored. She never talked about feeling the odd-woman-out. Never seemed to do anything but revel in her differences. This new side to Lauren was not only a surprise but also not very attractive. Oh, she felt for the insecurities she'd always known Lauren must harbor, because let's be real, everyone was insecure in some way. What she couldn't accept was the self-loathing yet self-centered turn her rant had taken.

Harper had her own questions. "How can you question if your parents love you? Ack! For goodness' sake, Laur, your parents are the best. This is not about you."

As if slapped, Lauren jerked her body and faced her friend. "How can you say that? My whole life is a lie."

"Stop. Just please stop." Harper shut her eyes.

"I thought you were my friend."

"I am your friend. Your oldest friend. Your best friend," Harper insisted. "But you gotta stop, Laur. This isn't about you. This is your mom's to deal with. It's between your parents—well, it would be if your dad was still alive. But it's still their story, not yours."

"I'm a product of that story," Lauren insisted. "I'm in the middle of this."

"You aren't. Can't you see? You've always been loved. You've always been supported. Your dad had his own demons he must not have felt comfortable sharing, but that doesn't take away any of the love or affection he had for you or your mother," Harper said, trying again to make her friend see sense. "What do you think he did to you?"

Lauren was affronted enough by her friend's candor to stop talking and think for a moment; the friend who was never unkind, never anything but supportive of whatever harebrained, uncomfortable scheme Lauren put forth. If Harper was that passionate about her view, there must be something Lauren had missed.

Lauren's mind spun. Her mother had weeks to think about all this and find peace—not that Lauren was sure if she had yet. Lauren had minutes. She deserved to flounder and rant a bit, she reasoned. Her mind struggled and eked out a memory Lauren thought of as the defining moment of her existence. Eleven-year-old Lauren alone with her father after a karate lesson.

"When I was eleven, Dad picked me up from karate," Lauren said, hiccupping, calming as she recounted the memory she had never shared with anyone.

*"Tell me, firebrand," her father said, settling into the SUV's driver seat, and turning to her before starting the vehicle. He used his favorite name for her. Her particular zest for life was equal parts impressive and frustrating for her parents; they had explained this to her many times. She knew she kept a lot inside, but when something had to come out, she had to let it out. What no one realized was she thought about things deeply and for a long time before she dared share a thought or opinion. She never wanted to be wrong. Felt she always had to be perfect. It was a little scary with a family full of such smart, successful, and well-connected people. Everyone knew her dad and mom, even her sisters and brother. Everyone respected them. She had a lot to live up to.*

*"Nothing to say," Lauren mumbled.*

*"What did I see in there? What did your teacher say? You had that guy. You let him win," her dad pushed. She knew he wasn't chastising her. He would never do that; he never told her she wasn't good enough. He wanted to know why she acted the way she had.*

*They had sparred in preparation for a tournament the following week. Her dad saw her allow that boy to take her down; Sensei definitely saw it.*

*Sensei took her aside at the end of practice and told her to never let anyone make her feel she had to hold back, never pretend she was not good enough to fit in. Anyone who expected that was not someone whose company she should desire. He hadn't mentioned the takedown, hadn't pointed to a specific example. He let his words hang in the air and told her he expected all of her present at the upcoming tournament. No holding back.*

*"Do you like that boy? Is that it?" her dad asked. "If you have to let him feel powerful to notice you, he's not for you, firebrand." He shook his head, lips pressed firmly, staring intently at her. He wasn't going to let this go.*

*"No."*

*"Then explain it to me. What happened? Did you lose focus?"*

*It was now or never. Either that or they would never get to the pizza place for lunch. She was really hungry.*

*"It was* her*. Not him."*

*"Who's her?"*

*"She likes him. If I beat him, she won't like me. I like* her*." Lauren stared at her dad, willing him to get what she was saying. Really get it.*

*Realization dawned on her father. His mouth formed an "O" and then one side of his mouth tipped up in a lopsided smile. "Ah, you like the girl. I see. But what I said still holds. If you have to lose for her to like you, she's not for you."*

*"That's it? You don't care it's the girl I like?"*

*"Hate to break it to you, firebrand, but I figured a long time ago this was probably how it was going to be. Some people like boys. Some people like girls. Some people like both. Some people only like someone if they like their personality or mind. There's no one way to like someone. It doesn't matter to me or your mom who you end up loving, just that they love you in return and treat you well."*

*"You're sure Mom won't care?"*

*"Positive. She's the least judgmental person I know. She won't care one way or another." Her dad grinned and messed up her hair. "She accepts me the way I am, right?"*

*Lauren wasn't sure that was a good example. Her dad was tall, lean, a full head of dark hair, and very handsome. He was also smart. Of course, her mom accepted him.*

*"Don't look so skeptical. Have I ever lied to you?" Hank asked.*

*"Nope."*

*"Then focus on you being you and don't worry what other people will think. The best people—your people—will accept you without you being weaker or dumber than them or liking a girl rather than a boy. Always be who you are, firebrand," her father said again for emphasis. "Ready for pizza?"*

*Well, that went differently than she had expected. She was kind of disappointed it was such a nonevent. She had built the moment up so much in her mind, she expected more of a discussion, more time spent figuring out what she wanted.*

*Nope. Just acceptance.*

*A grin broke out on Lauren's face. "Let's go. I'm hungry! Oh, and Dad? I'm gonna win at the tournament."*

Looking back at that short conversation in her father's SUV eight years ago, as she related it to Harper, she could see far more meaning in it than she ever realized. "Do you think my dad was building the foundation, so I'd accept him someday, you know, if his secret ever came out? Why didn't he take his own advice and be himself?"

"Sounds to me like your dad was a complicated man. Also sounds like he accepted who he was and did the best he could. If we look at not only his words—which were all the right things, remember—but his actions too, you know, I still say he loved your mom and chose her. There's no doubt in any of that, that he loved you unconditionally. That's more than we can say for my parents." Harper couldn't help but throw her situation in there.

The door opened at that moment. Both Alex and Maddie pushed through the doorway. Alex immediately went to her daughter's side and sat on the bed. Maddie kneeled in front of her and grabbed her hands.

"Excellent questions. Excellent analysis." Alex squeezed her daughter's shoulder in a hug and winked at Harper. Alex tried hard to hide the pain she felt inside. She was tired of feeling gut punched. "I'm so sorry you overheard any of my conversation with Maddie," she said.

The older women had heard the scuffling outside the door when Harper pulled Lauren from the floor. They weren't sure if anyone had heard what they discussed, but after peeking around the corner, watching Harper walk Lauren into their room, and hearing Lauren's sobs, there was no longer a question. When they heard the conversation on the other side of the teenagers' door, Maddie stopped Alex from bursting into the room, and they did their own eavesdropping.

"You should have told us." Lauren's face was scrunched, pained, as she accused Alex.

"Maybe, but I don't think so. Not your worry, Lauren. None of what happened. Not what I learned. Not the questions I will never have answers for. None of it changes one iota of your relationship with your father or how he felt about you. There is no question in any of this about his love for you. Don't ever forget that," Alex said, trying to reassure her youngest child.

Sounds of laughter and pounding feet rolled through the cottage at the same time they heard the screen door slam.

"If you want to think some more and talk to me later, I'm not going anywhere." Alex hugged her daughter and stood. Maddie told her she'd be in the kitchen in a few minutes.

After Alex left, Maddie squeezed Lauren's hands until the girl looked into her eyes. "Sucks to be an adult, huh?"

"Yeah." Lauren sniffled.

"Never a good idea to listen at doors, baby girl." Maddie tipped her head and pointedly stared at the girl. "Not sure if you overheard the whole story. Your mother's not the bad guy. For sure, it's not your story."

Lauren wanted to continue to argue her point but was beginning to see the merits in what her mom, Maddie, and Harper tried to tell her. It hurt, even if it wasn't her story. Not only did being an adult suck, but never getting answers from the one person who took them to his grave sucked more.

"Our parents are human too." Maddie concluded with those words and rose. "Fix your face and get ready to eat." She followed the order with a kind smile, kissed Lauren on the top of the head, and was gone.

Harper waited until Maddie left, then stood to follow. "No one lied to you, Lauren. Your mother was lied to, if anyone." She hesitated a moment, then said, her tone envious, "You're so lucky."

"You keep saying that. This is not lucky. This is hell."

"No. This is life. And you've got everyone cheering in your corner," Harper said. "I want that for Allie. My baby does not deserve to be ignored by her grandparents and unwanted by her sperm donor. But that's the hand she was dealt. I'm going to do my damnedest to make sure she feels like the luckiest girl in the world. Because she's got me. She's got your family. We will always love her—unconditionally. Can you do that, Laur? Can you love your mom and dad unconditionally? Me? My daughter? We're all human. We're all going to disappoint you at some point."

Harper left the room and shut the door firmly, taking all the air with her. Lauren struggled to breathe.

## 20

ighter. Alex felt lighter. The oppressive pressure on her chest was not unbearable today. No nightmares plagued her sleep. Alex felt rested for the first time in months.

There *was* a heavy pang of regret that Lauren had overheard her conversation with Maddie. She would deal with that later. This was something she had no desire to share with her children and would rather have shouldered alone. Was this in deference to her years with Hank? Was it embarrassment that she may have been complicit somehow? Or was it simply humiliation?

Whatever the reason, she still felt lighter than she had since the night she received the phone call and showed up in that hotel room, faced with a situation akin to an out-of-body experience, or, perhaps more aptly, a nightmare from which she could not wake.

It was time to start a new painting. This one was not an island scene. Not a landscape. She didn't create a sketch first. When the brush stroked the canvas, her wrist flipped up and down as if her hand was possessed, creating of its own accord. She was surprised what was in front of her by the time she heard children's voices waking up inside the cottage. A city scene took shape. Reds, grays, and black prominent. An outdoor café with gentlemen seated comfortably in their anonymity, unaware the artist captured them. The artist obviously the outsider looking in, uninvited.

Alex put the paints away, cleaned the brushes, and closed her tackle box underneath the bench seat, away from grabby hands. Easel, turned away from the inside of the screened porch, faced the north side of the cottage where anyone rarely walked. The path that ran next to the cabin along the top of the ridge was too close to the steep, tree-dotted, drop to the lake. It also led to the outhouse no one would voluntarily use.

By the time anyone else made it to the kitchen, she was well into her third mug of tea, warming her hands against the ceramic, staring into space. To her grandchildren she appeared to have all the time in the world to hear about their latest adventures and what they planned for the day ahead. Her patience was something her children only hoped to emulate, though she was glad they couldn't read her mind. As far as she was concerned, they had already mastered the art that alluded her.

Cameron had his eye on the camera screen, slowly panning the room, motion staid when he reached his grandmother's hands wrapped around the steaming cup of milky black tea.

"Capturing enough for a documentary?" she asked kindly.

He nodded and continued silently recording, moving out of the kitchen, and capturing either the movements of the others or their conversations; she wasn't sure of his focus. The plot would be revealed at some point. Regardless, the activity had captivated him enough to hold his interest for weeks on end. No more mention had been made of Wi-Fi, except when he asked to download editing software Maddie recommended.

"It's a cereal kind of morning," Charlie announced, setting several boxes on the counter along with bowls, spoons, and milk. All except the youngest of the cousins would be able to get their own breakfast. Charlie plopped onto the stool next to her mother, mug in hand, glad the kettle was already hot and ready for her tea.

"Bad night?" Alex assumed.

With a glance around—no children were within hearing—

Charlie sagged with her elbows on the counter. "You could say that. Dreamed about James again. I don't know. Maybe it would be easier if there had been a body to bury. Do you think he's visiting me?"

"Well, if he is, he's not haunting you. There's nothing malevolent about James." Her mother neither confirmed nor denied.

Charlie groaned. "No, the dreams aren't bad. They're disconcerting."

"How so?"

"It's like he's reaching for me, smiling, but I can't reach him. Then I hear his voice and I'm stuck in some maze I can't find my way through to get to him," Charlie said. "I don't know. I feel so good when I first see him, but when I can't get to him, I wake up frantic and can't breathe."

Before her mother could say anything comforting or intelligent, or even make light of it, Charlie said, "I know! A psychiatrist would have a field day with me."

"Not necessarily. But maybe you should consider going to a therapist, have someone to talk to. Maybe one who also specializes in dream analysis," Alex said, knowing before she said it what her daughter's reaction would be.

"Yeah, right. No thanks. I haven't met anyone yet who can tell me anything I didn't already know. I don't want to do that again."

"Well, if they don't go away, at least think about it," Alex said mildly, mug to her lips.

Charlie glanced sideways at her mother, head propped up in her hands, elbows still on the counter. "For you, I'll think about it." Still noncommittal. Better than an outright "no."

No more chance for privacy, the kitchen was soon teeming with activity. Lots of cereal poured and protein bars grabbed.

The screen door slammed behind Maddie. Alex was surprised to see her friend up and coming in from the outside. She thought for sure the woman would spend the first two or three days on California time, if not the whole trip.

"I always forget how beautiful and peaceful this place is. We should have a writing retreat here," Maddie enthused, getting her coffee from the single-serving contraption, adding the requisite milk and sugar, before sitting next to Charlie at the counter.

Charlie perked up at that idea. "Can I get in on this?"

"Sure! I need to engage your mother in some creative endeavors that could be quite lucrative. You too, if you're interested—you're a great writer, Charlie."

Alex added her own stipulations. "I'm interested. But I don't want people we don't know or don't like here. It can be us and *maybe* a *select* few others."

Hand waving over her head, as if that was a given, Maddie concentrated on her coffee.

Lauren avoided the kitchen and headed straight for the boathouse. She lifted a kayak into the water and dipped the paddle with long, strong strokes meant to escape into the reeds and lily pads. Her mind was still jumbled with what she felt, how she thought she should feel, and the reactions to the story she'd overheard—her own reaction playing over and over.

Remembering her best friend's reaction felt like a slap in the face all over again. She was not prepared for that. It was uncomfortable to have to try to think like an adult, look at different perspectives, and not stay in her own head, swim in her own grief. She dipped the paddle deeper and harder. Maybe if she exhausted herself, she'd have no space for recriminations, no energy to remember.

Her father's face haunted her restless night. Her mother's easy smile floated in front of her, made her feel angry that the older woman was not outraged, while also being angry her mother had not shared the secrets. Even in her emotional state, Lauren knew what was swirling in her brain and pressing on her chest was not rational. She knew she needed to get a grip.

"Paddle harder, Lauren," she gritted through her clenched teeth.

A muskrat scurried from the bank and almost landed on the kayak hugging the shore, startling the teenager from her self-imposed angst. Lauren leaned back, face screwed up, dark hair sticking to her forehead and temples with the perspiration begin-ning to gather from the exertion of paddling furiously. "UGH! Don't come up here and freak me out!" The creature was as startled as she was.

Now that sticking to the privacy of the shore was less appealing, Lauren paddled furiously to leave the false safety of the reeds and lily pads. She headed for the choppy open water and from there toward one of the more deserted coves tucked into the curving mainland shoreline—somewhere she could be alone in her own head.

On the other side of the lake, sails loudly flapped in the wind, like bed sheets on a clothesline, snapping crisply, violently, until Colin could bring the boat about and fill the sails. Relieved, his quick glance at the other sailors aboard this windy morning showed they ducked appropriately and remembered the safety lessons he tried to instill in them, as his father and grandmother had in him.

Earlier he thought he saw Lauren disappearing around the end of the island. He heard part of the blowup the day before through the back window when he was making his own escape to the treehouse. He wasn't terribly proud of himself for eavesdropping, but when he heard the sobs, he wondered if someone needed help. He almost wished he hadn't heard any of the sordid story. If anything, he felt badly for his grandmother and conflicted about Hank.

But out on the water, wind high today, Colin felt free. There was peace out here, even with the wind and whitecaps. Even with cousins in the boat, their faces turned to the wind, as happy and eager as he supposed he appeared. For the time, there was just this. Nothing else intruded.

On a pass in front of the island, back on shore he saw Jaspar and Cassie jumping up and down in front of his mother, gesturing wildly toward the lake. He presumed they were pleading to go waterskiing. Charlie's head shaking firmly "no" made him laugh. There was no way she was taking the kids out until it calmed a little bit. The water could be choppy during low winds, but this would pound the motorboat and the skiers mercilessly. The sailboat skimmed through the water, bow rising and falling periodically, spray coating the sailors, but mostly it cut through what would be more difficult for other craft.

Years ago, he and his mother had traveled to South Africa, where his father and team had a few days downtime. His younger brother and sisters stayed stateside with their grandmother and Hank. He, his mom and dad, and his father's friends had taken a large sailboat out into the bay, wind high, waves higher, sharks visible every once in a while behind and beside the fast-moving yawl. He remembered his dad's friend insisting one particularly big shark was racing them; if they lost, someone would be fed to the shark. Of course, the SEALs won.

According to his dad's teammate, Colin had nothing to worry about; they always won. His memory was clear that he knew someday he would be a member of the Teams and win too. Older now, he knew they didn't always win. Not everyone came home. But, as his dad said, what they believed in, the service, was important enough to try.

The wind today felt the same to him, blowing memories in and out, no time to feel bad, only to be part of the nature surrounding them, part of something bigger and broader, older, ancient. That was okay with him. It felt ... right.

What wasn't right, he realized, was that he had not seen Lauren or her kayak in some time. He used the rudder to steer to outer portions of the lake, the less used coves, wondering where his young aunt had disappeared. There was no overturned kayak so far; that was good.

In one of the more secluded coves, usually used only by fishermen, the whitecaps less there, he saw her in the kayak, paddle resting over the craft. Using the wind in the sails to slow the boat, he tacked, keeping her in sight, until he caught her attention. He waved. She waved back, lifting the paddle and beginning to move toward the sailboat.

When she got close enough to be heard, Lauren's sarcasm was in full effect. "What are you, the cavalry?"

"Wrong branch." Colin shook his head, the boat now rocking in the waves at the head of the cove. He would have moved closer but was afraid to beach the sailboat if it was too shallow.

"Whatever!" Lauren rolled her eyes, getting closer to the sailboat. "Did someone send you to rescue me?"

"No." Colin shook his head again. "It's pretty rough. I wondered where you went."

Lauren hated to admit she was a little worried how she'd get back to the island, and that she'd left without her mobile phone tucked into the waterproof pocket of her shirt.

"Want a tow?" Colin asked.

"How about you just help me get on board without falling in the lake?" Lauren said. Grace and Andi leaned down and held the kayak, trying to keep it still enough for Lauren to pull herself out and not have the kayak bang violently into the boat. The large whitecaps were smaller at the mouth of the cove, but they still rocked both boats. Colin reached to help his aunt sprawl on her belly and roll inside the sailboat. Rather than tow the smaller craft, they lifted and balanced it across the sailboat.

"Thanks," Lauren said, breathing heavily from the exertion. "I didn't think it was going to get so rough."

"Glad Colin saw you earlier and wondered where you went," Andi said. "That wouldn't have been fun getting back across."

Lauren agreed. "Guess I'm out of shape. My arms feel like rubber."

Colin set a path toward the island. The mood was broken, and he wanted to get to shore to unload the kayak and his crew. Maybe he could escape to the treehouse without anyone noticing. He loved his family, enjoyed their loud, exuberant approach to everything in life, but sometimes he craved the silence of his own thoughts.

Once back, everything and everyone unloaded, the others beat a path to the cottage, ready for lunch after all the fresh air and excitement of being on the rough water. Colin disappeared behind the cottage, on his way to the quiet of the almost completely rehabbed treehouse in the woods. They were waiting only on the tin roof promised by Maitland. For now, the wood and tarp served its purpose just fine.

Later in the evening, Indy escaped to the kitchen by herself. It was time to experiment with some recipes of her own. Plus, she thought she could get a head start on breakfast. *No cereal tomorrow,* she silently promised. She worked diligently, measuring ingredients, her lips pursed in concentration, flour spotting her face and her white-blonde hair.

The counter was testament to her efforts, showcasing a little bit of everything she concocted. She knew the chocolate chip pancake batter was done and put it in the industrial-size refrigerator, ready to make pancakes in the morning. She did the same with the sausage and egg mixture she made, planning to put the casserole dish in the oven in the morning. The cookie batter was almost ready when she heard her mother shout for her. It was time for bed.

It was so hard to mix the cookies. The stiff dough was a challenge. Too much of a challenge to finish tonight. She put that in the fridge too.

In a hurry, she stored the ingredients in front of her, wiped the counter, and ran to get ready for bed, flipping the main light switch to the off position—the one over the sink in the corner still burning bright—slamming the kitchen door tightly behind her. The pirate bottle opener stood guard, as he had for more than three-quarters of a century.

**21**

Eek. Squeak. Little footsteps. Eek. Squeak. Screech. Screech. Screech. Scritch. Scritch.

Tory and Alex turned to one another. Eyes wide. They stood on the screened porch staring at the closed kitchen door. Normal sounds of children and adults came from behind the living area door, voices, laughter, grumbling. The kitchen sounds were not normal.

Tory was up early, morning sickness in full bloom. Alex had held her niece's hair behind her head, cool washcloth against her neck, as the young woman dry heaved again and again. There was no painting this morning. No early mugs of tea before the rest of humanity woke.

So, who was in the kitchen?

Alex decided her hesitation was ridiculous. This was her island and whoever was in the kitchen didn't belong here. She would get to the bottom of the strange sounds. She pushed the door open, the effort made harder by the overturned chair in front of the door. When she pushed it out of the way, she tried to see through the fog of powder flying through the air.

Gray squirrels and a couple raccoons ran rampant in the room. They appeared to be scolding one another and grabbing whatever

166

they could from the counter. Cabinet doors hung open. Pots and pans were scattered across the floor.

"Shoo! Shoo!" Alex yelled, trying to scare the creatures into abandoning their playtime and her kitchen. She was a little afraid to approach. Didn't raccoons carry rabies? Would they attack if cornered? She had never paid attention when her father watched those nature shows on television. Emboldened when she saw the straw broom on the floor by the door, she picked it up and began swinging it, clearing the air in front of her with each swish, moving forward step by step.

"Shoo! Shoo! Get outta here!" Tory took up the yelling behind her aunt.

Alex pushed farther into the room, broom swishing in front of her, yelling. The woodland creatures scattered, disappearing behind the counter. When Alex and Tory made it through the dining area and reached the other side of the counter, they saw what they hoped was the last squirrel rush into a cupboard and disappear.

"I'm afraid to look in that cupboard. What if they're hiding inside?" Tory whispered.

"Nah, they're more afraid of us than we are of them," Alex said. Then noticing the incredulous look on Tory's face, she rolled her eyes and added, "Well, at least let them think they are."

With great trepidation, Alex bent at the waist to look in the open cupboard all the animals seemed to have disappeared through, ready to jump back and run if beady eyes met her gaze. What met her was a big hole in the back of the cupboard. She surmised, when the contractors put in the new stove, taking out part of the cabinetry to make room for the larger appliance, they cut holes to accommodate some sort of new piping. One hole was made bigger by the gnaw marks she assumed the squirrels had chewed. Another hole was big enough for the raccoons to get in. Now the strange odor she had noticed in the kitchen made sense. Animals.

"Umm, Alex?" Tory said, looking around the kitchen, taking in the mess for the first time.

Alex stood and, much like Tory, surveyed the room, turning her body the full 360 degrees.

"Wow!" Charlie exclaimed from the doorway.

The kitchen was a disaster. Not only did flour float through the air, but it was also scattered across the counter and the floor, along with sugar, chocolate chips, bananas, eggshells, cereal spilled from boxes pushed from the open pantry door, the trash can upended. Dish soap spilled out, dripping from the counter to the floor, little animal pawprints tracking it across the tiles.

Indy pushed her way around the adults gathered in the doorway, peered around Charlie's legs, a high-pitched sound coming from her throat, and she ran outside crying, not a word spoken.

Sage took in the sight, remembered the flour on Indy's face and in her hair before her bath, put together the missing pieces, and took off after her daughter. It took time to find the six-year-old. She hid behind the tree the treehouse was built in, legs pulled up to her chin, forehead resting on her knees as she sobbed. She would have been in the treehouse, but she was neither tall enough to reach the first rung nor strong enough to pull herself up to the ladder.

Sage dropped to the blanket of old leaves covering the ground and put her hand on Indy's shoulder, racked violently by her sobs.

"It'll be okay," Sage said. "Want to tell me what happened?"

"It's my fault!" Indy cried. "Aunt Aimee will never let me work in her restaurant now."

"Indy, shh. That's not true. Tell me." Sage encouraged her daughter and rubbed a soothing hand against the little girl's back.

Indy explained how she prepped for breakfast this morning, excited to feed everyone by herself, and how she made other things she had hoped to finish today.

"I put it in the fridge, Mama, I really did," Indy said solemnly through her tears. "But I guess I forgot to put away the sugar and maybe the flour canister wasn't closed. Maybe some other stuff was left on the other counter. I had to hurry because it was bedtime."

"Well, I doubt the squirrels got in the refrigerator. The rest could have happened to anyone, Indy. The sugar gets left out all the time with all these people here," Sage said. "Come on. Get up. Wipe your tears. You can apologize to Grandma and help clean up. Okay?"

Indy pushed to her feet and trudged back to the cottage. Inside the kitchen, cleanup was underway. Indy pulled on her grandma's shirttail and related her part in the debacle, contrite and apologetic.

Alex knelt beside the girl and looked into her eyes. "This wasn't your fault, Indy. If anyone's at fault, it's the contractors who left the hole in the cupboard."

Charlie called from the open refrigerator, "Did you do all this, Indy?"

Indy looked up, nodded, and waited to be berated.

Charlie broke out in a grin. "Well, hallelujah! We have real food for breakfast! Great job, Indy!"

"See, sweet girl, you saved the day. This is not your fault. I doubt very much you had the cereal boxes out last night." Alex smiled kindly, Indy shaking her head in a vehement no. "The animals got in because there's a hole in the cupboard. Then they played and ate. We just need to close the way they get in, so it doesn't happen again."

"So, are you ready to show me what we need to do with this food once the stove is cleaned up?" Charlie asked.

Indy nodded, tears forgotten, and got to work. She glanced at the pirate bottle opener beneath the counter when her shoulder brushed against it. Did he *wink* at her? She was sure he winked. But as she focused on him, waiting to see it again, the pirate merely faced ahead, looking mean and unapproachable, as always.

Maddie entered the kitchen yawning. "You've got some loud squirrels here. I think the entire population of island squirrels are under my window having their own town hall."

Everyone stopped what they were doing, looked at one another, then started laughing so hard tears fell, some dropping to the floor, the laughing starting another round of hilarity. Maddie looked at them all like they'd lost their minds.

"It wasn't that funny. I'm serious," she said. Then, surveying the room and people in front of her, she became suspicious. "What are you all doing anyway? Isn't it breakfast time? You look like you're spring cleaning."

"Sit. I'll get your coffee," Charlie offered, swiping at the tears in the corners of her eyes with the back of her hand.

Alex told her friend the story about the animals in the kitchen, while Indy stood on a chair to pour the chocolate chip pancakes on the griddle and flip them at the right time. The egg casserole was already in the oven, cheese added.

Maddie pouted. "I gotta get on Eastern time. I miss all the good stuff."

Charlie snorted. "Yeah, like cleaning."

Cameron moved to Maddie's side. He held out his camera and shared what he'd recorded this morning, from the end of the animals, Alex and Tory scurrying in the kitchen, complete with broom as a weapon, to the flour fogging the air, and the subsequent cleanup, all the way to Indy cooking from the chair.

"I didn't see you behind us this morning, Cam," Alex said, surprised. Cameron gave her a one-shoulder shrug and continued watching the screen and Maddie's reaction.

"He's like a ninja with that camera. He sees everything and no one sees him." Andi rolled her eyes and helped set the table.

Maddie was now howling with laughter. "Were you two really afraid of a couple little itty-bitty squirrels?"

Tory and Alex scowled. Tory said, "There were more than a couple and there were raccoons too!"

This made Maddie laugh louder; even Cam managed a half smile, one side of his mouth tipping up.

Quietly to Cameron, Maddie said, "You're capturing some decent stuff. You've got the makings of a good movie on your summer here."

Equally quiet, he said, "While you're here will you help with some of it? See if I'm getting the editing right?"

"Absolutely!" Maddie enthused and gave the twelve-year-old a quick hug. His tan face reddened a bit from the affection, but his smile belied how he felt.

From a morning fraught with drama, the day could only improve,

Alex thought, trying hard not to jinx it. She now had two consecutive days disrupted with drama, then add in Tory's soon-to-be-ex-husband's uninvited visit, and Harper's early labor—though that ended up a happy drama—and wished for no more for the rest of the summer.

After breakfast, most of the kids stayed inside playing games or reading quietly. Lauren sat at the kitchen table and played Fish with Indy, Savannah, Donovan, and Harmony. Harper fed Allie and watched the game, helping Harmony. After the lively morning, no one seemed to mind a break. Alex found a piece of plywood to temporarily keep the critters out of the kitchen and nailed it inside the cabinet.

Aimee arrived after all the morning hoopla. Charlie filled her in on the latest adventures her sister had missed after she picked her up on the mainland. The two then joined their mother, Maddie, Tory, and Sage on the flat ground outside the cottage to relax. They sat on the weathered old bus seats under the trees.

An acorn landed at Alex's feet. *That* was one of the trees she forgot about—the tall, straight oak trees that stood at the top of the hill on the flat surface.

Another acorn landed in Tory's hair. A tiny piece of branch with three leaves hit Aimee in the forehead. The sound of angry chattering echoed in the trees. The acorns came in faster succession, hitting the women sitting on the benches.

"What the heck?" Charlie grabbed the latest stick with leaves that landed in her wavy hair and stood up suddenly, looking overhead. A squirrel ran down the side of the tree closest to her and stared at her, squawking squirrel babble, before turning around and running back up. She was sure the thing was going to jump at her.

"We're under attack!" Maddie informed them, holding her arms over her head as the acorns, sticks, and leaves rained down.

"That's ridiculous—" Alex started and then an acorn hit her again, harder, on the shoulder. "Hey, that hurt!"

"Told you so." Maddie smirked from under her arms.

Charlie grabbed acorns and began throwing them directly at the squirrels she could see. The squirrels shot more down at the women.

"I think they're mad you kicked them out of the kitchen," Aimee laughed. Then an acorn hit her in the cheek, and she jumped up, ready for battle. "Hey! No fair. I wasn't even here this morning." Reasoning with the squirrels was hopeless. They all threw acorns and sticks back toward the invading rodents, trying to scare them away.

Finally, the acorn shower slowed and then came to a halt, the squirrels beaten back. The women sat back on the bus seats, wary the evil little creatures would return. Then it started. One small snort. A little chuckle. A high-pitched giggle. A snicker. A titter. Then all out hilarity. Who gets attacked by vengeful squirrels? The Newberry women, apparently. No one would believe this.

Cameron quietly recorded from afar, crouching on the path that led to the outhouse. At first, he thought the adult women were nuts. Then he saw they were being pelted with nuts. Then he saw the squirrels. Nature and civilization at odds. Might make for some cool video.

The women sat outside on those bus seats talking until the kids raced out of the house, swimsuits on, towels flying behind them, running down the path to the lake, jumping over familiar tree roots in their race to the bottom. The women followed at a more leisurely pace, enjoying a lazy day.

**22**

———

en's voices floated up the hill from the dock. Alex put the finishing touches on a new canvas, squinting through the screen toward the water. One voice was louder than the others, her brother Maitland.

She met him halfway down the hill. "How did you get here? I didn't hear you honk."

"Good morning to you, little sister," Maitland greeted her, kissing her cheek. "I caught a ride with the guys from the dock at the north shore gas station. They're here to put the roof on the treehouse."

"When did the treehouse become such a big project, Mait? It's always been however the kids can build it," Alex scolded.

"I always wanted the expansion, and this roof will last at least fifty years. Come on, indulge me a little, Alex. Why can't they have a tree-house that's not half falling down every summer. Where's the harm?" Maitland cajoled.

"Well, it's a little late now if I wanted to stop you, don't you think?"

"That's the spirit," Maitland said, taking her acquiescence as acceptance. He moved in front of the contractors carrying the roof pieces and ladders, leading the way.

Colin, Andi, Gavin, and Cassie ran out of the cottage. "Is that Uncle Mait and the roof?" Colin asked.

"Yep," Alex said.

"Sweet!" the kids chorused, running toward the treehouse.

"Hey, stay out of their way, all right?" Alex called after them.

"Uncle Mait promised I could help," Colin yelled back over his shoulder.

Alex looked toward the sky and shook her head. She was going to let her brother deal with this one and keep the kids safe; it was his project, after all.

The contractors were a lot more patient than Maitland expected. They answered Colin's questions, showed him what they were doing and how to seal the metal. The other kids wandered away once Maitland caught Cassie by the waist and pulled her off the ladder in an aborted scramble to the top, swinging her around before he set her down. "Sorry, kiddo, only your big brother up there this time." They figured they would come back when the work was done. That would be more fun anyway. The beach called, in the meantime.

"Will this really last fifty years?" Colin asked.

"It will."

"Wow. I'll be older than you before we need a new one," Colin called down to his great-uncle.

"And I'll be dead," Maitland said under his breath. That was not a pleasant thought.

Once the roof was finished, the contractors took their ladders and tools and climbed into the boat to return shoreside. The kids all yelled their goodbyes and thank-yous. Maitland chose to spend the day on the island. Someone would take him to the far north shore after dinner.

He sat down on his daughter's beach blanket and got to the point. "How's our plan coming?"

"I've prepared everything I can," she said. "I forgot how much fun law school applications aren't."

"References? If you need any, let me know and I'll make the calls."

"It's okay, Dad. I sent email requests to my references to see if they're still willing to provide one."

"Any more contact from that son of a bitch or his attorney?" Maitland asked.

"Dad," Tory sighed, glad Van was splashing in the lake and not within earshot. "I did what we said. No contact other than through my attorney. The restraining order seems to be working. Mark hasn't shown up here again."

Maitland nodded his approval. "Don't get complacent. You never know when he may decide to come out here and try to get you or Van back."

"He doesn't want me anymore, Dad." Tory sighed, a slight pain shooting through her chest.

"Well, don't count on it. That woman he was seeing on the side doesn't want him anymore either," Maitland declared.

"How would you know that?"

"I hear things. When she realized you weren't going to roll over with the settlement, she put him on notice. And Teddy, Grant, and I may have pulled all family investments we had with their firm," Maitland said, casually mentioning his and Alex's two older brothers.

Tory gasped. "This is bad. If the firm partner told Mark, he's going to blame me. He's going to show up and make me pay for embarrassing him."

"Hey, hey. It will be fine. We're playing hardball, remember?" Maitland soothed his daughter, rubbing her back gently. Tory's body remained stiff, though she tried to fake a smile for her father.

Luckily, at that moment, Van raced up and grabbed his grandfather by the hand. "Come in the water, Grandpa! Throw me!"

Maitland chuckled, stepped out of his boat shoes, slipped his dark polo shirt over his head, and allowed Van to pull him into the water. Waist deep, Maitland stopped and scooped the little boy up over his head and threw him a few more feet out into the lake. Van came up sputtering and yelled, "Again!" as he swam back to his grandfather.

The other small cousins thought that looked like great fun and lined up chanting, "Me next! Me next!"

Tory sighed with relief. Her son unwittingly rescued her from further inquisition. She worried Maitland's actions would enrage her soon-to-be-ex, as if that could get any worse. The last thing she wanted was another confrontation in front of her family. If she could think of a way Van and her unborn baby would never have to see the man again, she would make it happen. Unfortunately, she couldn't think of anything. All she could do was hope he would lose interest. It's not as if he ever had any interest in Van anyway, unless someone he knew and thought he could use would be at one of Van's T-Ball or soccer games. He had nothing to do with the school, except when he wanted to try to get the principal's business—Tory had been mortified.

Tory knew his girlfriend was more interested in money than people. For years she thought Beth was simply a co-worker who worked closely on some accounts with Mark. Maybe her dad was right; all was not good in paradise. Ugh. Tory was solid in her decision now. Mark could not come crawling back to her. She had not started the divorce proceedings—though she knew now she should have been the one to do it long ago—but she was sure going to finish them. That man would never touch her again.

She couldn't decide if the sun was hot, or her emotions were making her that way. Either way, she joined her father, son, and cousins' children in the lake. She splashed the kids in a happy display of summer fun, cooling her overheated body in the process, allowing the dark thoughts to retreat for the time being. Still not comfortable without the long-sleeve, high-neck swim shirt covering her, she breathed deep and promised herself, *one thing at a time.*

DINNER THAT NIGHT BEGAN, tension thick in the air. Lauren stared at her plate, not meeting anyone's eyes. Conversation happened around and over her. After one or two attempts, no one tried to engage her. The discussion turned to Alex and the company.

"Have you thought about what you're going to do with the company, Mom?" Aimee asked.

The entire table went silent. All eyes, even Lauren's, turned to the matriarch. Her brother stopped, fork halfway to his mouth. This was it, Alex thought. This was the beginning of the damned intervention she thought she had evaded.

"I have." She was delighted to see she surprised them with her two-word answer.

They all sat. Waiting. Not eating. Staring.

Aimee broke the silence first. "Well, are you going to tell us what it is?"

"I hadn't intended to in this setting," Alex said evenly.

Still, they stared. Waiting.

Alex sighed. She touched her napkin lightly to her lips and then replaced it carefully in her lap. She noticed a few of the grandchildren, who had not placed their napkins in their laps at the beginning of the meal, quietly slip them there now. That made her smile.

Staying as calm and even as she could, she said, "I think I want to step back from the company."

Everyone seemed to reply at once, just as she expected.

"Yes!" Aimee smiled triumphantly.

"Mom! No!" Charlie looked horrified.

"Why?" Maitland asked, baffled.

"Are you staying in Michigan?" Sage asked.

"What will you do?" This came from Harper.

"You're not old!" Colin threw in.

Alex raised her hands in the air to quiet the crowd. "I think it's time I pursue what *I* want."

"Is this because of my dad?" Lauren asked quietly, looking up for the first time.

Alex tilted her head and sent Lauren a kind smile. "Somewhat, yes. But not what you probably think. This company was always Hank's dream. We built it together. I believe we did a lot of good. But it's not my passion project. I want to paint more. Write more. Maybe collaborate with my best friend."

Maddie beamed and nodded at her friend's words.

"Don't worry, Charlie. I'm not selling the company. You can keep working there, if you want. In fact, you can pick up most of what I used to do. I'll chair the board. I'm going to recommend you and William be added to the board. Since I own the majority shares, I don't see that as a problem, do you? But working every day and handling the inane crises these politicians get themselves into? No, that's not me anymore," she said definitively.

"Where will you live?" Aimee threw out, fingers crossed under the table.

"I'm not selling any of the three houses or this island—never the island," she responded. "All three places hold special meaning for me and all of us. Who knows where I may need to be to feel inspired? And some of you may need one of these places someday."

"How come I'm not on the board or have a job at the company? Or why not Aimee?" Lauren challenged, chin high.

"Aimee has no interest," Alex said, and Aimee nodded in agreement. "And you're still in college. You need to find what path you want to take. But do you think you'd be happy working with clients, catering to their whims, helping make them better than they are?" Alex looked pointedly at her youngest daughter.

Lauren blushed. She remembered quite vividly the previous summer when she insisted on working at the company and making money for college. Within a matter of days, she had insulted a rising politician as being a bougie imitation of a real public servant, told her parents another did not have the brains of a jackass, and stormed out when yet another expounded on his version of a platform—not one Lauren could stomach. Her parents mildly suggested she might like to intern at an activist organization next time around.

"No? I didn't think so. Well, if you're interested when you graduate, you'll always have a place, and you can work your way up, like Charlie and William. You have time to decide," Alex said.

William and Charlie both worked there during high school and summers during college. Charlie joined full-time after graduation. William worked when he could during leave from the Naval Academy and knew a place waited for him, if he should want it when he got out or retired from military service. It was a training ground for William, who shared Hank's political ambitions for him. If he stayed in the Navy, Alex could easily see him someday on the President's Joint Chiefs of Staff.

"Maybe I should run for office someday," Lauren said.

Every adult, teenager, and preteen around the large table raised their eyebrows.

"What? I would be great at it! Lot better than what we have now," Lauren said stubbornly.

"The best public servants understand the art of compromise," Charlie said.

"What? You think I can't?" Lauren retorted. "Besides, compromise is overrated. What have we gotten with compromise? Delayed equal rights for women. Affirmative action rather than real action. Lower pay for women and underserved populations. People caring more about guns than the children they're killing."

"Mama, am I going to be killed?" Harmony asked, eyes wide. Savannah moved closer to Gavin, who silently put an arm around his cousin.

"Shh. No, baby." Sage soothed the little girl, shooting her passionate sister-in-law a warning look.

Lauren continued, unabashed. "I'm serious. Mait, you're a successful attorney. But you're a white man. Nothing is difficult for you. You're privileged. Hell, we're all privileged. But the patriarchy has a lot to answer for. It can't continue. Compromise doesn't change anything fast enough. The polarization in this country and around the world is ridiculous. Yes, we need to come together, but we need people pushing on the edges even more. People who care about people and don't put profits first."

Maitland jumped in while Lauren took a breath. "You think everything in my life has been easy? Or your mother's? Your brother's? I may be a white man and, yes, I agree the playing field isn't always even, but I do my part and do *not* condone or participate in discrimination in any form. My firm's female associates make the same, in some cases more, than their male counterparts. I don't care what color a colleague or a client is."

"This family is different than the average." Lauren persisted, pushing her point. "I know that. But it doesn't mean we shouldn't push to change more and change it faster. Maybe I'll stay on the fringes and be that catalyst for change. Maybe I'll run for office and push that way. But I will make a difference. I'm not going to pretend to be someone or something I'm not. I'm not willing to live in a world where it's not safe to go to certain towns, states, or countries because I like women. I'm not willing to live in a world where I have to hide or pretend to play the game. I'm not going to be my father and play the game where someone else created the rules. I won't.

"A world view that says hetero-normative behavior is the only *normal* way to be is insulting and lacking in any historical reality. Because people are scared of what they don't know or haven't experienced is not a reason to legislate against an entire body of people. What happens between consenting adults in the bedroom or elsewhere is no one else's business. Not that long ago blacks and whites couldn't intermarry. Are we going to go back to that idiocy?

"Another thing ... because heterosexual men have no consequences when it comes to sexual reproduction, and privileged women have been brainwashed or made to fear, they cannot be allowed to make the decisions for other women or couples. It's wrong. Choice is just that—a choice. Some people choose to have a baby in inopportune circumstances." She looked compassionately at Harper. "And others choose what is best for their lives. What is so hard to understand about choice? Whatever happens is between that person, their doctor, and their God; no one else gets a say. We cannot continue to allow bedroom politics. It's no one's damn business!

"So, yeah, I have a lot to say and I'm not willing to die and have this country be the same or worse than when I was born." Lauren ran out of breath. She gulped deeply. Only then did she notice no one had taken a bite since Aimee first halted the conversation. "What?

Am I wrong? Everybody, eat. It's getting cold." Lauren took a big bite without waiting for the others to catch up. Oh yeah, she was back. She would use the anger and warring feelings about the revelations surrounding her father to fuel her outrage and platform for change. Slowly, the room began to eat and conversation continued as before.

Alex was secretly delighted her firebrand daughter had taken the spotlight off her. Once again, she avoided the complete intervention. Because sure as the sun rose and set every day, someone was going to ask about how she was *feeling*, take the temperature of her grief.

Well, she really didn't feel a lot of grief but would rather not admit that. Her anger had all but dissipated, but the ambivalence about her life with Hank was something that still bounced in her skull. Though now it felt like an empty room rather than a painful swirling of thoughts. She was confident that would fade as well—as soon as she completely accepted she would never have the answers.

Cameron had quietly lifted his camera from his lap and captured the beginning of his grandmother's intervention and then his aunt's entire heated monologue. Leaving the camera on the table next to him, it recorded the conversation while he ate.

Maddie leaned over and spoke into Cameron's ear. "You know, you're going to have to be careful what you include in this movie. It's a skill to know what to leave in, what's edgy, but to not drop over that edge and hurt people."

Cameron merely met her eyes, gave her a small smile, and continued his meal.

# 23

Darkness covered the island. Very few stars shined through the cloud cover. By the time Maitland was ready to head home, only one pleasure boat cruised the lake, lights on, the music and laughter rolling across the water from their pontoon.

"Let's see if we can join them," Maitland suggested to his sister.

"What's up, Mait? Don't want to go home yet? You can stay, you know," Alex offered.

He sighed, a smile crossing his face. "Maybe you have the right idea. Maybe I should pursue other interests too."

"Come on. You love the law. If you want to give it up, I'll be whole-heartedly in your corner. But really?"

Maitland was silent for more than a moment and turned to watch his daughter coming down the hill after them. He responded before Victoria reached them. "Nah, I'll stick around until Tory finishes law school and joins the practice. But I might take more time to build treehouses and pick my grandson up from school and get ice cream."

Alex patted her brother's back and stepped down into the boat. She tried to remember not to jump; her knees weren't what they once were. "Are you coming with us, Tory?"

"No, I have to get back up there before Van realizes we're gone and wants his grandpa to read him a story," Tory said, out of breath from hurrying down the hill. Darn, this pregnancy was sapping her energy faster than when Donovan was in utero. "I wanted to hug my dad one more time."

"Ohhh, honey," Maitland said, opening his arms and pulling her against him. Her newly rounded, firm belly bumped up against him and he felt a protective pang shoot through his system. His daughter deserved so much more. He felt incredibly guilty for not pushing and prying before now.

"Love you, Dad. Thanks for being here." Tory hugged him tight.

"Love you too. Remember what I said. Watch yourself. Stay aware of your surroundings," Maitland implored. He looked around as he said it, as if the monsters of her childhood nightmares could come out of the reeds or trees at any moment. Or maybe just one current monster.

"Way to make me paranoid, Dad. But I hear you. I will," Tory promised.

Andi ran down the dark path at breakneck speed. "Grandma, wait. I want to go with you." She jumped into the boat. Maitland gave his daughter one more squeeze and stepped onto the boat seat, then sat next to his sister who was in the driver seat, as always. *Good thing I'm comfortable in my manhood,* he thought to himself. Then he chuckled, wondering what Lauren would make of that.

Tory watched the boat pull away, lights on, bow and stern. She stayed on the dock, taking a moment for herself. Breathing in the heavy, charged air that spoke to possible rain headed their way, she allowed her shoulders to relax. The motorboat turned around the island and was out of sight once she moved from the end of the dock. She no longer heard the motor spewing the wake behind them, spiriting her father across the lake, just a low hum of the motor. And the party pontoon must have moved to the north shore because their music was out of earshot.

One more moment alone, she gave herself. One hand absently caressing low on her belly. It was so dark and silent she could believe she was the only one left awake. The occasional voice drifted from the cottage above. She could see why her aunt took refuge here after Hank's death. This place was filled with the magic of her childhood. But now it held all the possibilities of entering adulthood on her terms. Something about being here made it all seem achievable.

A small splash came from the opposite direction where her father had disappeared; the water likely displaced by a fish jumping for a mosquito. She kept her eyes shut, head bent back toward the night sky. A slight bump against the end of the dock jarred her out of her reverie. That was some fish, she thought.

"Hello, Victoria."

The moon came out, shining brightly on the lake at that moment. She swung around, body freezing at the sound of the familiar voice. He quickly wrapped a rope once around the boat cleat screwed to the dock to hold his boat in place. She noticed the motor was not engaged and the lights were not on. The bastard must have hidden in the dark in the reeds. What she thought was a fish had to be him dipping a paddle in the water to maneuver to the dock in silence.

"You're not supposed to be here, Mark," she said, tense.

"Why did you do that, Victoria? Why would you take out a restraining order? I told you what to do, why couldn't you do it?" Mark said, his voice an unreasonable calm. "How about we go for a ride and talk about it?" He reached out a hand toward her but made no move to grab her.

"You have to go, Mark."

"Remember when we used to take the boat out in high school? Make love under the moon? No one knew. We can do that again," Mark mused, his tone taking on a singsong quality.

"I'm not going anywhere with you," Tory said, afraid to move backward and cause him to move and grab her.

"Mommy! Where are you?" Van's little voice called from the cottage's screen door. "Is Grandpa gone?"

"Go back inside, Van. Grandpa's gone. I'll be up soon," Tory yelled up the hill, praying her son did not run down the hill toward her.

Relief fluttered through her chest when she heard him say, "K," and the screen door slammed behind him.

"That's my son, Victoria. How about I go get him and we'll all go home? Would you like that?"

"Leave him alone, Mark. Just go."

"Then get in the boat, Victoria." Mark's tone more resolute, on his way to losing his cool.

"Mark, please, just leave." Tory was disgusted with herself when she heard the pleading in her voice. Old habits truly did die hard.

Mark took two steps in her direction. She moved backward slowly; she did not dare turn her back on him. Two more steps. His were larger and he grabbed her arm in a painful hold.

"Beth told me she lost the baby. That's your fault, you know. We just wanted an easy divorce. All you had to do was sign the papers, hand over the house, give me the money I deserved. All the stress caused her to lose *my* child," Mark said, voice hardened with anger.

Tory had the presence of mind to know she had nothing to do with Beth; the woman had her own agenda. She doubted she was even pregnant in the first place. It was the greedy woman's leverage to get Mark to leave. Mark would never have left on his own; he valued his control over Tory too much to let go that easily. In a twisted way, Tory supposed she should thank Beth.

At that moment, Mark looked down, noticed Tory's belly, enough of a baby bump to protrude in the telltale sign under her tight long-sleeved T-shirt. "What's this? Is this your way to get more child support from me? How about I just take the baby and then we can raise it as our own? You'll never see it. You're not fit to be a mother."

"What is it, Mark? You want me back or you don't? I don't think you ever loved me. You just wanted someone to control." Tory gathered steam. It had been many years in the making.

Mark raised his hand so quickly she didn't see it coming. After so many years, she should have expected it. It came crashing down against her temple and cheek. Flailing her arms, trying not to fall into the water, Tory reached out to grab Mark's arm for leverage, but her nails raked down his cheek first. She could see the blood pool to the surface immediately.

Mark looked stunned as he touched his face, but the shock only lasted a second. He drew back and punched her in the stomach and then an uppercut to her jaw. The young woman stumbled backward under the weight of the blows, her feet stumbling off the dock. She fell back, slipping underwater. She could see gray pulling at the sides of her vision.

As she sunk down, she willed herself to stay conscious through the fuzzy haze of impending darkness. No one would save her. No one knew she was in danger. She had to stay awake. She had to save her baby. To do that she had to save herself. When she floated to the surface, she was under the dock. She held fast to one of the pilings, well, as steady as she could as consciousness faded.

Way far away, she heard Mark's singsong voice. "Tory? Tory, where are you? I'm so sorry, sweetheart. I didn't mean it. You just make me so angry. Please, Tory, come back. We'll go home and forget about all this. Okay? Come on, baby." He pleaded but then stopped. Tory could feel the vibrations more than hear an engine coming through the water. Mark must have heard it because she felt the dock move and then heard an engine start and move away.

"Please, please, let my baby be okay," Tory cried silently, blackness pulling her under, no matter how hard she fought to concentrate.

A boat pulled up to the dock and Tory used the last of her strength to push out from under where she held the piling, "Help, please ..." Her voice faded as she floated on the water and the darkness finally consumed her.

"Oh my God, Grandma! I think it's Tory," Andi exclaimed, trying to see in the water as the moonlight waned, slowly extinguished by another cloud.

Alex moved quickly out of the boat and peered over the side of the dock. Her eyes widened when she spotted the floating body. "Tory?" No response. Alex jumped into the water and wrapped an arm around her niece, swimming and then pulling her to shore, where she could drag the unconscious girl onto the beach.

Water dripping from her jeans, sweatshirt, and swamped sneakers, Alex knelt next to Tory and moved her cheek to the woman's mouth, hoping to feel her breath, and put fingers over her carotid artery in her neck at the same time. She felt a pulse and glanced over at Andi. Even in the low, blue light from the moon struggling to show behind the storm clouds, they could see Tory's face and eye beginning to swell.

"Tory, can you hear me?" Alex asked. No response.

Alex pulled out her phone and pressed a well-used number. "Mait, thank goodness I caught you before you didn't have a signal. Turn around. Something's happened."

"What? Is something wrong with Van or Tory?" Andi heard her great-uncle's voice boom through the phone.

"Tory. She's alive but get here now! I'm sending Andi back with the boat to get you," Alex hung up and looked at her wide-eyed granddaughter. "There's no time to get anyone else. Go get Mait back at the general store dock, then the two of you get the doctor. He's in the cottage next to the judge. Mait knows. Now go. You can do this." Alex assured her granddaughter while communicating the urgency.

Andi nodded and ran back to the boat. She pulled the rope messily wrapped once around the boat cleat, clearing it, and jumped in. She turned the key for the engine and remained standing as she pulled away. She raced toward the north shore, going faster than she'd ever driven. Usually, she was happy to be a passenger when one of the adults or Colin drove, no responsibility to look for other boats, skiers, the odd swimmer. She thought she saw a boat near the other end of the island, but no boat lights were shining, so she decided it was only a shadow playing tricks on her imagination. The severity of the situation spurred her on, acutely conscious of what else might be out there.

Her great-uncle was already standing on the dock as she came alongside faster than was safe. He jumped in and moved her over, taking the driver's seat. He wheeled around so fast Andi was surprised he didn't swamp the boat. She glanced backward and saw Jared, the grocer's grandson standing on the dock with his hands in the air, questioning what was happening. Earlier she had time to talk with him privately while her grandma said goodbye to Mait. She would explain to him later—when she understood herself what was going on. For now, the bow was so high as Mait raced across the lake, she hoped he could see if anything was in front of them, because she couldn't.

"We have to get the doctor next to the judge," Andi shouted above the engine and water noise. She could smell the boat fuel as strongly as she could smell the lake water churned up by their wake.

Maitland clenched his jaw so tight, Andi was worried he would break his teeth. He finally spit out, shouting back, "What the hell happened?"

"Don't know. I found Tory in the water when we got back," she said, holding tight to the side of the boat. Even in the moonlight, Andi could see her great-uncle's fingers turn whiter around the steering wheel. "Grandma pulled her out of the water and she's breathing. But she was unconscious when I left."

"I'll kill him," Mait growled under his breath.

"No one was there with her," Andi assured him, not sure to whom he was referring.

"You're sure you didn't see that no-account husband of hers?"

"Mark? No, I didn't see anyone when we got there."

"Doesn't mean he wasn't waiting when we left," Maitland said, more to himself than her. He looked around the lake, searching for a boat, any boat, any clue. He thought he saw a boat at the end of the island but couldn't be sure. Storm clouds impeded the moonlight, and it could be a shadow

Mait pulled back on the throttle as he skimmed the water and came up next to the shoreside dock.

"Can you hold it here while I get him?" Mait asked the teenager.

"Yes." Andi gritted out the single word as the boat lurched forward with the force of the wake they left. She struggled to hold on; slivers embedded in her fingers.

Mait didn't seem to notice and jumped to the dock with the agility of a much younger man. Adrenaline spiked with not knowing what was wrong with his daughter.

The front of the cottage opened and an older man with white hair gleaming in the motion-activated light of his patio stepped onto the planks. "Mait? Is that you? Where's the fire?"

"Neal, you've got to come with me. Now. Tory's been hurt."

"Let me grab my bag."

Thirty seconds later both men raced to the boat and jumped in at full velocity. Maitland once again spun the boat around and raced toward the island. Andi saw the judge step out of his house and move toward his own boat. She was pretty sure he pulled away from his dock and followed them.

Alex had managed to call Charlie to come to the beach and bring a blanket, without scaring the rest of the family. The last thing Alex wanted was Van to see his mother unconscious.

As the boat pulled up with the doctor, Tory's eyes fluttered open and then closed again. "Owww."

"Lie still," Alex said.

"I feel like I've been hit by a truck." Tory slurred her words and tried to sit up, but the pain struck and made her lie back.

The doctor knelt next to the young woman and used his flashlight in her eyes.

"Ow. Stop." Tory mumbled.

"Glad to see you're with us, Victoria." The doctor chuckled. Then he was serious again as he continued checking her. "What hurts?"

"My face. Oh no! My side! My baby—is my baby okay?"

The doctor saw no blood through her light linen trousers, still wet from her plunge into the lake. He lifted her shirt and with the flashlight saw the skin already bruising on her lower ribs. He could not feel a break but did not want to take chances with the pregnant woman. "We can call an ambulance, or your aunt or father can take you to the ER. I'll ride with you."

Tory wanted to protest but also needed to know her baby was okay. She nodded her assent. "What about Van?"

"Don't worry about him; we've got him," Aimee said. No one had seen her quietly slip down the hill and join those on the beach.

"What happened?" Maitland demanded, cradling his daughter's

upper body in his arms now that the doctor had ascertained she didn't have a broken neck.

"Dad," Tory whispered. She knew she had to but did not want to relive the experience or her continued humiliation.

"Tory, we have to know," the judge said firmly.

She sighed and shut her eyes. A few minutes ago, the whole night was fuzzy. Then it came rushing back.

"Mark. No lights on the boat. Engine wasn't on. He was on the dock before I could get away." Tory tried to explain before she related the violent treatment at Mark's hand.

Then she told them what happened. Everyone's faces were drawn, lips pressed firmly in tight lines. Tory could feel her father's body stiffen as he held her in a sitting position.

"I told you, that son of a bitch. I'm gonna—" Maitland started but Alex hushed him.

"We know, Mait. We all feel that way," Alex said, acutely aware of the judge's and doctor's presence.

"Come on, young lady, we need to get you to the hospital," the doctor said softly.

"I'll call the sheriff," the judge offered. "They'll probably meet you there and want a statement." He turned to Alex. "You need to go too, Alex. They're also going to want to talk with Andi."

"Can't I go and if they really need Andi they can come here tomorrow?" Alex asked. She did not want to traumatize her granddaughter any more than may have already happened.

"I'm okay, Grandma. I can go with you," the teenager assured her.

"Mom, you and Tory are soaking wet. You need clothes," Charlie said.

Maitland cut in, "How about you get them both clean clothes and follow us? I'll take them in the truck and blast the heat."

Aimee silently handed her mother another blanket to wrap around herself and they helped Maitland get his daughter situated in the judge's boat, leaving Charlie to follow. She would not be too far behind since she would leave from the south shore and Maitland's truck was parked at the north shore.

"Do you want me to go with you?" Aimee put her arm around her daughter.

"I'm okay, Mom. Grandma's with me. You need to take care of Van," Andi replied.

Aimee nodded, already resolved to text Andrew at the restaurant and have him meet the family at the hospital and be there when the police questioned their daughter.

Hours later, ultrasound done, skull x-rays completed with a lead apron draped over her midsection to protect her unborn child, and an old-fashioned diagnosis of bruised ribs because they did not want to chance any harm to the fetus, Tory was relegated to a hospital bed overnight for observation.

The sheriff and a deputy had talked with Alex and Andi, Andrew standing protectively behind the two women, and were waiting until the tests were complete to get Tory's statement. They'd asked the medical staff to scrape under her fingernails and to see if any traces of evidence were left in her head wound, even though she had briefly been submerged in water, just in case they needed it.

The doctor entered Tory's room before the sheriff and deputy could begin their questions. Maitland stood at the bedside, Charlie and Alex next to him. Andrew sat with his daughter in the waiting room. He had offered to take her home to sleep in her own bed, but Andi insisted on going back to the island. So, he had waited, not willing to leave her alone until her grandmother and aunt were ready to leave.

"Tory, you have a mild concussion and you're going to have a whopper of a headache, maybe some nausea, but there's no brain swelling, which is good. The ultrasound, well, uhm," the doctor started.

Tory blanched and interrupted him before he could finish. "I heard the heartbeat; I know I did."

"Yes, you did. But it wasn't a heartbeat—" the doctor started again.

"What was it then?" Tory interrupted again.

"Let the man finish," Maitland said gently, his hand moving to his daughter's shoulder.

"Sorry."

"I was saying, there isn't one heartbeat. There are two. You're having twins." He handed the ultrasound photo to Tory and pointed to both fetuses. Tory reeled with the news, eyes wide. The bright light made her pounding head hurt worse.

"Hasn't your OB/GYN done an ultrasound yet? The two beats are distinctive and so are the fetuses," the doctor said.

The young woman stared at the sheets. "No. I confirmed that I was pregnant, but then I was trying to figure out how to tell my husband. I haven't been back."

"Ah, well, you're going to need regular visits now. The blow to your abdomen did a number on your ribs, but there was no damage to either fetus, placenta, or the uterus. We're lucky you didn't drown. I guess the babies made you more buoyant and kept you face up until your aunt could get to you," the doctor said, only half joking. "You'll stay here the rest of the night for observation. I should be able to discharge you by midday tomorrow, barring any complications between now and then."

"Thank you, doctor," Maitland said, shaking the man's hand.

Sheriff Kevin Clarke cleared his throat. "Okay, Tory. We need to get your statement now."

One more time, Tory went through the awful night, recounting each horrible moment in detail, until she woke up on the beach, drenched, next to her aunt.

Maitland walked the sheriff and the deputy out. The sheriff assured him they had already issued an all-points bulletin for Mark Wright. They did that when the judge called. Sometimes connections were particularly useful.

"Find him. He could have killed her," Maitland ordered. "I'm pretty sure he thinks he did."

The sheriff nodded. The deputy looked pained but tried to hide it. The kid was going to have to get a better poker face, Maitland thought offhandedly. He vaguely remembered the deputy had been in high school with Tory and Mark, played football with Mark. If he found out the deputy tipped off his soon-to-be-ex-son-in-law, he would have his job.

In the meantime, he was not leaving his daughter's side. If Mark tried to get in the hospital room, he might not leave. Maitland was determined.

"You can go back to the island now. Thanks for coming in for Tory," Maitland told his sister and niece in the hallway outside Tory's room.

"We don't mind staying and taking her with us tomorrow," Alex said.

"I'll bring her back. I promise," Maitland said. "I'll feel safer if I stay here tonight."

Charlie nodded and pulled her mother's sleeve before she could argue. She handed the bag with Tory's clean clothes to her uncle. "She'll need these when she's discharged."

"If I get my hands on that monster—" Alex started, but Charlie shushed her.

"I know, Mom. Same."

Back in the room, Tory was still in shock. "Dad, twins! What am I going to do?"

"This doesn't change anything," her father assured her. "Besides, I'm sure Charlie will be happy to give you pointers."

"It doesn't change anything?"

"Not a thing. Just one more little person to love," Maitland said.

Tory fell into a fitful sleep, only to be awoken an hour later by the nurse checking on her. Her father still hovered, wide awake, from the bedside chair. She noticed he had moved it between her and the door. She wanted to tell him he didn't need to do that; even Mark couldn't be stupid enough to try to get to her here. Though, she would have thought the same about the family island. Sleep claimed her thoughts again.

**24**

---

The night of Mark's attack and subsequent disappearance weighed heavily on the island residents. Even the youngsters, with no knowledge or understanding of the incident, picked up on the mood of their elders and stifled their exuberance. The light rain that fell outside didn't help lift the mood.

Charlie rose early and kept an ear out for the telltale honk from the shore that would signal Tory's return. She was uneasy about their departure from the hospital. She knew her uncle would protect his daughter, and the medical staff would be on the lookout for any complications, but she wasn't there and that did not sit well with the woman. The sooner Tory was back, the sooner Charlie could breathe. She had always been close to her younger cousin and mentally kicked herself for being so wrapped up in her own life she did not see the signs of her cousin's steady withdrawal from the world or the physical signs of her abuse. It didn't matter she lived 700 miles away. What mattered was her inattention. She vowed she would do better, be better.

The surprise announcement Tory was having twins was one more way the two women could bond. Charlie was sure the younger woman's head must be spinning, and not only from the blows she had received. Twins were an incredible miracle, but she knew firsthand how daunting the thought was.

The kitchen door opened, and Alex slid next to her daughter at the counter. Everyone else was in the living area or bunk rooms reading, playing games, or conversing. Maddie followed, plopping next to her friend.

"Well, that was quite the night," Maddie said, stating the obvious. "You two could write a screenplay about this." The looks on Alex's and Charlie's faces shut her down. "Okay then, maybe not." Trying to keep the smirk from breaking through, she tried again. "I'm just saying, once you step back from this, it would make for good content."

"Our personal lives are not open for distribution," Alex said.

"I'm saying, give it some time. See how this all plays out. It could be a good way for Tory to sell her story and be set."

Charlie snorted with laughter. "That's almost as bad as reality TV."

Maddie shrugged, not at all offended by her chosen family's disdain. "I never said the majority of viewers had the same highbrow tastes as you two."

"I'm not highbrow," Charlie protested. "I just don't like things that make me cringe." After a beat, she added, "Or that appeal to the intelligence of a gnat." If that made her highbrow, she could live with that.

"Well, I wasn't talking a reality show." Maddie defended her position. Alex and Charlie both burst into laughter.

Quiet eventually returned to the kitchen, each caught up in her own thoughts, each caught in the mood of unease that silently wrapped around them like a spider web spun at night.

When a horn honked from the southern shore, Charlie jumped up, grabbed her waterproof sailing jacket, snagged a couple of beach towels to dry the seats, and jogged toward the lake. Alex and Maddie were not far behind, each zipping their windbreakers. Maddie threw the hood over her head, covering her braids.

Before the screen door slammed, Van stood in the doorway, hope on his little face. "Is that my mommy and Grandpa? Is she okay?"

Glancing through the trees, Alex could see her brother's black truck. "Looks like it, Van. Your mom is going to be just fine. Go back inside before you get wet."

"Okay." Van smiled for the first time since he was told his mother was staying in town with his grandpa for the night. He made it clear he did not like her being away from him, and after Aimee probed a little, she was sure the boy knew more about his parents' problems than anyone thought. That was an adult discussion for another time.

For a storm, the lake was relatively calm. This was more the gentle, cleansing kind of rain, not the high wind and brutal whitecaps with powerful waves kind. Alex could not think of a better metaphor for washing away the torrent of the last twenty-four hours.

Maitland stood by the passenger side door of his big truck, Tory inside, out of the rain. His head was on a swivel, looking for lurking danger, as if he expected Mark to jump from behind the trees or a neighbor's house. He waited until the women docked the boat before he opened the door, covered his daughter in a giant rain slicker, and carefully guided her to the boat.

"Dad, I'm not an invalid." Tory protested, though she appreciated his warmth and support. She wouldn't admit it, because that would have meant more time in the hospital, but she was not all that steady on her feet. She could swear her belly grew several inches overnight.

"Know that. Just let me be your dad," he said tersely, aware of every movement in his peripheral vision. "I was your first protector, you know."

"My only protector," Tory murmured, then regretted it when she felt her father tense even more. Maitland felt responsible for falling down on the job, not knowing what was happening as his daughter scrapped all their long-laid plans and became more distant.

Tory only blamed herself. Her family's guilt compounded her own for putting them in the position to feel it at all.

"Any sign of the son of a bitch?" Maitland asked as he handed his daughter into the boat. She was stiff, and her bruised ribs ached with every movement. Her head pounded and she wanted to lie down and forget the confrontation, forget the sheriff and his questions, forget the deputy who was Mark's football buddy in high school and shot her accusatory looks when he thought no one was watching, forget the hospital where she couldn't rest with the constant checking of her status.

"Haven't seen hide nor hair," Alex assured her brother.

Maddie broke in, attempting to break the tension, but also curious. "Do people really say that? Is that a thing? Where does it come from?"

Charlie laughed; leave it to her mother's best friend to have overwhelming curiosity about the etymology of an old saying when everyone else was straining under the weight of the worry that a soon-to-be-ex-husband could jump from the shadows at any moment. Alex rolled her eyes at her friend and wrapped a blanket over her niece and her giant rain slicker.

"I think I should come with you," Maitland said.

"Dad, you have a trial to prepare for, don't you?"

He shrugged. "I'll be fine. This is more important. At least until he's found."

"We'll be fine—I'll be fine," Tory insisted.

"Maybe you and Van should come stay at the house. I'd feel better," Maitland said, tapping his toe on the edge of the boat from where he stood on the dock, rocking it more than the small waves. This was at least the fifth time since the doctor discharged her that he had brought it up.

"I feel safest at the island. Really, he's not going to show up with anyone else around. He's proven he's a coward."

"She'll never be alone, Mait; we promise," Alex said.

The longer they argued the more the rain dripped down their hair and faces—except Maddie's, who still hunched under the hood of her waterproof windbreaker, and Tory, who was bundled under the hooded rain slicker and a blanket.

"Okay. But I don't like it. Text me regularly," Mait said and turned back to his truck.

The women started slowly across the lake, not wanting unnecessary bumps to jar Tory.

"How are you—really?" Maddie asked.

Tory grimaced. "I want to see Van and lie down for a while. A hospital is a terrible place to sleep." She touched the left side of her face gingerly. She had made her dad pick up concealer at the pharmacy, but the ice pack overnight had not diminished the swelling enough to make it unnoticeable. Her eye was swollen, as was her cheek, the bruising there and her temple beginning to show prominently, though the concealer helped.

The rain was easing by the time the women made the trek up the hill to the cottage, someone on each side of Tory, keeping her steady. Donovan ran out of the cottage before Aimee could stop him, screen door slamming behind him.

"Mommy!" His little legs almost got tangled and tumbled him to the ground in his hurry to reach his mother, but he caught himself in time, only to stop short when he got within a yard of the women. His happy face clouded as he looked at his mother and noticed his great-aunt and Maddie both had a hand on her arms. In a voice far quieter and more subdued than he'd ever used, he asked, "Is Daddy here? Did he hurt you again?"

Charlie stepped around the three women and scooped Van into her arms. "Hey, buddy. Your daddy isn't here and he's not going to hurt anyone, okay?"

Van looked into Charlie's eyes, stared hard, looked to his mother then back to Charlie, his eyes squinted as if judging the veracity of her statement. Coming to his own conclusion, Van said, voice low, but stronger, "Mommy, Daddy hurts you. Was it him?"

Victoria felt complete dread crawl up her spine. Her little boy knew. How she thought she had kept him from the worst of it, she didn't know. She also realized the concealer had not done a good enough job. *I guess I've been delusional,* she thought to herself. To him, she said, "Van, I'll be fine. Don't worry."

"Where's Daddy?" Donovan persisted.

"I don't know, baby. I haven't seen him since last night."

Donovan struggled down from Charlie's arms and planted himself in front of Alex. "You're in charge here, Aunt Alex. Aimee says you're the mutt or something; that means you're the top dog."

Alex searched the other faces, wondering why she was a mutt. They looked as clueless as she felt. Then it dawned on her. "Matriarch. I'm the matriarch."

"Yeah, that. Top dog," Van nodded, his little face clearly showing he thought the adults were slow. "That means you get to tell Daddy he can't come here and can't hurt Mommy anymore. You'll keep him away, right?"

There was a collective intake of breath as all realized the gravity of what the little boy expected of her. Alex solemnly nodded, looking the little boy directly in the eye. "Yes, Van. I'll protect your mommy and you. We all will."

Donovan stared her down for a few more moments, seeking the truth in her eyes; seeing what he sought, he finally turned away, took his mother's hand, and continued up the path to the cottage. Tory tried hard to keep the tears from falling. Ugh, pregnancy hormones made her even more emotional than usual; that and the last twenty-four hours came close to breaking her. Oh yeah, and she almost lost her life, she remembered ruefully.

She settled in the bedroom. As much as she wanted to be strong and sit with the others, her body craved rest. She propped pillows behind her to lean against. Van sat on the edge of the bed holding her hand, not speaking. At some point he seemed to relax and realize she was all right, kissed her, and joined the other kids in the living room.

The oppressive atmosphere had lifted, and the noise level rose in the living area. Charlie brought a mug of mint herbal tea and set it on the nightstand, then threw herself on her own bed, since she shared the room with her cousin.

"How are you really doing?" Charlie asked.

"Tired. Sore. Scared he might come back," Tory said. "He was really mad at me."

"I don't think it's you. He's just angry and trying to blame you for his own failures," Charlie argued.

"Yeah. Maybe." Tory tried to convince herself this was his problem, not a fault in her character that caused his behavior. Knowing it in her brain was one thing; feeling it, after years of being told she was less than, was another thing all together.

"They really can't find him? Are they even trying?" Charlie questioned.

"That's what the sheriff told my dad this morning. He came back to the hospital before I was discharged. I guess he was up all night with his deputies, the city police, and even got the state police involved. No one has seen him—at least that's what everyone said." Tory took a sip of tea, then placed it back on the nightstand. With a sigh, she shut her eyes, unable to keep them open any longer.

Charlie quietly got up and squeezed her cousin's forearm. "Sleep now. We'll keep watch. He won't get to you here."

"Thank you," Tory whispered and was asleep immediately.

That night, Charlie brought a bed tray with Tory's dinner back to their bedroom.

"I could have come to the table," Tory protested, not wanting to be waited on or cause any more trouble for her family.

"Nah. You need to rest and heal." Charlie dismissed her concerns. She sat on the side of Tory's bed. "Mind if I keep you company while you eat?"

"Please." Tory nodded, not wanting to be alone with her own thoughts any longer.

"Other than Mark showing up, what else is bothering you?" Charlie asked. "I know there's something.

Tory chewed, taking time to think before she replied quietly. She didn't want anyone who could be lurking in the hallway to hear this conversation, particularly her son.

"What if Van or one of these babies is like Mark? I mean, what if I can't stop it from happening?" Tory said. In high school, even college, she didn't think Mark was the monster he was now. Though, when she really thought about it, there were warning signs she missed along the way. The controlling behavior had always been there, if not the violence.

Charlie narrowed her eyes as she thought. "Are you worried about the whole nature versus nurture argument?"

"Yes, I guess that's it. I mean, they have his blood running through them, as well as mine."

"That's not going to happen. Look at Van. He's a loving, well-adjusted boy, who is determined to protect his mother and the babies. You're the one who has spent the time with him. You're the one who's shaping his character." Charlie tried to dispel the notion. "Environment counts."

"Environment counts; but look at your own twins. They were born at the same time, raised the same way, and they couldn't be more different."

"But they're both still loving caring human beings. They may have different personalities and interests, and I'll give you that some of that is more than likely hardwired in their DNA, but we have influence, as do their friends, and society. We can only set the example and the path, but eventually they have to be the ones to choose it. It becomes a choice, I believe. If someone is naturally an angry person, they can be an angry jerk or they channel that energy into something more positive. And there's always therapy," Charlie said.

Tory laughed at the last part of her cousin's statement. "Yeah, there's always that." Then her face turned serious again. "I'll do everything I can to make sure they're good people ... everything."

"I know you will, Tory," Charlie said. It was a solemn topic, and she understood the young woman's fear. "We'll all help too. You know we will."

Once again, Tory was reminded of the importance of family and how fortunate she was that they hadn't left her behind during her self-imposed exile, imprisoned within the walls of the big, sterile house she had never wanted. Hunger was the last thing she felt but finished the plate anyway—she was eating for three now and needed all the energy she could muster.

She hadn't been asleep for long when she felt the mattress dip a bit. Little fingers lightly caressed her swollen temple. A child's lips gently kissed her cheek. The voice that usually had one volume—loud—softly said, "I love you, Mommy." Then she felt him put a hand on her swollen belly and kiss through her shirt, whispering, "I love you too, babies." Someone must have told him she was having twins. Tory slept.

## 25

A baby's cry pierced the cool morning air; the sun had not yet had the chance to warm the waking island.

Lauren opened one eye and saw Harper rise and bring baby Allie back to bed with her, pulling the blankets back over herself as she fed the growing girl. Mornings were never Lauren's thing, but Harper reveled in the joy and quiet of her time alone with the baby, whispering a conversation only the baby could hear. Her eyes would open wide and stare at her mother, as if waiting with bated breath for whatever wonderful utterances her mother would impart that day.

Lauren turned over and slept longer. She didn't want to intrude on the private time. She also wanted to sleep more. She really did not "do" mornings.

Later, more sounds woke her again, young voices calling to one another. This time when she looked to the other bed, mother and child were both gone. The bed neatly made, her great-great-grandmother's quilt work displayed, as it had been since before her mother's birth, possibly since before her grandmother's. The one good thing about getting up late was she had the bathroom to herself. This morning, dread filled her. She had no idea why. Well, maybe she did.

Everything was changing around her, and she was not in control of any of it. She had her own decisions to make. School would start again soon. She couldn't decide if Harper, her life's circumstances changed irrevocably, was leaving her behind, or if she would be the one to leave Harper behind. Did it have to be that way?

They had made plans a year ago, before they started college. They would study abroad. Travel Europe like other backpacking students. Maybe go to graduate school, maybe not. Move to either DC or New York after graduation and be young professionals living their best lives. That had changed with one fraternity party, Lauren thought ruefully. Now she wasn't sure of anything.

By the time she entered the kitchen, Harper's smile was bright as she carried on an animated conversation with Sage and Aimee, baby Allie alert and quiet, seemingly fitting in better than Lauren herself.

"Allie, look; Auntie Lauren is here." Harper turned her arm to point Allie toward her best friend.

Lauren thought she heard something about babies not being able to see very far, but she played along and waved at Allie from across the room.

"We're heading down to the lake; are you three joining us?" Aimee asked, grabbing her water bottle from the clean counter. 1000 Everything was always clean, clinically clean, when Aimee was around. Lauren laughed internally when she imagined Aimee's reaction if she had confronted the squirrels and racoons in the destroyed kitchen. Lauren admitted to herself she never wanted to be first up in the morning and definitely not first in the kitchen, though her mother assured them all she had, at least temporarily, closed the opening through which the animals had entered.

"Yes," Harper said. Lauren hadn't said much since her long monologue at dinner a couple nights before. And though she seemed fine, Harper knew the phrase *still waters run deep* could easily have been crafted based on Lauren Robertson. "How about we take the rowboat out? Or we could kayak," she suggested.

"What about Allie?" Lauren asked skeptically, looking at the baby.

"I'm sure one of the others will watch her. I can put her in the shade in the portable playpen and she'll probably fall asleep again."

"Okay. Let's go." Lauren perked up. Maybe she'd be able to talk with Harper and sort through all the things she'd been thinking.

The lake was smooth as glass this morning, water still and an inviting blue green. Situated in the rowboat, Lauren handling the oars, the two rowed out in the lake, far enough away where no one could hear their conversation. Harper was surprised how quiet the lake was this morning. Even sailing had the sound of wind in your ears. This? This was peaceful, and she relaxed in the moment.

Once Lauren began to feel the small trickle of perspiration down the center of her back, she stopped rowing, propped the oars on the sides of the boat, and leaned back, turning her face to the sun. The sky was a solid blue blanket, the even color blue, solid from horizon to horizon, that always looked fake in paintings but was oh so real.

Lauren broke the silence. "Everything has changed, hasn't it, Harp?"

"Because of your dad?" Harper questioned.

Lauren sighed. "Not just that. I mean, you have a baby now. How are we going to continue with the plans we made?"

"A baby is a big change, but one I planned for as soon as I found out," Harper said, not sure where the conversation was going.

"I know that." Lauren sighed again, this time sitting up and opening her eyes. "We were going to have internships starting next summer. Then study abroad for a year. Backpack around Europe. Move to DC or New York when we graduated and start our amazing careers."

"Ah," Harper said, finally understanding. "Those were broad outlines of plans, Laur. We were kids. We hadn't even started college yet."

"My brother and dad made plans that are years into the future for William's life. Planning for the future isn't just a dream," Lauren argued.

"Yeah, I know. But life hits bumps. It's messy. It doesn't always go as planned. Anywhere along the journey there could be factors that change the trajectory of our path. Allie just happened to be my first curve in the path. I have to put her first."

"I know."

"I still plan to have an amazing life, Laur. Maybe I can't study overseas now. Maybe I can't backpack around Europe now. It doesn't mean I won't ever. Who knows? Maybe I'll do graduate work at the Sorbonne in Paris and take Allie with me, get an au pair," Harper said, trying to show her friend the possibilities.

"Without me," Lauren said dejectedly, stabbing her toe into the bottom of the boat.

"And you can do your junior-year abroad. I won't stop you. I don't think you shouldn't go just because I can't. We'll still be best friends. We may have to go it alone on our own paths for a little while. I'm not holding you back, Laur," Harper said gently. "But I'm not holding myself back either. I'm recalculating my options, readjusting my journey to include my daughter."

"So, I need to keep pushing? Not make sure my plans include you?" Lauren asked, somewhat terrified at going it alone.

"Yeah, you should. Our plans could come back together or maybe they never diverge, but never hold yourself back because you're waiting for me. You'll resent me someday if you do that. I would never forgive you if you did that." Harper smiled brightly.

A few moments passed with the rowboat rocking gently in the slight movement of the water. The oars still rested on the sides, and Lauren sat with her hands knuckles down on the bench seat staring back toward the island. She could make out the women in her family and their kids sitting on the beach, some swinging their legs on the dock while they talked and laughed. The women were all settled in their lives and careers. She realized she was beginning hers and that petrified her. What if she chose wrong?

As if reading her mind, Harper broke the silence. "You know, there are no wrong answers. Your mom told me that after I had Allie. She said there are only different paths. The worst thing I could do is not move forward. You too, Laur."

Lauren thought about that a bit. Chewed it over in her brain. Tried to see how it tasted in her mouth. "Forward. I can do that. I just don't want to lose you. You're my best friend."

"And I always will be. Don't miss out on anything. We'll have lots of interesting things to talk about all along our paths. I promise," Harper said. She leaned forward and held out her pinkie finger. Lauren rolled her eyes at the classic move from their childhood but extended her pinkie toward her friend and locked the digits in the age-old assurance of a promise not allowed to be broken.

"I do have one other thing. It's probably not a big deal." Lauren hesitated.

"What?"

"Um. I mean. Um. It's *kind of* about my dad." Lauren wasn't sure how to talk about this. It seemed that speaking her greatest fear might give it wings to come true. That was the last thing she wanted. "Um. What if what killed him is genetic? What if I have it? I might have a time bomb in my head and not even know it." There. She got it out. She ducked a little, glancing to the sky—no storm clouds brewing; no imminent lightning to strike her down. That was a good sign.

"Oh, Lauren. You need to talk with your mom if that's worrying you!" Harper exclaimed. "Maybe the doctors told her if that sort of thing is genetic or if it was a fluke."

"I guess. I didn't want to worry her or make her think I'm a hypochondriac or something."

"She won't."

"I mean, what if I have it? Do I want to know? Will I live my life differently?"

"Are you talking about creating a bucket list or something?"

"Yeah, sort of. I mean, maybe I'll want to learn to ride bulls. Or skydive—I've always wanted to do that. Maybe race a motorcycle across Africa. If I could die any day, maybe I should do everything I can and make it count, you think?"

Harper knit her eyebrows and looked hard at her friend. "Or maybe you should live every day to the fullest. It shouldn't matter if you're going to die or not. I don't know why possibly dying would make you want to do things that could kill you!"

"I don't know, maybe I'd be defying death that way."

"Or speeding it along. No. Talk to your mom. Maybe there's a way to screen for that," Harper said, not wanting to talk about this subject any longer.

Lauren briefly wondered if having a child suddenly made you more mature and less willing to take risks? She smirked at her friend and dropped the topic. She kind of thought the adrenaline rush from some of those things would be incredible, whether she was dying or not.

Lauren gripped the oars in her hands and began to row back toward the island. She would woman up and talk with her mother. She had enough sentimentality for today and was done worrying about the future for the rest of the summer. Though she admitted to herself the time left was short; even she could get through those weeks with no more drama. Now she knew they would not necessarily share the same path, she could still move forward with what they planned, by herself now, because her plans had not changed, at least not yet.

Once back on land, Lauren pulled the rowboat onto the shore. She caught sight of her mother with her sketchbook, sitting away from the others. She steeled her back and marched toward the older woman.

"Mom, got a minute?" Lauren breathed.

Alex finished what she was shading with the edge of her pencil, flipped the sketchbook closed, and looked up at her daughter, giving her an indulgent smile. "Sure. What's up?"

Lauren dropped to the ground and crossed her legs, making her body as small as possible, not realizing the protective body language she displayed. Alex, a great reader of body language after years as a journalist and political coach, braced herself for what was to come.

She didn't have to wait long. Lauren, in typical Lauren fashion, was direct. "What if I have an aneurysm like Dad? What if I have a time bomb in my head?"

Alex put an arm around her daughter. "Oh, Lauren, I had no idea you were thinking anything like that."

"Well, I am!"

"I did ask if your dad inherited it. But without any siblings, it's difficult to tell. It's unlikely though, since neither of his parents and none of his grandparents died from that. It doesn't mean it couldn't have been hiding, but they all lived long lives," Alex explained.

Lauren chewed on her lip and thought about that. "So, it's unlikely."

"Yes."

"But still a possibility?"

"Well, yes. But so is getting hit by a bus." Alex tried to alleviate her youngest's anxiety.

"But it could happen," Lauren persisted.

"If you're really worried, you can be screened for it," Alex said. The doctor told Alex that when she posited that she could have one too and no one would know until it was too late. She decided she didn't need to be screened, but fully understood if her daughter wanted it.

Lauren worried her bottom lip a little more. "Is it better to know? I mean, should I be getting in everything I want to do now before I die?"

"Are you thinking of things like skydiving or buying a motorcycle?" Alex asked, a smile playing at the corners of her mouth.

"Maybeeee."

"Well, I think if you're worried, we'll set up the screening. But it doesn't change how you live your life at all. We should be living life to the fullest no matter how much time we have. No one ever knows, Laur. Life and death are intermingled; anything can happen. Best to not waste what time we have, whether long or short," Alex said. This was one lesson she wished she could impart to all her children and grandchildren, but until faced with death, most people didn't get the message until late in life; some never got it. Alex thought that was a waste. The death of two husbands left no doubt in her mind.

"So, no motorcycle?" Lauren teased her mom.

"No motorcycle," Alex said. Then her eyes twinkled with the smile that spread across her face. "Unless it's my motorcycle."

"Mom! No, you can't do that," Lauren protested, aghast.

"I can do a lot of things, Lauren. It's just a matter of what I choose," Alex said, not agreeing with her child. She was *not* old until she decided she was old; that would probably be never.

**26**

———————

After another long day playing in the water and sun, the kids of the Newberry clan were ready for dinner and downtime. Lauren seemed to find some peace, after talking with her mother and her friend the previous day. Her mother had already called to schedule the brain screening for before Lauren returned to school.

With all calm, and still no word about Mark's whereabouts, Alex and Charlie stole time to disappear together after a late dinner, twilight sinking on the horizon, the dark rising. They took the motorboat to the widest part of the lake and turned off the engine, letting the boat drift. Even on a smaller, inland, freshwater lake, the moon pull seemed to have a small effect on the wave pattern and where they lapped against the shore. Or maybe the moon only affected the humans.

Tonight, the sky was filled with millions of stars and the moon was bright. The women stretched on the seats and faced skyward.

"I really miss James." Charlie sighed, wondering yet again if her late husband would make his presence known. Maybe he was looking down on them from the bright sky. Maybe he was right next to her, close enough to touch her, but in a different plane the living couldn't breach. So often she could feel his warm touch on her face or his hand on her lower back or holding her hand, even though her rational mind told her that was impossible.

"I know you do."

"Sometimes I think maybe we should move to Michigan. Change it up."

Her mother laughed. "That would make Aimee's dream come true."

"But I don't really want to uproot Colin in high school," Charlie said, voicing her concerns. "I don't know about the company either. How's this going to work?"

"What do you mean?" Alex asked.

"Hank ran most of the day-to-day operations and the analytical side. I think he did anyway. I'm not sure anymore. I know he took on certain clients himself. You worked your magic with creating their voices, giving them substantive things to say, advised on crises. I do a lot of what you do and work with some of the analytical side for the clients I handle. I know all of that." Charlie paused, then laid out her concerns. "But Hank was CEO. Who's going to do that now? If you're really stepping back, what does that mean? Would we be better off selling it?"

Alex continued staring at the sky. "I guess we should figure this out. One of the managing directors is taking care of the day-to-day for now. There are very few elections this year, as you know. It's why you and I are both able to be here this summer." Alex turned her head to shoot her daughter a smile at this last statement. She knew Charlie had been working remotely, seamlessly handling client needs—the modem was plugged in some days when she knew she hadn't done it.

"It's not difficult to work remotely these days," Charlie agreed. "But there is something to be said for face-to-face some of the time."

Alex agreed with that sentiment. "Do you want to be CEO?"

"Are you serious? What about William? What about some of the guys who worked with Hank and you from the beginning?"

Alex wryly thought about Clay, Hank's long-time executive assistant and longer-time lover. "William hasn't shown any indication he wants to get out of the military any time soon. Anyway, you've been there since the beginning, if you count the summers in high school and college. Why would you think one of the guys would be better suited? Please don't tell me because they're men!"

"Of course not," Charlie exclaimed. "Well, darn, maybe I have an unconscious bias of my own. I guess that did cross my mind, that it would be a man. That is *so* wrong. Please don't tell Lauren or anyone that even crossed my mind!"

"My lips are sealed."

Charlie thought some more. "I guess I never thought about Hank being gone or you stepping down. I thought you'd always be there. You're not old."

"Thanks. Maybe you could convince your sisters of that."

"Well, I'm older than them and have a dead husband. Maybe I have a different perspective," Charlie said.

"That you do," Alex glanced over the side of the boat to make sure they hadn't drifted too far. Settling back in the seat she said, "I really don't want to do it anymore. I even thought about stepping down from the board."

"Why? Did this whole Hank thing throw you for that much of a loop?" Charlie probed, alluding to the story that had recently been whispered among the island's adult residents.

"It's more that it was never my dream. I'm good at it; I'll admit that. But this company was Hank's dream. It's provided a good living and now a legacy for whomever of my children deem they want it, but I never did. All I've ever really wanted to do is create. Tell stories." Alex tried to explain it so her astute daughter would understand she was not abandoning them but rather moving on to the next Act of her life.

"Well, then you shouldn't do it anymore. I'm all about following your own passion; you know that." Now Charlie was curious. "You want to write screenplays with Maddie?"

Alex laughed, the sound light and pleasant. "Maybe. But I was thinking about books too. Maybe tell some other people's stories as magazine interviews or articles—if magazines are even relevant anymore with the new generations."

"More so the online type," Charlie allowed.

"And I want to paint. I decided I can tell stories through my paintings and words. I want to convey all the feeling and emotion in different mediums, whether visual or writing. It's time to start the next Act in my life," Alex explained further. "But know this: I won't leave the board until you're comfortable and ready for me to leave."

"You're serious about me being CEO?"

"I am. Are you?"

Charlie waited a beat, hesitating as she thought of her young children, single motherhood thrust upon her, and then thought of the work she already did, what she knew how to do. "I am."

If nothing else, Charlie would provide an example to her children that men and women are equal, that hard work matters, and that she loved them dearly. Even the type of work you do matters. In this case, she helped find, prepare, and present many of the leaders within the country. That was a kind of service of its own. At least that's the example she hoped to uphold.

"I'll make it happen at the next board meeting, so it's official," Alex said.

"Thanks for believing in me, Mom," Charlie said softly.

"Never had any doubts."

"James would have loved to see this," Charlie mused.

"Yeah, baby, he would. He was always so proud of you."

"Oh, Mom. What am I going to do? Sometimes I miss him so much I feel like my entire insides are empty and aching, so much it's hard to breath," Charlie said, showing a rare display of vulnerability.

Alex automatically compared that to her own situation. She didn't feel completely empty. She didn't have a hard time breathing. She realized she was going to have to come to terms with the fact her marriage to Hank had been generally good—it was comfortable, they were friends, and while they loved each other, maybe they hadn't been *in* love with one another. That was okay, as long as she recognized it. She had also had the other kind of marriage, one of passion and all-consuming love, with her first husband, Ian.

"You're going to keep going. Just like you are. No other choice," Alex said. That was what her family always did. Kept going. Stoicism ran deep. It was elevated to a core value. "For what it's worth, I think you're doing great."

"Thanks. I'm trying."

In her head, Charlie spoke directly to her dead husband: *Hear that, James? She thinks I'm doing great. I learned from the best—fake it 'til you make it.*

She could hear his voice, clear as if he were next to her on the seat. *"You're not faking it. You're doing it. One foot in front of the other."*

*It's so hard,* her mind whispered back.

*You know the only easy day was yesterday. Proud of you, babe.* His voice was still clear and warm, filling her emptiness for a moment, wrapping her in a hug that warmed her in the cool air. It was fuel enough to keep going. Enough to make it through the coming days. One foot in front of the other. One day at a time.

"It's getting chilly out here. Want to head back?" Alex asked.

"Yeah." Something caught Charlie's attention on the northern side of the lake. Police lights flashing. She wondered if there was an emergency with one of the older residents from the cottages along the shore or if, perhaps, they had found Mark. No, that couldn't be it. Why would he have hung around for days after the attack? If she were him, she would have been across the border into Canada already.

When they got back to the island, the firepit was burning, and the women were helping the kids roast marshmallows and make s'mores.

"Got enough for us?" Charlie asked, hope in her voice.

"You bet." Aimee nodded, holding out two more sticks and the bag of marshmallows.

They crowded close to the fire, warming themselves after being out in the middle of the lake after dark. Charlie's squishy white treat turned to char as it caught on fire. "It's okay, I like them burned," she insisted when Indy offered to gently roast one for her. She slapped it between two graham crackers with a piece of milk chocolate and sunk her teeth into the gooey goodness. She almost moaned. Another memory of childhood filling her mind from the sensory experience— the smell of fire roasting the sweetness of the marshmallows, the taste of the three parts of the dessert sandwich, the sight of the scene before her, the crackle of the burning wood.

"I wish we lived here all the time," Grace said as she leaned into her mother's side.

"In Michigan?" Charlie asked, surprised.

"No, on the island. I'd like to stay here forever." The nine-year-old sighed.

"Might be pretty cold in the winter," Charlie responded practically. "And you wouldn't see anyone for months."

"We have the stove," Grace argued. "We'd all be here; I wouldn't be alone."

"Yeah, I guess that's a nice dream," Charlie acquiesced.

"We could do online school. My friend Becca does that now. I still see her at dance class," Grace said, proving she had given this lots of thought.

"Online school is a possibility," Charlie agreed. In her mind, it may actually be more efficient than the traditional classroom, at least in elementary school, not that she would go that direction with her kids. She didn't have the temperament to be the teacher, or even facilitator, at home.

"Grandma would have to stay too."

Charlie glanced at her mother and agreed with Grace; her mother was a part of the magic that came with the island. She would have to stay too. *Not* that anyone *would* stay longer than the summer.

**27**

—

Morning came quickly following the late night the adults spent around the firepit. The younger kids had faded quickly after the initial sugar rush from the s'mores. The older kids had wanted to sit inside, privacy important sometimes.

Now, the light bright, another sunny day promised ahead, the women moved slowly, breakfast a staggered affair as each rose at her own time. Other than the baby, who seemed to be on a set schedule, and Harper by default, everyone else slept longer than usual.

By the time the first few made it to the lakeshore, morning was heading toward afternoon.

"Will you take me fishing?" Donovan begged Jaspar.

"I'll go too," Gavin volunteered. "We have dibs on the rowboat," he called to everyone and busied himself handing life jackets to Donovan, Jaspar, and Cassie. Jaspar grabbed four fishing poles while Cassie turned the dark earth over with a shovel, looking for earthworms she and Donovan could put in the plastic bucket they used for bait.

Jaspar called dibs on rowing.

"You can do all the work; fine with me," Gavin said.

Three sat in the boat, while Gavin pushed it the rest of the way into the water before leaping over the side and settling on a bench seat. Jaspar began rowing around the corner, to the west end of the island—closest to where the docks sat, but far enough they felt independent of the others.

Alex marveled at how well the children, older and younger, got along and how independent they had become over the last several weeks. She was still thinking about her grandchildren when a boat with the official sheriff's logo pulled around the far end of the island and made a beeline toward their dock. Her stomach dropped, prepared for bad news, though she hoped they were not there only to let them know they still had no sighting of Mark.

The sheriff and two deputies jumped out after they tied off on the main dock. The sheriff looked grim.

"Alex, we need to talk with Victoria," the sheriff said, all business.

"Do you want to go up to the cottage?" Alex asked. The sheriff shook his head no as Victoria walked to the end of the dock with Charlie close behind. Tory's face and temple had lost some swelling, but the bruises were even more prominent in the three days since her soon-to-be-ex attacked her.

The sheriff made sure none of the children were close before he began speaking. Alex noticed Colin hesitate as he moved the sailboat and a few of the kids out past the raft, ready for another day of sailing lessons and the freedom the wind and water brought. She waved to him to keep going.

"We haven't found Mark, but we have some news," the sheriff said. "A couple on the north shore hadn't been out to their cabin in a week and called us last night. Someone stole their boat. We found it early this morning abandoned in a large cove to the east. The fingerprints on the steering wheel were Mark's. There was no sign of him, and the boat was floating quite a ways from shore."

"He stole a boat?" Tory asked, incredulous. "Why would he do that? He knows people who have boats."

"Maybe he didn't want anyone to know he was coming to see you," Charlie suggested.

"But why abandon it? Why not take it back?" Tory quizzed them. It didn't make any sense.

"Well, that's the thing. There was blood. It was under the canopy and under the lip on the side, so the rain didn't wash it away," the sheriff said, lips pressed in a straight, taut line.

"And a gun on the bottom that looks like it slid under the back by the gas tank," the deputy friend of Mark's said. The sheriff shot him a look that clearly conveyed he should shut up.

"What?" Tory's eyes were wide as she tried but could not come up with what that meant.

"He hasn't been back here since three nights ago?" the sheriff confirmed.

"No, of course not. We would have called you immediately," Alex assured him.

"Has Victoria been with you the entire time?" the deputy asked, glaring at Tory. It was the first time he ever called her by her formal name since they'd known one another—which had been pretty much their entire lives.

"Yes. She hasn't been out of our sight since she got home from the hospital," Charlie said, not liking his insinuation. "Since he's a coward and won't approach her unless she's by herself, we made a pact to never leave her alone until you catch that bastard." Charlie stared down the deputy through narrowed eyes. She really wanted to push him in the lake. He was the type who gave police a bad name. Alex laid a hand on her arm and lightly squeezed.

"My guys and the state police are searching the lake and the shoreline now, and divers are in the cove where the boat was found, just in case he didn't make it to shore. The problem is if he went overboard three nights ago, that boat could have ended up there from anywhere with the storms we just had," the sheriff explained, his tone far less accusatory than his deputy's.

"Is there anything we can do to help?" Alex asked.

"Just stay close, okay? We don't know exactly what we're dealing with," the sheriff said, not unkindly.

"We're dealing with a—" Charlie started and was interrupted by her mother before she could malign Mark's character any more than he had done himself.

"Thanks for keeping us in the loop." Alex closed the discussion and stood on the dock as the sheriff and deputies reboarded their boat and motored east.

Victoria was stuck in her thoughts, trying to figure out the confounding situation. "Why would there be blood in the boat? I remember scratching his face when I tried to grab him when I fell after he hit me, but that wouldn't cause much blood. Where did he go?" Then a thought came to her, and her eyes widened in alarm. "The deputy said there was a gun. Did he shoot himself? Why would he do that?"

"I don't think we're going to have any answers until they find Mark." Alex rubbed small circles on Tory's back and tried to soothe her. As she knew from personal experience, asking questions that had no answers would only drive her insane.

"I think I'm going to be sick," Tory said, rushing from the dock, hand over her mouth, and found a place behind the tree in the reeds before the little she'd eaten for breakfast came up.

Charlie chuckled, patting Tory on the back. "I know this won't make you feel better, but my doctor told me that with multiples, the sicker I felt, the healthier the babies were."

"You're right. That doesn't make me feel better," Tory scowled.

The rowboat with the fishers came back with tales of the size fish they each caught and released. All were happy with their fish tales and ready to swim to get rid of the strong smell of fish on their hands and swimming suits. Tory was happy Van jumped into the lake with his cousins after they stowed the fishing gear, because if she smelled a strong fish smell, she was sure she would have dry heaves.

The sailors were out longer, getting in as much time with the good wind as they could. They stayed mostly on the west and northwest parts of the lake, away from the police boats Colin saw crowding the eastern side, though some crawled the shore around the entire lake's perimeter, methodically investigating in and out of the many coves. Deputies walked the ground on the shore of the cove where the boat was found, hoping to find footprints if Mark had swum to shore.

They heard a shout as the family trudged up the hill for dinner, followed by more shouts. The sounds came from the east end of the island. Several more boat motors were heard speeding toward the island. Colin, Gavin, Andi, and Cameron started jogging toward the forest that started behind the cottage and stretched to where the ground became marshland on the east side, only to be called back by their grandmother's shrill whistle, her thumb and forefinger together in her mouth. It was the loudest whistle they'd ever heard and not one of them could do it, however hard they tried.

Alex called her grandchildren back. "Uh-uh. Don't go over that way. Nothing good can come out of interfering in a police investigation."

Charlie looked worried. Tory was pale, and Aimee took her into the house to lie down before dinner. Charlie asked her mother quietly, "You don't think he's hiding on the island trying to get to Tory, do you? Desperate people are dangerous."

"I think he was dangerous before he was desperate," Alex said, equally quiet. "But I certainly hope he's not headed this way. Let's make sure everyone's inside. The sheriff will let us know if they find something."

"I'll make sure the doors and windows are locked," Charlie said. "None of this makes any sense. She was going to give him the divorce." Yet, from what Maitland had heard, Mark may no longer have wanted the divorce, if it was not going to be financially advantageous.

"All that mattered to him was the control he exerted over her," Alex surmised, beginning to come around to her brother's solution, the more she thought about it—not that she would voice that or invite the bad karma it could cause.

The women were tense. Occasionally, through the kitchen windows, they heard loud voices coming from the eastern end of the island. What they didn't know was whether anyone else was on the island or if all the activity was in the water near the shore. Later they heard the boat engines start again and the sounds of many different craft leaving. Alex and Charlie walked back to the dock, hoping someone would give them news. They weren't disappointed. The sheriff's boat pulled to the end of the dock, and he jumped out.

"Alex, I guess you figured we had news."

"We were hoping," Alex replied.

He nodded and then looked at the even wood planks of the dock before meeting the matriarch's eyes. "We found a body partially submerged in the lily pads at the end of the island. I'm sorry to say, it looks like it may be Mark, but we won't be sure until the medical examiner gets him to the morgue."

"You can't tell?" Charlie asked, all sorts of horrific thoughts going through her head, including maybe the man tried to blow his head off with the gun they found in the boat and that might be why they couldn't identify him.

"He could have been in the water for almost seventy-two hours. Between the bloating from the water and the damage from the fish, we can't say for certain," the sheriff said.

Charlie grimaced, sorry she asked. She also mentally added a note to herself not to eat any fish the kids caught for the rest of the summer ... She preferred catch and release anyway.

"Will you tell Tory, or do you want me to tell her?" the sheriff asked.

"We'll take care of it," Alex said. "And if there's any way you can make sure she doesn't have to identify the body, that would be best. She's been through enough because of that man."

"Understood," the sheriff said. "I'll be in touch when we have more information."

"Thanks, sheriff," Alex said and watched the boat with the official seal pull away for the second time that day.

The women found Tory lying in bed when they got back to the cottage. Tears silently fell from her eyes when they told her. She wasn't sure if she was sad, shocked, or relieved. Could he have gotten counseling and been better? Maybe, but something inside her didn't believe he was redeemable. Maybe her nightmare would be over.

# 28

Sunrise, after a night filled with notes of tension and disbelief, seemed surreal. The sky brightened as the sun moved higher. The blue was prominent. Clouds were high, fluffy, and few. A gentle breeze wafted over summer-tanned skin, as if Mother Nature herself knew they needed comfort, a reprieve from the brutality most of them could only imagine.

The entire day, there was no news. No updates on the body, identity, or cause of death. The next day came and the same nothingness. Alex called her brother and spoke in low tones, only to learn he knew nothing more than they did. Nothing. She and he found it strange how tight-lipped everyone was being. Maitland knew everyone, including contacts within the state police, whose crime lab was involved. Nothing.

Frustrated, Alex reached out to Charles LeBrandt, DC detective and close family friend. He texted regularly throughout the summer, checking on the family, checking on her. Nothing intrusive. A simple, steady cadence of contact. He showed his support rather than said it. These days, Alex was far more comfortable with actions than with words.

**Alex: Body found at end of island. They think it's Tory's husband Mark. But no word on identity, cause, or anything else**

**Charles:Has Mait put in calls?**

**Alex:Of course ... sigh**

**Charles:Local sheriff?**

**Alex:And state police**

**Charles:Ahh. They could be backed up**

**Alex:Or? I sense an "or"**

**Charles:Or they're building a case**

**Alex:Against whom?**

**Charles:I wouldn't know, Alex ... but ...**

**Alex:But the wife is always a suspect**

**Charles:Yeah. If it wasn't an accidental drowning**

**Alex:This is a mess**

**Charles:Stay positive. It may be as simple as they're backed up**

**Alex:K. Thanks**

**Charles:I can come out there. I've got vacation time**

**Alex:Thanks, but we'll be fine**

**Charles:K, offer remains. Anytime**

**Alex:Got it. Bye, Charlie**

**Charles:Bye**

It didn't matter how many times her children or grandchildren told her the same rules of civility didn't apply in texts, she couldn't get herself to not say goodbye. She decided it was enough that she went against her own desire for complete sentences and punctuation.

Charles' assumptions were the same as her own, which offered little to no comfort. Somehow, even dead, Mark Wright was causing her sweet niece more pain. If it *was* Mark they found in the water ... it had to be him. The sheriff would not have said they thought it was if he wasn't sure.

Unable to bend results or time to her will, she picked up her sketchpad with a heavy sigh and made her way through the cottage. She was surprised to find Colin in the living area, sitting in one of the rocking chairs, feet on the seat, knees up—just like she used to sit—engrossed in the book in his hands. The book wasn't a modern thriller or the latest fantasy novel. The spine was cracked and peeling, the cover faded.

"What's that you're reading?" she asked.

Colin looked up with the surprise of someone so engrossed he hadn't realized anyone was in the cottage with him. "I found it on the shelf." He gestured with the book toward the corner bookcase. "Did you know this was published in 1878? It's about a pioneer family that pushed west."

Alex nodded, "I remember that book. I think it belonged to my great-great-grandmother. Look at the inside cover. It might have her name."

Sure enough, the name of the book's owner, the date, and who gave it to her were written in cursive, the blue ink faded but still clearly legible. "Wow," Colin said. "So, my great-great-great grandmother held this exact same book."

"Yes. And every generation since. I read it, too, when I was about your age."

"Wow," Colin repeated.

Alex chuckled and sat in a wingchair. Her grandson went back to reading. She captured this side of Colin, alone, reading, sitting in the same chair she had on days in the cottage with her grandmother. This was yet another aspect of the boy who patiently taught his siblings and cousins the art of sailing. She wanted to capture it on paper, this specific moment in time they shared together. Her sketch took shape—the large picture windows that made up most of the north wall, through which the trees rooted into the steep hill off the back of the island were visible in the background, and her grandson in the foreground, one more element in the drawing.

After a time, she quietly closed the sketchbook and wandered to the kitchen. Tory sat on a counter stool, running her hand up and down the mug of herbal tea in front of her. The pained look on her niece's face made Alex's chest constrict.

"What happened after he left here?" Tory asked, staring into space, for the first time since Alex entered the kitchen acknowledging she knew someone else was in the room with her.

"I don't know."

"Why was there a gun in the boat? Was he going to kill me if he'd gotten me into it? Did he plan to kill himself? Why?"

Alex spoke the truth. "We may never know."

"They think I did something, don't they? Why else wouldn't someone tell us what's going on?"

Alex remained silent, not bothering with another "I don't know."

"Maybe I should go. If I see him, I should be able to at least identify him," Tory said.

Alex, quick to dispel that thought, said, "You need to stay here. Let the police do their jobs. There's no need to put yourself through that."

Tory scowled, then nodded in acquiescence. "All they have to do is check for his knee replacement. Remember? The one from college that ended his football career. The one he said I caused because he'd been distracted, and it was my fault he took the hit? Don't they keep a record of product numbers or something?" Clearly her niece watched the same crime dramas she did.

"He blamed you for blowing out his knee on the football field?" Alex asked, incredulous.

"Yep," Tory said simply, as if it was a natural accusation.

"You do know that's ridiculous, right?"

"I'm getting there."

Alex noted the answer left unsaid, that part of her was still affected by that monster's accusations and lies. Time, Alex reminded herself. It would take time to unlearn the behavior reinforced by his fists.

Tory suddenly blanched, one hand going to her mouth and one to her stomach. She was not going to make it to a bathroom; Alex grabbed the trash can and held it in front of her, not sure what else to do. Anything the young woman ate or drank came up with the force of projectile vomiting.

Tory grimaced when she sat up. "I know Charlie said morning sickness lasting 24/7 past the first trimester is a good sign with multiples, but I'm really tired of this," she said, wiping her mouth with the paper towel Alex put in front of her before drinking from the glass of water shoved her way.

"They'll be here before you know it, and all this will be behind you," Alex said, not knowing how else to comfort her. She moved the tea a little closer, hoping that would calm her stomach. "Why don't you go lie down for a while?"

A shout came from the lake below. Alex looked out the kitchen window and saw Charlie walking out toward the end of the dock, meeting the boat pulling up. The sheriff was here. She saw Charlie shake his hand, then turn and look toward the cottage. Then the sheriff began up the path, Charlie close behind, yelling, "Mom! Can you come out here?"

Alex hurried through the screened-in porch, letting the door slam behind her.

"Alex, I need to talk with Victoria," the sheriff said, no preamble.

"She needs to rest. What's happening?"

"Please. I have to see Tory," he said firmly, though his eyes pleaded with her not to cause a problem.

"I'm here. What's happening? Do you have news?" Tory asked, stepping outside.

The sheriff turned to face her and indicated she should sit on one of the bus bench seats under the tall trees. Once she was seated, he waited a few beats before speaking.

"I'm sorry to be the one to inform you, but the body is Mark." He hesitated a moment, watching her facial expressions carefully.

Feelings are complicated and conflicting emotions raced through Tory's brain; at the same time tears silently crawled down her face. Part of her was relieved she would never have to worry about her children's or her own safety with him gone, but another felt guilty for feeling that way. Again, she wondered if he could have been redeemed. Then her thoughts turned another direction, and she wanted answers. What actually happened? The tears flowed, still silent. She felt struck mute, emotions clogging her throat. Instead, she waited for the sheriff to say something more.

Finally, he continued, forehead marred by tense lines, "I need you to go through the last night you saw Mark. In detail."

Charlie stepped in front of her cousin. "Is that really necessary? You have her statement."

"It is. Tory?" The sheriff gently moved Charlie to the side with a hand on her arm.

Tory stared at her hands a moment, then crossed her arms protectively over her baby bump. In a quiet voice, made an octave lower by the swelling in her throat that threatened to break out in uncontrollable sobs, she said, "It's okay, Charlie." Then she proceeded to walk the sheriff through the entire ordeal the last time she saw who she thought would be her ex-husband. Now, she guessed, he would be forever known as her "late husband."

She started with watching Alex and Andi pull away to take her father to the far shore, detailing Mark's silent approach ... the alternating darkness and blue light from the moon as it hid behind the clouds and then came out again ... her refusal to go with him ... his physical attack ... her trying to grab him to keep from falling into the water ... sinking under the water and trying to stay conscious ... Mark not helping her out of the water ... Mark rushing away when her aunt and cousin returned ... losing consciousness ... regaining consciousness on the beach.

Relating all the horrible details yet again caused her breath to catch in her chest; she was unable to get a deep breath and gulped for air, her vision swimming in and out of focus.

Charlie quickly sat beside her cousin and put an arm around the young woman's shoulders. "Breathe in deeply and hold; breath out; again," Charlie said, demonstrating as she talked, trying to stem the obvious panic attack.

Once Tory calmed, the sheriff continued, raising his hand against the protests from Charlie. "Tory, did you get in the boat with Mark at any time that night?"

"No! I wouldn't go anywhere with him," she said vehemently. "When would I have done that?"

"Your aunt was gone long enough for you to have taken a ride with him, maybe?"

"No!"

"Maybe he got you in the boat and drove away; you two struggled; he hit his head and went overboard; you left the boat to drift and got to shore, hurt by Mark during the struggle, and made your way back to the dock, where your aunt found you." The sheriff laid out a potential scenario.

"That's insane. He almost killed me. He left me to die," Tory said flatly, for the first time accepting that Mark could have killed her and driven away.

"What about the life insurance policy you have on Mark?" he pressed.

"What?" She looked genuinely confused. "Mark insisted on life insurance policies on all three of us around the time Donovan was born. That was six years ago. He pointed where I had to sign and that's the last I saw of them. He wouldn't even let me read the documents when I asked. I forgot all about them."

"You're sure? The policy is for two million, if he died," the sheriff said flatly.

Tory's eyes opened impossibly wide. "I don't understand! He said he was taking out just enough to cover final expenses and pay off the house, if one of us died."

"Sheriff—" Charlie was halted by the man raising a hand in the universal sign of stop, effectively silencing her.

"You're saying you weren't aware of the magnitude of the policy?" he pressed.

Before she answered, Alex broke in. "I think that's enough, sheriff. Tory will need an attorney before she speaks with you anymore. Just to be on the safe side." Alex added the last sentence, her voice filled with reproach.

The sheriff nodded. "That's her right. I'm not arresting her. I'm asking questions that if I don't, the state police will."

"They're working with you on this?" Alex asked. The sheriff nodded.

He turned to walk down the hill, then looked back. "I really am sorry, Tory." He made it a few more steps and then turned back yet again. "Mark's coworker, Beth Smith, said Mark spoke about the policies only last week and that Victoria was well aware of their existence and amount. I need you to stay in the county until we get to the bottom of all of this, Tory. The rest of the family, too, Alex."

"I have a question for *you*, sheriff," Alex said. "Did Mark also have a policy on Tory's life for two million dollars?"

The sheriff smiled a small smile. "He did." Then he continued down the hill with no more questions and no backward glance. His gait was sure and steady as he made his way to the dock. Even from behind, they could tell he held himself straight and tall, his broad back and shoulders barely moving. He waved and called goodbye to the others at the lake, sounding like the friendly man the family always knew him to be.

Alex reminded herself he was simply doing his job, but she hoped he broadened his search for the truth and didn't accept any simple conclusions or flawed logic just because they were easier and would close the case.

Tory was even more perplexed now than before. One thing she was not confused about was that she was considered a suspect and that wretched excuse for a woman, Beth Smith, was pointing the finger her way.

The day, once deceptively beautiful and calm, was quickly turning to an evening storm. The giant trees began to sway, their leaves brushing together so high above the ground, they sounded almost like a crowd at a football game, taking Tory's breath away—why the roar of a football game, of all things, something so intimately related to her late husband? Maybe that was why; talking of Mark conjured him. He managed to disturb her peace and space even from beyond the earthly realm. The sounds of the leaves high above the earth rustling in the wind usually comforted her. Not today. She shuddered.

Maddie walked the sheriff to his boat at the end of the dock, where a deputy waited. The sheriff had insisted on speaking with

Tory alone, telling the deputy she was more likely to be comfortable and open up with only him. The sheriff knew the man was a close friend of Mark's and didn't want him making anything harder than it already was—for Tory or for their investigation.

After waiting until the police boat was well on its way back to the north shore, Maddie hurried up the hill. Tory still sat on the bench, Charlie beside her. Alex paced back and forth, old pine needles and fallen leaves scrunching under her boat shoes against the hard-packed earth, soil tamped down with generation after generation walking, playing, and sitting in the flat space at the top of the hill.

"What was that all about?" Maddie demanded, standing in front of her best friend to stop her pacing and grabbing Alex's upper arms.

"They think I'm a murderer," Tory said, her voice hollow.

"Stop it. He didn't say that," Charlie admonished.

"Didn't he?" Tory asked. "It's what he thinks."

"Well don't put *that* into the universe," Maddie exclaimed. "I'm sure it only felt that way. No one would think you capable of that. Besides, he's a foot taller and has more than one hundred pounds on you."

"I agree. It's totally ridiculous," Alex said. "I'm calling Mait." She moved farther down the flat area to the other end where the hill sloped into the lake.

Her brother, after he was done ranting and threatening to knock sense into the law enforcement officers, agreed the whole prospect of his daughter not only killing, but being physically capable of killing, her monster of a husband, was preposterous. He was also prepared, in case they came to him, to reiterate his recall of the night in question.

Alex assured him he didn't need to come to the island and that Tory was holding her own. She flinched as she told him that, knowing it was a slight overstatement of Tory's state. But the young woman needed to know she had the strength to get through anything, and her father's presence would only stunt that necessary growth, in Alex's opinion.

*Huh,* she hummed to herself, *so this is the power in being the matri-*

*arch. I can orchestrate and decree as I see fit. This might not be so bad after all.*

The women wanted Tory to lie down or go into the kitchen with them to get tea. But she needed the fresh air and couldn't stomach another mug of herbal tea right now. As much as the wind had brought bad memories with the sound it made through the leaves, it also brought familiar, comforting smells that drifted across her—fresh water, a whiff of humidity, a tinge of gasoline, a slight odor of fish, the fragrance of green growth, the sweet scent of lily pad flowers.

This was *her* spot, her family's haven. Mark's death would not take this away from her. She had allowed him to take everything else, including her dignity. This would not fall to the tyranny he wielded even in death.

**29**

———————

*rateful. Three things. Then I can get up.*

**G**Tory opened her eyes in her bed. Her great-grand-mother's quilt pulled to her chin. She blinked and offered up that she was grateful another morning had come, and she had not been arrested. Then she added her gratefulness that her babies were progressing within her. And, finally, that so far Van had not overheard any of the women talking and didn't seem to know his father was dead.

She would have to tell him today. That thought made her lie cocooned in the warmth for a few more minutes.

Outside the bedroom door, she heard voices in the hallway.

"Hey, Col. Want to go sailing? You and me?" She heard Lauren ask.

"Yeah! Wind's good this morning," Colin said, obviously happy with the request.

The two raced down the hall and out into the living area, through the screened-in porch, on their way to the kitchen. They grabbed protein bars and bottles of water and were gone in a quick moment, not stopping long enough for anyone else to ask to join.

"You want to captain?" Colin offered the young woman who was his aunt but only four years older.

"Nah." She smirked. "You can do the hard work."

"Don't worry, I'll put you to work."

Once on the lake, mainsail bowing in the wind, they traveled at a good clip across and around the lake, too early for skiers to be out, fishers already ensconced in their favorite spots. Neither spoke for quite a while, simply enjoying the wind and the sound of the water as the boat sliced through it.

Lauren stretched out, limbs and face positioned to catch the sun. Her coloring was a little darker than her sisters and brother, taking on more of her late father's olive complexion and his dark hair. She tanned easily and enjoyed the summer's rays.

Colin's hair was getting longer than he liked. He usually kept it short on the sides, longer on top, much like his father had. This summer it had grown, the ends curling upward and tickling the tops of his ears and neck. The thing he liked most was rolling out of bed and hitting the lake. Andi told him he had the perfect beach hair.

"How do you do it?" Lauren asked suddenly.

"Do what?"

"Be okay."

Colin moved the tiller slightly, lessening the wind in their sail and slowing the boat to a more sedate pace.

He shrugged. "Why wouldn't I be okay?"

"Because you're a kid. You lost your dad suddenly. You didn't even get to see a body." Lauren sighed, blunt as usual.

Colin's posture stiffened. "I'm not much younger than you."

"I know, but that's not what I meant."

Colin waited. He preferred the silence to where this conversation was going. He also didn't like the implication that being okay somehow meant he didn't care about his dad. He was affected deeply by his death; he just didn't wear that on his sleeve for the world to see.

"I know you're being purposely obtuse," Lauren grumbled.

"Spell it out."

With an exaggerated sigh, Lauren sat up and turned to stare at her nephew. "I'm basically a mess since my dad died. I want to yell and cry and am mad at the world. Yet here you sit, your dad dead too, and you're all calm and mature. It's infuriating."

Colin smirked and teased her. "Guess I'm more of a grown up than you."

"I'm serious! Help me! How do you do it?"

Colin composed his face, trying to change from joking to serious like he would tack the sailboat, smooth. "I don't know. I guess I do what he taught me to do with everything—I put one foot in front of the other. One step at a time."

"Well, that's not so easy."

"I know. You just have to do it. I also try to focus on other people and not on myself, because that hurts too damn much." He did focus more on his brother, sisters, and mother, because it was far easier than thinking about his dad never walking through the door again. "It's not easy. It sucks. But we're not the only people in the world to lose a parent. There's nothing we can do about it."

"Maybe."

"I can let you in on a secret." Colin considered his words carefully.

"Okay."

"We have a Dead Dads Club."

Lauren sat up straighter. "You have a what? What's that?"

Colin shrugged. "Some of us who lost dads decided to form a club. We talk to each other. Mostly we make jokes about it and try to stop people feeling sorry for us. People don't know what to say when you make a joke about your parent being dead. Like, someone in school might say what a pain their dad is because he won't let them go to a party, and we'll say something like 'too bad your dad's not dead, he wouldn't be in the way then'—total sarcasm. Or, like, a kid will whine about having to mow the lawn, and we'll say, 'at least your dad's not dead.'"

Lauren looked horrified, like someone spit in her water bottle. Then, slowly, a smile spread. "That's kinda awesome."

Colin shrugged again.

Lauren hesitated, as if she was afraid he might refuse, before she asked, "Do you think I can join this club?

Colin tilted his head and pretended to evaluate her. "I don't know. Do you think you're ready?"

She nodded enthusiastically. "Well, I'm already sarcastic. And I gotta do something; I can't keep feeling like this."

"Then welcome to the club. Membership fee is one dead dad. You've already paid your dues."

She rolled her eyes. "You're really terrible underneath all that goodwill."

He spit out a laugh. After a beat, he said, "It's kind of hard to be part of this family sometimes."

"Yes," Lauren agreed and then hedged. "But what do *you* mean by that?"

"It's just, we have all these kick-ass women—multiple generations of them—and the expectations are so high. We're expected to behave a certain way. We're expected to accept all the tough stuff and get up smiling. Doesn't matter what it is, we *must* be strong. And then we're expected to support and serve other people. It's a lot of responsibility," Colin said. He was personally okay with it but suspected Lauren was struggling with those things in particular.

"Yeah, I get that. But it's not just the women; the men are pretty hard to live up to, too. Look at my brother and your dad." Suppressing a smile, she added, "You're going to be pretty okay too, you know."

"Gee, thanks for the vote of confidence."

They sailed in silence until Lauren said quietly, "Thanks for letting me in the club."

"No problem. You can initiate someone else."

"Kids of Dead Dads unite," she said, raising her fist in the air, the tightness in her chest lessening with the sheer act of irreverence. Colin merely shook his head and filled the sail, shooting across the lake again.

While the two of them sailed, Sage settled her kids on the beach, making sure Hudson and Jaspar had their life jackets fastened before they took the kayaks out of the boathouse.

Cassie and Grace had the new paddle boards ready to try, Alex's latest addition to the lake toys. The girls fastened their life jackets and attached the elastic anklets, kneeling and paddling smoothly until they were out deeper in the lake, Grace careful to go nowhere near the stand of tall weeds. Soon they were standing and paddling, balanced on the boards like pros.

Tory had grabbed Donovan's hand as he raced out of the cottage, passing her, ready to play in the water with Sage's girls.

"Mommy, let go! I have to catch up!" Donovan struggled to get out of her grip.

"Van, stop. I need to talk to you," Tory said, the seriousness of her voice stopping his struggle. He stared at her warily. She walked him over to a bus seat under the tall trees.

"Something happened," she said. Now his eyes were starting to show fear. His little body sat rigidly straight.

"Daddy got hurt and he's not coming back. He died and went to heaven," Tory said, her hands beginning to tingle, slightly panicking at how ill-equipped she was to have this conversation, and also not sure heaven was a place that would accept Mark. Was she causing her son irreparable damage? How do you tell a little kid his dad was dead?

Van seemed to consider her words carefully. He sat rigidly. His little jaw clenched, teeth grinding. Tory could already see the tell-tale signs he was growing up, his face looking more boy and less little boy, his jaw sharper, his face tan from a summer in the sun.

"He's really dead," he said.

"Yes, he is. I'm so sorry you have to go through this, Van," Tory spouted, trying to take the sting out of her news, though knowing there was no way to do that.

Van slowly nodded. "He's dead. He's not coming back?"

"No."

"He can't hurt you anymore? He won't hurt me?" Van asked for clarification.

"No, he won't hurt either of us ever again," Tory confirmed.

Van sat quietly for a moment, not moving. Finally, his rigid body relaxed, and he hugged his mother. "Good," he whispered. Then he jumped up and ran down the hill, yelling back, "I'm going swimming now."

Tory's mouth dropped. She was stunned. That was it? That was the sole impact of the news? Wow. Her son's honest reaction was one more slap in the face to how well she thought she had hidden what was wrong in their home. Most of the arguments were long after Van went to bed; he must have woken and heard or seen more than she thought. She clenched her teeth, mimicking her son's earlier posture. If she could make Mark die all over again for the damage he'd caused, she would.

"He's okay with it, isn't he?" Alex asked wisely, leaving her place on the screened-in porch.

Tory nodded.

"There's been a lot of death lately. It's not as if he doesn't know what it means," Alex reasoned. She thought over the last few years to her father's death, James', Hank's. The circle of life. They were all subject to it. And with such a large and long-living family, the younger members were all subjected to its effects sooner rather than later. She had some friends who never knew anyone who died until they were well into their forties. While sad, she tended to think earlier exposure was healthier.

"He's glad Mark's never coming back. God, Alex, my son must have seen so much more than I thought!" Tory shuddered.

Alex looked kindly at her niece. "Kids tend to do that. It'll be fine. You love him enough for two parents."

"Promise?" Trepidation rose in Tory's voice as she questioned her aunt.

Alex held out her pinkie to her niece. "Promise."

Tory managed a giggle at the pinkie promise. Then she shuddered again. "At least I know Dad didn't kill him since he was with you and then me the whole time."

"This is something to be grateful for."

At that moment a horn honked twice shoreside. Alex ducked and looked through the trees, across the lake. She saw Aimee step out of the car and wave to those on the island beach.

"Aunt Aimee's back," Indy yelled, no mistaking the excitement in her voice.

Charlie looked back toward the cottage and yelled up to her mother, "I'll get her!" Alex nodded.

"Time for my nap." Tory smiled and made her way to the cottage. She saw Maddie sitting on the porch, where she enjoyed the breeze and didn't have to contend with any bugs.

Cameron and Gavin walked out of the cottage the same time as Tory walked in. Gavin held the door, waiting for her to enter the living area before stepping down into the porch and closing the door behind him.

Cameron was lost in thought, looking at his camera screen. When he looked up, he smiled timidly at Maddie. "Hi."

"Hi yourself. What do you have there?" she asked, nodding toward the camera.

"Oh, I was looking through some of what I already shot." He paused and looked from the camera to her. He glanced down again without saying anything.

"Is there something you wanted to ask?" Maddie prompted.

"Um. Yeah. Um. Do you think you could go through some of the editing with me?" he stumbled. "I don't want anyone else to see it until it's done."

"A surprise for the family," Maddie said solemnly. She broke out into a grin and clapped her hands together. "Yes! I'd love to help!" Delighted she could do something other than worry about dead men, murder charges, and her chosen family, she hopped from her seat.

Cameron's face flushed pink as he granted her a rare, genuine smile. "Come on. I've got the laptop set up in the kitchen where we won't be bothered." He fairly skipped across the porch and up the steps into the kitchen, waiting until Maddie joined, and then closed the door behind her. As promised, his laptop sat on the far side of the table, where even if someone entered the kitchen, they wouldn't be able to see what he was doing.

The two sat on the table's matching bench, heads close, eyes glued to the screen. "This is what I've edited so far," Cameron said. "I wasn't sure if I should use order of events to tell the story or if I should use big moments."

He flushed again as he further explained. "I went order of events. It made more sense to me because everyone is getting tanner and changing, and I thought it would look weird out of order. What do you think?"

Maddie remained solemn, matching the seriousness of the boy's tone. "Chronological works. I agree with your choice."

They watched what he'd put together already. Maddie made some technical suggestions and showed him some shortcuts in the software. Cameron was an attentive student, lapping up her suggestions and praise for his work. She laughed at some of the antics building the treehouse, including Cassie trying to pull herself up to the first rung on the ladder, insisting she be part of the action. She responded appropriately to the more solemn moments, such as an edited version of Lauren's dinner table monologue; she was impressed he showcased his aunt's passion and sincerity.

Then Cam began going through some of the new footage to give her an idea of what was coming. He fast forwarded, adding commentary so she knew what she was looking at. Then he got to the part he had yet to review.

"Wait, back up. What's that?" Maddie asked, looking at the darkened laptop screen.

Cameron squinted and then sat back. "Oh, that's the night I set up the tripod because I was hoping to get the moon shining on the lake from the island. There was a storm coming in—hope I caught some lightning. I thought it might be dramatic. Pretty cool, huh?"

The two watched the slowed-down footage. Figures appeared in the frame, making their way onto the dock. Cameron nodded in recognition. "That's Grandma and my sister when they took Uncle Mait to his truck. And that's Tory on the dock when they left. Huh. I thought she went into town with Uncle Mait."

Maddie watched the screen with rapt attention. She didn't know how much the older kids knew, but it seemed Cameron hadn't listened at any doors or around corners for this one and was ignorant to the extent of what happened that night.

"Who's that?" Cameron said leaning forward, indicting a point on the screen. "Why aren't there any lights on that boat?"

The older woman felt her blood pressure rising, eyes glued to the screen, and didn't answer. The man tied off sloppily and got out of the boat with no lights.

Cameron snorted dismissively. "Col would have a fit if any of us tied off like that; what an amateur." He still didn't know what this was he'd captured. "Wait, isn't that Tory's husband, Mark?"

"Uh huh," Maddie replied. He was catching on.

They watched the body language and escalation of the scene. He hurriedly turned up the volume. Maddie was shocked they could hear the entire conversation. Then she was more shocked by what was said. The blows to Tory made them both physically pull away from the screen.

"What the hell!" Cameron slammed backward in his chair as he watched, revolted by what he witnessed after the fact. Maddie didn't bother to correct his swearing, more than feeling the same thing.

"He tried to kill her!" Cam said. Then more quietly he said, "I thought she fell off the dock in the dark and got those bruises."

They watched as Tory disappeared underwater and heard Mark calling for her to come back, apologizing, all the while blaming her for his having to hit her. Then they heard the faint noise of a boat engine, saw Mark's look of desperation, even in the blue light of the moon. They watched him jump back into the dark boat and move away before their own boat arrived back and docked.

They heard Andi's panicked cry when she saw Tory in the water, and watched Alex jump in the lake, grab her niece, and pull Tory through the water and onto the beach. The time waiting for Andi to bring Mait and the doctor back was agonizing. They knew Tory was alive, but still, the drama was big.

"You know you can't include this in your movie," Maddie said, at a loss for what else to say, as they waited for the next several minutes to play out and their boat and the judge's race toward the two separate shores.

"It's so good, though," Cam protested. She tilted her head and narrowed her eyes at him. He conceded. "Okay, fine. I'll only use the moon on the dark lake shots."

They watched until all was calm on the screen once again. Mark hadn't returned, and there was no way Tory had killed her husband. He left without her and then she wasn't alone again the rest of the night—in fact, she was in the hospital, watched over every minute.

"Cam, don't touch this yet. Go get your grandma and Charlie for me. Okay?" Maddie implored in all seriousness.

He nodded and slowly backed away, finally running to the lake where the two sat on the dock kicking their legs in the water, watching the kids swimming and others boating or paddle boarding. When he came to a fast stop next to them on the dock, out of breath, and said Maddie needed them in the kitchen, they did their best to get up and not alert anyone to anything wrong.

"Is Maddie okay?" Alex demanded quietly.

"Yes. But we found something. Come on," Cam said, his voice quiet but excited. No more questions were possible because the boy had already begun to run back up the path to the cottage.

The two women looked at one another quizzically and hurried behind. Sage and Aimee wanted to follow but had to watch the kids in the water.

When Maddie showed them the footage, Alex immediately called the sheriff's office, speaking to the dispatcher who said the sheriff was out. Alex insisted the sheriff call or come to the island. It was important.

Ninety minutes later the sheriff's boat pulled up to the dock. He jumped out, his long, muscular legs taking the one step without a problem, moving quickly up the hill to the cottage.

"What's going on?" Tory asked from the kitchen doorway.

Maddie, Alex, and Charlie were gathered around the laptop at the table, as if it might get up and walk away if they didn't stare at it. They had long since sent Cameron to find Gavin to swim or boat, hoping he wouldn't have nightmares from what he had witnessed on the recording.

"That's what I want to know." The sheriff echoed Tory's sentiments from behind, startling her. He stood on the step leading from the porch to the kitchen.

"You have to see this, sheriff," Maddie said.

"Maybe you should go rest longer, Tory. We'll call you for dinner," Alex suggested lightly.

Tory's face turned stubborn. "If this has something to do with me, I want to see too."

Alex sighed and acquiesced. The women made room for Tory and the sheriff on either side of Maddie, seated on the bench. Alex and Charlie stood stiffly behind them.

Maddie explained what they were looking at was a recording Cameron inadvertently captured the night of Mark's death and how the camera was on a tripod next to the beach. Tory gasped at the words. They wondered what she'd do when she witnessed her own almost-murder. She put her elbow on the table, her fist firmly against her mouth, steeling herself to watch whatever had been captured.

The sheriff nodded for Maddie to start the recording. The kitchen was eerily silent, other than the sound coming from the laptop speakers. The sheriff did an admirable job of keeping his face passive, but Charlie was keenly aware his body stiffened even more than she could have imagined his perfectly straight posture would allow when Mark stepped on the dock on the laptop screen.

Tory also stiffened when she first saw her now dead husband. She tried and failed to muffle her audible gasp when Mark struck her the first time. Then she was silent. Tears welled in her eyes. She tried to swallow and keep them from falling. She was sure she hadn't blinked the entire time the recording played.

"That should satisfy any questions about whether Tory went with Mark. He was clearly alive when he left the island, and she was in the water. She hasn't been alone again since," Alex said evenly.

"Has this been edited at all?" the sheriff looked at Maddie.

"No. It came right from the camera. You can tell by the date and time track and the counter, if you don't believe me," Maddie said.

"I'll need to take the original memory card," the sheriff stated.

Charlie choked out a laugh. "Cam is going to have a fit about that."

Maddie shook her head and waved her hand in the air. "It's okay. I'll give him a new card." She knew all the footage had already been downloaded to the laptop and saved in the cloud account, so it wouldn't matter, but no one needed that explanation now.

The sheriff stayed seated, not moving. Then suddenly, under his breath, he muttered, "That son of a bitch." He shook his head, trying to clear whatever dark thoughts had embedded there. Louder, he turned his head and purposefully looked at Tory. "I'm so sorry you had to go through that, Tory. I wish we'd known what he was like—I would have locked his ass up for a long time."

They all knew he couldn't predict what a judge or jury would do in a domestic case, but they agreed with the sentiment. Actually, Charlie wished someone had given him a taste of his own medicine a long time ago.

"Thanks, sheriff," Tory managed to whisper. Then, pain in her eyes, she asked, "Is it over now?"

"As far as I'm concerned, your part in this is. We still need to try to find out what happened, but it's clear you were nothing but a victim," the sheriff said, keenly aware he was saying more than he should.

Of those in the room, only Alex knew he considered a special place was reserved in hell for abusers. Growing up, his father, someone only a little older than Alex, had been like Mark. The sheriff relied on his grandfather, his mother's father, for the example of how a real man was supposed to act. It was no wonder he followed in his grandfather's footsteps and ran for sheriff once he had the experience. He never did find where his father disappeared to and never once tried to find him, assuming, like his mother, that his father ran off with one of his mistresses.

"Thanks, Kevin," Alex said quietly, calling the sheriff by his given name for the first time in days. Charlie added her thanks with a quick squeeze to his shoulder.

"Yes, thank you," Tory said, sniffling. Kevin Clarke had been eight or so years ahead of her, so they were never in the same crowd in school, but his grandfather was someone her father had respected, and her mother was friendly with his mother. It was hard not to know someone who you'd been around your entire life, Tory thought absently. She wondered what it must have been like for Charlie, growing up very differently and only in their hometown for short stints at a time. She still seemed to know all the old families, but it was different when everyone knew your business. That thought skidded to a stop in her head, realizing everyone would soon know her most personal, humiliating secrets. She better stiffen her backbone if she was going to get beyond the pitying and gloating—she expected both.

"I'm going to do my damnedest to get to the bottom of this," the sheriff said, rising from the bench.

"Stay sitting. I'll get you a coffee," Charlie offered, knowing her mother would not want to touch the single-serving contraption, as she called it. "I'm sure you're going to have a long night ahead of you."

The sheriff sat back on the bench. "Much appreciated, Charlie."

"Let me get you something to eat. I doubt you've had much time to eat in the last few days," Alex volunteered, not waiting for him to accept the offer. "Aimee brought back a pan of Andrew's lasagna and garlic bread."

Alex knew he didn't have anyone at home waiting with a warm meal. The man was a bachelor. She remembered hearing something about a broken engagement, but that was years ago. Maybe she should take a page from his book and keep her heart locked up. It might have saved her the heartache Hank caused at his death. But then, she couldn't regret their firebrand of a daughter, so she guessed she could not completely regret Hank.

"I should say no, but I'm starving," the sheriff admitted, relaxing, if only slightly, around the women for the first time since this whole tragedy had begun.

"You're going to try to eat too, Tory, while those babies are letting you keep it down," Alex said. Amazingly, Italian food was one of the things Tory didn't have trouble eating. She guessed the babies liked it.

The tension eased in the kitchen, and Maddie cheerily explained to the sheriff the documentary Cameron was shooting of their family summer on the island, the reason the footage had been captured at all. "Alex gave him the camera to keep him busy. Put all that preteen angst to an artsy use, one we hope he'll continue through all the teenage anxiety we expect Aimee and Andrew are going to get." Maddie and everyone else laughed.

"I wish more people would figure out a creative outlet for their angsty kids," the sheriff said.

"Well, let's see how this movie turns out. We may all look like shrews at the end of it," Alex laughed.

Maddie winked at the sheriff as she teased her friend. "Oh, I think you'll be surprised. And no, I'm not telling."

**30**

———————

The following days felt lighter, the specter of death less pressing than when they had first arrived, all worried how Alex was handling Hank's death, and Lauren grieving the father with whom she had far too little time.

Then Mark's demise and the questions surrounding it had added to the heavy feeling. It was probably particularly lighter now because Tory's name was cleared. No one cared the reason, only that the atmosphere was better, happy. The weather even cooperated, with warm sunny days and starlit nights.

"We're going to camp out in the treehouse tonight, okay?" Colin asked his grandmother, Gavin close by his side.

"I don't see why not," Alex said. There was no reason to be worried for their safety, now that Mark wasn't roaming loose.

"Can I come too?" Hudson asked, hoping the older boys didn't shut him out.

"Sure." Gavin welcomed him with a wide smile.

The cousins had all become closer this summer, probably due to time, proximity, and no interlopers. They had to rely on one another and had no one else to play with.

"Me too," Andi said. She was unusually quiet today, often casting her eyes to the lake.

"Not me." Cam shuddered. He imagined the mosquitos buzzing his head, and the thought of falling to the ground scared him—though he wasn't going to fall with the solid walls and new railing on the other side. It didn't matter; it was still a possibility. Heights were not his friend.

"I'm coming," Cassie proclaimed.

"I thought we were sleeping in the living area tonight, eating popcorn, and watching movies?" Grace reminded her twin.

"Oh yeah," Cassie frowned. She tried to figure out how to do both.

Aimee and Charlie headed to the lake. Both realized their days were numbered at their island haven and they wanted to get in more skiing time. Sage offered to spot while Charlie drove, Aimee ready to show off her slalom, choosing to get up on one ski rather than drop one.

"Way to go, Aims!" her mother hooted from shore as Aimee gracefully rose from the water on one ski.

Charlie looked back briefly, smiling broadly. Her sister was a vision of grace on waterskis, or one ski, as was the case now. As much as Charlie liked the sport, she'd never be as good as her younger sister. She noticed Harper and Lauren stand up from their blanket on shore to watch longer as the boat and skier rounded the island, admiring the display.

The farther they went into the lake, the more daring Aimee became, the look on her face pure joy. She leaped over the wake, flying through the air and landing easily on the water, ski skimming the surface. She even did a 360, showing off completely, laughing when she made it. Charlie was sure her sister could go for hours without falling and without tiring. After several more turns, Aimee let go of the rope and gracefully sat down in the water.

When the boat came back around, she said, "Your turn, Sage."

"Are you sure?" Sage asked hesitantly. She liked to ski, but she didn't want to cut into the time Aimee and Charlie had planned for themselves.

"Absolutely," Aimee said, handing her ski in and then pulling herself up the back ladder, water streaming from her tanned, lithe body. She squeezed the excess water from her dirty-blonde hair, the same color hair as her older sister and younger brother.

"Okay, if you're sure." Sage grinned, making sure her life jacket was fastened tightly, very glad she wore a one-piece bathing suit today and not her bikini.

Aimee handed two skis over the side and Sage got ready, putting the rope between the skis and leaning back in the water. The boat took up the slack, then she yelled, "Hit it!"

Charlie pushed forward, heavy on the throttle, pulling her sister-in-law from the water. Not as smooth as Aimee, but close. Charlie shook her head, envious of their sheer gracefulness. She was no slouch on waterskis, but she was aware of her limitations. She preferred driving the boat anyway. Going fast. Really fast.

Sage treated the wake like moguls on a snow-skiing hill and relaxed into the bump over, rather than using the wake as a ramp to jump like Aimee. She stretched out wide beyond the wake and brought herself over again and again, crossing the wake lines, skiing wide behind the boat, waving to those on shore and other boats as she was pulled along.

Seeing Sage waving made Charlie laugh at how friendly she was, even being towed at a high speed behind a ski boat. She would be right at home if William did choose to run for office someday. A final time around, Sage let go just beyond the docks and island beach and drifted until she sank into the water. She waved her sisters-in-law off and told them to go on without her, carrying the skis to shore.

Charlie and Aimee laughed and sped away, ignoring the kids' shouts that it was their turn. "Hurry up, go before they realize we're ignoring them," Aimee urged.

Aimee's wet, long hair was now pulled into a ponytail, while Charlie's shorter curls whipped around her face, giving her a perpetual wind-blown look. Charlie turned the boat into a large, empty cove, no cottages dotting the shoreline here, and killed the engine, letting the boat drift. She sat back and turned her face to the sun, Aimee already sprawled on a seat in the back of the boat.

The cove was quiet, the trees blocking noise from the rest of the lake. The water here was almost still and reflected the blue of the sky. It was also deep and dark. Charlie glanced overboard and couldn't see beyond the first foot or two.

Aimee opened one eye and glanced around. "Do you think this is where they found the boat Mark borrowed?"

"Stole. He stole it."

"I bet if he'd lived, he would have returned it. So that's borrowing. But do you think this is the cove?"

Charlie scowled. "I don't know. Maybe."

"Maybe someone killed Mark, dumped the body, and then abandoned the boat here and swam to shore," Aimee posited.

Charlie's scowl deepened. "Now you're creeping me out. I'm not going to stay in this cove if a killer is watching us."

Aimee snort laughed, which caused her to laugh louder. "Well, what do you think happened to him?"

"I like to think he either killed himself or he hit his head and fell overboard. I'd rather not think another person was involved, thank you very much," Charlie said, now shooting furtive glances around the quiet inlet.

"Wouldn't that be a nice tidy answer. Want to wrap him in a big red bow too?" Aimee joked.

"Only if we get to present his head to Tory," Charlie said and then grimaced, the image in her mind making her feel bad about the entire discussion.

Charlie sat up and started the engine, pulling slowly out of the cove. She headed to a different part of the lake and found an equally quiet spot, but far from where the police found the boat. Aimee shot her sister a look and burst out laughing. "My brave big sister is a closet chicken!"

"Am not," Charlie said, reverting to the childhood response.

"You totally are. You so moved us because the killer could be watching." Aimee kicked her legs against the seat, laughing so hard she howled.

"Shut up, goofball." When the younger woman kept laughing, Charlie rolled her eyes and conceded, "Fine, okay, you freaked me out. Happy now?"

"Yes," Aimee agreed, still laughing. While five years younger, she could watch horror movies and sleep just fine after. Charlie always escaped, refusing to watch, claiming to be tired or have homework. Aimee loved chipping at that chink in her sister's armor; watching Charlie squirm when not totally in control was a life-long pastime and she didn't often get the chance.

The ski boat rocked gently, water lapping against the painted wood. It was enough to lull the women to sleep if they let it. Both kept their eyes shut, faces warmed in the sun. Aimee worked on the tan she couldn't when shut inside the restaurant. She was grateful the planning commission had granted their permit to add an outdoor seating patio before the summer months. When she chose to work the floor, rather than greeting guests or helping Andrew prep in the kitchen, she tried to snag the patio and feel the sun and breeze on her skin.

Charlie was a little more circumspect about the sun. She appreciated it but was conscious of all the people she knew on the East Coast who died from skin cancer. Her own skin never tanned dark, only gained a golden hue, and stayed that way, further convincing her the paleness that came so naturally to her was a sign to be careful with the sun's rays. She noticed she was more careful about a lot of things, particularly since the official car arrived in their driveway and two service members solemnly delivered the news that James would never come home again. She was acutely aware her children had only one parent left.

So, while she still enjoyed the speed of the ski boat and driving a little faster than necessary when the kids weren't in the car, her devil-may-care days were behind her. At least that's what she told herself. Maybe she could pick up where she left off after the kids were grown and solidly on their own paths.

*Charlie.* She started, clearly hearing James' voice say her name on a sigh. The kind of sigh he used when he wanted her to think differently.

It was then she realized Aimee was talking, "...and why can't you do that?"

"Huh?" Charlie responded.

"You aren't listening to me." Aimee pouted.

"Sorry. I zoned."

"I think you and the kids should move to town," Aimee said.

"We have a house in Virginia," Charlie responded, her rote response to the request.

"There's no reason you have to stay there now. You can live anywhere."

Technically correct, Charlie could work from anywhere and travel to where she needed to be at any given time. Technology made it easy to stay in touch with their staff and clients. However, the kids were settled, weren't they?

"It would be great for all the kids to be here," Aimee said. "It's home."

Charlie tended to think of the area as their ancestral home, where the foundation of their family grew strong and some of them branched out. A place she visited every year, sometimes multiple times a year. But in her soul, she felt like a nomad, never settling for long—not that she would tell anyone that.

*Charlie.* There he was again, a heavy sigh in her brain. What was she supposed to do differently? What was she missing?

"You and Andrew decided to settle here, but you know we had many homes growing up," Charlie tried lamely to explain.

"This is the only place that ever felt like home to me," Aimee admitted.

"DC used to feel like home to me," Charlie said, surprising herself that she used the past tense.

Aimee sat up and grabbed her sister's hand, taking the opening she heard in Charlie's words. "Why can't you use this as homebase?

You'll have to travel if you stay with the company anyway. No reason you can't do that from here."

Charlie laughed, no real humor in the sound. "You just want us all in the same place. I don't know if I can do small-town living."

"Why? What's so different?" Aimee demanded.

"Uh, everyone knows everyone's business," Charlie tried.

"And DC isn't a fishbowl?" Aimee countered. "Come on, it's not like you're an anonymous intern there. You have a community, but are they really yours?"

When Charlie stayed quiet, Aimee started ticking off items on her fingers. "The military families move around; once they move on you keep in touch through social media, text, and email anyway. The politicos move in and out, depending on who's in power. The ones who stay—are they really your people? You said your circle changed once you became the widow."

Charlie winced at this last point, not that it wasn't true, just that it poked an open wound. She said, "I'm the third wheel now with other couples."

"Just think about it. That's all I'm asking," Aimee pleaded. In a smaller voice she said, "I want my sister back."

Charlie felt that plea in the pit of her stomach. She and her sister were so different in so many ways—outlook on life, careers, interests. But one thing had become very clear this summer: family was important. Love may be infinite and encompass lots of people over a lifetime. But time was finite and there was only so much time with the ones you love. She realized she really liked her younger sister's company and would like to have it on a regular basis. But how realistic was that? Aimee and Andrew were embedded in the community, with their business, their friends, their time already spoken for. Would they even have room in their lives for her if she were around all the time, rather than the carved-out periods during the year on which they knew to rely and for which to plan?

"I don't know. There's a lot to think about," Charlie hedged.

She had felt a pull, not sure what it was, for months now. She was no longer the newcomer, fresh out of college, eyes bright, youngest in any room. She was also no longer the wife of an elite operator, keeping the other wives and girlfriends centered when the team was deployed or on a mission. She was alone as the single mother of four children. And she was soon to be CEO of a company that had the power to do a lot of good—another change for her.

The wind felt like a warm caress against her cheek, so much like the way James used to support her jaw and caress her cheek with his thumb. She shut her eyes and leaned into the breeze.

Aimee watched her sister out of half-open eyes, like when they were kids and she didn't want the older girl to know she was tracking her every move. The older they got, the less the five years difference in their ages mattered.

She felt like she made headway with Charlie today. Next, they needed to convince Sage. If her sister came home, and they convinced Sage to move as well, the added benefit was that Alex would have no reason to spend more time anywhere else.

When they returned to the island, they saw a kid parade heading toward the treehouse, each carrying a sleeping bag, as well as other essentials, such as the battery-powered lantern, flashlights, snacks, water.

Cameron recorded the journey from cottage to forest. Aimee noted he'd stuck to his guns and no sleeping bag was under his arm. She was secretly glad to see her son was coming into his own, not caring about peer pressure—even from his cousins—and finding his own path. She would be forever grateful to her mother for the camera and chance she had given the boy to find himself and his art, and to Maddie for her mentorship and encouragement. Now she and Andrew would need to show an interest and keep up the encouragement; one more exhausting element to add to her exhausted life.

Work was hard. Kids were hard. Life was hard sometimes. She physically shook her head, dispelling the "overwhelmed" feeling that took her down a dangerous path of negativity. Negativity led to pessimism and a small business owner, particularly in the food industry, could not afford to be pessimistic. She knew that. The overwhelmed feeling that began the avalanche always led to one place:

wondering if she would ever measure up to her siblings or her parents, wondering if she was enough, wondering why her dreams never seemed as big as theirs.

A hard elbow to the ribs brought her out of the spiral. Charlie stared at her. "Where did you go? It didn't look very good."

Aimee shrugged and planted a fake smile on her face.

"Oh no. You don't get to do that. What's wrong?" Charlie looked toward where the kids disappeared behind the cottage. Guessing, she said, "Are you worried about Cam? He seems to have found his place this summer. He'll be fine."

Aimee smiled, this one real, if small, "Yeah, he has. But that's not it."

"What then?"

Throwing her arms in the air, Aimee huffed, "I feel like you all left me behind. I'm the one with the small-town dreams. I'm the worrier. I'm not the warrior." She meant that in the true sense of her brother and the metaphorical sense of her sister.

Charlie was gobsmacked. "Seriously? What is all this about small town versus big city? I have a revolving community. You have a life. Since when are your dreams not important? You're the one who went for it and opened a restaurant. All I did was go into the family business, didn't even follow my own dreams. You're an entrepreneur, little sister. You're amazing. And you're the only one who doesn't see it."

Charlie stomped up the hill. Aimee stood with her mouth open, staring after her older sister. Here she had always slightly envied her sister's life, imagining the Kennedy Center galas and all the election night parties, thinking her own life was small. Was Charlie right and no one else thought that of her?

"Sheesh. This summer is a freakin' emotional roller coaster," Aimee said aloud to herself. She huffed up the hill.

**31**

———

Hand over hand, Colin lifted the five-gallon bucket at the end of the rope into the treehouse through the trap door. The essentials for their campout were placed in the bucket and hauled up until everything was inside and ready for the night. Alex had sent extra blankets, afraid the kids might get cold.

Hudson completed every task the older cousins gave him, excited to be included. The encouraging winks Gavin and Colin shot his way made him grin; he felt like he was worthy of their company. He set the battery-powered lantern in the corner, out of the way. He looked around and realized the space was much bigger than when the rehab started.

Colin noticed his appraising looks around the treehouse and grinned. "It's bigger because Uncle Mait always wanted a bigger tree-house. So now it is."

Gavin sat down and opened the cooler. "Should we have dinner? I'm starving."

The others laughed. Gavin had spent most of the day exploring the lake with Jaspar. The two tried to out-paddle one another, and exploring one inlet led to the exploration of three more. Then they hugged the shoreline around the main part of the lake. Gavin's arms and legs had to be killing him, Colin surmised. Not that his younger brother would ever admit it. He also doubted Jaspar would last long with the movie marathon planned for the evening in the cottage.

Gavin handed Hudson, Colin, and Andi their sandwiches. They sat cross-legged, patting one another on the back about how well they had restored the treehouse and talking about who was better at swimming, diving, skiing, sailing, rowing, and fishing. All the things important in a kid's life when they spent the summer on a lake in northern Michigan. The same things that had been important for generations.

In silence, they watched the sun set over the water behind the trees on the west side of the island. The trees were thinner and fewer on that end. The docks, boathouse, and beach were on the south shore, close to the west end.

"It's really pretty tonight," Gavin marveled, eyes set on the horizon he could see through the trees.

"Reminds me, we need to do another sunset sail before it's time to leave," Colin said, making a mental note.

Hudson frowned. "I wish we didn't have to leave."

"Summer's almost over," Andi said.

"I know. But it's been great being with all of you," Hudson said.

No one disagreed.

Once the sun set and the gloaming disappeared, the lantern cast long spooky shadows in the treehouse, and the trees appeared far more menacing than they had by light of day. They could hear the nightlife in the nearby trees and in the soft crinkle of the many seasons of leaves on the ground. They told ghost stories. No one made fun of Hudson when he moved his sleeping bag next to Colin and leaned in close. Gavin fell asleep almost immediately after claiming kayaking all day had not made him tired.

Suddenly, Andi jumped up. "I have to go to the bathroom. I'm going inside. I might stay there," she mumbled. Colin and Hudson chuckled, assuming she was either cold or scared by the stories, of which she told the most, so they didn't feel sorry for her.

They watched her flashlight disappear around the corner by the cottage's walkout basement storage area. Colin settled, sitting with his back against a wall. Hudson scooted up next to him.

"Think this is how the pioneers felt?" Hudson asked.

Colin vaguely remembered a unit on pilgrims and then one on pioneers when he was Hudson's age. "I think they worked a lot harder."

"Yeah. Probably. But I bet they lived a lot like this."

"Except without the stove and refrigerator," Colin reminded him.

"Oh yeah. Without those."

They stayed in companionable silence for a while. Hudson stared up at his older cousin. The younger boy ran a hand through his white-blonde hair and squirmed in his seat.

"Something bothering you?" Colin asked.

"Nah," Hudson said. Then he asked, "Have you thought about what you're going to be when you grow up?"

"Yeah, you?"

"Yeah. What do you want?" Hudson pushed.

"If I keep my grades up and get good recommendations, I'm planning on the Naval Academy. Maybe then try for the Teams," Colin said, rarely telling anyone his plans for after high school. If he played it right, he would graduate a year early and enter the Academy at seventeen.

"You want to be a SEAL?" Hudson asked, surprised. Colin figured his younger cousin was surprised because Colin's dad had died in service.

"I do. But it's really hard."

"That's what I want too," Hudson said solemnly. "Naval Academy first. Like my dad and your dad and our first grandpa we didn't meet."

"Yeah," Colin said. He understood completely and felt the same sense of duty.

"Sometimes I worry about leaving Mom with all the other kids," Hudson admitted. "But I hope my dad will be home by then."

"I know what you mean," Colin said, nodding in the dark. "It's not so easy being the oldest, is it?"

"Nope."

Colin recognized the same seriousness in Hudson that he knew he had himself. He firmly believed they would both make it. He liked that Hudson looked out for his mom. That made him feel even closer to the boy, even though they were separated by a seven-year age difference. He kind of wished Sage and William's family lived closer. While they all lived in Virginia, he and his family were in Northern Virginia right outside Washington, DC, and Hudson's was near Norfolk, more than a three-hour drive.

Colin nudged Hudson, a grin, spreading across his face. "But it's kind of fun to be the boss of the others, isn't it?"

Hudson barked a laugh. "Yep." The younger boy offered Colin a cookie from the cooler. After eating his own, he pulled the sleeping bag over his head and went to sleep. Colin could tell the younger boy was out by his deep, even breathing. He knew it was only a matter of time before his brother Gavin would start talking in his sleep. Gavin did that a lot when his father was deployed and even more now.

Colin thought he saw a small light by the dock but couldn't tell for sure through the trees. The noise of motors passing by on the lake was pretty common, fishers heading home, joyriders out for an evening ride. He dismissed the light as his imagination working overtime after all the stories and the shadows in the moonlight.

Down by the lake, Andi cast a look over her shoulder as she admonished the boy in the boat to turn out the light until after they pulled away. She jumped in next to him and he quickly made a U-turn, heading back toward the north shore. She gave Jared, the grocer's great-grandson, a brilliant smile, which he returned. Both felt they got away with something.

The lake was calm tonight, only a light breeze. She was dressed as she had been in the treehouse, with skinny jeans, a green Michigan State sweatshirt over her white tank top, and sneakers.

Jared used the lever on the motor to steer his great-grandfather's fishing boat. He pointed the bow toward a different place on the north shore, a mile or more east of his grandfather's gas station, store, and the house on the lake his great-grandparents lived in year-round. Andi could see the glow of a bonfire. As they pulled closer, she could hear the excited voices of teenagers. When they pulled up and tied off on the dock, she recognized some of the partiers as high schoolers and even recent grads probably home for the summer from college. A thrill zinged through her body as Jared took her hand and moved toward the party.

Thoughts of her parents and family all but gone, Andi was determined to prove her independence. She also thought she could really like the new boy by her side who always smiled at her, making her think they shared a secret. Her footsteps stumbled a bit when she saw a girl across the bonfire who she had a crush on all last year. The girl was a year older and already in high school, but Andi admired her from afar all year. Now she saw she had her arm around another girl. They might be friends, but they looked awfully cozy to Andi. That sight made her lean closer into Jared, who at first tensed in surprise but then let go of her hand and put his arm around her.

Jared accepted two plastic cups of cheap beer from the older boy working the keg and handed her one. Andi tried to act cool and pretend it wasn't her first beer, holding back the cough she immediately felt rise when she downed her first mouthful. She smiled and laughed along with everyone else, the summer magic making them all feel invincible.

Across the lake, Andi could make out the outline of her family's island bathed in moonlight.

On the island, Colin, the only one still awake in the treehouse, could hear the occasional shout or laughter drifting across the lake. He looked out the window on the north wall—another Maitland addition—and could see a bonfire on the lake's shore. He could tell a party was in full swing. Lying back on the wooden floor, deep in his sleeping bag, he tried to sleep.

It was hours later on the north shore when sheriff's deputies showed up and began corralling teenagers. In the chaos that ensued, some escaped through neighboring yards, a few got away in their boats. Jared was pulling a tipsy Andi into the fishing boat when a deputy grabbed the rope and kept them from leaving.

"Where do you think you're going," the deputy growled.

"Home?" Jared asked innocently.

The deputy lifted his hat and stared at the two teenagers, both flushed from beer, the bonfire, and probably now adrenaline. "Aren't you George's great-grandson? Yeah, it's you. Son, aren't you living up here because you're already in trouble downstate?"

Jared dipped his head, whether in embarrassment or anger, the deputy wasn't sure and didn't care.

"Get out of the boat."

Andi had pulled her hood over her head and now it fell as the deputy took her hand and pulled her up on the dock.

"Andi Dumont? I wouldn't have expected you here. This isn't a place for a girl like you," the deputy tutted.

Andi scrunched her nose and tried to think through the floating feeling she had in her head. What did he mean by a girl like her? What she did know was that this was not good. Her dad was going to kill her. Starting high school grounded was not an auspicious beginning.

The deputy made a phone call after he made sure they were on the dock and not getting away. He spoke quietly into the phone and clearly did not like what he heard. He gestured to one of the other deputies and had a quick discussion. The other man nodded and stepped into the official sheriff department boat no one had seen pull up to the dock.

"Let's go, you two," the deputy said gruffly, holding an arm while each stepped into the bigger boat.

"What about my grandpa's boat," Jared asked, panic in his voice.

The deputy untied it, and they towed it behind them, stopping first at the grocer's house and leaving the fishing boat there. Jared turned to her and whispered, "I'm so sorry, Andi." Remorse was clear on his young face. Then he was out of the boat, escorted by the deputy.

Andi couldn't hear what was said as they handed Jared over to his great-grandfather, who, by the looks of him, had been pulled from sleep.

When the deputy returned, they headed toward the island. The rocking of the boat as they crossed the lake did not agree with Andi's stomach and she leaned over the side and threw up over and over again. She was never drinking beer again. The deputies laughed and she realized she must have said that out loud.

Once at the island, lights on the boat bright and still flashing, further humiliating the teenager, they began the trek up to the cottage. She thought she could make out Colin's form standing next to the basement, silently watching. At the door the deputy raised his hand to knock. Andi stopped him, "It's open; I can just go in."

"Oh no," the deputy grinned. He seemed to be enjoying this part. "I'll let you go in and get your mother, but if you don't come back, I'm waking the whole place up. Got it?" His face and voice had turned deadly serious with the last part.

"Got it." She groaned and stepped in through the screened porch door. A minute later her mother and Aunt Sage followed her to the porch, her grandmother and Charlie trailing closely behind. Andi swore the matriarch had bat hearing. Charlie had been up by herself in the living area reading.

"What's going on?" Aimee asked the deputy, though from the smell of beer and vomit coming from her daughter, she could guess. Aimee was in sleep pants and was glad she threw a sweatshirt over her T-shirt before leaving the bedroom.

"Party on the north shore, Aimee. Sorry, but Andi here was there with George's great-grandson," the deputy said. He looked a lot sorrier with her mother than he had with Andi.

"I'm so sorry," Aimee rushed out. The deputy had been in her class in school—unlike Charlie, Aimee spent her entire high school years in Michigan, graduating from the local high school before setting her sights on culinary school.

"Thank you for bringing my granddaughter home," Alex said graciously.

"You can thank Sheriff Clarke. Other parents are picking up their kids at the jail. He said to bring her here and to take George's grandson to him. He also said if they stay out of trouble, this won't go on their record," the deputy informed them.

"She will not get into any more trouble. Thank the deputy for being so generous and bringing you home." Aimee looked pointedly at her daughter. "Then go to bed."

"Maybe a shower first," Sage advised.

"I'm sorry. Thank you for bringing me home and not arresting me," Andi said, staring at the deputy's shoes. She turned and hurried toward the bathroom.

"I'm really sorry about this. She was supposed to be on a campout in the treehouse," Aimee rambled.

The deputy, for the first time, smiled and laughed, "Come on, Aims; it's nothing we didn't do, huh?"

Aimee turned red and looked behind her, making sure Andi was gone. "Don't tell her that!"

The deputy laughed even harder. Shaking his head, he turned from the door. "I think you're safe for a while. She puked all the way back here. Doesn't like beer much."

"Well, there's that," Aimee said, finding one thing to be grateful for in all this.

They watched until the deputy was back down the hill and he and his partner pulled away from the dock.

"Ugh!" Aimee covered her face with her hands.

"Oh, it's not that bad," Alex said.

"She was with a boy, Mom. A boy we don't know. They were drinking. Got there in a boat. At a party with a bunch of other kids. Anything could have happened."

"But it didn't," Charlie interceded. "You can ground her tomorrow. Or hey, how about you make her tell Andrew herself. That would be a fun punishment."

"I'm glad you're finding this funny," Aimee grouched.

"With everything else we've faced the last year, even in the last month, yeah, it's kind of funny. And fairly innocent," Charlie said smugly. When a deputy is at your door in the middle of the night, it could mean all sorts of things, none of them good. This was way better than where Charlie's head went when she saw the deputy standing there.

Aimee threw her hands in the air. "Ugh! I'm going to bed." Sage gave her sister-in-law's shoulder a comforting squeeze and followed her back to the bedroom they shared.

Alex waited until she heard the bedroom door shut and the shower running before saying quietly to Charlie, "You thought someone died."

Charlie sighed. "Yeah, I did."

Her mother gave her a half hug.

"Do you blame me? Deputy at the door in the middle of the night. Not knowing what's going on. Someone dead or hurt seemed like the logical answer. I know I shouldn't have laughed at Aimee's expense, but I was so relieved. I mean, come on, this was the lesser of many evils," Charlie said, defending her reaction.

"No argument here," Alex said. Late night visits or calls were the stuff of nightmares, in her experience.

The two women waited until they heard Andi go to bed and headed that way themselves.

Colin pushed away from the cottage, just out of sight of the screened-in porch, and made his way back to the treehouse. He didn't want Hudson to wake up and find he wasn't there.

**32**

―――――

With both the kitchen and living area doors open to the screened porch, Sage made sure to clang lots of pots and pans as she began breakfast. It hurt her ears, but she promised Aimee she would wake Andi as loudly as possible without going into the bunk room and banging a pot next to her pillow. The room she slept in had windows that were close to the kitchen. With the windows open, it was as good as being next to the bunk.

"No. No. Just no," Andi groused and pulled a pillow over her head.

"Breakfast time," Aimee sang at the bunk room doorway.

"Not hungry."

"Up. Now. Food is good for a hangover," Aimee said and left for the kitchen, fully expecting her daughter to dress and follow.

"Hangover. That's what this is," Andi thought, then was mortified by her memory of the night before. In the bathroom, Andi pulled on her swimming suit under shorts and a T-shirt. She brushed her teeth and then dragged herself to the kitchen, not at all ready for the lecture or teasing that was sure to ensue.

Sage slid a plate with scrambled eggs, bacon, hash browns, and toast in front of her. A glass of water and two ibuprofen were already waiting on the table. Her eyes rounded and her stomach turned over.

"Drink the entire glass of water and take the pills first," Aimee advised her daughter. "Believe it or not, the greasy food will help."

"Hey, my food is not greasy!" Sage protested.

Aimee rolled her eyes. "Bacon is always greasy."

The teenager was unusually quiet. She did as she was told. After she made an attempt to eat the food, she realized the women were right. She felt a miniscule degree more human—that was better than nothing. Her mother slid onto the bench next to her, and Andi realized the easygoing kitchen banter was about to end.

"When you're done, you're going to call your dad."

Andi's fork clattered to the plate. "Me? Why?"

"You're going to tell him about last night."

"You didn't tell him?"

"Nope. You're going to. You think you're old enough to go off with some boy we've never met, party half the night, get hauled home by the police; you're old enough to woman up and explain it to your dad." Aimee looked unusually pleased with herself. Her big sister had some good ideas, occasionally. Andi lowered her head to the table and groaned.

A few minutes later Andi paced among the bus benches, hoping her cousins didn't hear her humiliation. Aimee stood in one place, arms across her chest, smirking as she watched her daughter and caught one-sided pieces of the conversation. "Dad ... Dad ... I'm sorry ... No, Mom hasn't met him ... Dad, no!... Please, no ... I promise I'll help you clean the kitchen for a month ... Please ... I won't ... I really won't ... I'm sorry ..."

"Here, he wants to talk to you." Andi pouted, holding out the mobile phone to her mother and slumping on an old bus bench seat. Out of the corner of her eye, she saw her cousins carrying sleeping bags and camping supplies to the house. She thought Colin watched her the entire time he climbed the slope by the side of the cottage, but she didn't meet his eye—couldn't yet. She just wanted the day to be over.

Aimee said into the phone, "Yeah, she looks properly chastised."

Aimee could tell Andrew was frowning when he responded, "Good. What the hell, Aimee? She snuck off the island?"

"I know."

"What is she thinking? She's fourteen years old. Have you met this boy?"

"I think she thought a boy was interested in her, and no, I haven't." Aimee noted her over-protective husband was more concerned about the boy than the drinking. The son of an American mother and French father, some of Andrew's views were more European than what he called hypocritical American judgment. He explained to Aimee when they first met and married in Paris when she was eighteen—a total surprise to her parents—that from what he'd seen, Americans condemned in public that which they pursued in private.

"Well, I want to meet him and apologize to George. How do we know this wasn't her idea?" Andrew insisted. "I'll get away and be there this afternoon."

Aimee rang off and stood in front of her daughter, arms crossed again. "Come on."

"Where are we going?" Andi asked warily. Aimee noted the sheen of tears in her daughter's eyes.

"Let's take the boat out, just you and me. I think we're overdue for some mother-daughter time."

Andi followed her mother to the lakeshore in silence. Once far out on the lake, Aimee took a play from Charlie's book and turned the engine off and floated. It promised to be another beautiful, warm, sunny day. The lake was fairly desolate in the morning light, no other boats sliced through the water, other than the fishers quietly casting their lines in their favorite isolated spots.

"What's going on in that head of yours?" Aimee asked, settling onto a passenger seat in the back. Her daughter stretched out on the other side of the boat, face to the sun.

"Nothing."

"Not buying it. Why didn't you ask if you could go to the party?"

Andi sighed heavily, making her displeasure with the direction of the conversation known. "You wouldn't have let me go. Or I would have had to take Colin."

"You don't know that because you didn't ask."

Andi opened one eye and turned to stare pointedly at her mother.

"Okay, well, you're probably right. But you still should have asked. And why did you drink so much?" Aimee continued.

Andi mumbled something Aimee didn't catch.

"Come again."

"Argh! I saw Brittany with another girl, okay? I was upset. And now you know! Your daughter likes girls! Hate me now?"

Aimee sat up and reached out to touch her daughter's arm. "Hey. Why would I care if you like girls?" Inside, Aimee was reeling. Who was Brittany? She remembered seeing a girl who was a year or two older than Andi at the restaurant a few times; it was memorable because whenever she came into the restaurant, Andi disappeared into the back. Was that Brittany? And how was Jared involved in this?

"You don't care?"

"No."

"But you and Dad have this big love story and are always all googly-eyed with each other—that's embarrassing, by the way."

"You can have your own big love story someday, if you want. It can be with another girl. One thing I want to know though, so you *don't* like Jared?" Aimee pressed gently.

Andi groaned, big and long. "I don't know! Yeah, I kind of do. He's really cute and he's smart and he seems to like me—at least he did before all this happened."

Aimee tried to wrap her head around the conversation she started. Now she wished she had listened more closely to her sister Lauren when she explained the continuum of human sexuality.

"So—you like boys *and* girls."

"No! Yes? Oh, it's complicated. I thought I liked girls; I mean they're pretty and my stomach flips around when ones I like talk to me. But the same thing happened with Jared. Maybe it doesn't matter to me? Why does it matter if someone's a boy or girl? Why can't we all be just, I don't know, human?" Andi said, then continued before her mother could answer, "I mean, isn't all this really pushed on us by a puritanical society? You and Dad always told Cam and me there's no such thing as 'boy' toys or 'girl' toys, they're just toys. Maybe we should all just be human beings and nicer."

Aimee smiled. "Maybe we should. You can like whomever you like. Maybe you're someone who likes *the person* and not because they're a boy or girl. Or maybe you'll find you like both. Your dad and I just want you to be happy. And *not* lie to us and sneak out. And *not* drink to hide your feelings. That's dangerous."

"I really, really, really don't like beer. It's gross." Andi groaned again. "And I won't be sneaking out again—Dad says I'm grounded until I'm eighteen."

Aimee tried hard not to laugh. She suspected her husband would give in long before then, once he saw his daughter was back on the straight and narrow.

"Mom," Andi started tentatively. Aimee didn't have to wait long before Andi continued. It seemed the day for true confessions. "I don't know what I want to do when I grow up. Everyone else seems to know. I just know I don't want to own a restaurant. Are you okay with that?"

"Of course, that's okay. That's your father's and my dream, not yours," Aimee said. "Most people don't know what they want at your age. And a lot change their minds over and over before they find it. It's okay. And it's okay to try a few things."

"Really? Being part of this family is *so* hard. I feel like everyone has it figured out but me."

"That's not true, and it doesn't have to be hard. The family is here to support you, not make you feel you can't live up to their standards." Then Aimee confessed, "I used to feel like that. I didn't go into the family business. I wanted my own thing. I got married so young. But I judged myself; no one held it against me. Don't make your life harder like I did."

"It feels that way sometimes. And I feel bad that Cam makes me so mad. He's so moody, and you and Dad always try to find ways to make him be a part of things. I can't always cater to him. Then I feel bad."

"Oh no, no, no. You don't need to feel bad about your brother. You'll both find your way. I'm sorry if we made you feel like we put him before you. We love you both—equally," Aimee hurriedly said, her own guilt ramping up. "You'll be in high school this year, so you'll have some separation from your brother for two years. It will give you both a chance to find your own ways."

Andi looked out at the water and then back at her mother, eyes serious, "I think Cam found his this summer. That camera."

"Maybe. We'll see if he stays interested. But either way, it's not your responsibility. You just need to love him like a little brother," Aimee said, hoping her daughter understood. *Why does this parenting thing have to be so hard?*

Mother and daughter floated, chatting about other less weighty topics. Andi was much more open to conversation once she realized she was not going to be a complete disappointment to her parents. When it got too hot lying in the boat, they dove overboard and splashed one another in the lake, swimming until they tired.

When Aimee's mobile phone rang, she glanced at the name. "Your dad's here." She powered up the boat and moved toward the north shore.

"Why are you going this way?" Andi sounded panicked.

"He's at the lake grocery store."

"No! Take me back first."

"Don't be silly. Got to face your actions head on, Andi," Aimee said, sounding like a mother.

Andi chewed on her lip until they pulled up to the grocer's dock. Her father handed in a few bags, then jumped into the boat, kissed her mother in a long kiss, making those eyes that made Andi's own eyes roll. Then he turned to her and stared. She stared back. Andrew opened his arms and his daughter jumped up and leaped into the hug her father offered.

"What are we going to do with you?" Andrew whispered rhetorically.

"You already grounded me. Unless you don't mean it now?" she asked with hope.

"Not on your life. You're grounded." Andrew laughed. His talk with the grocer went well. The older man apologized to him for his great-grandson and then introduced Jared. Jared apologized profusely and explained he had hoped to meet some other kids before school started, thus attending the party. He also admitted he liked Andi and was sorry he got her in trouble. Andrew told them his daughter made the decision to go and was just as much to blame. He also made Jared promise not to sneak out with his daughter again, threats implied rather than stated.

"But I can stay at the island the rest of the summer, right? I don't have to come home today and work at the restaurant, do I?" Andi said, that thought only now crossing her mind.

Andrew made a show of looking at his wife, the two conversing silently, as if deciding her fate.

"No, you can stay. But if you do anything so stupid again, I'll come get you and you'll be at the restaurant with me from morning to night until school starts," Andrew finally said, in all seriousness.

"Thank you!" Andi jumped up and hugged both her parents. "I promise. No more trouble."

"Um, can I fill your tank?" a hesitant teenage voice sounded from the dock behind them. Jared stood there, shifting from foot to foot, looking from their eyes back to the dock, not sure where to settle or how he would be greeted.

"Hi, you must be Jared," Aimee said, holding out her hand to shake the boy's. "I'm Andi's mom."

"Nice to meet you," he mumbled, shaking her hand quickly. Then he stood straighter, quit shifting his feet, and looked Aimee in the eye. "I already told Mr. Dumont, but I'm really sorry about last night. It won't happen again." Then he looked at Andi, shyly. "I'm sorry I got you in trouble, Andi. I had a lot of fun with you, you know, before."

Andrew cleared his throat. "I think my daughter shares equal blame, but thank you for taking responsibility, Jared."

"Not your fault," Andi agreed hurriedly. After he filled the boat's tank with gasoline, Andi gave him a little wave goodbye. "Guess I'll see you in school." Jared gave her a single nod and smiled, aware of Andrew's stare. They pulled away and headed back to the island.

Andrew swam with his wife to the raft after handing the bags of groceries to his daughter and the other kids to carry to the kitchen. She told him about her talk with Andi. Explained all the angst over sexuality. He had a flare of anger in his eyes. "*Merde*. See, this is what I tell you about Americans, so constipated. Why is this a big deal? I really don't understand. Live and let live."

"I know. What was it your father said to me when we met? Eat well, laugh often, love a lot. That sums up nicely how it should be."

"I agree. What I don't like is that our children feel the double standard, no matter what we believe," Andrew said. Aimee waited for it, and yes, here it was. He said, "Maybe we should move to France."

She kissed him gently on the mouth. "We can't run away. There are problems everywhere."

"I know." He sighed, relaxing against her. "She knows we don't care who she likes or loves, right?" Aimee answered her husband affirmatively before diving off the raft and taunting him to join her. His olive complexion glistened in the sun; his dark hair fell over one eye as he chased his wife through the fresh water of the inland lake.

The two were still horsing around in the water like a couple of kids, when they heard a boat's motor turn around the bend at the end of the island. Curious, they swam quickly toward shore and the boat with the sheriff's official symbol reflecting cleanly on the side. They got to the dock shortly after the boat idling at the end. The sheriff was already on the dock, Charlie and Alex moving toward him. The sheriff motioned to the deputy and told him he'd radio when he needed a lift back.

Aimee noticed Tory held back, standing on her blanket under a tree next to the beach but not moving forward. Harper sat on the blanket, baby Allie asleep in the playpen next to them. Donovan played with Savannah and Harper in the sand on the small beach. When he saw the sheriff, the little boy took off at a run toward the dock as fast as his legs would take him, overtaking and passing Charlie and Alex. Tory's eyes widened, "Van, come back. No running on the dock!"

## 33

Before the sheriff could greet the women, a little boy, dark hair in need of a trim, raced down the dock and skidded to a halt mere inches from his legs. The little boy looked up slowly, taking in the long legs and muscular torso, having to tilt his head all the way back to see the sheriff's face. The man looked down at him.

"Hi! Are you one of the good guys?" Donovan said loudly.

The sheriff fisted his hands on his hips, eyes knit together, as he stared back into the boy's blue eyes. "Yes, I am. I'm Sheriff Clarke."

Donovan held out his little hand to shake. "I'm Donovan, but everyone calls me Van."

The sheriff took the boy's small hand in his own, swallowing it beneath his fingers, and shook it with the seriousness in which the boy offered it.

"Can I call you Van?"

Van nodded. "As long as you're one of the good guys." He then said, "I want to be a police officer, like you."

At that revelation, the sheriff squatted down on his heels, meeting the boy eye to eye. "That's great, Van. How come you want to be like me?" Not many people these days encouraged their kids to go into law enforcement; unfortunately, they had good reason, and it made him angry that the bad and corrupt in a faulty system now defined people like him who still believed in "serve and protect." He imagined kids in Detroit would have a very different opinion of his chosen profession. Still, he was grateful there were kids like Van.

"Because you're one of the good guys, silly. I'm going to protect people. That's what you do, right?" Van said this last part as if he might have gotten it wrong.

"That's right," the sheriff nodded.

Van looked relieved. "Good! I'm going to protect my mom from now on and the babies." In a low voice, unusual for him, he asked, "Can I tell you a secret?"

The sheriff nodded, and Van leaned in to whisper in the man's ear, hands planted on his shoulders. "My daddy was a bad man, but he's dead now. I know it's your job to protect people, but don't feel bad, nobody knew my mommy needed help; it's not your fault."

The sheriff's eyes widened, and he felt choked up at the little boy's candor and forgiveness. "Thanks, buddy. I appreciate that."

Van leaned back, patted the sheriff's shoulders, and looked him directly in the eye again, man to man.

"Van, can you come help me with Allie?" Harper called, hoping to divert the boy's attention from whatever new revelations the sheriff brought. It never seemed to be good when he visited the island.

"Gotta go. Harper's giving me baby lessons, so I'll know what to do with our babies when they come," Van explained and ran back the way he came.

Andrew and Aimee climbed up the ladder onto the dock behind the sheriff. Andrew greeted his friend. "Kevin, what brings you out here?"

"Just what I was going to ask," Charlie said, eyes narrowed.

The sheriff blinked a few times before he stood. "Think we can go to the cottage with Tory? Away from little ears?" He noticed Cameron hanging off to the side, closer to the boathouse, staring into the viewfinder, his camera obviously running.

The adults moved toward the path to the cottage. Andrew and

Aimee snagged towels on the way. In unspoken agreement, Sage, Harper, and Lauren stayed behind with the kids.

Once seated in the kitchen, Maddie already there reading a book in her endless pursuit of bringing new content to the screen, the sheriff cleared his throat a few times. Unbidden, Charlie handed him a cup of coffee, sensing something big brought him to their island.

Alex thought anything had to be better than the nothing they already knew, more questions than answers.

The sheriff took a long sip of the hot, black brew, nodding his thanks to Charlie. "Tory, we found Mark's car. It took a bit, but let's just say Beth Smith, his coworker, has been a little more forthcoming now that he's—he's gone."

"Dead. He's dead. You can say it," Tory said without feeling, granting permission. "And while we're being brutally honest, you can call her his mistress, or slut, whichever you prefer."

"Whoa, who are you and what did you do with Tory?" Aimee expelled her breath, eyes wide. Andrew placed his hand on his wife's back, supportive and a silent request for her to let the sheriff talk.

Tory blushed red, rising through the summer tan. "Sorry. This is all so new, and I was so *stupid* for so long." She never thought she would call another woman such a derogatory name and searched her brain for another way to describe her. "Maybe I should have said 'self-centered psycho' instead?"

Andrew barked a laugh, unable to help himself. "I agree with my wife's cousin. This is a good description." Andrew also knew Beth from the restaurant and was not a fan, long before the new connections to the family came to light.

The sheriff cleared his throat again and took another fortifying sip of coffee. "Now that Mark's dead, Ms. Smith realizes she has nothing to gain by keeping secrets. She suggested we look in the garage at her great-aunt's cottage on the northern side of this lake, not too far from where he stole the boat. Her great-aunt went to the nursing home last year, so it's been empty while the family argues over what to do with it. She claims he must have stolen the automatic garage door opener when he was at her condo. He told her he was going to make Tory sign the original divorce petition 'or else.' She claims she had no idea what he meant."

"Ha! Right, she didn't," Maddie exclaimed, heavy on the sarcasm.

"Anyway, we found his car. There was a suicide note inside—" A collective gasp rose from everyone in the kitchen.

"He planned to kill himself?" Tory said in disbelief. "Why?"

The sheriff looked at the table for a beat and then raised his head, making sure to meet each person's eyes before continuing his story. "It wasn't his suicide note, Tory. It was yours."

As he expected, the room erupted in chatter.

"Wait, sheriff, I didn't write a suicide note." Tory practically begged him to believe. Then the meaning dawned on her, and she fell silent. Her arms dropped to the table in front of her and she stared at her hands, knuckles turning white from gripping so hard. "He meant to kill me. Make it *look* like suicide. That's why he had the gun. For when he got me in the boat."

The sheriff nodded, lips pursed in distaste, feeling bad for having to tell the young woman the truth. "Appears so. We're still not exactly sure what happened to him after he failed to get Tory in the boat. But it looks like he hit a submerged log—there was some damage to the underside of the boat—and probably hit his head and fell overboard. Cause of death was drowning.

"He called the life insurance company a couple weeks ago to make sure the suicide clause was no longer valid since the policies were purchased six years ago. Maybe he figured since you were already in the water, presumed unconscious, that he'd get the payout anyway and didn't have to kill you. What we do know is that he promised Ms. Smith he was taking care of the 'problem' and that he would be free of his marriage and have a nice sum of money to bring to their relationship."

"He was a monster," Charlie said, rubbing her hand along her cousin's back.

"What did the suicide note say?" Tory suddenly asked.

"I don't think you need to read that," Andrew said.

"No. I want to know. I want to know what he thought he'd get away with," Tory insisted.

The sheriff, though agreeing with Andrew, understood Tory's desire to know. Anything he could do to bring closure to this part of her life, he would try. He held out his phone, a picture of the note on the screen. Tory took the phone with trembling fingers and read silently to herself, before handing it to the others. In script close to her own but not exact, her name signed at the bottom, the note read:

*To my family,*

*I'm sorry it's come to this, but I can't take my life any longer. I've failed everyone. This will be best. Please let my son know how much I love him as he gets older, but he will be better off with Mark and his new family.*

*Victoria Newberry-Wright*

Tory, though numb once again because of the monster she'd married, thought it ironic that he bothered to sign her complete, hyphenated, last name. He always hated that she did that, as if he wasn't good enough for her to take his name only, hanging on to a vestige of her past.

She barely heard her family's reaction as they read the final note Mark wrote, though, she supposed, it could have been written by Beth. Mark had learned to forge her signature long ago, so maybe not. The varied intakes of breath as they read registered as background noise in her brain. The sheriff seemed to sense she was ready to move on.

"The body is being released today. Do you want me to have the funeral home pick it up?" the sheriff asked. She noted he did not say "pick *him* up," dehumanizing her monster even more. She almost laughed at the appropriateness of his pronoun but realized they might think she had finally lost it all together.

"Do they take it to be cremated?" Tory asked, not a clue how this worked. "I don't want a viewing. Cremation. He hasn't talked to his parents for years—I think they moved to Florida. If his older brother wants a service, they can do it, but I don't think I can do this." Tory's voice trembled, close to breaking. It was all too much. Even if this was the end, it was too much. Too much for too long.

"I'm sorry, Tory," the sheriff said, emotion crowding his voice for the first time.

"Thanks, Kevin." Tory used his name, feeling this man deserved to be humanized at this moment. It had to be hard on him too. He knew everyone around the table. Grew up with them.

"I told the insurance company to release his insurance payout to you. Apparently, Ms. Smith contacted them and said it should be released to her, since she was the fiancée. They told her that's not how it works," the sheriff said, a sardonic smile graced his face at that revelation. "You and your kids will be fine."

Tory looked up at him with those words. Somehow, she knew he wasn't talking about the money. At least someone believed she could get past this horrible nightmare her life had become.

"I need to talk to my dad. I want the house sold. I don't want to go back there," Tory said.

"I'll go with you to get anything you want to keep," Charlie said.

Tory wanted to tell them to get rid of it all, but there were things she needed—some artwork, family jewelry, her son's things. Most of it she wanted to burn—the furniture she hated but Mark had insisted upon, the clothes in her closet he insisted she wear, the family photos he placed on the shelf to perpetuate the lie, and all of his belongings.

"We'll help too, clear it all out," Aimee declared, picking up on Tory's mood.

"Thanks. I think I'm going to lie down. Sheriff, can you tell my father all this?"

"Kevin, you can tell him when he gets here," Andrew said. He had watched Alex text her brother to get to the island immediately. "And please, stay and eat with us."

"I really should go," the sheriff hesitated.

"No, please stay. You have to eat." Alex insisted, nodding at Andrew for thinking to include the man.

"I'm grilling ribs and barbeque chicken." Andrew tempted the man further.

No sane person would turn down Andrew's cooking. The sheriff agreed and radioed his deputy that he wouldn't need the boat to collect him. He would get a lift back to his cruiser when Maitland and Andrew left later that night. He stood quickly when Tory rose from the table; his father may have been a bastard, but his mother and grandparents raised him to have manners.

"I'm glad you're staying. Van will be excited," Tory told the sheriff quietly, before she left the kitchen and disappeared to the bedroom area.

Maitland must have broken every speed limit between town and the lake. The sheriff said a small prayer of thanks none of his deputies or the state police patrol cars roaming the area had stopped him. Maitland laid heavy on the horn when he pulled onto the shore-side lot, his mood belied by the long, loud honking meant to alert the islanders to his arrival.

Within minutes, Alex collected her brother and talked him down enough that he wouldn't upset his daughter or grandson with his foul mood. He really wished he could kill his late son-in-law again himself for the pain and agony he had caused. The only good things were that he *was* dead, his daughter would not be drawn into a nasty custody fight—one he had no doubt would have been meant to hurt her, not for want of his son—and that his daughter would get the insurance payment rather than her dead husband.

Regardless of the adults' mood and the sheriff's presence, the day remained sunny and warm, the water placid; not a day for sailing, much to Colin's chagrin. He wanted to escape the obvious tension emanating from the cottage where the adults talked. The only hint of rain clouds came as the sun was setting and Maitland, Andrew, and the sheriff were dispatched back to their cars—Maitland to the family land on the south shore, and Andrew and the sheriff to the north shore grocer's dock.

During the barbeque dinner, the sheriff chuckled to himself that Andi avoided him like he had the plague. The one time he caught her looking at him, he had winked and smiled, knowing the teen was still reeling from her experience with his deputies the night before.

Andrew saw the exchange and guffawed, making his daughter even more self-conscious.

In bed that night, everyone else tucked away, except her daughter Charlie reading in the living area, Alex pulled out her mobile phone and texted the DC detective Charles "Charlie" LeBrandt.

**Alex:More news. Found suicide note when they found Mark's car**

**Charles:He left a suicide note?**

**Alex:Not his. From Tory**

**Charles:...**

Alex waited, watching as the rotating ellipses of him texting back persisted, then disappeared. Soon her phone vibrated in her hand with a call.

"That calls for a phone call, not a text," Charles LeBrandt said with no preamble.

Alex filled him in on what they had learned that afternoon. He whistled through his teeth. "I'm sure Maddie is champing at the bit to make this into a script." He laughed.

"She may have mentioned that."

"I'm just glad it's over now," Charles said. "Tory can get on with her life."

"She can. She already said she wants to sell the house and move," Alex said.

"I can imagine it holds one too many nightmares for her and Van," Charles surmised correctly.

"Oh yeah."

After a pause, Charles asked, "And what about you?"

"What about me? I've gotten a lot done on my sketch project. Oh, and Andi got a police escort home from a party she snuck off to last night." Alex told him all about Andi's drama.

Charles laughed again. "I can just imagine Aimee. She must have been mortified. But it was a good catalyst for their talk. That's a good outcome."

Talking to Charles was always so easy. She appreciated how much he knew about each individual in her family and marveled at how well he remembered the details. She briefly wondered if that was a product of his detective training.

"All these things have been a good distraction for you. Even the drama," Charles said, returning to the serious conversation.

"Yes, it's kept their intervention from happening."

"Alex." One word, her name, said as if it were a complete thought.

"What?"

"Have you been able to deal with everything that happened before you got to the island?"

"Nothing to deal with," Alex said, her chin lifted and jaw tense, stubborn, even if he couldn't see her.

"Alex."

She sighed dramatically, a sigh worthy of her grandkids. "Why do you know me so well?"

"Because I do."

"Yes, you do. Always have," Alex said. "I'm okay. I still have my moments of anger, but it's better. I know I'll never have answers to my biggest questions. I'm trying to live in the land of gratefulness and focus on the good things—without Hank, there would be no Lauren. Without Hank, there would be no business for Charlie to take over. Without Hank, William would not walk back into civilian life with a concrete plan."

Charles chuckled. "Leave it to you to figure out how to be stoic and see the bright side at the same time."

"It's how I was raised. Woman up."

"Yeah, and I admire that about you," Charles said. More quietly he added, "I admire a lot of things about you, but then, I always have."

"Thanks. You're not so bad yourself," Alex said, returning the compliment. The easy conversation reminded her why he had been Ian's best friend and her best male friend ever since.

"You going to be able to sleep now?" he asked. His shift would come early in the morning. One of these days he'd have to consider retirement. He kept putting it off.

"For the first time in a long time, I think that answer's yes." Then she added, "Maddie leaves tomorrow, which makes me sad."

"You can visit her," Charles reminded her. It wasn't as if she had anything or anyone holding her back. "Which reminds me. When are you coming back to DC?"

"I'm not sure. I've been thinking about staying on the island all winter."

Charles took a breath before answering. He suspected her children would tell her it was a horrible idea. He did not disagree. But his response had to be more circumspect, more acknowledging of her reasons. "What's driving that desire?"

She expected him to tell her why she couldn't possibly stay on the island during the winter. His question threw her. She hadn't examined her reasons too closely. "Leave it to you to call me out without calling me out."

"Not my intent."

"No? Well, I think you're smarter than you think. I don't really know. It's just a feeling. Maybe I like the idea of the isolation. You know, hermit in my hermitage. I can paint and read and write all winter, and no one will be here to interrupt me. I can eat what I want or not eat at all if I don't want to."

"And no one will be able to reach you until the spring thaw, after the ice is gone on the lake. Unless, of course, it freezes enough to take snowmobiles or cross-country skis across."

"Oh no! I won't go out on the ice, and I certainly don't want my children or grandchildren to do that," she exclaimed.

A memory came to the forefront of her brain, dredged from the recesses. She was riding a snowmobile, following her grandfather. She was unaware he'd driven onto a lake; she thought they were in a wide-open field. The ice cracked in front of her, and she watched him sink beneath the surface. His friends had quickly thrown themselves belly down on the ice and slid a rope into the hole in the ice for him to grab. They pulled him out. He could have just as easily been drowned. Later that same winter one of her friends lost her father when his snowmobile went through the ice on a lake, and they didn't find his body until spring. It didn't matter that both those incidents happened on a different lake, she was still petrified of falling through.

"I know you won't, but your family is going to check on you."

"Well, then I'll rethink this. Maybe I'll stay until the first snow flies," she conceded. "I have enough food to last the winter though, so no one would need to check on me."

He laughed. "Yeah, I'm sure you do. Let me know if you want company after they all head home for the start of school."

"I may take you up on that," Alex said, surprising him.

"Night, Alex."

"Night, Charlie."

Alex relaxed into her pillow, ancient quilt pulled up to her chin. Alex could hear a gentle rain begin to fall outside her window. She could picture her eldest daughter sitting in the living room, warm yellow light from the table lamp, reading her book, knees pulled up in the old red rocker, same as thirty years before. Her daughter loved reading in that chair, particularly when it rained outside.

Alex hoped the other woman stoked the stove. Summer rain could sometimes chill the air. What she was most grateful for tonight, other than her loving family and friends, was that summer rain. Fresh water clearing the air, one drop at a time, cleansing any lingering toxins, and replenishing the lake that sustained all life around them.

## 34

The nighttime rain had cleared before sunrise. The sky was brilliant, sunlight reflecting pink on the lingering clouds. Cameron stood on the dock looking forlorn. Maddie had loaded her bag and satchel into the boat. She had hugged everyone else already and said her "see you later" because there was no "good-bye" with this family.

She put her hands on her hips and met Cameron's eyes, glare for glare. "Well?"

"You can't leave yet. We're not finished," Cameron said, voice dangerously close to a whine.

Maddie laughed. "That's why you're all pouty?"

"Not pouty. We were a team. You said."

Alarmed by her son's disrespectful attitude, Aimee was ready to step in, but Maddie gave her a slight head shake. She could handle this preteen.

"We still are. Ever hear of technology?" she said. "You've got this, Cam. You know what you're doing. If you need me, I'm only a text or video call away. Finish editing and, if you want, upload to the shared account I gave you, and I'll take a look. That work for you?"

"You'll really look?"

"I said I would."

Cam considered her answer and then agreed. Maddie laughed and flung her arms around his shoulders. "You're killing me, kid." To his embarrassment, she kissed the top of his head. He hadn't had another growth spurt yet and was still shorter than her five feet seven inches.

Aimee nudged her son. He said to Maddie's back as she climbed into the ski boat, "Thanks for all the help, Maddie."

"You got it, kid. Keep it up and you're going places."

Alex pulled away from the dock and took her friend to the shore. When they got to the mainland dock, Alex shook her head. "We should have taken back your rental car. It just sat here all these weeks."

Maddie laughed and hugged her friend tightly. "It's fine. I'm writing this whole trip off. You've all given me more material than I'll be able to write in a year! Even if you won't let me write *specifically* about all of you."

"You're incorrigible." Alex hugged back just as hard. She would miss her friend. Having her on the island felt natural. For the first time she considered this summer's aborted intervention and was happy it brought all the women in her family together for weeks on end.

"You wouldn't want me any different." Maddie continued the banter and climbed out of the boat. Alex handed up the bag and satchel. "Come to LA next, huh? Or we could meet in DC."

"Or you could spend the winter with me on the island."

"You're not doing that. And I am most definitely not doing that—too isolated for me. Wait, unless you haven't told me something, and Charles has finally retired and is going to winter with you?" Maddie threw the possibility out there before Alex could stop it from winging its way into the universe.

"Yeah, that's not happening. He's never retiring," Alex hedged. "We'll see. I may or may not stay. I've got a lot I want to do—in my solitary pursuits."

"Well then, you better write the next bestseller, or paint enough so we can organize a gallery showing," Maddie said in a clear challenge. She knew her friend. "I think those sketches you showed me could be their own exhibit. I'm serious," she said, when Alex gave her the "are you for real?" look. "So much emotion and such rich stories in each."

"Love you, Maddie."

"Love you more, sister." With that, Maddie walked to her car, straight postured, feet solidly on the ground. She loaded the trunk and drove away, hand waving out the window, leaving her chosen family—for now.

On the island, the twins dogged Colin's steps. He was trying to leave them behind without letting them know that's what he was doing. Andi had avoided Colin since the cops brought her back to the island the night before last. He wanted to talk to her before they all left, and his family drove back to DC. He knew that time was a few days away, but she was the closest in age of all the cousins and she didn't trust him; at least he didn't think she did.

"Col, stop. We have to talk to you." Cassie grabbed his arm.

"I'm a little busy, squirt."

"Just stop, please." Grace grabbed his other arm.

He stopped, looking skyward for patience. When he looked back down, his sisters were staring up at him. One short wavy hair, one long wavy hair, but the same face. It was a little unnerving, especially when they got this intense.

"We want to ask Van to join." Grace spoke first.

Now he was really confused "Join what? I told you I can't take you sailing today."

"Not that. The Dead Dads Club," Cassie said, rolling her eyes, as if he were dense.

Colin choked and coughed. Grace pounded on his back while Cassie looked at him like she thought he was ridiculous. "No, Cass, Gracie. I'm not sure that's a good idea. And how do you know about that?"

"Duh! We're members too, you know. Gav told us a long time ago," Cassie huffed.

"Well, he told us after he asked one of his friends to join and we kind of overheard it," Gracie, unable to tell even a small fib, explained.

That's good, Colin thought; he wouldn't have to pound on his little brother.

Colin hesitated. "I don't know. Van's been through a lot, and he's awfully young."

"He needs us," Cassie insisted. "He's already got the attitude. He's got to know we get it."

"Cass—"

"No, Colin. She's right," Grace said.

He threw up his hands. "If you think you can talk to him and he'll understand and not run crying to his mother, I guess it can't hurt. But you need to make sure he's ready to hear it. Now, can I go? I need to find Andi."

"She's hiding in the rowboat." Cass waved toward the boathouse, where the rowboat was pulled onto shore. The twins ran off in search of Donovan.

The rowboat's exterior was painted white, with the aqua interior paint cracking in fine lines. It had weathered wooden seats. Pretty much everything was still the same since before his grandmother was a child. Something about the old, well-kept "toys" his grandmother left on the island made it feel like home to him. It was another way to connect the generations.

They even all learned to sail on his beloved sailboat. His family took out larger craft on the Chesapeake Bay when they went sailing there on weekends, but this felt like it was his. A piece of his heart stayed behind every time they left, not that he would tell anyone else his mind conjured such sentimental notions.

In the rowboat, Colin found Andi lying on her back on the bottom, towel under head, and knees resting across one of the seats. She had a book held in front of her, blocking the sun while she read.

"Avoiding me?" Colin asked, getting straight to the point as he jumped into the boat, rocking it where it sat on the ground, and dropped to the back bench. He plucked the book from her hand.

"Hey, I'm reading that!" Andi protested, grabbing for the book.

Colin held the book out of reach. "I'll give it back—if you tell me why you didn't tell me what you were doing the other night."

Andi felt the air leave her chest. "I wanted something for me, okay?"

"You could have told me."

"Then it would have been for you too."

"I didn't have to go, just know what you were doing, in case something happened."

"Yeah, right. Then you'd be grounded too." Andi laughed without humor.

Colin considered it. "Yeah. I guess." He handed her book back.

"I learned one thing—I don't like beer." Andi grimaced. "And that my parents are cooler than I thought."

Colin laughed and jumped out of the boat. "Race you to the raft!" He peeled off his T-shirt and threw it in the boat. She jumped up, book forgotten, and peeled off her own shirt and then shorts. While Colin gave her a chance by running through the water from the beach and then swimming, Andi ran down the dock and dove in a clean slice.

In the cottage, the twins found Donovan eating a snack with Savannah and Harmony. They sat down for their own and waited for Sage to take the other two girls to the lake. Harmony, in particular, was restless and ready to go. She was so excited to be able to swim without her floaties, though her mother stayed close, as mothers tend to do. The smallest cousin thought it was great fun to toddle to the end of the dock and jump in with no warning, which made her mother's heart jump to her throat every time.

"Van, wait 'til we're finished," Cassie said as the others made for the kitchen door.

"What are you two up to?" Sage asked, well, sagely. She stared hard at the twins who were trying hard to remain nonchalant. While Cassie pulled it off, Grace looked nervous.

"Nothing. We'll be down with Van soon, after we finish eating," Cassie assured her aunt.

"Okay, but don't get into trouble. No using the stove or anything like that, promise?"

"Promise," Grace said, glad their aunt didn't press.

Once alone, Grace said, "So, Van, would you like to join a club with us?"

"What kind of club?" Van asked, paying more attention to his peanut butter and jelly than to the two girls.

The twins looked at one another and Grace nodded to Cassie. Cassie said, "Well, you know our dad died last year, right?"

"Yeah," Van said slowly, now paying more attention to them.

"Well, we found out there are other kids like us, you know, who know how we feel," Grace continued cautiously. Maybe Colin was right, and this wasn't such a good idea.

Van piped up and said, "My dad is dead now. But he wasn't nice. Your dad was nice. When he was alive, he did stuff with you guys. I bet you're all sad." Van looked back at his sandwich and then said in a voice so quiet they had a hard time hearing him, "I'm not sad. Does that make me bad?"

"No!" Cassie responded first, eyes huge with surprise. "You're not bad at all! We all love you!"

Van considered this and then smiled. "I love you guys too." Getting serious again, he said, "I didn't like my dad. Mommy says he's in heaven now where he can be happy, but I don't think he's good enough to go to heaven. I don't want to see him there."

Grace knew it; they were in too deep, but now they couldn't stop. "Well, if he's there, our dad's there and he would never let him hurt anyone we love."

"Really? I liked James, a lot."

"Us too," Grace said, close to tears now.

Cassie elbowed her sister. "Now back to the club. Since your dad is dead too, you can join the Dead Dads Club with us. It's just for people like us with dead dads. We can talk to each other, and we never let anyone else feel sorry for us."

"You'd let me join?"

"Yes."

"Okay." Van shrugged and smiled. "I like that. Does that mean you'll keep in touch even when you go back to where you live."

"Yes, we promise. We can video call on your mom's laptop until you're old enough to get a phone and text us," Grace suggested. She held out her pinkie, as did her sister, and Donovan used his own two pinkies, both sufficiently sticky with peanut butter and jelly, to link small fingers with his cousins. They all laughed and licked off the stickiness, back to kicking their feet on the bench that went with the table and eating their sandwich snack.

*Good job, Gracie.* Grace smiled even broader as she heard her dad's voice in her head. She asked him in her head, thinking telepathic communication would be kind of fun, to make sure Van's dad was not allowed to hurt anyone, if he was even there at all. She heard his resonant voice again. *I've got this, baby girl.* Grace sighed contentedly; it was the same thing she had heard him say time and again. She didn't know what she'd do when she couldn't remember what his voice sounded like, but then quickly pushed that thought away. It was too much to imagine.

Gavin popped into the kitchen. He'd had his own time alone in the treehouse that morning and was now ready for company.

"Anybody want to swim or take the rowboat out?" he asked.

"Yes!" Donovan yelled, hoping he would be allowed to go.

"K. But wash your hands. No sticky mess in the boat." Gavin grimaced and pointed toward the sink. He picked up the crusts to throw away in the woods, far away from the kitchen.

The next few days passed as summer days should: innocent fun, quiet time in the cottage, hot dogs and s'mores roasted on sticks in the firepit, games in the evenings, Franklin stove burning when the nights were cool. Colin even got his wish for sunset sails, his cousins and grandmother as his crew. Lazy days and cozy nights. The island magic wrapped them in its enchantment.

When Maitland texted that Mark's car had been released and his ashes were ready, Tory wouldn't let even that news bring her down. She was another step closer to her new life, leaving the old one in the dust. Her dad assured her Mark's brother had no desire to hold a service; she had expected as much—they'd been estranged.

Tory asked her father to get copies of the death certificate and sell the car. She didn't want to see it ever again—one more lavish lie that spoke to the wealth her late husband wanted to flaunt to the world, even though he didn't have it.

Maitland suggested he could put the ashes in the trash can and be done with it. Tory told him she'd pick them up and figure it out. Throwing the ashes in the trash was a step too brutal, even though he may have deserved it.

"I'll pick up the ashes when we come to town to clean my stuff and Van's out of the house tomorrow," she told her father. Harper and Lauren volunteered to watch the kids while she, Charlie, Aimee, and Sage quickly gathered the things she wanted. Her father said he'd leave boxes for them on her porch, along with the ashes.

Tomorrow she would take the next step. She would not break down when they got to the house. She would not freeze in terror, remembering the horrors she'd suffered within those walls. She would stick by these resolutions and be strong in front of the other women—and, really, for herself. He did not deserve one more ounce of tears or one more shudder of fear.

Resolved, she was jolted out of her head by the kicks in her abdomen. She could feel actual kicks from the babies, beyond the fairy-wing flutters. One more joy to celebrate and wipe away another on the bad register she kept like an inventory in her head. She hoped to eventually wipe out everything on the bad register, replaced with good and joy.

Lauren sat closest. Tory grabbed the surprised young woman's hand and placed it over her belly.

Lauren's eyes rounded. "They're kicking! Either that or you've got bad indigestion."

## 35

Tory rose early. Only her aunt was awake. The signs that the sun was contemplating climbing over the horizon were barely visible in small streaks of light. The sooner this day was done, the sooner she would never set foot in that house again. It was never a home, never that.

Alex sat on the bench seat of the screened-in porch, her sketchpad abandoned beside her. In her hands she held some sort of child's craft project.

"What's that?" Tory asked on her way to get the herbal tea that her babies seemed to like in the morning. Alex was lost in thought, surprised that someone stood in front of her.

"I was searching for paint tubes that fell out in the storage under the bench seat and found this under some very old magazines. My grandmother and I used to make these on rainy days," she said in an awed voice, holding up the project. Her grandmother had kept them.

One was a rectangular, light green, cardboard tray, the sides curved up. Inside was a scene of a flower, trees, and sun, made of different types of pasta glued to the colored tray. The other was a similar scene, but of what looked a lot like the cottage, on a purple tray.

"This is what grapes used to come on," Alex told her niece. "Green grapes on the green tray and purple grapes on the purple tray. I didn't like the purple grapes because they all had seeds back then. I remember my grandfather showing me how I could spit the seeds across the ground outside and see how far I could do it. He suggested contests with my brothers; I always tried to beat them. But I still didn't like the purple ones. Funny what memories a single object can dredge up, huh?" Alex shook her head, trying to ground in the present. "I can't believe these lasted all these years at the bottom of this bench. I still remember the day we made these two. My grandmother and I were here by ourselves. It was raining."

"This looks like something the kids would like to do. We may not have grape trays anymore, but I bet we can bring back some cardboard with us that would do the trick," Tory said. She was amazed the glue still stuck after what had to be more than fifty years. Only one piece of pasta floated loosely on the tray.

Alex nodded, and Tory noticed the sheen in the older woman's eyes. This time the tears that welled were sweet; at least she thought they were.

"I'll get us tea, and you can tell me more about what you and my great-grandmother did when you came to this special place," Tory said, moving toward the kitchen, happy to be the one doing the fetching instead of being waited on.

She listened as Alex told her about her childhood and why this island was her haven. So much of it sounded the same as what her generation and the children today experienced firsthand. Once again, she was amazed by the enchantment of the place. Maybe all that fresh water surrounding them kept the world away, if only for a weekend or a summer.

It was not long before Charlie, Aimee, and Sage were ready to go face Tory's demons.

The house looked innocent enough from the driveway. The perfectly symmetrical building stood tall and straight. She preferred asymmetry, but Mark liked the aesthetic. The white siding and black trim stood out starkly against the green of the trees and bushes. The front porch really wasn't wide enough for comfortable rocking or sitting and conversing, another nod to perception rather than function. The faux stone that clung to the house for four feet up on the front always annoyed her. She liked real fieldstone, but this was imitation, meant to be admired from the curb. The front door was oversized and double, designed to lull visitors into thinking what it opened to inside was ostentatious, belying wealth.

She supposed this was what money-types did. "Look at my house, my car, my watch ... I'm beyond wealthy, and I can do that for you too..." She shuddered. Never again.

Tory pushed the garage door opener and was relieved her father had done as she asked. Mark's car was nowhere in sight. Charlie pulled into the triple-wide driveway behind her. All four women exited the vehicles and waited while Tory took a deep breath and collected herself, steeling to the onslaught of emotions she expected.

"Let's do this," she said and took deliberate steps toward the front porch. One foot in front of the other, like a runway model. The boxes were there, along with the packing tape and boxes of packing paper. Leaning against the wall beside the door was an unobtrusive, rectangular, plain, pine box, slightly smaller than a bread box. She realized with a start that it must be the urn. Leave it to her father to have picked the typical pine box. Well, he was right. Expensive urns were ridiculous when the ashes were only going to be scattered to the wind.

Charlie took the keys and unlocked the front door, pushing in first, as if she could dispel the demons before Tory stepped into the room. Tory was surprised when both feet stood in the expansive entryway. No demons attacked her. Mark's voice didn't scream in her head. All she noticed was the stale air, but even that wasn't so bad since the air conditioning had been left on. Mark had obviously been here since she left on that last day of kindergarten, the air conditioning and the hint of his aftershave in the air her clues.

Her cousins got busy building and taping some of the boxes, ready to pack her things in them. "I wasn't going to, but can you pack my pots and pans and baking dishes? They're under the stove and in the cupboard next to the oven. I like those."

"What about the table services and utensils?" Aimee asked.

"Nope. He picked them. I hate them. Oh wait, the pasta bowl and individual-serving dishes that match it—I bought those; I want them. They're in the back of the bottom cupboard next to the fridge. I also want to take the Waterford crystal from the hutch in the dining room," Tory continued, pointing toward the dining room. "That was mostly from my mother and grandmother."

Aimee and Sage grabbed boxes and packing paper and got to work on those few things Tory mentioned.

Tory headed to the bedroom, Charlie tagging closely behind.

With a quick look around the room and a deep breath, Tory began pulling sweaters, jeans, a few work outfits she had picked herself but never wore, boots, and shoes, and placed them on the bed where Charlie packed them into the suitcases she found in the closet. Everything else stayed in the closet or drawers. She almost gagged when she looked at the silky lingerie in her dresser, but then pulled out the ones that had gone unworn and threw them in a suitcase with her underwear and flannel pajamas.

She added her jewelry box to the bed, along with four quilts her great-great-grandmother had created, and she'd kept hidden on a closet shelf. While in the closet, she grabbed the fireproof lockbox that held all the important papers she might need. She lifted the two pieces of black and white photographic artwork she had chosen from the walls. The rest was modern art chosen by her dead husband and would never see the inside of wherever she ended up.

On the trip to the living room, she vaguely noticed Sage and Aimee packing up Donovan's room. It was so bright and cheery, primary colors in bright blues and reds and yellows accenting the room, nothing like the reality they had lived through. They figured she would want most of that so the boy would feel at home at his grandparents and when they had their own home again.

Tory did the same thing in the living room, taking only her

artwork and the pictures of Donovan. She debated leaving the family photo album but threw it in the box at the last minute with the albums from her childhood. Maybe someday her babies would want to know what their sperm donor looked like.

She sat back at that thought—it was the first time she thought of him as merely a sperm donor. She took the CDs that were her choices, even though most of her music was now digital. She also took the small unit that played satellite radio, CDs, and cassette tapes. Who knows? She might come across some of her mixed tapes from high school sometime. That was back when Mark took the time to create the tapes for her and she still thought he was sweet. A time she thought she was in love.

*No. No tears,* she admonished herself.

The women made short work of what could have been a long, dreary day. Tory stuck to taking only the few things on which she had decided.

"Only things left are my dad's tools—they're in the toolbox in the garage. I'll need those someday. Oh, and there's one box of Christmas ornaments out there I want because they came from my mom and grandma." Tory looked around, satisfied with her decisions.

They added the pieces she wanted from the garage to the small collection of suitcases and the few boxes that sat in the living room, *Fragile* marked carefully on the box of crystal wine, whiskey, and martini glasses and matching decanters, along with a couple of Waterford bowls and vases.

When they opened the front door, Maitland was poised to walk in. "Look who I found driving by." He motioned behind him to Sheriff Kevin Clarke, this time out of the brown uniform. "He's going to help me haul what you're keeping to my truck."

"Afternoon, ladies," the sheriff said, picking up the closest box, then looking around skeptically. "Are you sure this is all you're taking?"

"Yes," Tory said adamantly.

"All right then. This won't take long," the sheriff said. Each of the women, except Tory, who they wouldn't let lift anything, helped carry and made the work even shorter.

"What about everything else?" Kevin asked, her cousins wondering the same thing.

"I don't care. Give it to charity. Burn it. Sell it. As long as I never see it again," Tory said, a stubborn set to her jaw.

"We can see what the homebuilding charity in town can use. They could sell the clothes in their shop too, I bet," Kevin suggested to Maitland. The older man agreed. Tory had studiously avoided Mark's side of the closet.

The rest the charity didn't want, they would leave to a home belongings or junk buyer who would offer a price for everything that remained, though Kevin doubted there would be much left for anyone to buy.

"As soon as it's all out, we can get it staged and on the market," Maitland said, surprised at the ease of what could have been a traumatic experience. What he would come to understand was his daughter was done with trauma and drama.

After everything she wanted was out, Tory took one last look at the gleaming hardwood floors, the expertly painted walls, the furniture meant for a showroom rather than comfort, the kitchen with all the modern conveniences and more, then backed out the door. She handed her dad the keys and walked with her head held high to her vehicle.

Kevin watched in admiration; he wished his mother had had half as much determination as this woman.

Charlie followed, her cousin's dead husband in her arms. "Hey, what are we going to do with the remains? Should we scatter them behind the boat at the lake?"

Kevin and Maitland were both about to say that sounded like a good idea—quick and easy, and it *was* where he died.

Both were glad they hadn't voiced their agreement when Tory stated vehemently, "No! We are not going to pollute our family's special place with his toxicity! I'll figure something out. Soon.

Because I am not sleeping in a room with that thing." She waggled her hand at the box.

"Well, thank God for that, considering I'm sleeping in that same room," Charlie snarked. She settled the box onto the floor of the back passenger seat.

"Thanks for helping," Tory called out to her dad and Kevin as she shut the door and started her vehicle. As an afterthought, she rolled down the window and tossed her dad the garage door opener clipped to her sun visor. "The realtor will need this."

Then the two vehicles with the female cousins rolled out of the driveway and stopped at the local diner for a late lunch.

"Seriously, what are we going to do with the ashes?" Charlie whispered when the four were seated in a booth at the old-styled diner with red vinyl seats, Formica tabletops, and non-working miniature jukeboxes at each table.

"Well, I have an idea, but I don't think you're going to like it," Tory said. They all waited for her to explain. She rolled her eyes and told them her plan.

"The last place, and maybe the *only* place, Mark was ever happy —and a time I was happy with him—was on the football field. High school and college. I was thinking about scattering them on the high school football field. It's close and holds only happy memories. College was where he blew out his knee, and it's too far away anyway."

The other three stared bug-eyed. Aimee recovered first and whispered tersely, "Are you crazy? They won't let you scatter human remains on the football field!"

"Well, I wasn't going to ask!" Tory shot back, whisper shouting.

A slow grin spread over Charlie's face. "Yeah. This could work."

"Now you've lost your mind too!" Aimee spit out, whisper shouting back.

"No, listen, it's just a box of ashes. You know 'ashes to ashes, dust to dust' and all that. It's basically dirt." Still whispering, Charlie grinned brightly. "We can leave the island tonight after dark, sneak onto the field when no one's there, and voila! No one has to sleep with remains tonight. Yes! We're going to do it!" Charlie warmed even more to the idea and rubbed her hands together in a manner reminiscent of a movie villain.

"We could get arrested," Aimee insisted in an adamant whisper.

"For what? Trespassing on public school grounds?" Charlie asked, still whispering.

"I don't know! There must be a law against spreading human remains," Aimee whisper argued.

"Ashes!" the other three women whisper yelled back.

Aimee threw her hands in the air. "Fine. I'm in. But don't tell Andrew; he may have to bail us out."

The four women touched their water glasses in "cheers," then Charlie held out her pinkie finger and they all solemnly joined pinkies, forming a pinkie swear circle and sealed their deal. They giggled. Tonight was the night they would be rid of Mark Wright forever. Tory was even being sweet and picked a place he'd been happy.

When they rose to leave after burgers, fries, and the chocolate malts that marked their childhood, they saw the sheriff, still in his jeans and T-shirt, in the booth behind them munching on his own burger.

"When did you sneak in?" Charlie asked suspiciously, the other women blanching.

"I didn't sneak. I was hungry," Kevin reasoned.

"Why didn't you join us?" Charlie asked.

"You didn't notice me while you were busy conspiring."

"We weren't conspiring!" Aimee protested.

The sheriff shrugged. "Well, whatever it was you were whispering about and all pinkie swearing to. I remember when you used to do that as kids. Must be some serious stuff."

Charlie wondered if he was purposely trying to bait them or if he really hadn't heard what they talked about. They were whispering, after all, she analyzed.

"Just typical cousin stuff. It's not often we're away from all the kids," Sage said, sounding perfectly reasonable.

Kevin smiled and nodded. "Be careful driving back to the lake."

"Will do. Thanks again for earlier, Kevin," Tory said brightly and pulled her cousins toward the door. Nothing or no one was going to rain on her parade today.

# 36

The kids waved excitedly when the women returned to the island. They sat through the late afternoon diving contests, swimming races, and paddle board wars until it was time to go to the cottage for supper.

Clouds were starting to blow in from the west and the wind picked up. Now, if only the rain held off until they could complete their mission. They thought the sun would never set. One of the perks—and tonight a drawback—of being so far north was the summer light lasted well into the night. Now that it was August, the days were a little shorter and nights a little longer, though the real change would be noticeable in late September.

Nonchalantly, after most of the kids were settled in the bunk rooms and the few others gathered in the living area, Aimee made sure Lauren and Harper were willing to keep an eye on the kids for a few hours while the other women took the boat out for a night ride. They didn't need to know the "ride" was only to the shoreside dock and back after their mission was complete. Alex had been noticeably absent since they finished eating; they assumed she was taking time alone in her bedroom—they could see the glow from the bedside lamp under the door.

"Why are you all dressed that way?" Colin asked, glancing up when the women entered the living room.

They stared at one another and burst into laughter. They all had on either black jeans or black leggings and black sweatshirts. "We might get cold on the water. We're going to be out for a long time," Charlie answered her son, not exactly lying.

Colin narrowed his eyes but shook his head and went back to his book.

They picked their way carefully down the path. No one wanted to trip on a tree root or pine cone before they completed their mission. The night was much like the one when Mark died; the moon shone brightly but then was covered by clouds. The wind was still high, but no rain had blown in yet.

"You might need these." Alex stepped from behind the boathouse, arm outstretched. The four women jumped, startled.

"Mom! I almost peed my pants!" Aimee shrieked.

"Maybe you should have gone to the bathroom before you left the cottage," Alex said wryly, in perfect imitation of their childhood road trips.

The women gathered around the matriarch to see what she was holding. She handed each of them a black knit beanie, then pulled one over her own curly hair, much whiter than at the beginning of the summer. Three of the four had blonde hair that was all too noticeable in the moonlight. The hats were a good idea.

"Uh, what are you doing?" Charlie asked carefully. She noticed the older woman's black jeans and black sweater. And were those black combat boots?

"Coming with you."

"Mom, no! We're probably going to have to scale a wall or climb over a fence or something," Aimee protested. "Wait! How do you know where we're going?"

Alex tsked with her tongue. "Aimee, you should know by now that 'whisper shouting' is not really a thing. I heard you talking since you got back. I figured it out."

"Oh," Aimee said, chagrined. "You're still not coming."

"In the words of your dear children, 'you're not the boss of me.'" Then she reached behind the boathouse and pulled out a portable, folding ladder and handed it to Charlie. "I wasn't sure if we'd need this or if a step stool would do. But I think this is better than a step stool, depending on the height of the fence. It might be hard for a pregnant woman to get over a fence." She indicated toward Tory, and the others felt silly for not thinking of that themselves.

All four women stared at her with mouths open. Charlie recovered first, a small smile creeping across her lips. Her mother was the definition of classy badass.

"Are you coming or not? We want to beat the rain," Alex said and walked to the dock, stepping into the ski boat. They scurried behind her. Fully in charge, no one questioned her authority, and she drove the ski boat to the southern shore where all the vehicles were parked.

Internally, she thought, *well fake it 'til you make it worked again*— she hadn't expected them to give in so easily to her participation. Charlie, yes, the others, no. Charlie always did see her mother as a formidable equal; she sometimes thought the others only saw an aging woman who had lost two husbands. Charlie was correct; she was formidable and would be until the day she left this earth.

They used Charlie's larger vehicle and drove toward the high school. Alex quickly texted *Rabbits on the loose* and immediately felt silly with the code. But "rabbits" did sound better than "cats," neither of which could be herded, much like the women in her family.

She quickly received a response: *Copy. Path cleared.*

Smiling to herself, she tucked the phone in her pocket.

Once at the school, Charlie pulled off the road onto the long drive and turned off her lights. "Why won't all the lights go off?" she groused. "Ugh! These new vehicles!" She had to be satisfied with the dimmer lights in place of the bright headlights, happier when they parked, and she turned the vehicle off all together. She carried the ladder up the slight incline to the high school football field.

Sage ran ahead and tried the gate at the end of the drive the school used to move equipment, supply the snack shack, and on which the marching band approached the field on game nights. It was padlocked. "Well, unless you have bolt cutters, we have to climb or find another way."

"We're not *breaking*, only entering," Aimee hissed.

"Come on, the fence used to be lower over here," Tory called. She was glad the night hid the embarrassment that rose to her cheeks as she remembered sneaking out here with Mark during high school. She was well-acquainted with under the bleachers, behind the snack shack, and even the press box. Mentally she pushed those memories to the recesses of her mind and looked for the best place to get inside the field.

"When did they add such a high fence behind the bleachers? There's nothing back there except the woods," Aimee groused.

"Probably when kids found it was a good way to sneak in," Charlie said.

Tory really had not thought this through enough. With her pregnant belly, climbing the fence would be difficult, but getting down on the other side would be even harder. She hoped her aunt's foresight with the ladder would help.

"Here! Over here!" Sage called, whisper yelling again, which, in this case, was yelling. She found a line of fence that came to her chest. It faced the school and was out in the open, but this late, in the dark, no one in the building, they should be able to get over the fence, complete the mission, and get out unnoticed.

"Let me go first," Sage said, swinging her legs to the top of the fence, touching briefly, and dropping on the other side.

"I forgot you used to run hurdles," Aimee said, impressed.

"Yeah, when we stayed in one place long enough for me to make the team," Sage said, involuntarily cringing when she remembered her disruptive childhood. "I think this is more from William teaching me to run the obstacle course with him."

"Oh, there is that," Aimee agreed, nodding wildly. She helped Charlie unfold and stabilize the ladder.

In the meantime, Alex had a toe in the chain link fencing, climbing more gingerly to the top, hoping there weren't any sharp bits sticking up like the one on which she had sliced her hand open when she was a kid sneaking in behind one of her brothers and his date. She still cringed when she thought of the stitches and tetanus shot. She remembered her brother glowering at her in the emergency room for interrupting his date—the girl long gone—and her father laughing at her antics, her mother simply holding her other hand.

Aimee noticed her mother climbing. "Mom! Stop! Wait for the ladder!"

"I'm fine." Alex dismissed her. At the top she realized she should really have waited for the ladder but was not giving in now. She swung her leg over the top and stuffed her booted foot into a toehold to carefully step to the ground. There, no undo impact to her knees, no embarrassing falls. She was pleased with herself.

"I think I can do it like Alex," Tory said, studying the fence.

"Just use the ladder to get up and when you come down the other side we'll catch you," Charlie insisted.

"You'll catch me?! Yeah, right." Tory laughed. Charlie went before her and dropped to the ground, ready to help on the other side. Aimee held the ladder still. Tory still thought her aunt had the right idea. Once up the ladder, she gingerly reached her foot to the other side and grabbed a toe hold, then carefully moved her hands to the top, and stepped down one more toehold before dropping the shorter distance. Sage and Charlie were there to catch her, though she was off balance, and they all fell, the other two cushioning her fall with their bodies.

"Oomph," Tory huffed and then burst out laughing as she rolled to a sitting position on the short-clipped grass.

"Dang, you're heavier than you look," Sage said through her laughter.

"Uh, guys, forget something?" Aimee asked from the other side of the fence. She picked up the pine box urn, forgotten against the fence.

Tory's eyes went wide, "Oh wow. Yeah, seriousness now. Remember why we're here."

"Yeah, to get rid of the son of a bitch," Charlie muttered. Her mother sent her a withering glance. Charlie reached up and took the pine box.

"Hard to believe a whole person is reduced to this," Charlie mused, lightly shaking the box.

Aimee climbed over. The five women looked around, their eyes accustomed to the darkness, assessing where the best place would be to complete their mission. Their noses wrinkled at the strong smell of the fertilizer someone had covered the field with to make the natural turf grow evenly.

As the moon came out from behind a heavy cloud, the wind picked up, and Tory pointed to the fifty-yard line. "Let's start there and scatter all the way to the end zone."

"You're giving him a final touchdown?" Charlie asked, following her logic.

Defensively, Tory shrugged, chin held high. "Why not?"

Charlie replied, "Not criticizing, just noting the symbolism. Cool with me."

While the younger women chatted and figured out logistics, Alex felt her pocket vibrate. She turned her back and read the text: *Make sure stand upwind.*

Well, that was good advice. She responded: *Copy that.*

At the center of the fifty-yard line, Charlie set the pine box on the ground and unclipped the top. She was surprised the inside held a heavy, clear plastic bag with a twisty keeping it closed. "Well, that would have been good to know. I've been worried about spilling it all day."

Sage giggled, which started the others. When they had calmed down, Charlie carefully lifted the bag and untwisted the tie, hefting the bag in the crook of her arm. "How are we going to do this?"

"Let's just shake it out as we walk," Sage suggested, not wanting to touch the ashes.

Alex felt the wind on her face and pointed. "You need to turn to the other side, so the wind doesn't blow at us."

"Ewww. Yeah," Charlie and Tory said at the same time as they both realized what Alex had just implied. The women all quickly turned, Aimee and Sage slightly behind the others.

"Should someone say something?" Sage asked, not knowing the propriety of scattering ashes in the middle of the night on a dark, empty football field.

"I don't know." Tory hesitated. Then she said simply, "We brought you where you were happy. Please rest in peace and leave us in peace."

Charlie added, "Ashes to ashes, dust to dust, this was hallowed ground for you, made more hallowed by the ashes we leave to enrich the field of play." When Aimee stared at her like she was nuts, Charlie merely shrugged.

Charlie and Tory both held the bag and began scattering the ashes into the wind as they quickly walked the fifty yards to the end zone. Once there, they flung the ashes that remained and took a symbolic knee. That seemed enough. No bad karma would be coming their way for messing with remains, even the ashes type. They were all silent, stayed in place for a few beats before folding the plastic bag and collecting the pine box as they moved as one back to the fence. Getting back over was less fun, the energy gone from the air.

"Can't we leave the pine box on the field? People could wonder what it's about, you know, like Stonehenge," Charlie suggested.

"No!" Aimee screeched. "Someone would recognize the box as the one Uncle Mait bought."

"Oh," Charlie said, disappointed. The two of them reached over the fence and brought the ladder to their side. Once everyone was on the other side, they grabbed the ladder once again, pulled it over the top, and folded it until portable.

Tory felt the heaviness inside lift as the wind picked up and swirled around them. They glanced back and watched as the dust—probably the remains—was picked up from the ground, churned in the air, and flung outward. "Let's go," she said, hustling her family back toward the vehicle. The path back was a little harder because the moon was gone. They could smell the rain in the air, and the skies opened as they slammed the doors shut once inside Charlie's SUV.

"Well, that was good timing!" Sage said, pulling the beanie from her head and shaking out her long, naturally bleached-blonde hair.

"How do you feel?" Alex asked Tory.

"Good. I think. More peaceful." Tory stared out the window, looking back toward the football field.

The others started talking animatedly, the adrenaline high from pulling it off successfully.

Alex felt her pocket vibrate again. She surreptitiously glanced at the message: *Good job.* She stuffed the phone back in her pocket. Sitting in the third row by herself, she looked behind her and thought she saw a pickup truck move onto the roadway from the trees next to the field and head the opposite direction. She smiled. He was a good guy, even if he hid it well.

In the pickup, Sheriff Kevin Clarke drove toward home. His heart returned to its normal rate. For a long minute he thought he was going to have to lift Tory over the fence, so she didn't hurt herself or the babies. When he called Alex earlier to tell her what he overheard in the diner, he hoped she would make sure the operation went smoothly.

For his part, he had sent the usual patrol cars to other parts of the county for the couple hours surrounding the women's caper. Now he could breathe easy. No one would be the wiser; besides, what did it hurt anyway? As Charlie said, ashes to ashes. He would have been happy putting the pine box in a dumpster, as Maitland originally suggested, but Tory being Tory, she just couldn't be that heartless. He was okay with that.

## 37

"**G**randma," Cameron called to the matriarch from where he sat at the kitchen table. She turned on her stool at the counter and raised her eyebrows in the universal "what's up?" look.

"It's done," he said proudly.

"Your movie?"

"Yeah. I just finished the last edits Maddie suggested," he said excitedly. He smiled a lot more now than he had at the beginning of the summer. His brown hair, in need of a cut, flopped over his eye, just like his father's, and the sides reached his shoulders, unlike his father's.

"You like Maddie." Alex patiently returned his smile.

"She's awesome. She knows everybody in the movie business!" Cameron gushed. Then, shyly, he asked, "Do you want to see it before everyone else?"

"Do you want me to? Or do you want to have a big reveal on the television screen tonight after we eat?"

Cameron raised his thumb and index finger to his lip, staring at the laptop, as he thought through the merits of both. "I'll let you wait with everyone else. You're sure they'll want to watch it?"

"I'm positive. This is a big deal, Cam. Everyone is in it, right?" she decided to doublecheck. You never knew when someone would fall out with someone else and purposely leave that person out.

"Yeah, everyone," Cam confirmed. "Okay, I'm going to go swimming. Want to come?"

"Sure," Alex said and rinsed her mug in the sink before following the boy to the waterfront. She was shocked when he threw his T-shirt on the beach, ran off the end of the dock, and did a cannonball. Normally they had to cajole him to get in the water. Not now. He was acting like any of the other kids. She followed his example and did her own cannonball, even though her preference was to slowly let her body acclimate to the colder temperature of the water. They both swam to the raft, Cameron arriving before his grandmother.

They watched from the raft, water dripping from their bodies, as Charlie spun by with Sage on skis. Jaspar and Gavin were in the boat yelling encouragement, waiting for their turns, while Aimee spotted.

Later in the afternoon, with everyone back on shore or swimming, Jaspar and Donovan came out of the boathouse with fishing poles over their shoulders. "We thought we'd catch dinner tonight," Jaspar announced, grinning widely.

"No!" Charlie, Sage, and Aimee yelled at the same time.

The boy jumped back; the smile left his face.

"Sorry, Jaspar. We shouldn't eat fish from the lake right now. Just catch and release, okay?" Alex said smoothly.

"Why?" Donovan asked.

"The smell of fish cooking will make me sick right now," Tory said, scrambling for an excuse. "Pregnancy does that."

"Oh, makes sense." Jaspar shrugged. The two boys wandered beyond the beach where the reeds grew and looked for a space where the trees cleared so they could cast without interference.

The women laughed, releasing nervous tension. The other kids looked at one another and shook their heads, assuming the women had lost it, something they suspected often, as kids do when they watch adults.

The afternoon and evening could not pass fast enough for

Cameron. He waited nervously to show his masterpiece to the family, slightly worried his cousins would make fun of him. When the time came, they all gathered in the living room, Aimee and Sage passing out bowls of popcorn and water bottles. Cameron had set up the feed from laptop to television earlier. All he had to do was press *Play*.

He debated whether to say anything and instead, decided to let his work speak for itself. The opening credits listed it as a *Cameron Dumont production, Maddie Owen as executive producer*, the title simply listed as *Home for the Summer*. The entire family grew silent as the early scenes unfolded, first with a shot of the island from the shore to set the context for the movie, then scenes of the family playing in the water, swimming, racing, sailing, kayaking, skiing, having paddle board wars, fishing. They watched shots of Van and Harmony learning to swim confidently, the pirate bottle opener guarding the kitchen, Aimee cooking, and Sage being so gentle and patient with all the children.

The soundtrack mixed a summer music jam with the natural flow of the conversation in the scenes. He even included the footage Andi captured when Colin rescued him from drowning. The happy sounds and low tones that greeted new baby Allie when she arrived on island, Lauren's impassioned monologue at dinner, the treehouse renovation from broken down to work of art, Alex griping she wouldn't use the single-serving contraption in the kitchen with the kettle whistling and steaming in the background, squirrels and raccoons destroying the kitchen, Van talking to his mother's belly, the sheriff smiling with the family at the barbeque, games in the living room, various cousins reading in the rocking chair, rain pouring down, the lake choppy and trees bending in the wind—all tastefully shot and narrated with actual conversation. The night scenes were brilliant and moody, the moon shining on the choppy water, the firepit, nights with s'mores or hotdogs, rowdy dinners around the extra-large kitchen table, Gavin snoring and talking in his sleep in the treehouse—courtesy of his big brother. The final shot was of Alex, unaware she was being recorded, sketching in her pad, her easel and latest painting next to her, mouth set in a firm and determined line.

Then the final shot ended with the old cinematic circle, reminiscent of silent movies in the 1920s, getting smaller and smaller around the scene and then fading to black.

The final words popped up: *The End...for now*. Final credits rolled: *Cameron Dumont, director and editor, Maddie Owens as executive producer and creative consultant*, and *the women and children of the Newberry clan as themselves*.

Silence reigned supreme as the movie ended. No one said a word or even looked away from the now black screen, and Cameron worried he blew it. Then Colin began clapping. Everyone clapped, loudly, and then the cheering was overwhelming. Everyone was patting him on the back and hugging him. Several people were wiping their eyes.

Andi hugged him, something she rarely did, and whispered, "You did *so* good, Cam."

Aimee let her tears flow freely and praised her son. "Wow, Cam! Just wow. I can't wait for your dad to see this."

For once, Cameron did not feel on the outside looking in. He had a place in this family after all. Alex was amazed how well the project turned out and was more than happy she had suggested Cameron use the camera.

ONLY A FEW MORE WAKEUPS ON their island haven, the family spent the time left sharing the fun times, soaking up the sunshine, relishing the rain on the roof, playing games, eating good meals.

Lauren and Harper, who had to return to college, were the first off. Alex felt a momentary panic that Harper would be overwhelmed caring for baby Allie without all the support she'd had for the summer. Then she breathed in and hugged her chosen daughter goodbye, remembering they all had to make their own way.

"You're stronger than you think. But call if you need anything, even just to talk," Alex whispered in Harper's ear, then kissed Allie on the forehead.

"Thanks. For everything, Alex. I will," Harper whispered back and hugged the woman in a one-armed squeeze.

"Mom." Lauren breathed, tears in her eyes. The one word spoken with so much emotion, it almost made Alex cry.

"Go get 'em, firebrand. The world is waiting," Alex said with feeling to her youngest daughter.

"Mom." Lauren breathed again, hugging the woman tightly to her. "Thanks again for the car! I'll call when we get there." Earlier in the day, Maitland had delivered the small SUV Alex had bought for her daughter. She wanted Lauren to be mobile, especially if Alex decided to stay on the island for the winter. Lauren had no father to count on any longer.

"See you for Thanksgiving!" Harper waved as she adjusted the car seat in the backseat of the new vehicle. They'd already packed the rest of their bags and gear in the rear area. They pulled out of the gravel drive carefully, honking the whole way, ensuring the entirety of the lakeshore residents noted their departure. Alex waited to return to the island until she could no longer see the vehicle.

The firepit was stoked with logs that night, and they sat around roasting marshmallows. The firelight bounced off the trees in an eerie glow, creating shadows that made the smallest of the children crowd closer to the adults. Everyone seemed keenly aware the night was one of the last for their summer together.

"I don't want to go back to Virginia," Savannah whined. "I want to stay home."

"Newport is home, Savvy," Sage said, hugging her daughter's shoulders.

"No, it's not," she disagreed. "It's where we live in a house. It's not home. Home is with the rest of the family."

"Yeah, I agree," Grace said quietly, leaning into her grandmother's side from where they sat together on a log. Charlie felt a pang, the same pang she had felt all summer. She couldn't settle on what was best for her kids and her—stay in Northern Virginia or move to Michigan. She didn't want to upend Colin's high school years, particularly when he was doing so well academically and was enjoying both his hockey teams so much.

"We can come back for Thanksgiving," Charlie offered Grace.

"And Christmas?" Gavin asked, upping the ante.

"We could probably do that," Charlie agreed.

"We could do online school and live anywhere," Grace reminded her mother.

"So you've said," Charlie said.

"I like the idea of being with *all* of our family," Cassie said.

"If we were here, I could work with Aunt Aimee and Uncle Andrew when I'm old enough," Indy added.

Aimee beamed at the little girl. "And we'd love to have you."

"Not helping," Charlie whispered through her teeth. Her sister sent her an angelic look and batted her eyes, causing all the adults to laugh. Everyone knew Aimee's desire to get everyone in one town. They thought she would probably like it if they were all in the same house, or at least on the same street.

After the children went to bed, Sage confided in the others. "Maybe the kids and I should move here. They're happy. I'm happy. William can take his leave here until he decides to retire."

Aimee was shocked and tried not to get too excited. "Are you serious?"

Sage nodded, not completely settled with the idea. "I mean, William and I will have to talk it over more, but I brought it up the last time we video conferenced, and he thought it might be best for the kids to be closer to family, especially given how many months out of the year he has to be gone. His only other suggestion was to move closer to Charlie and the kids, but Northern Virginia is so much more expensive than Michigan."

Alex listened and tried not to sway any decisions with her own words or sentiment. She would be happy as long as her family was happy and secure.

"Ohhh, I love it when a plan comes together," Aimee squealed.

"It's not for certain yet. But if we're going to do it, we need to decide soon to get the kids enrolled in school," Sage said.

"The kids can stay here with me. Then you can go cancel your lease on your house, pack up, and get the movers," Aimee offered, knowing her sister-in-law and brother had chosen to rent a house in Norfolk since neither had wanted to buy in that area.

"We don't have anywhere to move to yet," Sage protested.

"Well, we can look. You'll need to decide if you want to rent or buy." Aimee continued her planning.

"You can stay in the house in town until you decide exactly what you want," Alex offered. "It's a big house, and there's plenty of room for all the kids."

"I don't want to invade your space," Sage said.

"You wouldn't be," Alex assured her daughter-in-law. "You forget, I grew up with multiple generations in one house. Besides, I'll be here at the island. I haven't decided what I'm going to do yet—where I'll call homebase." She saw Aimee glare at her but was thankful her middle daughter didn't try to argue with her choices for now.

"William was going to try to video conference tomorrow, so I'll see. I did check, and the hospital and several doctors' offices are looking for trained nurses, so I should be able to find a job." Sage smiled, relaxing now that she was closer to a decision. She never had somewhere she called home and longed for her children to have a more stable environment than her hippie parents provided her or than the moves military life had given her own children.

"You know, home is wherever family is, either your own unit or the broader family. That's what's important. Your parents moved you around, so you crave stability. My parents stayed in one place; I craved adventure. Now my own children seem to crave that hometown stability—Aimee's here; I know Charlie is worried about disrupting Colin; even you and William are trying to find stability despite the military life. Whatever you decide, your kids will eventually do their own thing. It's taken me this long to realize neither path is right; it's only deciding what's right for you," Alex said, taking a deep breath at the end of her statement.

"When did you get so wise?" Charlie teased, once again amazed that her mother hit the nail on the head.

"I've told you. It's always there, but we don't realize it until we're in our fifties!" Alex said then laughed.

Charlie remained silent, but she might consider moving in two years, the summer before Gavin began high school. Colin didn't know that she knew he hoped to graduate a year early and go directly into the Naval Academy—his guidance counselor let it slip at a conference in the spring. She was waiting for him to tell her. It was all contingent on whether he was accepted, and she couldn't see any reason he would not be. His father, uncle, and grandfather were graduates. His grades were stellar. He had extracurricular activities and was a top-notch ice hockey player—had been varsity since he was a freshman and played on a travel team with older kids. No, she'd keep her own counsel for now. Who knew what two years would bring?

Sage was stuck in her own thoughts again, feeling, possibly for the first time in her life, she could rely on people beside herself and William. This summer may have been about supporting Alex, but she could not deny it had changed her in ways she would not have imagined three months prior. They'd included her as if she was a full-blooded sister.

The next day it was decided. The kids would enroll in school and go with Aimee and Andrew until Sage could wrap up moving their household.

"Are you really going to stay here for the winter?" Colin asked his grandmother on their final sail of the summer, just the two of them.

"I haven't decided yet, but it appeals to me," Alex told her oldest grandson.

"Why?"

Alex thought for a minute before replying. Colin was quiet, waiting for her, not filling the space with idle chatter. "I'm not completely sure, but I like the idea of spending some time alone, getting my thoughts straight about how I want to live now that I'll step down from an active role in the company. I'm thinking about writing a book and I want to spend more time painting and drawing."

"You could be alone at your house in DC," Colin reminded her.

"And I'd be close enough to attend all your hockey games."

"Well, yeah, but that doesn't matter. But when I'm at the Naval Academy, I'll want you to come to watch me play—if I make the team." Colin qualified his statement, not wanting to sound too arrogant or to jinx himself.

"I have no doubt you'll make it, if that's what you want," Alex said. "I may stay here all winter and find I hate it; in that case, I'd never do it again. But at least I'd know."

"So, you want to test if the magic is only in the summer or if it's year-round," Colin said.

Alex sat up straighter at that insight. "I hadn't thought about it, but yes, my gut says that's exactly what I'm looking for!" More contemplative, she added, "And I feel really close to people I loved who are no longer with us when I'm here."

"Can you hear their voices?" Colin asked, thinking about how he heard his father's voice in his head, knowing it was probably his memory conjuring his father.

"Sometimes. Yes, I can. My grandmother and your grandpa Ian especially," Alex said. She thought it was interesting she was having this conversation with her fifteen-year-old grandson when she had not been able to have it with her own children. Maybe he was too young to be judgmental. Maybe he was an old soul. Maybe it was because he still admired his grandmother. Whatever it was, she could feel her decision settling inside her, all the way to her bones.

"You do realize Aunt Aimee is having visions of Uncle Mait having to call in a helicopter rescue to get to you because it's the only way off the island in the winter, unless the ice is frozen enough to walk across, and she says you won't do that." Colin smirked. His dirty-blonde hair blew in the wind, the type of wind she and her grandson loved for sailing.

"I figured as much. And no, I will *not* cross over on ice. Way too dangerous. Don't you ever do it either!" she admonished.

"I love you, Grandma. I'll miss you if you stay here all winter. But I get it," Colin said and then came about, the two sailing in silence until it was time to dock.

The summer came to an end. Sage, Aimee, Charlie, Tory, and their families all departed the same day. Hugs, spoken "I love yous," and shouts of "see you at Thanksgiving" were said over and over until the last of the four vehicles left their shoreside lot. Alex watched until the last car pulled out onto the road and was gone from view before taking the red wooden ski boat back to the island. She tied off and sat on the shore watching the last of the summer residents get in their skiing and fishing.

Her pocket buzzed with a text message. She smiled when she saw Charles LeBrandt's name on her screen.

Charles: Alone again?

Alex: Yep

Charles: Intervention?

Alex: No! I made it unscathed

Charles: Lucky you

Alex: Indeed

Charles: Deafened by the silence yet?

Alex: LOL. They just left!

Charles: It's why I asked (smiley face)

Alex: Suppose you're right. The longer they're gone the less deafening the silence

Charles: Now she understands

Alex: Don't you have to work?

Charles: Tonight

Charles: I'm thinking about retiring

Alex: You've been thinking about that for years

Charles: True. But you talking about this last "Act" got me thinking

Alex: Have you figured anything out?

Charles: I'll let you know. LOL

Alex: SMH (shaking my head, in case you aren't up on text acronyms)

Charles: Hey, did you give them your sketches?... Ignoring your dig that I'm old

Alex: I decided to wait. Maybe make a book for Christmas

**Charles: They're really excellent, at least the photos you shared. Maddie's right, you should plan an exhibit**

**Alex: I don't think I'm that good**

**Charles: Disagree**

**Alex: I'll think about it**

**Charles: LOL. I'll text in a couple days to see if you're stir crazy yet**

**Alex: I'll be here**

**Charles: See ya**

**Alex: Bye**

Alex moved up to the cottage to find something for lunch.

## 38

Alex felt particularly inspired, the lake around her quieter, nature closer, after the summer ended. The trees with leaves changed color, brilliant reds, yellows, oranges, and browns, which gave the island a different feel. She was glad the pines stayed green all year; it was comforting. She sketched more, the profiles of her family in various poses and activities, capturing the light and personality of each one of them.

She found more time to paint. The cityscapes took shape, with their bolder and darker colors, some even completely created in shades of gray. When she looked at them, she realized she was working out her anger, confusion, and frustration on the canvas. The scenes were clearly depicting her feeling of isolation in the city, her looking on as her late husband went about his life, a life from which he partially locked her out. She acknowledged the paintings were fraught with emotion. Anyone who knew her would sense she felt left out of the scenes she painted, an interloper spying on others' lives.

The juxtaposition with the city scenes compared to her canvases of the lake and landscapes, and sketches of her family, were stark. She represented pain and joy in her art. When she recognized it, she felt a hole inside her begin to heal, a hole she hadn't even realized was there. "Better than a damned intervention any day," she said out loud.

She pulled out her phone to text her friend Charles LeBrandt again and moved into the living area with the Franklin stove heating the room, the late fall wind now too strong and cold to sit comfortably on the screened-in porch.

Alex: You and Maddie may be right

Charles: Of course we are! LOL. What exactly are we right about?

Alex: Maybe I could do a gallery exhibit

Charles: Excellent!

Alex: I'd have to be vulnerable though. Exposed

Charles: And you hate that

Alex: Sigh. Yes

Charles: Nothing wrong with that, Alex, vulnerable is relatable

Alex: Sigh. Yes

Charles: LOL

Alex: You don't have to be so smug

Charles: Sure I do. It's not often I get the chance with you

Alex: Maybe I'll try writing the political thriller we've talked about for the last 10 years

Charles: The one Hank told you not to waste your time on?

Alex: Ouch. Yes

Charles: Sorry. I hated seeing you put yourself second with him

Alex: I didn't even realize I was doing it until now. I had a breakthrough looking at what I'd painted without thinking or planning what I was painting

Charles: Sounds promising. Can't wait to see these paintings

Alex: I'll send you pictures

Charles: Did you send the sketches to have the book created?

Alex: I did! Did you know you can do it all online and they'll send me all the copies so everyone can have one?

Charles: LOL No, but it doesn't surprise me

Alex: Maddie hooked me up with the place to do it

**Charles: Of course she did**

**Alex: I'm going to go think about writing now**

**Charles: Good luck**

**Alex: Talk soon**

**Charles: I'm here**

October turned to November and then on to December. She could smell winter in the air. Autumn had always been her favorite season and it was now gone.

Alex had plenty of wood stacked inside on the porch, and more under the lean-to at the side of the cottage. There was more than enough to last this winter and next, if not longer.

The pantry was full of canned vegetables—thanks to Andrew and Aimee—as well as her soup, tuna packets, pasta, condensed milk, and everything else nonperishable, including an entire shelf designated for her tea, the freezer full of meat. She was set.

She spent days working on the political thriller, her fingers flying over the keyboard, similar to her brush on a canvas. She felt she had so much inside and not nearly enough time to make it all happen.

This final Act of hers was going to work out. She felt it, tasted it.

Back in October she hadn't been able to wait any longer and hired the people to pull out her three docks and store them until next summer. The sailboat was back in the boathouse, up on the platform. The ski boat was also stored in the boathouse. The rowboat too. Her only transportation now was a motorized inflatable dinghy; it was light enough for her to pull up on shore. Once the ice began to form, she would have to put that in the boathouse too.

Her phone dinged as she looked around her in awe. The first snow was flying. Large white flakes fell. The lake below was gray and stormy, white caps higher than she had seen in quite some time. Luckily, the Franklin stove threw off enough warmth to take the chill out of the cottage air, as did the electric heater in the kitchen. Detective Charles LeBrandt's name on her incoming text made her smile.

**Charles: Are you surviving? I saw on the weather app you're expecting snow**

**Alex: It's already here. Surviving yes**

Charles: What's wrong

Alex: Nothing

Charles: Alex?

Alex: It's pretty quiet out here

Charles: I thought there's a storm raging

Alex: I mean there are no people, except the ones I'm creating in my head for the book

Charles: You aren't talking to them, are you?

Alex: I might have to (smiley face)

Charles: Want me to come out and keep you company?

Alex: You have to work and in another month I don't think we'll be able to get a boat across

Charles: Told you I can retire

Alex: I think this must be how the pioneers felt

Charles: LOL. Yeah, I suppose so, minus the space heaters...and internet...and electricity

Alex: Yeah. Yeah. Winter might be crazy

Charles: Maybe, but at least you'll know if you want to live there year round

Alex: I would have made a bad pioneer

Charles: LOLOLOLOLOL

Alex: Not funny. I don't like not being good at something

Charles: You're an extrovert. You need people

Alex: NOW I remember that

Charles: You wanted to be alone to figure things out. You have

Alex: No more hole in my chest

Charles: No more hole. No reason to stay if you don't want to

Alex: My choice

Charles: Always has been

Alex: Good talk. Going to write now

Charles: Any time

One thing Alex was clear on—if she stayed the winter or if she left, it would be because it was what *she* wanted. She would miss Colin's hockey games and spending days with all the grandkids. They kept her mind young.

She smiled as she thought about making her own children a little uncomfortable with her decisions. It kept them on their toes. And, if she wanted to be perfectly honest, it served them right. Her decisions. Her terms. No acquiescing to anyone else.

That decided, she settled in with her tea and her laptop, ready to spin more intrigue in the capital city fraught with it. One thing was certain, she was having a grand time writing the political thriller. If nothing else, she was amusing herself greatly.

The snow came down harder outside. Looking out the large picture windows in the living area, she could barely see the far shore to the north through the storm. The lake was even choppier now. She remembered now she never liked snow much, but maybe it wouldn't be so bad since she didn't have anywhere to go. She pulled her great-grandmother's quilt over her legs as she sat in the old red rocking chair, laptop on a portable desk in front of her. Feeling less isolated and more ensconced in family and tradition, she settled in for a long writing session.

The matriarch looked out the window again and smiled to herself, just as the generations of matriarchs before, the fresh water of the lake lapping at the shore below, hearing the distinct sound in her mind. She was at peace. Rejuvenated. She felt the magic. She'd have to tell Colin it wasn't just a summer thing.

She then scoffed, talking aloud to herself, as one is wont to do when living in isolation, "I'm not old. And I'm certainly not dead. This Act is going to be my best." More quietly now, "Watch me."

She closed her eyes and summoned the memories of the insecurities overcome, the demons fought, the tragedy experienced, the sorrow wrought, the truths faced, the strength discovered, the growth achieved, and the joy found by three generations this past summer, each healing the other and themselves. Stronger together, her family by blood and choice.

She whispered a heartfelt, "Thank you. I'm grateful..." Letting the words be carried to God and the universe.

# ALSO BY MICHELLE S. MORRIS

<u>A Timber River Thriller (Series)</u>
Comes Around (Book 1)
A Quiet Town (Book 2)

# NOTE TO READERS

Since so many have asked, as readers there is a lot you can do to support the authors you love. If you feel so moved, please take the time to leave a review on Amazon and/or Goodreads. It doesn't have to be long—only a couple of lines make a world of difference to authors. In this era of algorithms, it means more than you know.

I enjoy talking with book clubs (in person and via videoconference) and joining podcasts that inspire, encourage, and connect.

You can follow me for the latest news on book releases and my musings on:

Facebook: Michelle S. Morris, Author

Instagram: @michelle.s.morris

Amazon (to purchase books, leave a review, or follow me)

# ACKNOWLEDGMENTS

My readers, who continue to be carried away by the story and come back for more, you make this journey possible and pleasant, giving me the lift to write the next. Thanks in advance to everyone who leaves a review on Amazon and/or Goodreads.

Loree Ann Richardson Noel, for embracing my pursuit of happiness and purpose. You are the best example and strongest mother a woman could hope to have. Always the first eyes on my work and the one who sticks with me through everything life throws our way. Melanie Nolan and Christopher Morris, my siblings who stand strong in their support and belief in a world where both family and the arts matter. Ciara, Benjamin, and Jamie Cowan, whose unfailing belief in their mother is humbling. A special call-out to Ciara for enduring my writing of this book and my numerous pleas to "listen to this section" and ensuring I had it right. Thank you to my first cousin once removed Sandy (Richardson) Winstead for her discerning eye and belief in my new direction, and her husband Mitt Winstead for sharing his experience in the publishing world.

To have someone believe in me enough to jump into the fray is huge. Michele Hutchinson stepped up as my patron and partner in this business. She brings the organization to my creative brain, ensuring I am able to keep writing my novels ... and keeping a schedule that has my production up (as well as my heart rate).

As always, my early readers are greatly appreciated for giving me feedback, what works and doesn't, and marketplace relevance: Lenore Troia, Torin Lee, AnneMarie Laorenza, MacKenzie Morris, bestselling author of Hannah's Dream Diane Hammond, Nancy

Renko, Steven Garcia, Michael Lage, Michael Salsbury, Joan Beck, Gayle Garrison, and Veronica Adomeit.

Thanks to my friend Scott Willems, who pushed hard for me to keep writing and become the novelist I always thought I would, and his wife Sara for cheering loudly in the background. Though not the first published, this was the first fiction novel I put to paper. Scott has kept up the encouragement and tough love through each book and through the rewrite of this one.

A huge thank you to my editor and proofreader, Sheri Wisniewski, who gave me the biggest compliment she could have when she told me there were times in working on *Fresh Water* that she got so caught up in the story she just read and forgot she was editing. (Then went back, of course!)

Noelle Nevins of Abbeo Design has been a complete joy with whom to work. She listens, is creative, fair, and has an enthusiasm that bubbles over—just the type of energy I love. And it gets even better—her mother grew up in Michigan not too far away from where I did and is a big reader and book club member who gets excited when Noelle's projects are book covers. Small world, indeed.

My Starbucks friends, Maegan Felix, Becky Fegan-Dinsmore, and everyone under the management of the spectacularly welcoming Gary Moore in West Branch, MI, have kept me caffeinated, supported, and feeling like I belong in my seat, allowing my imagination to wander and my fingers to fly over the keys.

Rochelle Lombardi and Brandie Glauber, owners of Going to the Sun Gallery in Whitefish, Montana, whose art—their own and the artists they show—provided great inspiration. Brandie owns the cozy apartment where I spent six weeks alone writing my husband and my story (publication in the future) and beginning "Fresh Water." Thanks to them both. One of Rochelle's wonderful sculptures was my reward for completing the book I went there to write.

It takes a village and mine is solid.

# ABOUT THE AUTHOR

Michelle S. Morris writes thrillers, contemporary and women's fiction, underscoring the power of resilience and connection. She worked in politics—first job at the White House—and as a journalist, then as a communications executive with global companies, now a full-time novelist. Born in Northern Michigan, she's lived most of her adult life on the East Coast, from DC to Connecticut, with a few years in San Francisco, and a magical year in England. Michelle's late husband was a musician from Dublin, Ireland, and they have triplets. Having traversed the globe, she's learned to embrace her inner nomad and considers Northern Michigan and Southeastern Connecticut home.